RACE AGAINST TIME

Celebrating his forty-fifth birthday, lawyer Stephen Kennard appears to have everything money can buy and more. A successful practice; an attractive wife; a winning racehorse; and a seat on the board of a Public Company.

Slowly but surely, however, Kennard is riding for a fall. It begins when he is stopped by the police and held for drink-driving. Yet there is far worse to come.

Professional disaster, financial ruin, social disgrace, even matrimonial difficulties, all become part and parcel of Stephen's life until finally only Trisha Martin, a young investigative journalist, is left fighting by his side. Then Stephen Kennard takes the biggest gamble of his career in a race against time—a race he dare not lose.

RACE AGAINST TIME

RACE AGAINST TIME

by
Mel Stein

Magna Large Print Books
Long Preston, North Yorkshire,
England.

British Library Cataloguing in Publication Data.

Stein, Mel
    Race against time.

    A catalogue record for this book is
    available from the British Library

    ISBN 0-7505-0770-5

First published in Great Britain by Judy Piatkus (Publishers)
Ltd., 1994

Published in Large Print March 1995 by arrangement with
Judy Piatkus (Publishers) Ltd. and Mel Stein.

Magna Large Print is an imprint of
Library Magna Books Ltd.
Printed and bound in Great Britain by
T.J. Press (Padstow) Ltd., Cornwall, PL28 8RW.

For David, a true friend and partner—
and Jeff, with apologies for not changing
the name.

'Those friends thou hast, and their adoption tried,
Grapple them to thy soul with hoops of steel.'

(Hamlet, I.iii. 59)

Chapter One

The horses circled the parade ring in obedient steady procession. It was difficult to believe that in a matter of minutes they would be transformed into smooth-running machines with all the power, grace and beauty of custom sports cars.

'Would jockeys please mount?'

They strutted in wearing white breeches and multi-coloured silks standing out against the manicured turf, and approached trainers and owners. Though jockey and trainer had long before agreed tactics and prospects there was still the ritualistic necessity for lip service to be paid to the poor mugs who paid the bills—the same poor mugs whose money would inevitably vanish into the bookmakers' satchels, as the optimism of all but one of the trainers proved ill-founded.

Stephen Kennard leaned casually on the rails, watching the horses closely as one by one they left the paddock for the start of the race. Even though his own horse was not due to run for another hour, he was already a part of the scene, already drawn into the magic world of the race track, so different from the world of the office and board-room in which he usually passed his days.

Unwillingly he dragged himself away from the ring—not as he would have liked to mingle with the bookmakers and fight for a price on the horse of his choice, but back to the hospitality tent where he'd just finished lunch. At least the name on the board outside gave him some satisfaction: Kennard & Wightman. His solicitors' practice had come a long way since the day he and his old school friend Jeffrey Wightman had put up their first sign in the North London suburb where their practice had begun over twenty years ago. Twenty years in partnership with the same man...it was like a marriage, only you saw a lot more of your partner than your wife and you relied on him a hell of a lot more. If your wife made a mistake and reversed into the neighbour's car it was an apology, a bottle of wine and an insurance claim. If your partner fouled up for an important client it could be a short sharp farewell to anything up to a quarter of a million pounds' worth of fee income a year. The nineties weren't like the seventies when clients were falling over themselves to be represented. This was the harsh world of recession and liquidation, when even the biggest client wasn't taking risks, when even the most generous was negotiating you down on your charges; this was a world where a lawyer had to go out and get the work.

Still, Kennard & Wightman had been less badly affected than most firms. Stephen himself was still a director of the publicly quoted Sidney Developments Plc, which he had helped to float on the Stock Exchange seven years ago, and even in bad times they still brought in a fair amount of business. That was no reason to be complacent, though. Jeff Wightman's idea to flatter their prestigious clients by taking them out for a day had been eagerly seized upon by Stephen when he knew his own horse was going to run at Lingfield.

At that time he'd no idea that Montpelier King would have developed the way he had. A big rangy colt, he'd looked slow and gawky when he'd been left at the start of his first race, but he'd spun around and made up enough ground to leave two or three horses behind him. He'd been eighth next time out in a big field of twenty-three and almost everything that had finished ahead of him had gone on to win or be placed. Then on his third appearance it had taken a big effort by his young jockey to pull him back to sixth place when he could easily have been third. Rory

O'Donnell, his trainer, was a great believer in placing horses to win at generous prices. Odds-on favourites who won might upset bookmakers, but they didn't do a lot for his reputation amongst owners looking for a quick killing.

If Montpelier King had been in the frame on his third outing he might well have started favourite on his next visit to the racecourse. The way O'Donnell planned things they'd get at least 6-1 against him this afternoon. A grand to win, six thousand pounds in the pocket. It wasn't as if that sort of money would change Stephen Kennard's lifestyle, but there was still the same thrill of winning he'd had when he was a kid. In those days he'd read his illiterate Russian-born grandmother the runners from the *Daily Mirror* and then gone up the road to place her illicit bets at the local barber shop.

'A shilling each way and a tanner each way for me.' It had meant just as much to him as the grand he intended to bet today, more perhaps when your whole pocket money was only a shilling a week. A tanner, a bob...forgotten coins in a part of a forgotten life. His grandmother, long buried, a slight embarrassment to his parents right until the end, parents who strove to be more English than the English, yet still reverted to Yiddish expressions in times of stress.

'They're at the post,' the racecourse commentator said in his perfectly enunciated tones. Stephen hurried into the marquee determined at least to watch the race on one of the many TV monitors positioned thoughtfully for the racegoer who didn't want to muddy his (or more likely her) shoes.

Jeffrey Wightman bustled over towards him.

'We thought you were taking a last-minute ride in the race. Come on, Steve, I need your help. Half the people here are your clients and you know I'm lousy with names.'

Jeffrey wasn't lousy with names at all, but he wasn't that great with people. They'd been friends since the first year at their Grammar School in the East End of London and together they formed a kind of Janus mask, not just in personality but also in looks. Stephen's mind moved like a ball spinning around the roulette wheel, often appearing to click into place at random, yet slotting too often into the right space for it to be just chance. Jeffrey was more methodical, his slightly plodding dull approach in school transformed in legal practice to a methodical analysis, which if somewhat lacking in flair, almost inevitably got the right conclusion. Stephen was always prepared to leave his back uncovered to take the glorious chance, safe in the knowledge that Jeffrey was there to bring up the rear guard. It was the mid-field genius operating in front of the reliable sweeper and it worked.

Physically they made an odd couple. Stephen was tall and muscular, although putting on a little weight as the expensive meals and the drinks that went with them outmanoeuvred the squash and tennis matches that filled what little time he had. He wore his black curly hair long at the back; his habit of pushing his fingers through it at times of stress meant it was permanently unruly. Even in moments of anger he was unable to keep the look of compassion out of his large brown eyes, and with his dark skin and strong arms he looked more like a Latin American tennis champion than a Jewish lawyer who was celebrating his forty-fifth birthday that very day. He was very conscious of his own image. Though nobody else would have thought him overweight, he had just promised himself to cut out bread for the rest of the month and to take the exercise bike down from the loft after catching sight of himself on one of the TV monitors on the course.

The bike had been a fortieth birthday

present from Cathy, his wife, given to him after she'd first had cause to suggest he had a hint of a paunch. They'd been lying together in their bedroom in the cottage on a Saturday afternoon with the children playing in the garden, their cries coming faintly through the shutters, blurred and distant, part of another world. Her hand had played with the hairs on his chest, her face buried into his neck. He felt her fingers move down his body and was immediately aroused; but her hand had stayed on his stomach, kneading the excess flesh she found, like a baker preparing dough.

'What's that?' she'd asked.

'Nothing,' he'd said, and from then on the roll of fat around his middle, which obstinately refused to respond to treatment, had been designated his 'nothing'. His family were not ones to let him off lightly, for only last month, as they holidayed for a weekend in the South of France, his daughter had spotted what she perceived to be more than one roll of flesh and had promptly renamed him 'Mr Michelin Man'. He took it squarely on the chin. If he had a problem with his weight he would address it; if a problem was addressed it could be dealt with.

Jeffrey, on the other hand, made little or

no effort to deal with his figure. He was, in any event, shorter than Stephen, and definitely plump if one were being kind and fat if one were not. Yet his rotund form had an appeal. It gave him the air of a cuddly cartoon character. Women loved to cuddle him, female clients adored him—so much so that while Stephen had been married to Cathy for nearly nineteen years, Jeffrey had three broken marriages and innumerable affairs behind him, each of the marriages ending because of an affair with the heiress apparent. While Stephen was cleanshaven Jeffrey had grown a neatly trimmed beard on holiday some ten years ago which he kept because, together with the gold rimmed spectacles that he did not really need to wear, he felt they gave him an intellectual look.

Jeffrey always dressed impeccably and expensively, and today at the racecourse was wearing a dark blue double breasted blazer which he'd bought especially for the occasion, grey trousers with knife-like creases, and a red silk tie neatly knotted against a blue button down shirt, which itself had probably cost more than Stephen's suit. Yet despite his impeccable appearance it was Stephen who won the heart of the clients. It was Stephen who would be called in to trouble shoot when a client was dissatisfied. It was Stephen

16

who, somehow or other, would always produce a major new client to bolster the practice income. It had been unlike Jeffrey to speculate, but speculate he had in property, and after one or two successes he'd had one major failure. He'd actually owned a share in the horse when Stephen had bought it, then had sold it when he needed to raise money. Typically Stephen had got an independent valuation then virtually doubled it to help Jeffrey out. It was that kind of friendship.

Jeffrey put his hand firmly on Stephen's shoulder and guided him over to a gaggle of clients who were just finishing their after lunch liqueurs.

'What do you fancy in this race, Stephen?' asked an elderly man with a music hall, walrus moustache.

'Whatever you're not backing, Gerry.' There was a wave of laughter and Gerry Mortimer, Chairman of Sidney Developments, joined in with them as all of his previous selections during the day's racing had trailed in forlornly at the rear of the field.

Jeffrey stepped back a pace or two and left the stage to Stephen. Somehow his personality always lit up a room or a meeting, and however many people were present, however well or not he knew them, he always managed to take control.

Even at school, although Jeffrey had beaten him hollow in the subjects that needed basic learning, Stephen had triumphed at English where his imagination could run riot. Imagination and flair, that was how Stephen had built up his practice. Never claiming to be the best lawyer in the world but always giving the client the feeling that he would outsmart the opposition. Most practices couldn't stand more than one Stephen, his mind forever moving on, his administrative ability zero, his boredom threshold even lower; but then Kennard & Wightman only had one Stephen.

He picked up a glass, thought about climbing on to a chair, then changed his mind, preferring to stand in the middle of the marquee, a star performer at the theatre in the round. He smiled straight at his brother Anthony, five years his junior and the tax specialist in the partnership. Tony blinked back at him from behind old-fashioned horn rimmed spectacles, his thoughts doubtless a million miles away. He tended to live in a world of his own, his face only showing animation when he thought of a new tax-saving device. This might well happen during the course of a totally unrelated conversation and cause some consternation. Stephen remembered only too well an occasion

18

when an established client had been telling Tony about the long and painful death of his wife from cancer. Tony's reaction had been to cry out with delight, his face wreathed in smiles, as it suddenly dawned upon him that the interpolation of a Dutch Antilles company into a particular transaction would save another client five million pounds. It had taken Stephen a lot of explaining, several lunches and more than a few bottles of vintage wine to retain the affronted widower.

'Ladies and Gentlemen,' Stephen began, his voice well modulated, with a resonance that would have done justice at the Old Vic. A hush settled over the room as Stephen turned to take in the whole gathering, caught in an imaginary spotlight.

'Let's drink a toast as I formally welcome you to this afternoon of the sport of kings. Let us drink to Montpelier King in his race, and let us, the partners in Kennard & Wightman, drink to you, their clients, who have made this all possible.'

He emptied his glass in one dramatic gesture and like a Greek chorus the words came echoing back to him:

'To Kennard & Wightman.'

Stephen Kennard, lawyer, racehorse owner, bon vivant, at forty-five years of age was at the peak of his career.

19

Chapter Two

Although there was another race before Montpelier King took centre stage, Stephen longed to get away from the throng to visit the horse in his box before he was brought out into the parade ring.

Sarah Lawrence saw his anxiety to get away and locked her arm through his.

'Don't tell me our little Stephen is trying to escape from all these nice people?'

'You know me all too well, Sarah.' He removed her arm, in what might have appeared to those who did not know him an absent-minded gesture, but little Stephen did was ever unpremeditated. Sarah did look striking this afternoon, her long auburn hair newly permed, makeup applied in such a way as to hint that she could be dangerous. Her eyes were almond-shaped behind glasses without which she was incredibly short-sighted. Today she had dressed to kill, although her intended victim was undesignated. Her red trouser suit with its inevitable designer label, a silk print blouse, all topped off by an eccentric black velour hat creating a combination which she only just managed to carry off.

Now in her thirties, she looked much older than the twenty-one-year-old who'd been one of his first articled clerks when he and Jeffrey had set up their practice. Her interview had been unforgettable.

'And why do you want to join our firm in particular, Miss Lawrence?'

'I didn't, in particular.' There was a pause. 'You were just one of the names I was given by the Law Society. I liked your choice of paintings in reception—and you have an interesting selection of magazines and newspapers. I'm tired of reading the *FT* and *Punch* while I'm waiting to be interviewed. I actually walked out before one yesterday because the only *Punch* they had was a month old. I enjoyed reading *Private Eye* while I was waiting for you, and I've always thought that the *Express* tells you everything you need to know about what's going on in the world—don't you agree?'

Inevitably he'd offered her articles. How could he have done otherwise? And now she was the matrimonial partner in the practice, their 'token woman' as Jeffrey put it in his less tolerant moments. It was her natural superiority that made her such a good divorce lawyer. The women who came to her assumed she wouldn't make the same mistakes as they had; the men who instructed her realised

21

the inadequacies of their own spouses. Yet the general clients didn't take to her. In her early days with the firm she'd done some ordinary litigation and the complaints had come flooding in to Stephen.

'She's so bloody arrogant...'

'She treats me like an idiot...'

'She makes me feel like a child...'

It had fallen to Stephen to tell her that she must stick to family law.

'It's their loss,' she'd shrugged, crossing her legs and watching as Stephen's eyes were magnetically drawn to the dark shadows between her thighs. There had been a time when he had been welcome there, a time when what had started as a brief office affair had threatened to explode into a marriage-destroying romance, but he had drawn back from the brink, shocked and frightened by what he saw as he peered down into the abyss of adultery. Cathy, the children, the family, friends, his name, his reputation, the solidity of his life and marriage—he had no real heart for infidelity. The lies, the excuses, the guilt, were all too much for him, as indeed for some time was the pain of telling Sarah it was over. He put it off, time after time, until finally it was she who spoke the words.

'You want it to end, don't you? Well, I'll accept that. It's your loss'—The same assured tone as she'd used about the practice's non-matrimonial clients. She'd known that she was as good in bed, as she was at her job; she'd known that what she had done with him, for him, Cathy would never have dreamed of even in her most abandoned moments. She'd known that he'd want her back, and he had, but he had won every struggle with his conscience and never suggested they try again. Yes, she'd said he could end it, but she'd imposed a condition, played a bitter card in a move that he'd not expected from her.

'I want a partnership. Don't think because this has happened between us that I'll allow it to drive me out of the practice.' She'd got her partnership, and he justified the decision by the fact that Jeffrey did not resist. As far as Stephen was concerned that showed that she'd been given her position on merit, and to be absolutely fair there had never been a day on which he'd regretted the decision. Her commitment to the practice was unquestionable, her drive and determination bringing countless divorces to a successful conclusion for her clients and securing their ongoing commercial business for the other partners in the firm. She never mentioned their affair and although she had never married he made no inquiries into her personal life. The odd man was brought to a social function, but rarely the same one twice. Sarah Lawrence was a woman intent upon her career—a man may have helped her in creating it but no man was ever going to destroy it.

She walked a few yards with him away from the marquee.

'Just cover for me, Sarah. I need equine company.'

'Why didn't Cathy come today?' The question seemed innocent, but there was a hint of malice in the tone. Stephen shrugged.

'Racing's not really her scene. And she's got the children home, and we're going away for the weekend...'

'And...and...' She was taunting him a little now.

'And, as you well know, she's never been very keen on my clients and the practice.'

'And your partners,' Sarah said, smiling, a few glasses of champagne giving her a certain degree of licence.

'It must be nice to be an artist and not to have to get involved in the grimy old world of commerce, not to have to get down into the pits where the filthy lucre's made. OK, I'll do your work for you, or rather your wife's work. Give the horse a big sloppy kiss for me.' She fumbled in her bag. 'Oh, and by the way, happy birthday. I didn't forget.' She gave him a small parcel and turned away without waiting for a thank you. Stephen didn't open it immediately but dropped it into the pocket of his jacket. He watched the shape of her buttocks moving inside the tight-fitting suit and sighed momentarily, remembering the sound of her clothes falling to the floor, remembering her love of silk next to the skin, and hearing the gentle whisper of her last piece of underwear as she rolled it down her legs and flicked it away with her foot.

'The horse...concentrate on the horse,' he told himself. It was as good a way as any of blotting the thought of an undressed Sarah out of his mind. He crossed behind the parade ring and into the stable area where the horses were brought in readiness for the next race. There was nothing like an English racecourse on a fine spring day. The trees were in blossom, the crowds were celebrating their release from winter, there was warmth in the sun, an excited anticipation of the year ahead as classic trials gradually formed the betting market for the Derby and the Oaks.

Montpelier King was only a two year old and had certainly not been bought with any thought of next year's Derby.

Stephen had been in several syndicates over the years, groups of friends and clients who had owned horses—some of them reasonably successful, some out and out disasters. The Archer had won ten races for his first syndicate, on the flat, over hurdles and over the jumps, while the aptly named Never Again had never actually seen a racetrack after continually breaking down in training.

Stephen mumbled an identification to an uninterested racecourse security man and made his way to Montpelier King's box. Rory O'Donnell was busy with the usual pre-race tasks of ensuring the saddle was tightly fixed, that the horse was properly shod, and most of all that he was beautifully and perfectly turned out. Rory prided himself on how his horses looked just as much as how they ran, and if the race carried a prize for the best turned out horse, Rory's stable was tipped as hot favourite to win it. In fact the lad here was a lass, blonde, pretty in a red-faced, country sort of way, a pert bottom enclosed in tight blue denims as she bent down to ensure there was no swelling around the horse's hocks.

'How's the King, Rory?' Stephen immediately fell into the racing vernacular, realising how much more comfortable he felt nowadays in the company of his trainer than his clients.

Rory O'Donnell looked nothing like the typical Irish leprechaun that racing fiction had created. He was five foot eight tall, just a little shorter than Stephen, his face thin and cleanshaven, eyes piercingly blue, sandy hair expensively cut to match the equally expensive leather jacket that he wore despite the sunshine. Unlike most trainers he did not favour the trilby hat and waxed jacket, and even the shoes were Bond Street. The accent, though, was pure County Cork, unaffected by the twenty or so years he had spent training in England after gaining experience with Kerry McCourt, the most successful trainer in the Republic.

'Raring to take his throne, Stephen.' Not for Rory O'Donnell the deference of 'Mr Kennard'. He didn't train for anybody unless he felt he could call them a friend, and you didn't call your friends by anything other than their first names.

'He's all ready,' the girl said, her voice tinged by a West Country accent.

'All right, Lorna, take him out.' The girl patted the horse, put her face next to his in an affectionate nuzzle and led him out on to the narrow sanded pathway around the green sward. Stephen stood on the grass and felt a thrill of pride and possession as the horse walked confidently past him. Horses tend to grow darker as they get older but this one was nearly black already. His intelligent head looked all around him, and although this was only his fourth visit to the racetrack he seemed to know exactly what was required of him. A couple of the other horses were beginning to sweat up, and one in particular was almost covered in lather, his mouth tinged with froth, bucking rather than walking.

'Looks excited,' said Stephen.

'First time out,' Rory commented, 'no chance. There's our danger.' He nodded in the direction of a small well-built colt, much lighter in colour but also exuding well-being.

'That's John Montgomery's runner, Silenzio. Well bred. John thinks he's got real potential but today's trip might be a little short for him at six furlongs. A few of the cognoscenti are said to be having a bit of a plunge on him.'

'Any other dangers?' Stephen asked.

'Well, they've all got four legs. There's one I like—River Demon. Nicely bred. I bought his half brother in the January sales. That's the one I think we've got to beat.'

Stephen nodded. He liked Rory, liked the way he didn't always tell him what he wanted to hear as did so many other trainers. Humour the owner, that was the name of the game. When Rory was sure, though, he was really sure. Stephen didn't ask why and he didn't ask how, but when Rory categorically said a horse would win he usually did. There was no logic about it because there were other trainers in a race who were doubtless equally confident, who would earn the similar conviction from their owners that they were always right, but then that was a matter for them. Rory O'Donnell was Stephen's man.

Rory signalled Lorna to take the horse across to the main parade ring. Stephen suddenly realised that he'd neglected his guests for almost half an hour. Another race had passed and he'd no idea how his non-gambling partners would have coped.

'I'll see you in the ring,' he shouted back over his shoulder as he almost ran towards the main racecourse. It was unlike him to put his client connection at risk. He'd fought hard to get them and the one thing he'd always prided himself upon was never losing a client, unless it was due to death or a corporate takeover. Perhaps it was something to do with being forty-five, a mid-life crisis that made him favour his hobby over his work. He was over-reacting, he knew it, it was only half an hour, but then he felt he'd been acting oddly all day. For once in his life he did not feel totally in control and he didn't like the sensation.

'So you've remembered us have you?' It was Gerry Mortimer, Chairman of Sidney Developments, putting into words what everybody else was too polite to say. He'd met Stephen halfway between the marquee and the parade room.

Mortimer was a short plump man, almost seventy years old but looking twenty years younger despite his grey hair and moustache. It was the eyes that did it. A lively, alert, dancing hazelnut colour always looking mildly amused by life even when closing the toughest of business deals.

He peered at Stephen over the top of rimless glasses that gave him an academic look that was very far from the truth. Gerry Mortimer was educated in the school of life. He'd been in the rag trade from the age of fourteen, and had been a friend of Stephen's father Len right up to his death ten years ago. It had been at Len Kennard's funeral that Gerry had first decided to instruct Stephen. He'd fallen out with his old solicitors over the scale of fees he was being charged and had decided it was time for a change.

'He was taking me for a ride. I don't mind paying through the nose for the best, but he wasn't the best—just tried to fool me into believing he was. If he'd only said to me: "Gerry, it's all getting a bit too complicated, I need to take on a corporate whizz kid to deal with your matters," then I would have understood. I would even have borne the cost. But, no, he wants to be able to muddle through and still charge me top whack. Now to my mind that's not only greedy, it's also dishonest. You play it straight with me, young Stephen, and we'll go places. Lie to me and I'll not only leave you but I'll leave you crucified. *Farshteyst?*'

He had a habit of slipping the odd Yiddish word into his conversation just to remind whoever he was with of his roots, or perhaps to remind himself. He had come a long way from Stamford Hill in North East London, where he'd been brought up. Now he lived in a huge mansion in Hadley Wood, had a chauffeur-driven Rolls-Royce, a villa in Marbella, and had seen himself slipping into the top hundred richest men in England according to the most recent *Sunday Times* listings. He and Stephen had gone places together. It had been inevitable that when Stephen masterminded the company's flotation, he should be asked to join the board. But Gerry Mortimer had wanted it to go further than that.

'Leave the law—it's a *shmutsik* profession anyway. You're all a load of vultures picking at bones—the bones of a company, the bones of a marriage, the bones of an accident—come and work with me full time. I'll make it worth your while.'

'And my partners?' Stephen had asked.

'Do you need their permission? If they got such an offer I can't see that they'd think twice—not that they'd get such an offer, you understand. You're the jewel in the crown in that firm. Don't sell yourself short.'

'I can't do it to them.' Stephen had been adamant, and had felt better for it. He'd gone so far as to discuss the offer with Cathy and she'd left the decision to him. To be fair to her, when it affected his life she always left the decision to him. Other wives might have seen it as an opportunity to be financially secure for life, but as far as she was concerned he had to be happy. Wives like Cathy were few and far between and that had been what had ultimately finished his affair with Sarah.

And so Stephen had remained a solicitor while Sidney Developments went from strength to strength. He had earned out of it, of course. The fees generated by the almost frenetic level of activity within the company meant that Sidney was the biggest client of the practice; the share options that Stephen had taken when his partners had hesitated meant that potentially, one day, he would be very rich indeed. Yet for the moment Sidney was just one client, if the biggest, and one thing Stephen had learned from his early days in practice was that it was dangerous to rely too heavily on just one client. Solicitors have no contracts with their clients, and however much he trusted Gerry Mortimer, doubtless his previous solicitor had felt just the same.

Now Jeffrey wanted them to merge, with another firm, wanted to use their client strength as a power base to build an empire; he was insisting that they talk to the City practice of Greystone's, but so far as Stephen was concerned he was merely paying lip service to the discussions. He liked the practice the way it was. Maybe they did need to take on a few assistants with partnership potential, but that was the way to expand—from within—not artificially with strangers.

He pushed all thoughts of work to the back of his mind and threw his arm around Gerry Mortimer's shoulders.

'Come on, Gerry, I know how much you love horses. Come into the parade ring with me. Then we can join everyone else in the box to watch the race.' He'd made sure that a box would be available, at least to watch Montpelier King, for he had no intention of following his own horse's fortunes on a TV monitor.

'Sure I'll come with you. I need to talk to you Stephen. You can even charge me for the time if you like. We must talk about D'Arblay. It's getting out of control. All this is very nice, but don't neglect your business.'

'Are you lecturing me, Gerry?'

'I wouldn't bother. You wouldn't listen. I hear you're forty-five today. *Mazeltov.* You're a big boy now, but sometimes an *alte kaker* like me, we can give a bit of advice. You've never done badly by me, but right now we need to concentrate—when I say we, I really mean you. This D'Arblay deal is vital.'

'I know, Gerry, I know. I'm going away for the weekend straight from here, but first thing Monday morning you'll have my undivided attention. Day and night.'

'Night and day?' The old man smiled and sang, in a not unmelodic voice.

'That too. You know you ought to be in vaudeville. Come on, let's get my horse on the road. You can help my jockey up if you like.'

'I don't like.' And still arguing, the two of them made their way into the middle of the parade ring.

Chapter Three

Stephen kept himself slightly apart in the private box. He was still mindful enough of his responsibilities to answer questions that were put to him, but he felt a distance, an embarrassment, between himself and his non-racing companions. It was like taking a girlfriend to a cricket match and her asking in a very loud voice where the goalposts were.

'They're going behind.' The voice of the racecourse commentator cut through the noise of the crowd, which then fell to a hush before rising again to a roar of excitement as the starting stalls sprang open.

'They're off.' The clipped emotionless tones, totally neutral, refusing to reveal which horse might carry his money.

'Silenzio the first to show, then Sweet Life, followed by River Demon on the rails, Montpelier King handily placed just behind the leaders.' Stephen wanted to turn around as he heard the King's name and say: 'That's my horse, mine. I worked for it, I earned it. It shows just how far I've come.' Instead his binoculars focused on

35

his white racing colours with the distinctive black scales of justice on them, which he'd argued and persuaded the Jockey Club into accepting.

'Silenzio continues to lead, River Demon moving alongside him, Sweet Life is fading, Montpelier King is making good progress. They're into the final furlong. River Demon goes on by a length, Montpelier King now in second place, Silenzio back in third, River Demon by half a length from Montpelier King, River Demon, Montpelier King getting up, they've gone past together, it's a photo...'

Stephen still held the glasses to his eyes, replaying the final strides of the race. They were almost on the winning line but not quite, and the angle could be difficult.

'What do you think, Stephen?' A chorus of voices all asking the same question, all the inquirers holding their betting tickets in their hands, having loyally placed their money on their host's animal.

Stephen was curiously superstitious about things like this. He'd thought the King had got up but it was as if he was back at school, being asked how he'd done in an exam where he knew he was bordering on a Grade A. The answer was invariably: 'Bit difficult, wasn't it? Not quite what I expected.' Now he looked around slowly and shook his head. 'It was very close, he had a lot of ground to make up.'

He felt rather than heard the sigh of disappointment. Nobody here was short of a bob or two yet he knew that they were more concerned about their winnings than whether or not the horse won for his sake. He was getting cynical in his middle age. There had been a time when he had wanted to be friends with his clients and Cathy had despaired as dinner party followed dinner party, an invitation being issued as an automatic reaction to any sizeable new instruction. Now he would be pleased to be away from them—the property men, the accountants, the stockbrokers, the analysts—even his own partners. He just wanted to be away from here and with his family.

'I'll be back,' he half shouted at everybody and hurried down to the winner's enclosure. He elbowed his way through the crowd, drawn irresistibly towards the steaming horses. The bookmakers as he passed were laying odds against the King, a bad sign for they were rarely wrong in their analysis of a photo finish. They had their men positioned dead on the line taking a mind's eye photograph every bit as accurate as the highly technically developed print upon which the judges relied.

As he got to the enclosure even the

jockeys were looking confused. Bryan Morris, the rider of Montpelier King, exchanged a few words with Richard Eaves who'd been up on River Demon and shook his head. Slowly he led the King into the place reserved for the second.

Stephen took Rory O'Donnell's arm.

'What's he doing?'

'Relax, Stephen, we've won it. Eaves only thinks he has and Bryan hates an argument.'

'How can you be so calm?' he asked his trainer.

'Aren't you calm when you're asked to sort out a million-pound business tangle? It's my job.'

Once again, as if by magic, the crowd's noise fell to a whisper as the loudspeaker blared across the race track.

'Here is the result of the photograph. First, number five, Montpelier King, second...' The roar went up when the number was announced from those who had their money on Stephen's horse, the traditional whoops of excitement and triumph which greet every winner at every track around the country. All past losses were forgotten, only the present mattered. The ability to go home, to go to the pub, to go into the betting office next-door, to relate how much money had been won on this particular horse, forgetting how much money had been lost on hundreds before and how much money was still to be lost before the final bet. Stephen felt strange, experiencing the same emotion as when his oldest child Danielle had been born seventeen years ago. Cathy lying in bed well into labour and the child refusing to come into the world, turning in her private universe into the breach; the doctors telling him the baby was in distress, sending him away into the white antiseptic corridors then going about their business swiftly and efficiently; the moment when the nurse came to tell him he had a girl, that mother and child were well, the exultation, the relief—and then the restraint that he was showing now, as if it was the most natural thing in the world to be a father, the most natural thing in the world to be a successful racehorse owner.

Rory disappeared to make sure his jockey weighed in, the statutory check to make certain he and the saddle were the same weight as when they started. Stephen returned to the marquee where his guests had reassembled. The champagne was really flowing and he absent-mindedly emptied a glass as it was handed to him. Jeff was by his side, throwing an arm around his shoulders.

'Well done, old son. We've a whole bunch of satisfied customers here. There's no way we're going to lose this lot as clients for many a day to come, and at least two of our borderline invitees have told me of some major instructions on their way. It's all worked out beautifully.'

'Thanks to the horse,' added Stephen.

'Thanks to the horse,' echoed Jeff. He looked at his watch. 'Didn't you say you were off to the Cotswolds for the weekend? I think you've done your bit. Have another drink and then get on your way. I'm sure Cathy and the kids are going to be better company on your birthday than we are.' As he spoke Stephen's glass was refilled.

'Did I tell you I was off to the Cotswolds?'

'You didn't,' said Jeffrey, 'but then you didn't tell me it was your birthday either. Your super secretary saw to that. Here's your present. Have a good one.' He dug into his pocket producing a neatly wrapped present no bigger than a credit card.

'Are you sure you can manage, Jeff?'

'No problem. Now say your goodbyes, drink up and leave us to lose our winnings back on the last race.'

'Well, I suppose I'll miss the bulk of the traffic.' Stephen didn't really need persuading. It had been a good day, no need to spoil it by turning up late at the cottage. He didn't know what his wife had in store for him but he didn't really want

40

to risk upsetting her. She'd been none too pleased when he said he'd be going racing and would meet her in the country.

'On your birthday, Stephen. What about being with the family?'

'What about the family coming with me?'

'Come on, you know how much I like your clients. Almost as much as I like racing! It's a drag but we'll take both cars. I'll see you down there. Don't be late.'

Stephen took his leave to a flurry of thanks, handshakes and embraces. Only Gerry was a little less than gracious.

'This isn't a long weekend, is it, Stephen? I really need to see you first thing on Monday. Leave me your phone number in case anything explodes over the D'Arblay situation.'

'Nine o'clock all right for you?'

'Make it eight. We've a lot to do. And what about the phone number?'

'Breakfast at seven-thirty and we'll leave out the phone number. I just need a quiet weekend. All this excitement's not good for me now I've hit forty-five.'

'You can't help negotiating, can you. Stephen? very well, seven-thirty, and no calls over the weekend. Have a good time. Give Cathy and the kids my love. We don't see enough of them.'

Although he'd lost his wife the previous

year, the 'we' still slipped off Gerry's tongue. Stephen felt a pang of guilt. When Myrna Mortimer had been alive they'd often gone out to dinner as a foursome. Since her death they'd had Gerry over to eat just once. It wasn't deliberate, it was just a question of time. Friends and family... At the pace Stephen lived and worked it was always a question of time. He had to change that. Forty-five years old was a good staging place to make some new resolutions. What was the point of making money and working like a lunatic if you couldn't enjoy yourself, couldn't spend the time, let alone the money, on those closest to you? Things had to change.

On his way back to the car he made a point of seeking out Rory O'Donnell.

'How's the King?'

'He's fine. He's had a hard race. That's a bit of a horse you've got there, Stephen. I don't think we should push him, but I can see him being a serious contender for some high class races next year, maybe even the St Leger with his stamina.'

'So what's next?'

'Well, we'll give him a bit of a rest, two or three weeks, then there's a nice two-year-old race at Ascot over seven furlongs that I think we might have a go at. All the high flyers will be there but I can't see any harm in trying to find out just how good he is and how well he stays.'

'Sounds fine to me. I'll order my morning suit and top hat.'

'You do that, Stephen. You'll look the part, that's for sure. I must tell you this horse really excites me, and it's not often I say that to an owner.'

Stephen reached into his wallet and pulled out a bundle of notes.

'Give that to Lorna and the Head Lad.'

'I will.'

There was no question of Stephen looking after Rory—it wasn't that sort of relationship. The two men shook hands formally and the trainer looked straight into his eyes.

'I'll see you at Ascot then, I'm really looking forward to it. You know, you're a lucky man, Stephen. People own horses for years and years and never get so much as a place, let alone a winner. Here you are with your first horse on your own in the winner's enclosure. You've really got everything to play for. I'm not a jealous man but I almost envy you.'

'I'd swop with you any time,' replied Stephen, but he knew as soon as the words were spoken that he didn't really mean it.

He walked across to the car park,

switched the alarm off on his BMW, and with the road atlas on the seat beside him set off on his cross-country route to the Cotswolds.

'Everything to play for, Stephen,' he said to himself—and then, before he had gone a mile from the racecourse, saw in his window a blue flashing light and sensed the first drop of rain to fall on his parade.

Chapter Four

Cathy Kennard was not a happy woman. It was gone seven and she had already battled her way through London's traffic, suffered several major holdups on the M40 which appeared to be permanently undergoing repairs, and arrived in Oxford just in time for the start of the rush hour. As if that part of the journey wasn't bad enough, she'd been stuck behind a trail of heavy lorries and farm tractors for most of the distance between Chipping Norton and Moreton-in-Marsh, which would have been unbearable even if her children Danielle and Jonathan had not been bickering all the way. She couldn't remember how their argument had started, it was something to do with Danielle insisting on sitting in the front although Jonathan claimed she knew he got sick in the back. Even though Cathy was his mother she couldn't remember him ever being sick in a car during his fourteen years, but her pointing this out to him had only added fuel to the fire.

'You always take her side, Mum. Just because she's a girl.'

'And Dad always takes your side,' his seventeen-year-old sister had added.

'Well, Dad's not here. He's off with his rotten clients, watching his rotten horse,' Jonathan had paused, then used the ultimate threat with consummate timing.

'OK, Danny baby, if you want to sit in the front that's fine by me. I'll just remember to vomit forwards.'

'Well, you just do that,' his sister had replied. 'You make me sick anyway!'

And so it had gone on, non-stop, until Cathy had turned the Range Rover into the drive of the cottage between the villages of Stanton and Broadway. Normally she felt an enormous feeling of relief and exhilaration when she arrived in the country. The problems of the city were left far behind; all that greeted her were the rolling hills, the prospect of rising late, then long walks and leisurely meals in good restaurants which she neither had to cook nor clean up. Yet today was different. The irritation that had begun when the

45

children hadn't wanted to come with her had turned into a black mood, with a threatened migraine pounding at the base of her skull.

In her more rational moments she accepted that Stephen and she were growing apart from the children. It had begun with Danielle's adolescence, but now Jonathan had reached the same stage while Danielle had a seemingly inexhaustible string of male admirers, some of whom were equally attractive to Cathy.

'We're old enough to be left on our own, Mum. Why don't you and Dad go off for a nice romantic weekend?' had been her daughter's calm suggestion, while Jonathan's had been more predictable.

'I'm not going! It's boring. All my friends are here. The video shop's miles away there. I've seen everything they've got, and what I haven't seen is crap.'

'It's your father's birthday. He'll expect to spend it with his family.'

'Look,' her daughter had continued with a persuasiveness that promised well for a career at the bar, 'if Jonny's in this sort of mood it'll just spoil it for everybody. We'll get Dad a nice present, you take it down, we'll phone him and sing "Happy Birthday" and everybody will be happy. Jonny can go and stay with one of his little friends and I'll get Mandy to come and sleep over to keep me company.'

Cathy, though, had been insistent, although she couldn't say why. There was a stubborn streak in her which overrode a pragmatic approach to any problem. It was Stephen's forty-fifth birthday, he was her husband and the father of Danielle and Jonathan. It was right that they should spend the evening as a family—even if they weren't going to enjoy it.

She had booked them a table at the Lygon Arms in Broadway. It was Stephen's favourite restaurant, a sixteenth-century coaching inn where Oliver Cromwell had stayed, now owned by The Savoy, with a gourmet menu fit to match anything in London. The reservation was for eight. She knew Stephen's horse had been running in the three o'clock. Now there was not only no sign of him but not even a phone call. Thoughts of a road accident crossed her mind and were dismissed. By now the police would have been in touch, surely. Stephen was sufficiently organised to carry all his contact phone numbers on him. No, this was pure thoughtlessness. Once again work was taking precedence over family. The same old story, and birthday or no, she rehearsed the verbal onslaught he was about to receive.

It hadn't always been like this. They had met at school. Cathy had attended the sister school to Stephen's and their paths had crossed during a joint production of *Much Ado About Nothing* when she had played Beatrice to his Benedict. Their relationship had been very much like the lovers in the play: hate at first sight, gradually leading to an awareness that they were both physically and mentally attracted to each other. Stephen was eighteen, on his way to read law, Cathy a year younger planning to take an English degree. She had always been attracted to dark Mediterranean-looking men, in sharpest contrast to her own petite Scandinavian looks: a natural blonde, her skin fair and clear, untroubled by any teenage acne, blue eyes testifying to the rape of some Russian-Jewish ancestor by an itinerant Cossack. Yet despite Stephen's height advantage over her, despite the fact he was older by some fifteen months, she had the maturity, she had the control, and in those days she also had the ambition.

In 1967, before Stephen and she had met, she volunteered to go to Israel to help out after the Six Day War. She worked in the orchards, tirelessly, ceaselessly, until even the *Kibbutzniks* had told her to slow down, scared she might set a precedent they would not be able to match. She had grown up in the three months she had spent there—three months during which

48

Stephen had done his usual holiday job in a library.

She had seen the burnt out tanks lying in the roads to the border, had seen the boys coming back home from the war, the faces of school children and the eyes of older men. She had lost her virginity to a soldier, a boy called David, born on the Kibbutz, but now bearing a scar down the side of his face like a sword wound from a Prussian duel. He'd spoken little English and her Ivrit was equally limited but somehow they communicated, somehow he was able to show her the areas where the deadly attacks had been the worst, had been able to explain to her why they were fighting, why he could not cry for his best friend who would never come back from Sinai.

She'd never told Stephen about him, and when they'd finally gone to bed together he had been too polite, or too shy, to ask who had been the first. Twenty-three years ago, a memory, a lifetime...could it ever be recaptured? She shook her head in irritation. Concentrate on the present otherwise it all becomes impossible. But where the hell was he?

At seven-thirty the phone rang. It was Stephen.

'I'll be back soon. I'll explain when I get there.'

When he finally arrived and she saw the pallor of his skin, the look in his eyes, she bit back the angry words.

'I've been breathalysed! Hauled down to some God forsaken police station, treated like a criminal, and I still don't know whether or not they're going to charge me.'

She looked at him in amazement.

'But you never drink and drive.'

'I know. The King won, and somehow there was always somebody filling my glass.' He paused, tried to concentrate for a moment on what had happened, but his mind was too confused to conjure up accurately the sequence of events.

'Who was filling up your glass? The evil pixie? If you drank too much it was because of your own carelessness, not because of some mystical force. You could have killed somebody, you could have put all our futures at risk!' Her voice, rising to a shriek, brought the children running down from their rooms.

'Daddy, hi. Happy birthday. Pleased you could make it.' Danielle said with scathing teenage sarcasm. Jonathan, more physical, less mature, just threw his arms around his father and put his head on his chest.

'Happy birthday, Dad. What kept you?'

'His boozy clients,' Cathy interjected

before Stephen could reply.

'Look, I'm sorry I'm late. I'll go down on my knees if it helps. It really wasn't my fault. I felt perfectly OK. There was just a police car with nothing to do waiting outside the racecourse. He flagged me down, asked me where I'd been. I was stupid enough to tell him that I'd just come from the races where I'd owned a winner. It was strange, it was almost as if they were waiting for me and knew who I was...'

'The drink's really got to you, Stephen, hasn't it? Now we're talking conspiracy. Somebody feeds you drinks, somebody arranges for the police to be waiting, I suppose they dug up some old murder charge as well?'

'No, not exactly. I blew into the bag, it was negative, just. Nine times out of ten they wouldn't pursue it, but not today. They asked, very politely I may say, if I'd be so kind as to accompany them to the station and give them a blood or urine test—my choice of course. I gave them a sample of blood—somebody once told me there's less chance of the alcohol showing up in that. But even then they kept me hanging about. Then it was "thanks for your co-operation, we'll let you know". I was so confused I didn't even ask for a sample to take away myself...' His speech

51

slowed as he realised just how little he'd heeded the advice he'd always given to clients.

'It was all a nightmare. I kept telling them you'd be waiting and worried but they wouldn't even let me phone.'

'So why didn't you phone as soon as you got away?' Cathy was not to be that easily appeased.

'I'm not sure. I just wanted to put distance between me and them. It was only when I was quite near that I began to calm down. It's all crazy, it's really not like me, none of it.'

'So did they charge you?'

'No, they just cautioned me and said they'd let me know. What a way to spend your birthday.'

'Poor old Pops.' His daughter kissed him on the forehead. 'Why don't you have a nice drink, a hot shower, and then come out with your loving family?'

'I'm not sure about the drink, the rest of it sounds good. Where are we going?'

Cathy still looked peeved. It was an expression he knew of old. She was in a mood and would only come out of it when she was good and ready. Cajolement was not the answer.

'Give your father his birthday present. I'm going to phone to say we'll be late.' She flounced out of the room.

Stephen exchanged glances with his son and daughter.

'Go and have your shower, Dad,' his daughter said, 'we'll give you your present later.'

Jonathan still looked anxious. As a small child he'd very nearly died of asthma, and now in his teens moments of stress still sent him gasping after an inhaler.

'Are you all right, Jonny?'

'Are you all right, Dad?'

'I'm fine, honest. Just relax. Go and be nice to your mother. I'll be ready in fifteen minutes.'

'Sure.' His son flashed him a smile, his mother's smile. Stephen breathed a deep sigh of relief. Whatever had happened had happened. He was here in his own home with his family. Nothing could harm him now.

Chapter Five

As the waiter brought the birthday cake to the table nobody would have suspected that the four guests, husband, wife, son and daughter, were anything other than a perfect happy family group—and indeed half a bottle of champagne and two glasses of wine had brought back the smile to Cathy's face, particularly as she had seen her husband abstain even from his favourite Rully.

The rest of the diners looked on in a mixture of frostiness and polite endorsement. The elderly locals who came to the famous Lygon Arms once a month did not welcome an intrusion into their quiet meal, particularly from somebody they did not recognise and therefore did not regard as one of them. Most of the others were Americans, stopping off on their way to Stratford, mildly amused to see that birthdays happen even in the midst of English village life. Although the locals might not regard them as regulars, the hotel management did, and the head waiter had greeted Stephen with an effusive handshake that reflected his generous tips as well as his custom over the years.

'Mr Kennard, good to see you. We all had a little investment on your horse today. There's a bottle of champagne by your table with the compliments of the management.'

It was hard to explain that champagne was not top of his list of priorities for the evening's entertainment but the gesture was appreciated. Stephen asked about various members of staff and their families. Somehow he was able to relate to restaurant staff just as he was to the backroom boys and girls of the racing world. He had the ability to swop small talk, to ask personal questions as if the answers really meant something to him, and for the most part they did. Cathy was more remote, more in favour of the master-servant relationship that maintained a reserve and a distance but ensured maximum efficiency.

Stephen looked around the dining room, starting to unwind for the first time that day. It was false, of course, added to the genuine sixteenth-century part of the building as late as 1910, but it was still effective with its large minstrel's gallery and threatening array of Civil War weaponry around the walls. He liked the big open fireplace which tonight was unlit, but which in winter invited the guests to linger over their meals before braving the cold winds which whipped through the Cotswold night outside.

He laid his hand on his wife's and leaned across to kiss her.

'I really am sorry you know.'

'I know,' she said quietly, then in a bright voice added, 'Pressy time.'

Various parcels were magically produced from beneath the table, smuggled in whilst he'd been in the cloakroom.

'Mine first,' said Jonathan, his face

flushed and excited after half a glass of champagne.

'Why not? Yours is the cheapest,' he sister said unkindly.

'It's not a question of price, it's a question of value,' Stephen began.

'Come on, Dad, no lectures tonight. We're all here to enjoy ourselves, remember.' There were moments when Stephen didn't understand, when he felt he didn't even know his daughter nowadays. Was she being serious? Was it an attempt at a joke, was it sarcasm? A year or so ago he would have jumped down her throat, but now there was a grace and poise about her that made him hesitate. Instead of responding he made a great play of opening Jonathan's clumsily wrapped present.

'Jonny, thanks, they're really nice. I'll wear them next time I play.' He held up a pair of monogrammed tennis socks as if displaying them to an assembled crowd.

'Do you really like them, Dad?'

'Yes, I do.' He leaned across and kissed his son on the forehead. A tennis fanatic, he knew he really would use them and was touched by the thought that had obviously gone into the choice of gift with his son's limited finances.

Danielle smiled condescendingly. She looked increasingly like her mother: the same fair hair pulled back to accentuate the high cheek bones, the eyes with a hint of grey to dilute the blue, the nose so perfectly straight that even friends suggested she must have had plastic surgery—and the smile, the gorgeous smile that had so entranced him when he had first met Cathy. Even the voice was one with her mother's and many was the time Danielle had answered the phone and Stephen had said, 'Cathy?' When his daughter was in a playful mood she let him continue until some hesitancy on her part, a giveaway note, let on that he was explaining to his daughter rather than his wife just why he was going to be late home from work.

Danielle pushed across a flat package tidily wrapped in paper decorated with racehorses, the bow itself a work of art. Stephen carefully began to undo it, but found the paper tearing in his hands.

'There you are,' Jonathan said triumph-antly. 'I told you it was a waste of time and effort to wrap it up like that. Mine took me sixty seconds to do, hers took about sixty minutes.'

Almost automatically, Cathy sighed.

'Haven't you two had just about enough arguing for the day? Have a look at the menu and see if you want a dessert.'

Jonathan picked his up deliberately upside down and began to crane his neck at an impossible angle pretending

57

to try and read it. An elderly couple at the next table, strictly county, tutted. In response Cathy snatched the menu from her son's hand.

'Just behave yourself. You're old enough to know better. Next time we'll leave you at home.'

'Promises, promises,' he replied, giving an exaggerated yawn. 'I'll have the assorted ice cream with Dad's chocolate cake.' He turned his attention back to his father's efforts to get the parcel open. 'Haven't you sorted that out yet?—You'll be disappointed when you finally get to it anyway.' His sister elbowed him neatly in the ribs and he gasped for breath.

'The little beast is going to go all dramatic on us and have an asthma attack. Just watch.'

Stephen and Cathy looked at their son with more concern than his sister had shown. They knew asthma was no joking matter. It was they, not Danielle, who had sat with him for long hours in hospital rooms while he struggled to breathe, his colour gradually changing from blue to white to normal as their prayers were answered.

'Have a drink, Jonny,' Stephen said, pouring him some water.

'Do you need your inhaler?' his mother asked more practically. The boy shook his head, giving his sister a grim look that warned her he was going to seek his revenge just as soon as they were out of the restaurant and out of range of their parents.

'Don't make a fuss of me. You're too bloody overprotective.' It was a favourite phrase of his lately and calculated to annoy his mother, but then most things he did at fourteen were calculated to annoy everybody around him.

'I'm not, and don't swear.' Her voice was reduced to a whisper as she sensed the rest of the dining room looking on at what was fast becoming a spectacle.

'Stephen, just open your presents and let's go! It's been a long hard day—at least for those of us who were battling through the traffic rather than gallivanting around the racecourse with London's finest.'

He completed the unveiling of his daughter's gift—a Pavarotti CD.

'Great, Danny. I'll play it in the car on the way back.' He looked at his wife expectantly, and automatically she fumbled beneath the table and pulled out a square parcel. He opened it swiftly and efficiently, sensing that he had not finished wearing his hair shirt for the day. Inside was a perfect miniature of Montpelier King, right down to his racing colours.

'Cathy, it's beautiful. Where on earth

did you get it made?'

'You know, that little place in Broadway, just across from here.' She coloured a little, embarrassed that he was clearly so pleased with it. 'You like it?' There was the same note of concern that his son had demonstrated over his present, a need, he thought, to be reassured, even after all this time. He leaned over and kissed her full on the lips and sensed that rather than closing her eyes to receive the kiss she was glancing from side to side to see if anybody was still watching. She pulled away from him and pushed back her chair before any of the waiters could rush to help her.

'I think we ought to go now, don't you?'

'Mum, I've not finished my afters,' Jonathan complained.

'I'm sorry, I feel really tired. I'll get some fresh air and wait for you by the car. You have your coffee or whatever else you want. I don't want to spoil anything for any of you.'

Stephen reached out and took her arm.

'It's all right, I understand. It was a nice meal, a nice surprise. The presents were great. I'll settle up the bill and let's all have an early night.'

They collected their coats in a flurry.

'Look,' he said to the children, 'you two slip into the car. Let Mummy and me just have a walk on our own.'

For once they didn't argue. Stephen put his arm around Cathy's waist and guided her out into Broadway High Street. It was totally quiet, the street unlit, most of the shop windows now also in darkness. An American friend had once commented that they rolled the road up at ten o'clock and certainly tonight it seemed that way. They turned right and crossed the road towards the village green.

'What is it, Cathy? I've said I'm sorry.'

'I know. I'm sorry too. I didn't mean to spoil your birthday. I really didn't. I'd worked so hard to get everything just right and then...'

'I understand.' He stopped in front of a shop selling teapots, remembering the words of John Moore, his favourite Cotswold writer: 'Broadway is a whore.' He looked up the street, empty of cars, and could almost imagine himself transported back in time, could hear the rattle of the stage coaches coming down Fish Hill. If Broadway was a whore then he was pleased he was a client. He pulled Cathy towards him, and although for a second she resisted she eventually yielded to his kiss. They stood merged into one, like young lovers, as his tongue found its way into her mouth, his hands pulled her buttocks hard towards him. Breathless and flushed, she finally pulled away.

61

'We must get the children. They've probably destroyed the car or each other by now.'

'Yes, the children,' he sighed, and as he turned and walked back to the Lygon Arms, his hand in his pocket guiltily touched the unopened present Sarah had given him that afternoon and in the darkness he bit his lip, trying hard not to remember things that were past.

Chapter Six

They slept late on Saturday morning, even the children for once not stirring to the birds' dawn chorus and the chiming of the clock in the village church. Stephen fumbled for the alarm only to realise it was the telephone. He swore quietly, then saw it was nearly eleven and accepted that it was a reasonable time to call.

Cathy turned over and pulled the covers around her, disappearing into an anonymous heap by his side.

'Hello,' he said, his voice still blurred with sleep, his throat dry.

'Hello, am I disturbing you?' The voice was bright, young and female, and realising that perhaps Stephen did not recognise it, added, 'It's Trisha, Trisha Martin. Is this not a good time? You sound terrible.'

'No, it's all right. Just hold on, I'll take it downstairs. I was still in bed.'

He pulled on a dressing gown and made his way down the well-worn oak staircase that had so appealed to them when they first decided to buy the cottage. He ducked his head at the bottom two stairs as the landing bowed and curved dangerously low for anybody above average height, then picked up the phone in the lounge.

'I'm so sorry, but you did tell me to call, remember? I tried to get hold of you last night, but there was no answer.'

'It's no problem. I can't believe it slipped my mind. I should be up anyway. I hate burning daylight, as John Wayne once said.'

'*True Grit,*' Trisha added.

'Spot on. I thought you'd be too young to remember that.'

'I sat on my daddy's knee. Anyway, Stephen, I had to tell you—we won! Hook, line and bloody sinker.'

'I'm glad, Trish, I'm really glad. Not so much for you and me as for the Robsons. Those bastards really needed showing up.'

'I know. I'm running the story all this week. I even got the editor to agree to pay the Robsons. Not that money's ever going to make up for what they've been through. The judge said exactly that on Friday. We didn't finish 'til gone six but I think he didn't want to drag everybody back again on Monday.'

'Surprisingly thoughtful for a judge,' Stephen said with some feeling. 'I'm sorry. I should have phoned but it was an odd day.'

'Happy birthday, by the way. You'll find your present waiting for you at the office. I saw your horse won as well. Sounds like quite a good day to me, rather than an odd one.'

Upstairs he heard Cathy moving around. He felt a desperate need to keep her happy today, and if she came down and found him fielding what was basically a business call she was likely to explode.

'What were the damages awarded?'

'Five hundred thousand.'

Stephen let out a whistle.

'They should have settled when they had the chance.'

The stairs creaked, and as if sensing his anxiety to be away, Trisha said brightly, 'Look, we'll talk next week. I'll buy you lunch. I owe you that for all your help. I didn't mean to disturb your weekend. 'Bye.'

He replaced the receiver quietly, regretfully, not realising his face revealed his emotions.

'What are you smiling for, Stephen? You look like the cat who got the cream.'

'The Robson case. The clinic had to pay five hundred thousand.'

Her reaction could have gone either way, but yesterday's mood seemed to have vanished and been replaced by one of vague distraction.

'That's good. From what you told me they were real villains. Can you do the breakfast? I just need a bit of fresh air to shake off the champagne from last night.'

'Sure, no problem.' He was pleased by the delegation of the task, pleased to have something to do that wouldn't tax his brain. That was what being in the country was usually about: the ability to switch off, to do things he normally wouldn't dream of attempting, like cooking or washing up or even making beds, things that his clients would never have imagined him attempting.

He watched his wife disappear up the drive looking from the rear in her tight faded jeans like a teenager. He thought again of the Robsons and how they must be feeling this morning.

It had been over a year ago that he had first met Trisha Martin. He had been chairing a meeting of Breathless, a fund-raising asthma charity to which he devoted much of his spare time. Over

65

a glass of wine at the end he had felt himself under inspection. It was a young woman he'd never seen before, her hair a tousled mass of red that could not have come from a bottle, her face dotted with freckles that testified to some recent sunbathing, her make up a mere gesture to convention—a dash of red on the lips, a touch of mascara on the eyes—the individual features chaotic, the whole set in an oval face that was attractive in an unorthodox way.

Finally she came across to him and in a Northern accent said, 'You're Stephen Kennard, and I need your help.'

'That's lucky, I thought you were going to claim your five pounds. And you're?' He extended a hand in an old fashioned gesture of politeness.

'Trisha Martin.' She'd hesitated. 'Journalist.' She waited for a reaction as if she'd confessed to some contagious disease, but none came.

'Look, can we talk? I really do need your advice. There's a pub just around the corner if you've time for a drink.'

'Just one, I'm afraid. I've got some work to do when I get home.'

'You sound like me.' The girl had laughed, a pleasant honest sound, and his usual suspicion of journalists went out of the window. Stephen didn't like the Press. He'd seen what they could do to individuals, to companies, to whole families, just for the sake of a story, and by the time the apology was published or the damages paid they meant little or nothing. It was like giving a loaf of bread to a man sitting in the ruins of his own burned out home, surrounded by the bodies of those he'd loved.

She bought the drinks and he sat in the corner of a smoky room feeling a little awkward, a little guilty. Women didn't usually buy him drinks, and since his affair with Sarah he'd always been scared to be alone with an attractive one, as if he had lost the ability to trust himself. No matter how often he tried to convince himself that it ought to be as easy to have a conversation alone with a woman as with a man, he always failed.

Trisha lit a cigarette and saw his look of disapproval.

'I'm sorry. I should have asked if you minded, but to be honest even if you did I think I'd have had to light up.'

'How many do you smoke?'

'About forty a day.'

'Slow way of committing suicide.'

'I know.' She smiled, and whereas he would normally have felt that a stupid answer, Trisha's smile actually won him over.

And then it all came out. The Robsons were a couple in their thirties; he was a surveyor with a local authority, she was a clerical officer with the same council. They had one child, a nine-year-old boy. He'd been asthmatic from birth, then been afflicted by chronic eczema. They'd tried doctor after doctor, clinic after clinic, nothing had worked. Finally, they'd turned to private medicine and what was reputedly a specialist clinic in Hertfordshire, just to the north of London. The clinic was run by a Swiss doctor called Arndheim whose qualifications proved to be as dubious as his techniques. The owners were a mysterious Liechtenstein company who had nothing more substantial in the United Kingdom than a plaque on the wall. However, the Robsons were completely taken in and invested their life savings in a course of treatment that ended with their son, Robby, not only asthmatic but also bronchitic.

'This Arndheim character,' Trisha told him, 'was polite and regretful as the Swiss always are, but couldn't dream of returning any of the fees.'

'We are, of course, all terribly saddened,' she mimicked the doctor. 'In the short time Robby was with us he had become, so to speak, one of the family. However,

I have investors, you understand. They would never permit it, although if it were left to me...'

'It had all been different when the Robsons had first sat in the office. Arndheim had been confident then, not apologetic. He'd told them his clinic is different. It had succeeded where others failed. Their methods weren't always conventional but they worked.'

'"Is there any risk?" Sheila Robson had asked.' Trisha lit another cigarette. 'She's a nice lady, Sheila. She must have been attractive once, but now her hair's a bit too bleached, she looks permanently worried, too much powder on the skin—you've seen the type in supermarkets looking at the prices on everything. Anyway, Arndheim reassured her there's no risk at all, he's a man not used to having any doubts cast of his opinion. The Robsons ask how much it's going to cost and Arndheim looks suitably embarrassed, as if a skeleton had just been pulled clanking from a dark cupboard.'

'"I'm not really the right person to talk about that. I believe our hospital administrators have already discussed our rates with you in some detail. My concern is your son's health and on that, I'm sure you'll agree, it is impossible to place a value."' Again, the mimicry was perfect

69

and Stephen had felt as if he'd actually been there.

'Afterwards it was so different. Arndheim was going through the motions, reading from a script by lawyers and insurers. "These things happen. Nothing can be certain." He's like a vicar giving a Sunday sermon to a critical flock.'

'"What things happen?" the Robsons ask.'

'For the first time maybe Derek Robson is getting a bit uptight. Arndheim senses it, reacts accordingly, now he gets tough.'

'"I believe the problems have all been explained to you by the consulting physician." It's as if he doesn't want to get his hands dirty. The Robsons even remembered what the room was like. The walls were a delicate shade of pink, the paintings abstract, the desk large and suitably old fashioned. They've not understood what the doctors have told them and Arndheim is looking at them as if they're something the cat's brought in. He glances at his watch just long enough to ensure that they see they are holding up a very busy man.'

'"Well, I'm sure if you make another appointment the doctor will go through things with you again. Some things, however, I feel we'll never understand. They're in the hands of God." The parents are distraught. The kid's desperately ill, he's not the same child they brought in.

'Arndheim looks a bit embarrassed, but not for long. He wants these people out of his office, as far away from his clinic as possible; but he knows the rules and he knows he has to obey them: "Treat them kindly. Make them feel sorry that we did everything we could. Try to get them to leave feeling sorry for us rather than themselves or the child." Our friend Arndheim's not an emotional man. Emotion can't be measured in money, which makes it an unknown quantity.'

' "We did all we could." He rises from his seat, hoping he's concluded the conversation, but the Robsons stand firm, determined to understand their son's predicament. Mrs Robson tells it like it is.'

' "Robby wanted to be better. You said you'd make him better, not worse." '

' "My dear Mrs Robson, you're over-wrought. I understand it's been a difficult time for you. We tried to make him better, what happened wasn't our fault." '

'In fact the treatment had always been speculative, experimental, and rarely tried on human subjects. It had worked once in Switzerland and that was enough for them to try it again—for money. But this time the vaccine had been mixed

71

up with another one, whatever the hell it was—Arndheim could never remember—it reacted and Robby had been the victim of that reaction.'

'The parents leave in bewilderment.' Trish paused for effect. 'I can see now as the door closed behind them Arndheim breathes a sigh of relief. He waits a few moments before moving to the window and watches them walk away up the long drive, sad and forlorn figures slightly apart as if they're leaving room between them for their damaged child.' She looked at him to see if he was taking it all in.

He was. 'The Robsons have tried legal action already and found they earned too much for legal aid but not enough to fund what is doubtless going to be a speculative action. If this had been the States they would have had ambulance-chasing lawyers queuing up for a huge slice of the damages by way of a contingency fee. But you English lawyers, you're just not prepared to gamble, not prepared to ignore the good old Law Society rules and take the case on that basis. So the Robsons in desperation turn to the media and chanced upon me, little Trisha Martin. I'm freelance but I've worked in the past as part of an investigative team for a quality Sunday. Yes, I sensed a story, but more than that I realised that the coverage itself wasn't going to put the Robsons' money back into their empty pockets, nor going to produce any damages for Robby.'

'So there you are, you see. It's really quite simple.' She stubbed out her cigarette and turned her grey eyes full on Stephen. The effect was mesmeric. It was, of course, quite simple. Stephen would take the case on without a fee, and Trisha would get a newspaper to agree to pay all the disbursements in return for an exclusive from the Robsons who would also receive a fee if they won the action.

'So everybody gets something out of this except my firm?' Stephen said with a half smile, almost won over.

'Exactly. You've got lots of clients who pay you mega fees. Just charge them a little more. They won't notice. It's pure Robin Hood. And not everybody gets something out of it. I'm not taking a fee either.'

'You'll just settle for an enhanced reputation?' He didn't feel he could give in without a fight.

'It won't do your reputation any harm either,' she'd retorted. Stephen sniffed.

'Oh, great. I'll have a morning surgery every day for penniless litigants who've heard about my charitable works. We'll have Christmas three hundred and sixty-five days a year!'

'I thought you didn't believe in Christmas, Stephen, I've heard all about your work for Breathless, otherwise I wouldn't have come to you. You raised over a million for them last year in your spare time—I bet you didn't send them a bill. I've a feeling that under that lawyer's skin there might even be a heart.'

He gave her an odd look. She obviously knew he was Jewish yet strangers didn't normally refer to it. He wasn't known as the soul of orthodoxy, and from the way non-Jews talked around him knew he was rarely taken for one.

'No, it's Santa Claus I don't believe in,' he replied.

'Well, why not try and play the part? Maybe you can make him come to life.'

'Why not? He'd come up with no very good reason and had taken on the case. His own son was asthmatic. He knew what it was like to see a child fight for breath. There but for the grace...it hadn't been hard to handle. All he'd had to do was the mechanics. Trisha had done all the leg work, and done it extremely well.

'You should have become a lawyer,' he'd said to her as the case neared its conclusion.

'So should you,' she'd said, and as she spoke he realised how very nearly right she was. All the work for Sidney

74

Developments, the wheeling and dealing of public company life, the forays into the City, the lunches, the dinners, the social and political infighting—they were a world away from the legal challenges to which he had first responded, what now seemed a lifetime away.

And now it was over. The Robsons had their money back and enough besides from the insurance company to make life comfortable for themselves and their ailing son. The clinic would be closed down ignominiously, Arndheim discredited, the owners sent scuttling back into their offshore anonymity. Yet he felt an odd sensation of disappointment, not in the result but in the fact he no longer had an excuse to talk to Trisha on a daily basis. He'd looked forward to her calls, the chit-chat, the gossip from the life of a twenty three year old seemingly with no ties but with her eyes set firmly ahead on her career.

After the first meeting he'd liked to be with her, to be seen with her, for she was the sort of girl who turned men's heads and left them wondering why she should be with him rather than them. Now all he had to look forward to was a last lunch next week. After that there was no excuse of business, it would just be pleasure and the threat of broken promises. The promise he had made to himself to be faithful, the hollowness of any promise he could make to her. He shook his head to be rid of these thoughts. He was being fanciful. For her he had been just a means to an end, no more, no less, and now the end had been achieved there would simply be the final payoff.

He put his hands into his pockets and wandered out into the garden. The apple blossom was out in profusion. There'd be a good crop this year. Danielle sat reading a book, her head bowed, her silhouette a carbon copy of her mother's. Of Jonathan there was no sign. He'd probably rise at noon from the pit that was his bedroom and then claim he couldn't go into the garden because of his allergies. They tried to wrap him in cotton wool, his precious son, and got no thanks for it, yet when he wanted to use his physical condition to manipulate them, he didn't hesitate. Children. Ruthless creatures...like his clients, like the women in his life. The world was a harsh ruthless place.

Stephen needed to be alone, to walk across fields where streams meandered without direction, where cows peacefully grazed oblivious to casual walkers, where the hills rolled way to the horizon, where he could be left undisturbed by people. He laid out the breakfast things and then picked his favourite old straw hat off the peg, pushed an apple and a chocolate bar into his pocket, and without looking back set off towards the meadow.

Chapter Seven

The traffic into town on Monday morning was horrific. He'd wanted to leave late on Sunday night but Cathy had developed a headache, taken to her bed and slept through from seven in the evening. Even now she dozed by his side as the children grew more and more restive in the back.

'I don't see you being sick now that Mum's in the front.' Danielle began, firing the first shot.

'I don't feel sick with Dad driving,' her brother replied.

They'd had to leave Cathy's car at the cottage as she didn't feel well enough to drive and wasn't prepared to entrust her learner daughter with a trip that long.

'I'll come down on the train and collect it during the week, perhaps stay over. I just feel tired.' She did look pale and yet again Stephen felt a twinge of guilt. His lifestyle did not make for a relaxing existence. The irregularity of his hours, the phone calls at home, the paper work that cluttered his office and often filled their evenings. There had been too many cancelled dinners lately, too many phone calls asking her to find somebody else to go with her to the theatre. She'd been perfectly justified in her verbal assault on Friday evening. It would have to change. It would change. But first of all he had to get the D'Arblay deal out of the way.

Sidney Developments had begun as a small company in the rag trade, founded by Gerry Mortimer's father, Sidney Moskovitch. Gerry always claimed it had been his father's idea to Anglicise the name, but his father's tombstone read Moskovitch and Stephen suspected that Gerry's memory was supporting the easy lie. From an insignificant showroom based in Eastcastle Street, Sidney had built up a successful, if not sensational, company by creating a timeless style of clothing that had a consistency of design even though more esoteric individuals came and went within the company. When Gerry took over the running of the company in the sixties he'd been happy to adopt his father's formula. Even the names on the labels made a statement—Michelangelo, Caruso, Giovanni, Mozart. Not for them the mini skirt or the virtually invisible tank top. They still catered for the mother of the five year old who wanted to look smart and fashionable but chose not to reveal her buttocks and nipples, the smart girl about town who needed to impress the boyfriend's family. Even the middle-aged woman who wanted to knock ten years off her age went for a Sidney design. Companies came in the square mile of the rag trade, rocketed into the sky like shooting stars, then fell to earth and were gone. Gerry Mortimer watched them like the elder statesman he was, sometimes regretfully, sometimes with a smile of satisfaction when a particularly flash young man exploded in a shower of cocaine and debts.

Gerry's showroom became a psychiatrist's office for the troubled younger generation who thought his advice worth listening to, and even if they were potential rivals, he never refused to help. Sometimes his assistance went beyond just listening: a visit to a friendly bank, an introduction to an estate agent who knew of a cheap and available showroom, the loan of a designer when the money ran out to produce a range, even credit guarantees to help the young men get fabric when times were hard. If you were one of 'Gerry's boys', you were lucky indeed. There were those of course who envied him his success and popularity, who created the false rumours that he only helped in order to be in a position to buy up assets when a company failed, and yes, there were times when a cash buy-out was the only solution; but Gerry never made anybody sell, never called in his debts and never bought when there was somebody else prepared to pay a higher price. Yet the assets he acquired, the leaseholds of the showrooms, the flats in the square mile, all began to form a property portfolio that soon threatened to become a property empire.

For Gerry that was never going to be enough.

'I don't want to be a rent collector who also makes dresses. I need to do something that interests me, that's constructive.'

The interest came first in the shape of bingo halls and then in leisure centres, bowling alleys, health farms and tennis centres. Gerry, more than anybody else, sensed the pressures and stress that afflicted the businessmen of the seventies and eighties. He saw the property crash coming, reduced his borrowing accordingly, and realised that in a difficult economic climate people would still spend money on leisure. He was right and the steady and inexorable progress towards a public flotation on the Stock Exchange was inevitable.

Yet throughout this rise to success,

D'Arblay Leisure had been a thorn in Mortimer's side, a particularly poisonous thorn given his dislike of their Chairman, Toby Lipscomb. For years it had seemed to Gerry that whenever an opportunity for an acquisition arose, whenever he had a development in the offing, D'Arblay was there—and even if they didn't succeed in beating him to the post, invariably succeeded in pushing up the price. They had also gone to the market and although their results had never been as impressive as Sidney's, there was no doubt that they had cornered, and were continuing to corner, a more than meaningful slice of the industry.

Now a unique opportunity had arisen. Everybody spoke to Gerry Mortimer and during the course of one of those little conversations it had come to his attention that the relationship between D'Arblay's Chairman, Toby Lipscomb, and its Chief Executive Officer, Bryan Kinsey, was less than cordial. Some discreet investigation revealed, inevitably, that there was a woman at the bottom of it, a woman shared by both men. Toby had the woman at the moment, Kinsey wanted her, and if he wasn't going to have her, was going to make life as difficult as possible for his erstwhile partner. Lipscomb and Kinsey had built up the company together, but it had always been an uneasy alliance, a relationship forged on necessity rather than friendship.

Kinsey, it appeared, was prepared to sell his 25% stake in the company, but not to just anybody. He would only sell to somebody who would cause maximum damage to Lipscomb. Kinsey would take the money and run, knowing that as far as Toby Lipscomb was concerned, the company was valuable above money. Lipscomb was that kind of man, believing himself to be destined for a knighthood. Even his name sounded better prefixed by a 'Sir', as if his parents had chosen it with that honour in mind. Lipscomb was a committee man, a charitable benefactor whose photographs appeared with monotonous regularity in the newspapers: bowing to a Royal, opening the wing of a hospital, planting a tree in a new garden. Lipscomb's public efforts were public for that very reason: to massage his ego, to promote his image, to make him a man to be seen with, and D'Arblay was a perfect platform for his ambitions. Their health clubs attracted the right sort of people, their nightclubs gave him sufficient knowledge of the sexual peccadillos of the politically powerful to use as leverage, and their hotels, particularly those in the more attractive parts of the countryside, had eagle-eyed managers who could spot who had been staying where with whom. It didn't matter to Lipscomb which charities he supported: the object was not fund raising in itself, but to be seen to be fund raising. Without D'Arblay he'd be just another rich man. With D'Arblay he was a rich man sitting in the midst of a network of information.

Kinsey's plan was simple and he really believed he'd thought of it, even though Gerry Mortimer had planted it in his mind through a mutual female friend. He contracted to sell his shares to Mortimer, then went offshore to a suitable tax haven before he completed, to count his money for the next three years. With Kinsey's shares under his belt Mortimer would then speak to a few institutional shareholders in D'Arblay, and once they were on his side make a full bid. The lawyers had looked at the situation and satisfied themselves that the Monopolies Commission wouldn't be interested. It was just a question of getting Kinsey's shares at a sensible price then keeping the rest of the shares down long enough to make the bid viable.

That was Stephen Kennard's task for the week. Get Kinsey signed up in total secrecy, for any sort of leak at all would mean a movement in the shares. That in turn would push up Kinsey's price and might make the whole takeover financially impractical. It wasn't easy. Mortimer was pushing, but deals like this couldn't be done overnight. The Stock Exchange had strict regulations about one public company buying a stake in another where a takeover might result, and Stephen as lawyer and director knew he was treading through a minefield.

Cathy stirred by his side.

'Where are we?'

'Stuck somewhere between Oxford and Uxbridge. I can't believe these roadworks. They've had this bloody motorway up more often than Tower Bridge.'

'Don't swear, Dad,' said his son, 'you tell me off when I do.'

'Yeah,' said Danielle, 'but you used the "f" word. Bloody's not swearing. Shakespeare used it.'

'Can we leave the literary discussions? My head's exploding,' snapped Cathy. She tapped her fingers impatiently against the glove compartment, then switched off the radio.

'I think I'm going back to sleep. Wake me up when we get there—or for lunch, whichever comes first.'

The cars inched forward. The police had imposed a speed limit of 50 mph—an increasingly sick joke. Stephen glanced at his watch.

It was already eight-thirty and the traffic was going to get worse, not better. By the time he'd dropped the family off at home in Totteridge, it would take the best part of an hour to work in Holborn, so he was looking at nearly eleven. Gerry would be going through the roof. Stephen had already put off their breakfast meeting on the grounds of his wife's incapacity, but Gerry wasn't likely to be so understanding about this latest delay. And that added to a day out of the office on Friday, with all the calls piling up. It was going to extend the patience of Sandra, his long serving secretary, to its very limit. Sandra gave in her notice nowadays on a monthly basis, but after ten years he treated each episode like a minor matrimonial tiff.

'When you leave, Sandra, it'll be feet first,' was what he'd said the last time. Every so often he took her out to lunch or bought her a bouquet of flowers. It seemed to work in appeasing her, although the sort of pressure she'd be under this week might well justify jewellery rather than food and horticulture.

Cars were overheating and pulling off on to what had been the hard shoulder. Even the temperature gauge on his BMW was hovering just below the red danger level. Cathy snoozed on, half waking with a start each time her head dropped to her chest. Jonny had also fallen asleep in the back, where Danielle jogged to the noiseless rhythm of her headphones. Nine o'clock came and passed, then nine-thirty, and still London seemed ever more distant. At times like these Stephen regretted the luxury of the cottage—a regret that would be dispelled as soon as he broke free of London and passed through Woodstock on his next visit. But for the moment there was no freedom, just the torture of being in a humid metal box in a long line of other metal boxes.

At 9.45 the car phone rang. He sat up with a start, realising just how close he'd been to nodding off himself. That was all he needed! Hauled in and breathalysed on Friday, asleep at the wheel on Monday. He expected it to be Gerry, but instead it was Jeffrey.

'Steve, where the hell are you?'

'In a solid wall of traffic on the M40.'

'How quickly can you get in?'

'How quickly can a pig learn to fly? Your guess is as good as mine. I've got to drop the family off first, then as soon as I arrive I've a meeting with Gerry.'

'I think that may have to wait—we've got a problem.'

'What sort of problem?' Stephen asked almost not wanting the reply.

'I'm not sure. Something odd has gone on here over the weekend. Arthur's not come in and we can't get any sense out of the computer. I've checked the weekend deposits with the Bank and they don't seem to stack up.'

'What are you saying, Jeffrey?'

'Just that our accounts manager's not here, he's changed the codes on the computer on Friday and didn't tell Eddie, and I don't like what I'm hearing from the bank. Has that little piggy learned to fly yet?'

'I'll be there as soon as I can.'

He took a deep breath, then another, trying to calm himself. Arthur Kemp had been their accounts manager for ten years. They'd trusted and relied on him. There had to be a good explanation. Eddie Sims, his number two, was none too bright. Maybe he'd misunderstood whatever it was Arthur had done on Friday.

As if sensing his despair, the road suddenly reverted to three lanes, a sign apologised for any inconvenience, and Stephen was speeding towards the centre of London, speeding towards his office, speeding towards what in his heart of hearts he knew to be trouble.

Chapter Eight

Stephen and Jeffrey looked down at the bank of computers with the same expression on their faces that they might have worn if faced with the latest in Martian technology.

'It was easier when we just had a little man writing up the books, wasn't it?' Stephen said in a tone that was brighter than he felt.

He'd driven straight into town, put his complaining brood into a taxi, and turned his attention to the immediate problem. Gerry Mortimer was no longer asking for an appointment, he was giving ultimatums, and whatever happened Stephen had to be at Sidney's offices in Great Titchfield Street by two. That gave him just over three hours to sort out the crisis in front of him. He stopped only to open the neatly wrapped present on his desk. It was a caricature of himself, holding the scales of justice, beautifully framed. Trisha must have commissioned it specially, full of confidence that he'd win his case. He owed her a thank you, but even that would have to wait for the moment.

Eddie Sims, a plump, ruddy-faced individual in his mid-twenties, ran his fingers over, rather than through, his close-cropped hair. He was not an attractive person to be with for any length of time. At moments of stress he tended to sweat and right now his shirt was soaked with perspiration. His teenage acne, which had never really healed up, stood out red and raw and his eyes seemed to be bulging out of his head with the effort of concentrating.

'Come on, Eddie, you've always told us that you were a genius with computers. Now's the time to prove it. What was it you said when you pushed for a rise last month? Arthur's from the old school—you're the new breed? Show us what the new breed's worth.'

'It's not that easy, Mr Wightman. Without the password I can't raise anything on the screen. If you asked me for a printout on any account I couldn't give it to you right now. And to find the password—well, I'd just be guessing.'

'So guess,' said Stephen. 'You worked with Arthur. You know how his mind worked, what he liked and disliked, what was his favourite food, singer, woman. Which football team did he support?'

'Fulham.'

'Try that. Try Cottage. Go through the

Fulham first team. Try Johnny Haynes and Jimmy Hill. Even Tommy Trinder. Just keep trying!'

Stephen felt the frustration simmering inside him, knowing it was irrational and unfair to be angry with young Eddie but also realising that he was a natural target.

'What happens if we don't break the code?' Jeffrey asked.

'I'm not too sure. I suppose we take the last print out and do a manual reconciliation against the bank balances, then re-program. It's a massive job for the auditors and the accounts staff, and even if there's nothing missing I'm not sure we shouldn't be telling the Law Society.'

Stephen gnawed at his lower lip, a habit he thought he'd grown out of when he'd finished his last examination.

'You said the bank had some information that worried you?'

Jeffrey referred to a little notebook at his side, like a policeman giving evidence at a trial.

'When Arthur didn't come in and Eddie was drawing a blank, I phoned Arthur's home. He lives with his elderly sister. She sounded surprised because she thought we would have known Arthur was on holiday. He'd told her he'd saved up his time owing and was going on a cruise for a month.

She'd been really pleased because he never took enough time off and she thought a long rest would do him the world of good and recharge all his batteries.'

'Well, I'm pleased about that. Let's hope Arthur remembers to send us a postcard,' Stephen said grimly.

'I don't know how you can joke about this, Stephen, I'm not sure we even had Arthur bonded. I've asked my secretary to dig out the insurance policies.'

'Anyway, you established Arthur had taken his bucket and spade and toddled off...'

'That's right. So I phoned the bank to get the balances on the client and office deposits. They said we had three million pounds odd on client and two hundred thousand on office.' He paused, waiting for the figures to sink in.

'Yes,' Stephen urged him on.

'Well, on Thursday those balances were four million and five hundred thousand.'

Stephen felt himself go cold.

'Look, Jeff, we may have had completions on Friday. Monies could have been going out. And as for office—well, the rent was due, and so were salaries. It may not be as bad as we think—or bad at all. Let's not panic.'

'Steve, don't hold your breath. We were all out on Friday, remember. We gave

Arthur full authority in our absence. If there was one day he was going to go rogue on us, then Friday was it. We left him the keys to the store and he already had the combination of the safe. Maybe you're right and a few bits and pieces went out legitimately, but not the whole balance. I tell you, we're stuffed.'

'Maybe, maybe not. We have to tell the Law Society and probably the police as well,' Stephen said.

'What, right away?'

'I think so. Have you told Sarah and Anthony? They're in this too. And the junior partners.'

'I've only spoken to you.'

'Then let's give them the good news. I'll call the auditors and the Law Society, then I've got to fly. If this is going to be as bad as I think it is, we need every good client we've got.'

By the time Stephen reached him Gerry Mortimer was not a happy man. He'd resisted the temptation to move his corporate headquarters out of the square mile that was the heart of London's fashion trade. 'The trade's not done too badly by me, why should I abandon it now?' he'd always said. Today, with Stephen, he was less philosophical.

'What fucking time do you call this? You're getting too big for your boots.

Don't forget, I made you. Big man, you're a director of a public company, a racehorse owner. Big man! Well, big men can also be cut down to size. Don't forget that, *pisher!*'

Stephen tried to interrupt him, to calm him down, to placate. He'd never seen Gerry like this before, but he was not to be placated.

'*Pisher!*' His voice rose to a crescendo. 'To me you'll always be a *pisher* until you start acting like a *mensch*. I remember when you wet your trousers, and your father, *oleva sholem* gave you to me to change. He could never abide any sort of mess, your father, bless him. There was a *mensch!* He didn't know the meaning of being late.'

The mixture of Yiddish and English became more intense, as if he was regressing to his childhood, a nursery tantrum because his nanny had kept him waiting for tea.

'My father's late now,' Stephen said. Gerry looked at him as if had taken leave of his senses.

'You can joke? You can joke about your dear father? I don't believe you, Stephen. I wanted to call you on the weekend. Oh no, no business calls, a country gentleman in his home. His house is his castle. You don't belong in a castle—a *shtetl,* that's where you belong, hiding under the table when you hear the cossacks' boots. Then see what a big man you are. So I don't phone because we're having breakfast. Do we have breakfast? No I get a 'phone call, *I* get *schlapped* out of bed before I have to get up—because his wife's got a headache. So she had a headache last night to stop you giving her one? Believe me, with a *shmeckle* like yours I don't blame her! At least so long as it doesn't disturb my breakfast meetings. I call you on your car phone—oh, yes, Mr Big man has got a mobile—but he can't talk to me on it because he's on the motorway. And finally he turns up half an hour late—for what? You had a lunch appointment, you had some *shikse* you needed to service in a hotel. For what...'

Gerry had gone so red in the face that Stephen thought he was about to have a heart attack. He was puffing and panting like an elderly man who'd staggered up the escalator on the tube, his voice hoarse and breathless, the veins on his forehead dancing in a wild fandango.

'Can I explain now?' Stephen asked, then giving Gerry no chance to catch his breath told him of the disasters that had befallen him from the moment he'd left the racecourse. Gradually the old man calmed down and finally leaned over and squeezed Stephen's shoulder.

'*Gnug*. Enough. We've both had *tsores*. Let's get down to business. Your problems you can do nothing about. From what you've told me you're not at fault, and even an *alte kaker* like me knows that you have to be insured for employees' theft...'

'Jeffrey's not too sure.'

'Jeffrey. What does he know? I've told you before, he needs you much more than you need him. Where would that *verduste* practice be without you?'

'Jeff and I have been friends for a long time...'

'So? Stay friends. Finish being partners. I've asked you before and I'll ask you again. Leave practice. Come into the company full-time. Then you won't have me shouting at you because you don't turn up for important meetings.'

'You're right, Gerry—I'd just have you shouting at me all the time. Look, it's a kind offer...'

'...It's not kind. It's selfish. I need you more than Jeffrey. He'll muddle through. Let him do that merger he's talking about—but not with you there.'

'Greystone's, you mean? That's not a merger—it's a takeover. Besides, they're D'Arblay's solicitors. I don't even really want to talk to them—even to say no—until this deal is over. And by that time I suspect they won't be talking to me.'

95

It had been two months since Jeffrey had first told him that Greystone's were interested in a merger. They were a City firm, not large by City standards, but large for all that. Philip Greystone, the senior partner, was the latest in a long line of Greystones dating back to the middle of the eighteenth century.

The world of London lawyers is neatly divided. City firms are situated in that area between what was Aldgate and Blackfriars, extending just as far north as City Road but not beyond. They share a certain code, certain rules—whether in terms of dress, attitude or clients. Dark grey suits, usually pinstriped, are the norm, worn with suitable sober shirts and even more sober ties—bright braces are just permissible if kept under the jacket, which is never removed at meetings even on the hottest of days. Normally you have to live south of the river to become a partner, although nowadays Islington, and on rare occasions Hampstead, and some parts of Hertfordshire and Essex are acceptable. Jews are not encouraged and the true blue City firm sometimes manages to achieve a hundred partners without the hint of a Semite amongst them.

Clients are carefully screened. Institutions and insurance companies are welcomed, clothing manufacturers not. Public companies are regarded as their own particular territory, carefully protected by the enclave of City accountants and City stockbrokers who dissuade any entrepreneurial board of a Public or potentially Public company from instructing anybody but one of their favourite firms. Every City lawyer, once he dons his uniform and passes his masonic-like entrance exam, automatically believes he is superior to every other lawyer on the earth. A clash between two large City firms, each entrenched, each haemorrhaging their clients' money freely to score a point, is like a battle between two dinosaurs. At least that was the way Stephen often saw them: antediluvian prehistoric creatures, lumbering about their business while the world overtook them.

Even when Sidney had gone Public, the brokers, the underwriters and the financial advisers had told Gerry he had to use a City firm. He'd told them to put in writing why they thought Stephen's practice was not suitable. He awaited the letter, Stephen had his libel action all ready to issue, but the letter didn't come. Gerry Mortimer then, as now, was his own man.

A race apart from the City firms are the West End practices, generally representing successful commercial companies who are not quoted on the Stock Exchange or rich individuals who have a close personal relationship with a particular partner. Even the largest of the West End firms are half the size of a large City firm who, anxious to protect their own monopoly position, point out that very feature when extolling the merits of their own practice. Stephen knew that whereas a City firm would field up to half a dozen solicitors on a major transaction, he'd run it with just himself and one other, yet still he felt that he could compete with the best of them. The one area where he and the other West End firms scored was in their commercial approach. Point a City lawyer from A to C and he'll go there via B. Yet Stephen knew that B was not necessarily always the best stopping off point and indeed C was not even the most advantageous end to the journey. He was flexible, imaginative, able to rescue a situation for a client rather than kill it off. It was all a matter of approach. He felt a deal was there for the doing and there had to be a way to do it. Most of the City firms were trying to give their clients a lesson in law at their own expense, and if in so doing the deal fell by the wayside, then so be it.

This dividing line made the approach from Greystone's all the stranger. Yet their story was that they wanted Kennard & Wightman, and whatever else came with them, mainly for their commercial approach. They liked their attitude, they liked their ambition, they liked their mix of clients. What they would think about Arthur and the potentially missing money was another matter. Right now the two firms' paths were about to cross.

'So what do you think?' Gerry's voice brought Stephen back to matters in hand.

'I'm sorry, Gerry, about what?' He thought he might have missed something vital.

'About giving up your lousy profession and joining my lousy company?'

'I'll think about it. Let's get this bit of business over and done with, get my position sorted out, and I'll address my mind to it. What's the agenda for today?'

Gerry looked at his watch.

'What's left of it?' He couldn't resist the final dig. 'We're seeing Bryan Kinsey at four o'clock. It's all a bit like Deep Throat in Watergate. He's having someone ring us here in half an hour to tell us where to meet him. He thinks his phone may be bugged.'

'Maybe he just likes to feel important. Maybe he's paranoid.'

'Maybe,' Gerry said, 'but I've known Toby Lipscomb a long time, a long, long time, and believe me, he makes a dangerous enemy.'

'Who's being paranoid now?' asked Stephen. But as he saw the grim determined expression on Gerry's face he knew the time for joking had passed. It was time to get down to serious business.

Chapter Nine

The flat where they sat could well have been a safe house in a Le Carré novel. There was a plain sofa that converted to a bed, a small round table with four chairs, an open plan kitchen with just enough room for one person to stand, and a miniscule toilet and shower. There was no hiding place, no escape. The walls were white and pictureless, the window small, only begrudgingly letting in air and such light as escaped from the narrow gap between the narrow buildings and the house next door. Even the carpet on the floor had a colour that defied description.

'Nice place you've got here,' Stephen said with a smile.

'It serves a purpose.' Bryan Kinsey was not a likeable man. Clearly he'd once been fit and powerful, but his six-foot frame now ran to fat rather than muscle, stomach winning its fight against his shirt buttons and testifying to a surfeit of lunchtime drinking sessions. He could only have been in his mid-forties but his hair was completely white, and the bloodshot, alcohol-injected eyes gave him the look of a slightly crazed rabbit. His moustache was still dark, accentuating even more the colour of his hair, and somebody who loved him should have told him to shave it off. It might well have been that nobody loved him enough to bother because with his nicotine-stained teeth testifying to a sixty a day habit, he was going to buy rather than earn affection. However, if the deal that was on the table went through, then he was going to be able to afford an awful lot of affection. The woman who'd chosen Toby Lipscomb rather than him obviously had some taste.

Gerry and Stephen sat down at the table waiting to be offered something to drink, realised the offer was not going to be forthcoming and then spread out their papers. The other occupant of the room was a thin, weasel-faced man whose dark hair was sleeked back in the style of a forties film star with either Brylcreem or boot polish. He wore a large dotted bow tie that had the effect of appearing to support his scrawny neck. By contrast the lapels of his double breasted jacket were so wide that they made him seem as if he were about to take off. He introduced himself as Peter Repton, Kinsey's solicitor, and when Stephen took his hand it was like touching a newly deceased corpse.

Kinsey and Repton had been waiting for them a while and the ashtray on the table was already filled with cigarette butts, some only half smoked. There was a haze in the room normally only associated with all night card sessions and Stephen, a committed anti-smoker, felt his lungs tighten in the fug.

'Do you mind if I open the window a bit,' he asked, coughing. Kinsey grudgingly nodded his assent as if he objected to any interference with his private camouflage.

'Can we get on with this, please? We've got a lot of arrangements to make and you're already an hour late. It's no way to do business.' Repton had a short staccato way of talking, a man used to giving orders and being instantly obeyed. Stephen wondered if he was married and with what hang-ups his children would grow up.

'Right.' It was Stephen who took command, naturally and easily. Late he may have been but he'd had the time to get clear and precise instructions from Gerry. He knew what they wanted to achieve and a quick telephone conversation with

Anthony had given him an idea of how to achieve it.

'You have three million shares in D'Arblay...' Repton interrupted him. 'Could you address your comments to me and not my client? I'll be making the decision here.'

Kinsey lit another cigarette and blew the smoke straight across the table into Stephen's face. He broke into a paroxysm of coughing and Kinsey permitted himself the first smile of the meeting. This lawyer wasn't up to much. Repton was going to be too much for him, and if they maintained the intolerable conditions Kennard was going to be dying to get the meeting over—dying or dead.

Stephen took a deep breath, half choked again, then turned to Repton.

'Your client has three million shares in D'Arblay. He also has assignable options for another million. The three million represents twenty-five percent, the extra one million would be part of a dilution but would still bring him up to a twenty-nine percent shareholding. Obviously that sort of stake merely creates nuisance value and doesn't give control. Consequently we've valued it accordingly.'

'We?' the other lawyer queried. 'Oh, yes, I'd forgotten you're wearing two hats. I assume your client doesn't mind any potential conflict he may have?'

Stephen fought hard to control himself. He knew he was being needled, he knew this was all part of a carefully nurtured technique, and for his client's sake he had to keep calm. He turned to Gerry.

'Do you mind, Gerry?'

'Conflict away.' Gerry pulled out a large cigar and lit up, then returned fire by exhaling the thick blue smoke directly into Kinsey's face.

'I hope you don't mind if I smoke?' he said. 'Sorry, Stephen I interrupted you.'

He shuffled his papers to give himself a moment to regain his concentration.

'The shares at the moment are quoted at £3.15. If you were to try and sell you might get that price for the first thousand, then as the brokers and the market realise what they were selling the price would go down and down until perhaps it would reach £2.30, even assuming you could find a buyer for all your shares in what might best be described as a very tight market. So what we're suggesting is that we pay you £2.60 per share, cash on the nail, and you can assign the benefits of the options to us for nothing. Seven point eight million pounds—not a bad deal. I also understand you'd like to go abroad. We'll wait until you've gone non-resident, then we'll complete. You'll get all your profits free of capital gains and Toby Lipscomb finds himself with a new minority shareholder.'

'Is that it?' Repton asked.

'That's it.'

Repton made as if to rise.

'Well, gentlemen, thanks for coming, but let's not waste each other's time. I'm not stupid and nor is my client. We know you've got some institutional support lined up.' He referred to major pension funds and like who took shares in public companies for investment and would not hesitate to cash in if a big windfall profit came their way. They were easy to deal with. It was the small, long-term family shareholders who were in it for the duration rather than the money who could be the problem.

'You'll buy my client's shares at a knockdown price, then use that as a guideline for the others, launch a full bid for the company as you're obliged to when you go over the twenty-nine percent, and Lipscomb would not be able to resist it.'

Stephen didn't move from his seat. He would have been disappointed if Repton had reacted any other way.

'Look, we don't want to be unreasonable. The shares are steady at £3.15 now. However, we know there are a few skeletons

105

in the cupboard. A certain young lady, for example, well known to both you and Mr Lipscomb is, I understand, being courted by the Sunday newspapers for her story. Dirt will stick. It may not ruin the company but it's not going to improve your standing in the City. They'll run a mile from scandal as things are today. No other buyer would be so amenable as to get the money to you tax free. So we'll say £2.65 and that's it.'

Repton, to his credit, didn't panic.

'My client's looking for a certain figure. He wants to clear nine million pounds—£3 a share and you pay my costs.'

Stephen didn't even bother to look at Gerry.

'We'll stick at £2.65—and yes, we'll pay your costs.' He added the last as if he couldn't quite believe how undignified it was for a real grown-up lawyer to ask anybody but his client for costs.

'May I have a word with my client alone?' Repton asked, accentuating the 'may' to show his good breeding.

Stephen nearly burst out laughing. The first time he'd seen anything mildly amusing in life all day.

'What are the two of you going to do, lock yourselves in the loo? OK, OK, come on, Gerry, we'll wait outside.'

The landing was dark and evil-smelling.

Closing his eyes, Stephen could imagine himself in some Dickensian tenement peopled by caricatures culled from the underworld.

'I hope he'll buy himself something better with the proceeds of sale,' Stephen said in a whisper.

'You're sure this deal is going to go through?'

'He can't say no.'

'You weren't bluffing about skeletons in the cupboard then?'

Stephen just smiled. 'Did you think I was bluffing?'

'It was the first I'd heard about it, but then I'm only the client. I wish you'd discuss tactics with me first.'

'Do I need to if they work?'

'Let's see them work first.'

The door opened and a feeble shaft of light filtered reluctantly into the gloom.

'We're ready for you now,' Repton said.

They re-entered the room and took up position, unable to miss the two empty glasses that were now on the table.

'Been celebrating early?' Stephen asked. 'Funny, I would have thought we'd have heard the champagne cork through the door.'

'Do you pay him by the hour or by the quality of his comic material?' Repton asked Gerry. 'I do hope it's the former for his sake, otherwise he might be struggling to earn a living.'

'He earns a living, don't worry,' Gerry replied. 'Have you made up your minds, or should I be speaking in the singular?'

'£2.75 a share and you've a deal.'

Gerry opened his mouth, but Stephen cut in. 'Sorry, this isn't an auction situation. £2.65. The offer stands—or at least it does for the next five minutes.'

Repton and Kinsey exchanged glances.

'Very well. It's a deal. But we want some heads of agreement signed now and all the money deposited by noon tomorrow. I'll tell you when we want it released. I want my client here out of the country.'

'If you've got the share certificates that's no problem. Obviously I want to satisfy myself that there are no prohibitions or conditions on sale.'

'There's nothing,' Kinsey said, 'I've always made sure of that.'

It took just under an hour to write out an agreement that satisfied both parties. They signed, exchanged and then rose to leave. It wasn't a transaction where hand shakes were offered.

'I'll speak to you tomorrow then,' Stephen said to Repton.

'You will.'

Kinsey didn't seem like a man who'd just made himself over seven million pounds.

He gave Stephen a look that might have worried him if the two of them had been alone down a dark alleyway.

'Tell me, how did you know about the girl?' he asked.

'I have my sources,' Stephen replied, then closed the door behind him and stumbled down the dark stairs to gulp in the fresh air outside.

Chapter Ten

Toby Lipscomb ambled along a flower bed, snipping and tidying with a pair of garden shears as he made his progress.

'There, there, my beauty, that's better. Need you looking your best for the Minister's visit.'

He enjoyed talking to his flowers and plants. They never answered back so he could say what he liked, and if he didn't approve of a reaction then he could crop or destroy as ruthlessly as he chose. Yet he liked plants, genuinely preferred them to most people he knew. Plants were trustworthy, predictable. They were planted, they grew, and eventually they would die, but for the moment he simply wanted them to look beautiful. In two days' time he would entertain Sir Richard Kemp, the Minister for Health, and he wanted everything to be just right. The gardener had worked ceaselessly on the lesser tasks; his staff had bustled around the property, painting, polishing, replacing; his cook had been bolstered by the hiring of André de Chevois for the occasion, and all that remained to be done was to put the final personal touches.

Not many people who met him across a boardroom table would have taken him for a gardener, but then not many people knew exactly what did go on in the mind of Toby Lipscomb. He'd been born nearly fifty years ago in Plymouth, his father a retired naval officer, his mother a member of the famous D'Arblay family. The same D'Arblays who'd switched from Cavalier to Cromwellian to begin a family fortune, who'd concealed Catholic antecedents to support Hanover against Stuart, who'd figured in governments as disparate as Palmerston's and Balfour's, Campbell Bannerman's and Chamberlain's.

Lipscomb had never really known what it was like to want for anything, yet some would say he desired everything. Others would pay tribute to his generosity, his unfailing support of charities. His opinions were kaleidoscopic, shaken into a thousand different viewpoints, a tangle of colours and emotions. Put half a dozen people together who knew him and each would paint a different picture, finally having to acknowledge that perhaps they did not really know him after all.

A tall impressive figure, grey hair, slightly receding but styled in a distinguished manner, he wore delicate gold-rimmed spectacles. His moustache, neatly trimmed, finished off the military edge to his appearance, one not in any way hindered by the smart blazer and knife-edged trousers that he invariably wore in public. He had never married, perhaps scared that somebody living in proximity to him for any length of time might successfully probe beneath the urbane surface.

He was proud of his family name and tradition, yet never too proud to be prepared to use it in his quest for commercial success. D'Arblay had sprung from more illustrious roots than Sidney Developments. A Whitehall club founded in the eighteenth century had been its first asset, an acquisition by inheritance rather than purchase. The management had been mildly surprised when the young Toby Lipscomb, then only thirty, had taken a personal interest in the running of his newfound toy. At first they'd humoured him, listened politely,

111

then gone on in their own long-established ways; but gradually they'd seen men who'd been employed for twenty-five years make the mistake of laughing at him once too often and those men had rapidly fallen by the wayside, their hopes of a comfortable retirement shattered by summary dismissal. Younger more aggressive men took their place, the club prospered, and other similar establishments were acquired, all run along the same lines—a benevolent despotism, but one that worked.

In a way it was hardly surprising that Toby Lipscomb and Gerry Mortimer should so dislike each other. They were both aiming at the same objectives whilst coming from totally different directions. At some time in their lives a collision seemed inevitable. Like Gerry Mortimer with the fashion trade, Lipscomb became bored with clubs and diversified into leisure centres and from there into health farms and even private hospitals. It caused some surprise to the City when D'Arblay was floated. Lipscomb had run the company virtually single-handed, no decision, however seemingly minor being made without his personal nod of assent. Now he had to present to the City a board that included accountants, bankers, gaming experts and even a doctor, a board where the individual talents had to appear to merge and gell for the overall good. If the City was surprised by the principle of the flotation they were amazed by its success. From an original offer price of £1 shares rose consistently until they reached £6 when a two for one offer reduced the price to £3 but made Lipscomb an even richer man.

Bryan Kinsey had arrived with the first casino. He was good at his job, knew the industry inside out, and even more important understood the Gaming Board and their requirements. Whilst other casinos came and went, their licences revoked, their doors closed, the D'Arblay Group consistently sailed on through, their reputation unsullied. Nobody ever found D'Arblay touting, nobody ever proved that they gave inducements to their high rollers. No D'Arblay croupier was ever found sleeping with a member. Their success infuriated competitors to the point of hysteria. In City meeting rooms and at dinner parties, opinions were expressed as facts.

'D'Arblay had the board in their pockets.'

'Lipscomb pulls strings at the highest level.'

'Kinsey gets away with everything for which we're hung, drawn and quartered.'

But the mud didn't stick and even the few specks of dirt that occasionally filtered through were flicked away like troublesome flies by Lipscomb's elegant fingers.

Kinsey was anything but elegant. He'd learned his business in South Africa, in the rough and tumble unregulated world of Sun City where gamblers came from all over the world and in particular from the African continent. From out of chaos Kinsey brought order, and from order he brought gold. Lipscomb approached him and made him an offer he simply couldn't refuse, both as to the amounts involved and the way it was actually put to him. Lipscomb had his own particular approach to business that did not tolerate refusals, that merely suffered competition as a way to achieve ultimate triumph.

It had not been a marriage made in heaven but Lipscomb and Kinsey understood each other. They avoided trampling on each other's toes and rarely mixed socially, but as the company grew so did Kinsey's role. Then the girl came along. Like most women who have played a major role in history there was nothing really remarkable about Cheryl Stokes. A good figure, an average brain, a pleasant face, no more than an unexceptional croupier; but something about her triggered off a reaction in both Chairman Lipscomb and Chief Executive Officer (as he'd become) Kinsey. Kinsey was not particularly prepossessing

114

but he was Cheryl's boss and she needed the job. Consequently when he asked her out to dinner on the pretext of inquiring into the activities of one of her workmates she made no objection. Nor, after a couple of bottles of champagne, did she show much resistance to him taking her to bed. The trouble came when Kinsey mistook for love what she saw merely as an implied term of her contract. Lipscomb made no such errors. For him the distinction was clear and on a fleeting visit to the casino where she worked she caught his eye. Whether or not he even knew about her involvement with Kinsey was academic. She was there, she worked for one of his companies, so he took her.

Now Lipscomb looked back up to the house, tossing the gardening tools on to the immaculate lawn. He could see the girl sitting at the edge of the indoor swimming pool in the conservatory, the pallor of her skin arousing in him a sexual excitement that was only controlled by the fact that he knew he could have her whenever he chose. He was toying with the idea of taking her there and then by the side of the pool when the telephone rang. He immediately picked up the cordless phone that he carried with him around the grounds. The voice at the other end sounded animated, concerned, but Lipscomb simply listened and nodded

115

as if the other person could actually see him. Finally the speaker ran out of steam and Lipscomb pushed down the extended aerial. So Kinsey had sold his shares. Not just sold them but thought he could keep the news a secret. Lipscomb hadn't realised how much Kinsey had cared for the girl. If he'd only said, Lipscomb would probably have given her to him—when he had finished with her.

He tapped the second finger of his right hand against his lower lip, his mind moving with awesome speed. Always be one step ahead of the game, know your opponent's next move. He had a new shareholder in his company. He'd have to make him welcome.

Chapter Eleven

Back at the office Stephen had no time to enjoy the triumph of his negotiations. Jeffrey, Sarah and Anthony were closeted in the board room with Paul Levy, a partner in their auditors, Golding, Levy and Redford.

'Hello, Stephen, I won't ask how you are.'

Paul had also been at school with

Jeffrey and Stephen, and ever since he had qualified and set up his own firm there had been a steady exchange of clients between the two practices.

Paul sat with sheet after sheet of computer printout in front of him, a gleam in his eye as the professional challenge became more and more complex. There was a time when he'd been slim, they had school photos to prove it, but years at a desk and a penchant for chocolates and biscuits had helped create a paunch which could shelter a queue at a bus stop. His chest above his stomach was fairly normal in size then suddenly spread out to a huge neck upon which was perched a round moon-shaped face, the bald head adding to a cartoonist's dream.

Stephen didn't miss the computer print-out.

'That's right,' Jeffrey said, 'we found the code word. You were on the right track when you focused on Fulham.'

'What was it?'

'Rabbi,' Jeffrey replied.

'The Rabbi'—the Craven Cottage nickname for Jimmy Hill in his playing days. The Rabbi...could anti-semitism have been a motive for Arthur's actions? It was hard to believe but then Stephen's grandmother had always told him that all Gentiles are anti-semites at heart; she'd seen her own grandmother killed by Cossacks in a pogrom while they hunted for the family fortune that they knew all Jews kept concealed.

'Is it bad?' Stephen asked.

'It's not good.' It was Sarah who spoke for the first time. 'You should have told us first thing this morning, Stephen, we're partners too.'

Anthony said nothing. Anybody who did not know that there was a spark of genius in him would have thought him catatonic. He sat doodling on a pad in front of him, seemingly oblivious to the panic amongst his partners.

Paul Levy looked up from his papers.

'It's not easy to tell exactly what's been happening. We carried out our last audit three months ago. I'd stake my reputation on everything being in order then.'

'If it wasn't it's your negligence policy rather than your life insurance that will interest us.' Sarah said what friendship prevented Stephen and Jeffrey from saying, even if they might have thought it.

Paul chose to ignore the comment and continued to look nonplussed.

'It may well be that the only un-authorised transfers took place on Friday, though it's possible that there's been a systematic fraud even before that. All I've been able to do so far is look at Friday, see what transfers were made and then try and work out where they went. I've found something that worries me, a couple of inter-client transfers which I think were just a clumsy smoke screen, but then a million went out on a foreign transfer. I've told the rest of them already that you have to call in the police—and the Law Society. This is clients' money we're talking about.'

'There is some consolation,' Jeffrey added. 'I've checked our insurance policies. We're covered for up to £2,000,000 for employees' theft. We've £100,000 excess but against the background of what we could be in for, that's almost a relief.'

What Jeffrey meant was that the first £100,000 of any theft by a member of staff had to be paid by the partners. After that they were covered up to £2,000,000, and then they were on their own. Stephen just prayed that Arthur's efforts had fallen short of that magic figure. A hundred grand was not a loss they could bear lightly but it wasn't enough to wipe them out. At least it left them with a practice that in time would earn them enough to pay back any short-term borrowings.

'So what happens now?' asked Sarah, with an air of belligerency that suggested none of this would have happened if she'd been senior partner.

119

'I carry on with my investigations. The Law Society will want to ask some questions. They'll send somebody in as well, I would think, both a solicitor and some auditors, just to make sure there's not some deeper, darker fraud taking place. They'll obviously be a bit concerned about the lack of supervision, even if it was just for one day.'

'Oh, they'll be really pleased when they find out where we were on Friday—perhaps you'll be able to turn away their wrath with a hot tip for the five o'clock at Newmarket, Stephen.'

Sarah had gone white, her makeup invisible, just two red spots illuminating her cheek bones. At this moment she was regretting ever coming into the practice, and even more staying there after her affair with Stephen had ended. The way in which she'd negotiated her partnership had flown in the face of all her principles. Throughout her years at the London School of Economics she'd been known as a radical socialist. She'd seen what a right-wing government had done to her parents. Her farmer father had struggled for subsidies and watched his French counterparts become the bully boys of Europe, all the while working longer hours for less and less reward. Even today at seventy he struggled on at his Gloucestershire smallholding, forced to supplement his income with a farm shop selling fruit and vegetables to coach loads of tourists. It was a sad end for a man who'd had a love affair with the land. Her mother had only recently retired as a teacher and she too had fought against a system that closed local schools where they were still needed and swelled the numbers in their classes to unmanageable proportions.

There was a time when Sarah had been concerned that the law should be available to everybody. Even after she'd become a partner she'd still held a free weekly clinic in Stoke Newington where she lived, but then the pressures of private practice had meant she'd missed a session, and then another, until finally she'd been replaced by somebody more reliable, somebody younger. She wasn't young any more. Thirty-six. If you didn't have your first child by the time you were thirty-six then you had a problem; but she wasn't going to get married just for the sake of having a child. She would have married Stephen, and before him there had been Kenny at University.

Poor Kenny, South African, as firm a believer in the rights of man as she was, but Kenny had two disadvantages: he wanted to put those rights into action in the country where he was born, and

Kenny had been born black. In those days you couldn't change South Africa and you couldn't change your colour. Apartheid and blackness—two constants in life. He'd wanted her to join him in Johannesburg when the time was right, he'd written to tell her so, but the time was never right. Kenny Okadibo was frozen in time because in 1978, at the age of twenty-two, he'd died in a police cell while resisting arrest. Kenny, sweet, gentle Kenny, would have resisted nothing. For a while Sarah railed at the injustice of the world, wrote letters, drafted petitions, tried to encourage liberal lawyers in Africa to take action, but by then it all seemed hopeless and she'd met Stephen while Kenny Okadibo was finally buried in a grave she'd never seen.

And now she saw all this as a punishment, sent from a God in whom she didn't believe, a punishment for abandoning her principles, her political faith if not her spiritual one. She felt terribly trapped, and even if she didn't show it, not a little afraid. Although she only had fifteen percent of the practice she was on the line to the bank and to the world outside as if she had one hundred percent. Yes, she had an indemnity from Stephen and Jeffrey, who between them had seventy percent of the practice, but an indemnity was only as good as the people who gave it and if they were going to go down they were going to take her with them.

She felt like kicking herself for acting so far out of character. When she and Stephen had parted after a steamy guilt-ridden night of passion she had decided she wouldn't let their personal life interfere with her professional ambitions. At the time it seemed right. It would have been the easiest thing in the world to have cut and run. With her connections there were many opportunities in firms far more socially committed than Kennard & Wightman. Yet she'd stayed. Was it because something at the back of her mind suggested that if she hung around long enough Stephen would leave his wife? Leave Cathy. It was absurd. She'd gone through all the motions with that woman on social occasions, smiled the right smiles, said the things she'd hoped Cathy would want to hear, but still Stephen's wife didn't warm to her. Maybe it was just that, just because she was Stephen's wife, and with that unnerving instinct that honest women have, knew there had been something between Sarah and her husband. Sarah hated to admit it but she hated Cathy. She hated to see her with Stephen, hated to see her with her children over the years. The only consolation was that Cathy grew older as the children did, though even then she looked no older; while she, Sarah, seemed to have to take that little bit longer with her makeup every day to keep herself up to her own high standard of appearance, to allow her to face the day, to face Stephen.

Right now as she faced him she felt as if she wanted to kill him rather than his wife. He had a reputation as a hard negotiator in the world outside but within the practice he was a soft touch, and it was about to cost him dear—and not just him, but also her. Again the sinking feeling in her stomach as the reality of the situation came home to her. She'd been robbed, they'd been robbed, but it was the personal affront that rankled. She knew now what it felt like to be mugged, to lose your pride as well as your possessions. She felt abused.

Just then the phone rang. They all looked at it as if they knew it was bringing a message of disaster for them and them alone. It was Paul who brought the agony to an end and answered it.

'Yes, yes, he's here.' He looked around and if they had not known him better the partners would have sworn he was playing his own private little game.

'It's for you, Stephen.' The others seemed to take a deep breath at a temporary reprieve.

'I told the switchboard no interruptions.' Paul shrugged. It wasn't his practice.

'Shall I say you're busy?'

'Who is it?'

Paul asked the question, then raised his eyebrows at the answer.

'It's your mother.'

Stephen groaned. He'd forgotten to phone her that morning and if he didn't call her by ten then she became concerned that some terrible accident had befallen him, or worse still that she'd perpetrated some unknown offence that had upset her elder son. Anthony suddenly came to life.

'Oh, I'm sorry, Stephen. I forgot to tell you she called and wanted you to call back.'

Stephen looked at his brother and not for the first time in his life wondered if they came from the same seed. It was only in moments of desperation that their mother asked to speak to Anthony at the office. It wasn't a question of favouritism, although Stephen was her first born, Anthony her baby, and nothing could change that. It was simply a question of knowing that Stephen could be relied upon whilst Anthony could not.

Stephen's face wore a hunted expression, but there was no escape. 'Put her through.'

Her voice could be heard around the room even though there was no loud speaker and Stephen held the receiver tightly against his ear.

125

'Stephen, are you all right? I was worried. You didn't ring. I thought maybe something happened on the way back. So many crazy drivers in the morning, everybody in a hurry.'

Stephen knew of old that if his mother had nothing to worry about she would sit up all night thinking of something. It might be the weather, it might be a new pain she was feeling which a friend had experienced just before they fell victim to some terrible disease, it might be whether or not her grandchild had actually liked the present she'd bought for him or her. Stephen invariably replied when he was asked how his mother was, 'Not so bad as she thinks she is.' Now she carried on, without waiting for a reply, never listening even when he gave her one.

'Look, Stephen, I've been thinking about my will...'

'Again?' He had prepared over a dozen versions in the last three years, and as he'd pointed out to her time and time again, she didn't have that much to leave.

'Maybe, maybe not, but I don't want anybody falling out over the jewellery. Never let it be said that my death broke up the family.'

'Look, Mum, I'm really busy right now. I'll pop in on my way home from work.'

'What time will that be?'

Fay Kennard liked a bit of certainty in her life, something he'd never been able to give her.

'I'm not sure. Quite late. I'll ring you. I've really got to go.'

Giving her no opportunity to continue the conversation, he put down the receiver. The others looked at him accusingly as if he had no right to conduct his normal personal life, as if it was his personal life that had brought them to this situation.

'You won't be away early tonight, we've got that meeting with Greystone's,' Jeffrey said.

'You have to be joking! What are we going to tell them about all this?' Stephen replied.

'We tell them the truth. We've done nothing wrong.'

Stephen sniffed. He'd been looking for reasons not to proceed with the Greystone's merger, but this was not exactly what he'd had in mind: a firm so badly run that their accounts manager could magic away sums of money that they weren't able to calculate accurately.

'I think we should put them off. Tell them something vital's come up.'

Jeffrey was not to be budged. 'Stephen, I've worked hard on this deal. It's not every day we get the chance to hop into bed with

127

somebody as high class as Greystone's. I'm not putting it off.'

Suddenly, Stephen felt too weary to argue. If Jeffrey insisted on this merger then somewhere along the line there might well be a confrontation; but right now, as they sat around the room like broken marionettes with Paul trying to pull the strings, wasn't the moment. If they were to get through this they had to pull together. His eyes moved from face to face: Jeffrey, his mind already racing ahead to the Greystone's meeting; Sarah, the anger still etched on her face like a scar; Anthony, his eyes blanked out by his glasses, his notebook a mass of figures and diagrams. Stephen's partners, his ex-lover, his family, an unlikely quartet—yes, if they were to get through this they all had to pull together, but in which direction only time would tell.

Chapter Twelve

Philip Greystone sat at the head of the table, looking down his nose at the people ranged down the sides. His fair hair was impeccably combed into place in a manner so impossibly old fashioned that he managed to appear positively trendy. His high forehead gave him the look of an archangel, until one saw the hard businesslike eyes that were unlikely ever to welcome anybody to heaven. Although he was cleanshaven it did not appear that he had to work very hard at it. He wore a well-cut double-breasted blue suit that looked as if it had cost every bit of the one thousand pounds that had been expended upon it, and the neat pale blue shirt was set off by the spotted bow tie that he had at first daringly affected and then adopted as a City trademark. His cut glass accent had been nurtured by a succession of nannies, cultivated at public school, honed at Cambridge, and perfected by years of dealing with public company chairmen who sometimes had not shared Philip's benefits.

To his left sat two of his partners, Dennis Logan and Richard Stephenson; to his right were Stephen and Jeffrey. The room was perfectly air conditioned, the views, to the right over the river, to the left across the City, enough to distract even the most eager of opponents. Yet today the firms of Greystone's and Kennard & Wightman were not in opposition; they were, if some of the assembled company had their way, about to enter into a sort of matrimony.

'Shall I take the chair then?' asked Greystone rhetorically, given that he had already seated himself in the relevant position. 'I've taken the liberty of producing a working agenda.' He dipped into the file before him and extracted two beautifully bound sets of documents that looked more like an abridged version of the Bible than an agenda.

'I've had to exhibit some addenda, such as accounts, leases, projections, analytical breakdowns of client base, etc—the usual sort of thing.'

Jeffrey nodded as if every document he had ever seen was in such pristine condition, while Stephen wondered just what they were doing here. He felt as he had done as a small boy when he had visited a church during the course of a service—if anybody discovered who he really was then he was likely to be expelled. Suddenly he felt that there was no point in beating about the bush—once this City firm knew what had happened yesterday it would all be off. Until this moment that was exactly what he had wanted, only the catalyst was not exactly the one he would have selected for himself. Now he felt a tinge of disappointment that the courtship was to come to nothing. It had all been so flattering, if not downright surprising, when the approach had first been made.

The two firms had been on opposite sides, Jeffrey acting for a computer company that had been taken over by one of Greystone's public quoted clients. Anthony had dealt with the tax side and Stephen had been peripherally involved in some of the service contracts for the directors. Although a takeover of that nature normally meant the loss of the client, the transactions had in fact, proceeded extremely smoothly and been completed to the clients' mutual satisfaction and the opening of several bottles of celebratory champagne in this very board room. A week or so later Philip Greystone himself had invited Jeffrey and Stephen to his club for lunch and had put it to them that Greystone's had some surplus space while Kennard & Wightman were conducting City type work in the West End, that it had generally been pleasant dealing with them, and why didn't they commence some preliminary discussions with a view to a merger? Jeffrey had been enthusiastic, Stephen less so.

'It's a great opportunity for us. It'll convince the clients who only give us some of their work that we can deal with it all. It'll give us status, make sure everybody accepts we've really arrived. Not bad for two Jewish boys from the East End.'

'Jeff, I know you like a bit of poetic

131

licence but we never came from the East End.'

'Perhaps not, but spiritually what else are we? How else do people perceive us?'

Stephen was not convinced.

'You make us sound like a couple of market boys. Come on, don't forget your cut price conveyancing, it's all going very cheap today! Roll up here for your divorce bargains! Wanna litigate? We'll do it for you at rock bottom prices and only twenty percent commission! Leave it out, Jeffrey. What we've got here is unique. We've our own niche in the profession. We know our clients, they know us. OK, so we don't bring a barrage of specialists to a meeting, but when we're in doubt we go to counsel. The client never suffers. And how do you think some of our clients are going to cope with Fancy Dan City prices?'

Jeffrey began to dig his heels in.

'Stephen, for once in your life don't prejudge people. We're not going to bed with them, they're not going to be the mothers of our children, and you don't even have to break bread with them on a regular basis. Let's just talk to them, see how it stacks up financially, and then make a decision.'

And reluctantly Stephen had agreed. Financially...that was what was important to Jeffrey, but it was easy for Stephen to be cynical. He had money, more than enough, he didn't have ex-wives forming an orderly queue every month for maintenance like pensioners outside a post office. He didn't want a row. It was easier to agree. Talk was cheap...although for lawyers perhaps that wasn't so true. As he never tired of telling his clients when they argued about his current level of charges, all he had to sell was his time.

Philip Greystone tapped on the table, as if such an action was universally recognised for bringing a meeting to order.

'I believe we all know each other? As you'll see the first item on the agenda is the financial effect of such a merger in relation to our two practices. You'll see that we've prepared a combined balance sheet and budget assuming the merged practice operating from these premises, and also assuming a ten percent growth in turnover in the first twelve months. It's been prepared by our auditors, and again I've assumed they'll be appointed to the new practice.'

Stephen flipped through the document.

'I see their fees account for a fair proportion of our profit.'

'Yes,' Philip replied, 'they're not cheap. but anything good seldom is.'

'I've been with our accountants for a long time,' Stephen said, looking crossly

133

at Jeffrey who had clearly placed him in the role of defending counsel. 'They send us a lot of work. I'm not sure on either a moral or commercial basis we could drop them just like that.'

'Bravo,' said Greystone, without a hint of sarcasm, 'I do like loyalty in a man. The problem is that, however competent they may be, will they be able to cope with what will, even on a conservative basis, be a multi-million pound operation? I fear not. But I'm never one to ruffle feathers. Public companies exist with joint auditors. I'm sure we can find such a role for them for a year or two, and then compensate them by recommending the sort of work which they will feel comfortable dealing with.'

Stephen shrugged. He hadn't meant to become embroiled in the details. First he had the good news about the missing money to tell them. He took a deep breath. Bad news was best told quickly.

'Before we get into the question of auditors, I'm afraid I have to tell you about a problem that's occurred in our practice which may affect everything.'

Greystone lifted his eyebrows a millimetre or so higher, and waved Stephen on with what would have been designated a century or so before as a grand gesture of his hand.

'Our accounts manager has vanished,

together with a not insubstantial amount of our clients' money we fear. We have had to advise the police, Law Society and our insurers, but as the gentleman in question was a computer expert the full extent of the damage has not yet come to light.'

Greystone, to his credit, did not bat an eyelid.

'I see.' He looked towards his own partners as if they communicated telepathically, then, message received, continued in a loud voice: 'We would have been far more concerned if it had been one of the partners who had disappeared. I assume there are no allegations against you?'

Jeffrey eagerly shook his head, and to his own surprise Stephen found himself mimicking the gesture.

'Well then, I also assume you have insurance in place with regard to this sort of unfortunate incident?'

Jeffrey's dumb show continued.

'Therefore the clients need not know, and until your man is apprehended and charged I don't believe the public has to either. If we've merged by that time your name will no longer mean anything...'

Stephen returned to the fray.

'I see that practice name is sixth on the agenda. I don't think we should presume too much...'

'Of course not, of course not.' Greystone seemed eager not to offend. 'Look, my dear fellows, I feel for you. It's a little like finding the butler has been at the family silver, but it's not the end of the world—unless he was a particularly good accounts manager! They are like butlers, you know, terribly hard to replace. However, I must point out that what has happened to you would not have done so had you been part of a larger organisation, such as our joint practice would be. No one person would have absolute control in accounts then, and if you look at the suggested management structure you'll see a very strong finance committee responsible to the management committee—not even one managing partner who might go rogue on us. No, gentlemen, let's look forward rather than back. We are grateful to you for telling us. Now, if we can proceed with the agenda, we have rather a lot to get through.'

Stephen felt confused. The reaction was totally unexpected and remarkably civilised. Maybe there was something to be said for a public school education, and maybe Jeffrey was right: that a merger like this would be for the best in the long run. He poured himself a glass of water and addressed his mind to the figures in front of him. They too showed just what could be achieved by the merger. It was all becoming terribly convincing. So his head told him, but deep in his heart he still wanted things to stay just the way they were.

Chapter Thirteen

The alarm rang at its usual time of 6.15 am, although it seemed to Stephen he had only had a couple of hours' sleep. He sat bolt upright immediately, his body covered in a cold sweat, still suffering from a feeling of panic after a half-remembered dream. He sought for the memory, punched his pillow and then rolled over to wrap his arms around his wife for comfort.

Cathy pulled away.

'Leave me to sleep, Stephen. You roll in at four in the morning and then get up at the crack of dawn! You may be killing yourself but there's no need to kill me. Why didn't you phone?'

'If I'd phoned you'd have complained that I'd woken you up. I'm sorry, the meeting just went on and on. It's not like I was out with another woman. I was trying to do the best for us. This whole business with Arthur has really shaken me, apart from all the pressure that Gerry's exerting at the moment. Just bear with it. It'll all get better, I promise.'

Cathy stayed with her back towards him and although he couldn't see her face, he sensed there were tears in her eyes.

'When are you going to stop living at a hundred miles an hour, Stephen, and take some time to smell the flowers? You can buy me the biggest bouquets in the world, but if you don't get back and look at them and enjoy them with me, then it's not worth it. It's just not worth the candle. You've got a family, but not so's you'd notice. From Friday to Friday when do you see the children? And when you are here you fall asleep watching the television. You've got to stop for breath, Stephen, otherwise you're going to die for lack of oxygen.'

He let his hand stray to her breast and when she did not push it away, found himself aroused. She felt him hard against her buttocks and wriggled him into a position where he lay flat between her cheeks. Instinctively, he glanced back at the clock. He had a meeting with Gerry Mortimer at eight and it was already six-thirty. He knew if he started to move against her he would not be able to stop, yet he also knew that if he moved away she would feel neglected. Client or wife? Yet another choice. She contracted against him, drawing him on and in, her nipples hard and erect against his hands. He moved his right hand down over the flat stomach, his fingers running through the fine pubic hair until they found the soft wetness that was so familiar to him. There was a sharp intake of breath as his finger entered her while he probed harder from behind.

'Faster,' she said, 'do it harder.' She arched her back so he could enter her, then with a hidden strength flipped him over so he was on top of her and moving inside her. His mouth moved to her breasts, his teeth biting her nipples. Her nails raked his back, clawing his buttocks, pushing him into her like a woman possessed. Not for the first time in their lives he sensed he was being used in much the same way that a woman alone might use a dildo. He was inanimate, she was alive.

'Don't come! Make me feel you banging into me. Fuck me.'

It was the language of the gutter, the language of the whore. The sort of language that almost made him want to be a voyeur. From the corner of his eye he saw it was nearly 6.45. Selfishly, he moved more swiftly against her. She was really hurting him now, her nails biting into the sensitive part of his flesh at the back of the spine, then moving behind and digging into his balls. Yet he would not give himself a release, and the faster he moved the further he seemed to be from spilling his seed into her. For a moment he thought he might be there forever, pumping into his wife, their bodies hopelessly entwined. Then he felt her tense and come, muscles contracting. It was what he needed as he felt the sweet relief of ejaculation without any of the disappointment and despair that usually followed.

He withdrew from her at once. Normally she told him to lie within her even after he'd come until she was ready to let him go, but today he had to go. He kissed her perfunctorily and then, oblivious to her needs, was out of bed and in the shower, the hot needles of water stinging his skin like antiseptic on wounds.

When he returned to the bedroom she was lying on her side, her back to him again.

'Cathy, I'm sorry, I have to go to work.'

'And if I asked you to stay here this morning?'

'I couldn't. I want to, but I couldn't. Let's go out for a meal tonight. We could go to Le Gavroche—they'll always find me a table.'

She shook her head. 'I can't be bothered

with all the dressing up. Don't worry. I'll make something here. You don't have to take me out just because of a sense of guilt. Give me some idea of when you'll be home.'

'I'll be back early, I promise.' As he spoke the words he really meant them. Nothing would give him greater pleasure than to close the door of his office at five-thirty and be home by six. How many times in the past had he made just such a promise? How many times had he kept it?

As if to compensate and to reassure himself that all was well, he knelt by the side of the bed and kissed his wife full on the lips.

'I love you,' he said, and without waiting for a reply left the room.

By missing breakfast and taking liberties with the drive he got to Gerry's office just a few minutes after eight. He felt like death. Yesterday's meeting had gone on for far too long and despite himself he had come out into the small hours thinking he had conceded too much, given too much ground for Jeffrey to turn back now.

Greystone had been polite throughout, and his partners actually seemed like decent people, but it still felt wrong to Stephen, wrong for his other partners and wrong for the clients. Yet every emotive

141

argument he raised was brushed aside with logic and common sense. If Arthur had not vanished like this it would have been easy to say no, but now Stephen was not quite so sure. One thing was certain. He couldn't commit to anything until Sidney Developments had made their move for D'Arblay. The conflict would have been impossible: director of Public company seeking to take over another client company. It would end with them losing both clients, and Stephen up before the Stock Exchange and the Law Society.

They'd finally adjourned at 3.30 am, agreeing to meet again in a week's time. Even after the many hours they'd spent closeted together Greystone looked as unruffled as ever, his hair neatly combed, his trousers impeccably creased—a stark contrast to the open-necked, loosened tie appearance of Jeffrey, and Stephen's rolled up sleeves.

'I think we really are making good progress, gentlemen,' Greystone had said. 'And now I think a shower is in order, and a brief nap, before we launch forth into the trials and tribulations of another day.'

Jeffrey and Stephen found themselves on the pavement, mist rising from the river, the distant hoot of a foghorn audible from a boat, too late for even the homegoing nightclub traffic, too early for the office cleaners. A passing policeman eyed them curiously for a moment, then looked up at the building outside which they stood and walked on satisfied. Clearly he was accustomed to twenty-four hour usage by Greystone's and their clients, and indeed Philip had privately told them it was a rare night when the bank of secretaries did not work well past midnight and often until dawn.

'Well, Stephen, didn't I say it was worth listening? I thought they were really understanding about our present problem.'

'Yes, Jeffrey, they were.' Stephen had felt too tired to argue. All he could think about was the sort of reception he'd get when he arrived home. Argument, for argument there was sure to be, would have to wait for another day.

But not today because he knew he was going to be closeted with Gerry. Now that they had Kinsey's shares in their pockets they had to decide exactly when to make that public. Stephen had drafted the documentation on the basis of an irrevocable option to buy rather than an outright purchase contract. That meant that nobody need know about it until the time was right, although Repton, Kinsey's lawyer, was nobody's fool and had insisted upon an end date after which Kinsey could make them buy; but that end date was three months away, and with the money in the bank as security, already earning interest for Kinsey, he was far from unhappy.

The decision that Gerry and Stephen had to take was whether to pick off a few more shareholders, to get their ducks in a row as Gerry liked to put it, to buy a few more shares on the open market, or to come right out in the open and make what would inevitably be a hostile bid. The problem, as with everything in life, was the price. They'd paid Kinsey £2.65, the quoted price was £3.15. Any rumour of a bid, any pattern of selective buying by an unusual source, such as one of Gerry's off-shore trusts, would push the price inexorably upwards, thus making the whole operation just that bit more expensive, just that bit less commercial.

Gerry was already stripped for action by the time Stephen reached his office, shirt sleeves rolled up, a half-empty percolator of coffee, a plate with a few crumbs and smears of jam showing the remains of breakfast. Papers were all over the desk but in neat piles rather than strewn haphazardly, suggesting an agenda just as pre-planned as Greystone's if not as professionally presented. He sniffed and ostentatiously looked at his watch as Stephen came in.

'I said breakfast, not lunch.'

'Leave it out, Gerry. I'm fifteen minutes late. I'm pleased you waited for me to eat. Where's the rest of the food?'

'I was hungry—there's some coffee over there, you look as if you could use it. There was a time when early mornings suited you.'

'They still do,' Stephen replied, 'it's the late nights I can't take.'

He poured himself a coffee and took a deep draught of it on the way back to the desk, like a drug addict with his first fix of the day.

'Well, Gerry, I'm all yours. Let's get down to it.'

They worked for two hours like a well-oiled team, exchanging views, arguing points, respecting each other's ideas, each giving, each taking. Stephen enjoyed these sessions with Gerry, and as his patience waned with other clients in the practice, he enjoyed them even more.

It was just after ten when the phone rang. Stephen looked at his watch with surprise.

'Good grief, I didn't realise what the time was.'

'Shows you're enjoying yourself,' said Gerry, then in an altogether different tone into the telephone, 'I thought I said I wasn't to be disturbed?'

An explanation was offered and accepted. 'It's Chris,' Gerry said to Stephen by way of explanation. Chris Kennedy was a financial analyst whom Gerry had rescued from the redundancy heap after he'd been released by a large firm of City brokers, and handed the job of preparing the analysis and report on D'Arblay which formed the basis of his total game plan.

Kennedy looked the typical eighties Yuppie: cleanshaven, dark wavy hair worn long, an easy smile showing perfect teeth, a tribute to patient NHS dental care as a child. Now his working-class background was carefully hidden by a cultivated accent, a liking for bright shirts, brighter braces, and psychedelic socks. Yet he had a mind that Gerry at least recognised as being razor sharp in his field. The best thing about Kennedy was that he stuck to what he was good at. Point him in a straight line and he went from A to B and then on to C, happily working his way through to Z if so required. He didn't have a truly commercial bone in his body yet he could read into figures and half statements an encyclopaedia of facts. Balance sheets might be prepared by the brightest of accountants to satisfy even the most aggressive of shareholders, but Chris Kennedy would still be able to ferret out the true situation.

'I see,' Gerry said. 'Yes, yes, how much?'

The last words were said with a groan of despair. 'That can't be right,' he continued. 'Of course. I'm sorry, of course it's right. It's just well, not right.'

Stephen glanced towards Gerry to ask what was going on, the frustration of a one-sided conversation getting to him quickly.

'Hold on, Chris, I'm putting you on the loudspeaker. I've got Stephen with me. You tell him what you just told me, and let's see if he can make any sense out of it.'

Chris' voice, smooth and unruffled, came loud and clear over the loudspeaker.

'Hello, Stephen. As I've just told Gerry, D'Arblay's shares are on the move today and it's nothing to do with you. They're up thirty pence already this morning and from what I understand the buying's not over yet. Somebody put in some big overnight orders at £3.15, then bought again when 5p got put on, and kept on buying while the shares kept getting marked up. It's not a big market so even a few hundred thousand pushes them upwards.'

'Who's buying?' Stephen asked.

'I'm not sure. It's being done through three different brokers and it's almost as if they've chosen the firms where my inside information is the weakest. But I'll get there, don't worry about that.'

'I'm not worried about that,' Gerry said, 'it's the price I'm worried about. Where does this whole exercise become uneconomic?'

'Well, according to the last interims I reckoned they were worth at least £4, maybe even £4.50. I've not seen or heard anything to change my view on that, so there's still some way to go. Except I know you were banking on £3.50 being a maximum bid price and we're nearly there already, so that's looking a bit sick.'

'Thanks, Chris,' Gerry said, 'you're doing a good job. Just keep tabs on it and keep on calling us back. I'll tell the switchboard to be sure to put you through.' He flicked off the loudspeaker as the line went dead and looked at Stephen.

'Who the hell can be buying? Who'd want this company except us? It's specialised, it won't fit naturally in many places. It can't be Kinsey. He's committed to sell and he's hardly likely to throw sand in his own face by pushing the price up. Stephen, who is it? We've got to find out and we've got to find out quickly, otherwise this is going to collapse about our ears and all we'll be left with is a profit in the Kinsey shares.'

Stephen shook his head.

'I'm a lawyer not a clairvoyant. Let's leave it to Chris. If anybody can get to the bottom of this, he can.'

'If anybody can,' Gerry said with a hint of despair. 'And if nobody can...?'

He left the question hanging in the air as they returned to their task of plotting a course towards an island which had just moved beyond the horizon and off the map.

Chapter Fourteen

'So why hasn't Stephen been to see me all week?'

The speaker sat in a deep armchair which made her seem smaller than she really was and accentuated the impression of weakness that Fay Kennard liked to give at all times.

Her younger son Anthony blinked behind his thick glasses and wondered, not for the first time, just why his father had ever married his mother. He'd loved his dad, loved the way Len, unlike almost everybody else he knew, had actually understood him; but somehow it was as if his mother always had to put on an act for an unseen audience, even when there were just the two of them together. Now, following stage directions, she repeated her question.

'He's been really busy at work—we all have.'

Fay sniffed, suggesting she doubted his word, but then begrudgingly accepted it and countered with another thrust.

'I was never too busy for him when he was small. Now I depend on him, it's a different story. I remember one night in a pea-souper fog he was desperate for his favourite comic. I staggered out into the gloom. Two hours I was wandering around, and did I come home without it? No. Nothing was ever too much. And daughters-in-law—have I got daughters-in-law?'

'Mum, if you didn't go on about your health from the minute they arrived, they might visit you a bit more.'

Cathy and Louise, Anthony's wife, had little in common, meeting only on family occasions or when the practice social life demanded the attendance of wives. Louise was not Jewish, and although Fay complained about her failure to visit she omitted to mention the battle she had fought with her son when he'd first brought her home and told her they were about to get married. Not that there was anything wrong with Louise personally. She came from a perfectly acceptable professional background: father a successful tax barrister, mother a speech

150

therapist who didn't need to work but chose to follow a vocation. Fay, however, was not to be placated and had been implacably and consistently rude to her in-laws in such a way that suggested they may have been personally responsible for inventing and implementing anti-semitism and the Holocaust. After some five years of marriage she had moved on, as far as her daughter-in-law was concerned, from the guilt of her not being born Jewish to the ultimate sin of not producing any grandchildren. However much Anthony tried to explain to her that the fault lay with him rather than his wife, she refused to accept the fact and still described Louise as: 'The poor little barren *shikse,*'—a rare lapse into the yiddish she had so long ignored.

Cathy was guilty of greater crimes.

'She keeps the grandchildren away from me deliberately. Don't they deserve to get to know their grandmother?'

'Mum,' Stephen had explained with a patient reasonableness bred from many years of practice, 'it is not the children's idea of a good time to be shown for the umpteenth time photos of your grandparents' village in Lithuania. And if I recall correctly when Booba was alive you always wanted to pretend your roots were English.'

His mother had pretended not to hear

him. She had a convenient memory when it suited her.

'It's history. Children should know their roots. You and Cathy provide them with little or no tradition. Being Jewish is more than a question of lighting candles on a Friday night and serving up chicken soup. All the years we sent you and Anthony to Hebrew classes and you remember nothing. He married out and your children know nothing. When I die I doubt if you'll even say Kaddish for me. Your father would be turning in his grave.'

Len Kennard, however, in his lifetime had simply smiled at the alleged short-comings of his children. He'd worked hard in the ladies' wear business that he'd built up from scratch, and Fay, too, had had much to do with the development of the company. Yet, tired though he was at the end of a day, Len had liked nothing better than to come home and play with his two boys before sitting down and falling asleep on the horse hair sofa he'd inherited from his mother. Fay had been different in those days, still showing flashes of the attractive woman he'd married, her business mind razor sharp, a proud and loving mother, fiercely protective of her brood and her family as a whole.

It was after Len had died that she'd started to go to pieces. Her conversation became obsessed with death and illness, her objections to her daughters-in-law taking on a new ferocity, her complaints to her sons driving them initially to distraction and then almost to wry amusement. They both phoned her dutifully each day, morning and night, even from holiday.

'Just to make sure I'm still alive,' she complained when Stephen had tried to extricate himself after a mere twenty minutes of her recounting her bowel problems and the ongoing difficulties with the management company of the block of flats to which she had moved after her husband's death. Even that had been traumatic.

'I don't want to leave the house where my husband died. There are too many memories here.'

Len had quietly nodded off before the television some four years ago, woken with a puzzled but resigned expression as the pain of the heart attack hit him, said goodbye to Fay in an orderly fashion, as if he were just going out to buy an evening newspaper, and then closed his eyes for ever.

Eventually the boys had persuaded her to move out of the house.

'Mum, it's five bedrooms and three bathrooms. Unless you're thinking of adopting or sub-letting or remarrying a man with four kids, it's too big. And the area's not getting any safer either.'

Despite the money the Kennards had made Len had shown a reluctance to move from the comfortable detached family house he'd bought in Stamford Hill when that was the place to be, when North London was the escape route from the East End. Now the middle classes had moved ever further northwards. Finchley, Hampstead, Edgware, Southgate, until the wanderlust had taken them to Radlett, to Hadley Wood, to Bushey, to St Albans—a tribe dispersed, expanding little tributaries into the furthermost parts of the Home Counties. Stamford Hill became abandoned to the ultra-orthodox Jews and the incoming West Indians who lived side by side in an uneasy alliance that every so often broke out into a mutual racial skirmish. Too many old ladies were being mugged for Stephen and Anthony's liking and eventually, despite her protests, they sold the house and moved their mother to a purpose-built flat in Hendon where nothing appealed to her, where nothing was like the old days, and where nothing would ever fill the hole that Len's death had left in her life.

They'd sold the business, too, which perhaps was a mistake, for now, despite the comfortable nest egg from which she could live for the rest of her life, Fay had too much time to dwell upon her own problems. Consequently each ache became magnified, each minor annoyance which she would have taken in her stride in her prime became a major catastrophe which she could only overcome by summoning both her sons to her side wherever they might be. A telephone call in the midst of an important meeting to tell them the central heating had failed was not unusual, and just last week she had surpassed herself by telephoning Stephen four times in twenty minutes. When he had reluctantly taken the last call she told him that the newsagent had delivered the wrong paper and could he pop in on his way home to exchange the *Sun* for her beloved *Mirror?*

The boys had worked out an informal rota for visiting her and today was Anthony's turn. He reckoned an hour was enough. He'd already spent forty-five minutes, drunk two cups of tea and eaten two slices of cake that she'd forced upon him.

'I nearly killed myself making it, the least you can do is eat it.'

The talk was of trivia but beneath the frail exterior Fay Kennard still had the instincts that had taken her and her husband to financial success.

'It's not just that Stephen's been busy, is it? There's something else. I spoke to Gerry last night. He seemed a bit off himself but he agreed with me that Stephen's not right. Come on, Anthony, don't keep things from your mother. If I know I can help, if I don't know I can only worry.'

Gerry Mortimer had been a lifelong friend of Fay Kennard's. They'd been brought up together, although looking at the two of them now it was hard to believe they were both in their mid-sixties. Fay saw her pension as a passport to infirmity while Gerry regarded free fares on public transport as an excuse actually to use it for the first time in many years. At some time in the past there had been more between Gerry and Fay than mere friendship but whether that was before or after she had met Len neither of her sons had ever been able to ascertain. For a woman who was ever ready to gossip, on that matter she had kept her counsel remarkably well.

'There's something big going on with Gerry's company—and we're talking to another firm about a merger.' The last thing Anthony wanted to tell his mother was about the missing money. She would have got off her supposed sick bed and been round the district with a collecting box before the news was out of his mouth.

'That Gerry, he always wanted to run before he could walk! Did I ever tell you about the time we all went on holiday to France? Me, your father may he rest in peace, Gerry, his lovely Myrna...'

Anthony listened for a quarter of an hour to a story he'd heard innumerable times, but at least it rescued him from his mother's attempts to play private detective with regard to the practice. He looked down at his watch. The hour had gone.

He was anxious to get back to work. All that was going on around him was very unsettling. Anthony liked to have everything in order, everything tidy, everything logical. When faced with a complicated tax problem he simply applied the same techniques he'd used in chess. At the age of ten he'd won the London Schools chess championship, and had represented England at twelve. It was only when he'd played the Russians and the Americans that he'd seen how basic his own game was, and realising in his heart he'd never be quite that good he now played purely for pleasure. It had given his parents an enormous thrill, though, and although Len hadn't known a queen from a pawn he'd sat for hours watching his son represent their country, a gently satisfied smile only leaving his face when he realised that his boy had lost. Anthony missed his father now more than ever. He wanted somebody to talk to. Stephen was impossible. Stephen never took him seriously. Stephen didn't seem to take anything seriously nowadays unless it involved Gerry Mortimer and D'Arblay. Jeffrey only tolerated Anthony. He knew deep down that just as he had only become a solicitor because his parents wanted it, so he was only a partner in the firm because his mother had put pressure on Stephen. He in turn had fought and won his battle with Jeffrey, and Jeffrey was no more Anthony's potential confidante than Sarah. She frightened him a little, but then most women did, not least his own wife. Louise understood business far better than he did. She was a market analyst who worked long hours and achieved alarming success. Money poured in from bonuses and rises and he knew from the bank statements that arrived just how much she had in her separate account. Their lack of a family she brushed aside in public.

'Who's got time for families? All they're good for is to attend your funeral.'

But alone at night he had heard the stifled sobs; all too often he'd come into a room to see her red-eyed and sniffing. The tests had proved it was he who had a low testosterone count, and try as they had to follow the various specialists' treatments and advice, nothing had come of it but frustration. Only last week they had attended an IVF unit at a private hospital. All the faces of the doctors they had seen merged into one, but the latest seemed more hopeful, more positive, and so Anthony had yet again agreed to pay the money and pray. He knew his mother thought it was some kind of divine punishment for marrying out, and that in itself made him more determined to produce a grandchild for her—that and the thought of his brother's children, the thought that yet again Stephen had something he did not.

He stood up to go and saw the look of fear in his mother's eyes as he reached for his jacket.

'You're going?'

'I have to.'

She shrugged and for a second he felt a terrible wave of sorrow for this lonely woman, old before her time, building a barricade around herself from self-pity and bitterness. He kissed her on the cheek and went down the stairs to his car. As he looked up he saw her standing at the window, wiping her eyes. Scared to look back, he waved his arm out of the window of the car and drove away.

159

Chapter Fifteen

Jeffrey Wightman was not in the best of moods. He had a problem with the latest woman in his life which did not please him. Women were always a problem to Jeffrey. It was not getting them that was difficult, it was simply not growing bored with them. For Jeffrey it was the chase, the hunt, that was exciting; the first date, the first kiss, the first touch in a secret place, the discovery of just how far he could go in bed with them—and then, when all frontiers had been reached and crossed, the urgent desire to go on a totally new voyage of discovery. Yet the latest woman was different and not in a long time had Jeffrey felt the way he did now. He lifted the phone to dial her number then slammed down the receiver as he heard the annoying persistent engaged tone. It had been like that for the last half an hour and knowing the woman as he did he guessed she had probably taken the phone off the hook just to soak in a long hot bath. The thought of her naked body lying there, the water half covering those perfect breasts, made it difficult for him to concentrate on his work, but there was a lot to do and he had to get on with it. The phone call would have to wait. Let her worry about why he hadn't called, she'd get through to him eventually.

To the left of his desk he'd placed all the papers regarding the Greystone's merger. It was Wednesday afternoon and they'd already produced a coherent working paper implementing what they saw as the agreed course after Tuesday's meeting. He liked it, liked in particular how his name appeared so high up amongst some forty other names, like the financial arrangements that gave him not just a greater potential income, but also a greater drawing facility.

Solicitors' practices work upon the basis that each partner draws a monthly income on account of his share of the profits, then at the end of the year the actual profits are calculated, and provided he hasn't drawn more than his share the balance is credited to his capital account to be taken out when he retires. Greystone's, however, proposed better than that. They suggested a regular annual lump sum distribution after due provision for tax for some fifty percent of the surplus profit, and to Jeffrey that sort of income would be manna from heaven.

None of his ex-wives had remarried and paying them maintenance within his income from Kennard & Wightman was stretching him to the limit. Stephen had been good about it, but then Stephen was good about most things: the perfect partner, generous, understanding and creative. Yet there was only so much in the pot, and just recently it seemed the harder Jeffrey worked, the smaller the pot appeared. Greystone's would make life easier. They had the clients, and with Greystone's name behind them Stephen and Jeffrey would be able to expand that client base. Stephen would have to understand that, but Stephen at the moment was too tied up with D'Arblay. Jeffrey should have put his foot down long ago but he'd been scared not only to lose the client but also to lose Stephen as well.

They had a rule in the partnership that any business opportunity that came along was offered to the others. Stephen had offered him the chance to take D'Arblay shares but Jeffrey had been in the middle of his last divorce and had neither the finances nor the wish to offer a predatory wife any more assets. He'd offered Stephen the chance to take shares in Romney Developments, but this time it had been Stephen who'd said no, and hadn't that been a wise decision? Mick Romney had gone rogue on him, something Jeffrey had never believed would happen.

Romney had been a long-established builder with a good record of relatively small residential developments around the south coast. When he'd offered the chance to come in on a deal, Jeffrey had jumped at it; but the money had gone in and Romney had felt the pinch like so many other builders and simply re-routed the financing to keep other projects afloat. Robbing Peter to pay Paul had to come to an end sometime, and in the great game of larcenous musical chairs Jeffrey had been the last Peter to have his pocket emptied. It had been an uncomfortable and embarrassing final visit to the site to see holes dug, seemingly at random, unfinished walls, roofless houses, dirt tracks instead of roads, and Mick Romney simply holding up his hands as if an apology would sweep away the problem.

Stephen, as ever, had tried to help.

'We'll go to the bank, get a bigger overdraft, and you can take what you need. We'll tell them we're suing the bastard and it's just a matter of cash flow. And I'll buy your share in the horse. You never wanted it anyway. If it ever becomes really valuable I won't forget you once had an interest.'

Jeffrey had not been convinced there would be anything there for which to

163

sue. There was a queue ahead of him baying for Romney's blood as well as his money. Not only was he likely to lose his investment but there was also the question of the guarantee he'd given to the bank. The merger would solve all of his problems at one fell swoop, it was just a question of convincing Stephen—but Jeffrey knew of old just how stubborn his friend and partner could be. And it wasn't as if Stephen was that committed to the practice any longer. D'Arblay, his horse, his charity work seemed that much more important to him.

He looked at his watch. It was three in the afternoon and where was Stephen? He'd promised to be back to discuss Greystone's. They'd both blocked out the rest of the afternoon from their diaries, although at five o'clock they had an appointment with a solicitor and accountant sent by the Law Society which would doubtless be at worst unpleasant, at best embarrassing. He rang through to Stephen's secretary, Sandra, although it would have been just as easy to open the door and walk across the corridor.

'Where's Stephen?'

'He's at a meeting of Breathless.'

'He does know he's got a meeting with me at three?'

'It's in his diary.'

'So's Ramadan, but I doubt if he'd be able to tell me the date of it this year.'

Jeffrey found Sandra singularly unhelpful. Although she and Stephen argued like husband and wife she was unswervingly loyal to him. She was also incredibly untidy. Her hair sat like an ill made haystack on top of her round lumpish face, she smoked like a chimney, and the black jumper she invariably wore was dotted with so much ash it looked like part of a pattern. Her broad bottom fitted uncomfortably into too tight skirts, and the flat shoes she wore for comfort rather than fashion might well have been abandoned by a Russian peasant. There was no way she could be taken over to Greystone's office looking the way she did. Stephen would have to talk to her, and if she didn't respond then, ten years or not, she'd have to go. Jeffrey, for his part, liked his secretaries to look good, and indeed his latest appendage could well have come straight from an audition for *L.A Law* with her model-like figure, gazelle eyes, and permed auburn hair. She wasn't a bad secretary either which proved the point that Jeffrey was always making to Stephen: namely that you didn't have to look like the wreck of the *Titanic* to be efficient.

The phone rang and Jeffrey picked it up irritably.

'Jeff, it's me, Stephen. I'm sorry, I'm going to be a bit late. I'll be back by four, I promise. We'll squeeze in an hour before the vultures descend and if they leave any flesh on our bones we'll continue afterwards.'

'Look, Stephen, this is important. We've got a practice to run. It's not like you're actually out there earning money at the moment.'

'Jeff, I have to go. I left them right in the middle of some vital discussions. I'll be back for four.'

Not for the first time lately, Stephen ended a conversation with his partner wondering whether or not they were still on the same wavelength. Breathless was something dear to Stephen's heart, as Jeffrey well knew. Jeffrey also knew that amongst his fellow committee members were one or two powerful barons of industry who'd actually given them some instructions after working with Stephen in his fund-raising efforts. Stephen's reputation in the field of creative fund-raising was now European rather than just British. Six months ago Breathless had held its first conference in Dijon where representatives from groups in more than a dozen countries had been present, and the net result had been a planned Eurovision telethon appeal supported by international stars which was due to take place next month. The publicity was going to be enormous and although that was an irrelevancy as far as Stephen was concerned, it was not going to do the practice any harm.

Anything that eased the sort of agony that Stephen and Cathy had gone through when Jonathan was younger had to be worth the candle. The raging eczema that went hand in hand with asthma they could deal with, although there had been times when they'd sewn mittens on to the child's hands to stop his scratching himself to ribbons in the night. It was the mad rush to hospital when inhalers couldn't cope, the helplessness of seeing your son fighting for breath, of watching him drowning without water, the skin going blue, the mouth forming bubbling cries for help as the panic set in, until the oxygen took effect and gradually the crisis faded—until the next time. And there was always a next time, that was the problem. Summers were worst, particularly when the days were hot and humid or when the pollen count was high, but even the winters weren't entirely safe, for any small cold seemed to go to his chest and attack after attack of bronchitis meant him falling behind with his schooling. It was an endless circle of pressure, and the worry itself begot attacks, like the recitation of a dynasty in the Old Testament.

'He'll grow out of it,' people had said, but people didn't understand, and even Jeffrey, who'd spent so much time with them during some of his marriages or recovering from others, didn't fully grasp the nervous tension that assailed them every day. Stephen's work with Breathless wasn't really much in the vast plan of things but it was the best he could do and he was fully committed to it.

He knew he ought to get back to Jeffrey and managed to rush the rest of the meeting through by three-thirty, leapt into a taxi, prayed for a break with London's traffic, got it and arrived back at the office by four. Jeffrey was less than happy.

'Stephen, you know I'm the first to applaud the work you do—and believe me I understand why you do it—but when we've so much on here you've got to give *us* some commitment. We're on the brink of either setting ourselves up for life or getting struck off, and you're wandering off here with your horse, there with Gerry Mortimer, and now with your charity!'

'Jeffrey, you're right,' Stephen gave one of his disarming smiles that could be so annoying, yet usually persuaded people to forgive him anything. He ran his fingers through his hair in another gesture calculated to effect an apology.

'Come on, let's get on with it. I'm here. We've an hour now...'

'I won't be able to stay afterwards,' Jeffrey said a little shamefacedly.

'Why?' Stephen asked, half amused at the colour that had risen in his partner's cheeks.

'Spurs are playing tonight in a cup replay.'

Jeffrey was a Tottenham fanatic who'd not been known to miss a home game since he was seven years old. Stephen remembered the lies he'd told at school when homework had not been finished because he'd spent the evening at football, or the subterfuge he'd had to undertake when Spurs had played a match on the Saturday of Rosh Hashana, the Jewish New Year or the Day of Atonement.

'Of course, Jeff, I realise Tottenham Hotspur are a bit more important than the merger or the Law Society. Perhaps you'll tell Mr Blackstock who's coming at five that you can't actually go into details of the missing clients' money because you have to put on your scarf and bovver boots and stand on the terraces with a view to

169

kicking seven bells out of the opposition supporters?'

'You'll never understand football, Stephen. Just stick to your racing.' Jeffrey had tried to persuade Stephen that an executive box at Tottenham where they could entertain clients would have been a sound investment, and indeed when the whole idea of the racing day had been floated he'd tried again, but Stephen had been unmoved.

'Wrong image, Jeffrey. Not everybody likes football. The beauty of racing is that even if you don't like horses you can enjoy the social side. You can't actually do that at a football ground with forty thousand yobbos chanting obscenities.'

Jeffrey took out the proposals that Philip Greystone had prepared.

'Assuming the Law Society just gives us a smack on the wrists, almost everything Greystone sets out would be acceptable to me. For a year we run the practices as Greystone's in association with Kennard & Wightman, then it'll be just Greystone's...'

'I'm not happy about that. Our clients will perceive that we've been taken over. If this thing happens—and I'm still not convinced it should—then we have to make it look like a genuine merger.'

Jeffrey tried to restrain his impatience. Over the years he'd learned there was no point in rushing Stephen. There was a donkey-like element to his character. The more you pushed him, the more likely he was to dig in his heels.

'Stephen, you have to be realistic about this. They're bigger than us. That's a fact. We want to show our clients that we're bigger. That's a fact. After a year of the sort of service we'll give them, nobody will care what we're called.'

'Maybe,' Stephen sounded unconvinced, 'but then there's the profit allocations and the warranties. Although we'll draw equally, they want a points system at the end of the first year depending on what we've each actually billed and had paid. Then that could be reduced down if the income from our clients doesn't come up to their projection.'

'Yes, but their projections are conservative and reasonable,' Jeffrey said, his voice still quiet and cajoling.

'They're reasonable as long as our clients don't take a look in horror at the sort of bills they're going to get and then decide to walk. You've seen the hourly rates they want us to charge. Can you imagine how Bobby Goldstein with his launderettes is going to react to that? I'm not even sure I'm going to be able to persuade Gerry Mortimer to pay them.'

'Look, they said they were guidelines. If

171

an individual client won't stand it, and we want to keep the client, then we'll have to be flexible.'

Stephen was still not convinced.

'I hear what you say...' he said, mocking a response beloved by solicitors when it was implied that although one heard, one did not believe. 'Let's move on. I'm not so sure their figures are that marvellous—for a large firm they don't have a terribly wide spread of clients. It'd only take three of the big ones to walk out and we'd be looking down into a black hole—and that's if we're lucky.'

'And if we're unlucky?' Jeffrey asked in a resigned tone.

'Then we'd be falling down into it.'

They talked on for half an hour, Jeffrey enthusing, Stephen cautioning, until finally Jeffrey's patience snapped.

'Look, Steve. If you don't want to do this deal, why not just say so—and we'll all stop wasting our time.'

'And if I do say that?'

Jeffrey shrugged.

'What do you want me to do...put a gun to your head, say things will never be the same again? We go back a long way Stephen, I can't be like that. If it's no, it's no, but don't be negative just for the sake of it. I know you always accuse me of rushing into things, but this time

172

I've really thought it through, and what's happened with the money has shown just how thin is the tightrope we walk.'

Stephen pursed his lips. He could see how much his partner wanted him to say yes, but this was too important a decision to make out of politeness. It had to be right, it had to feel right, and at the moment it did not. He was just about to pronounce judgement and to kill the merger off once and for all when the phone rang.

'Mr Blackstock and Mr Lessiter are here.'

Stephen thanked his receptionist politely and turned to Jeffrey.

'Look, Jeff, this'll have to wait. The men with the big sticks are here from the Law Society. If we can't convince them we're guiltless then this whole Greystone's business becomes academic. Let's see them. I'll sleep on it and we'll talk tomorrow—after your football match. I know how hard you'll find it to keep your mind on things when your team's future's at stake. Let's have them in and get it over with.'

He lifted the phone.

'Jaqui, ask the gentlemen to come up.' And then, mumbling half to himself, 'Let battle commence.' He replaced the receiver to an imaginary fanfare of trumpets.

173

Chapter Sixteen

If Blackstock and Lessiter had the echo of the music hall in their name there was no hint of humour in their presence. They came into the room darkly dressed and shook hands as if it was an imposition rather than a pleasure. Well rehearsed, they simultaneously withdrew cards from leather wallets and pushed them across the table like gamblers knowing their bids had won.

'Trevor Blackstock, Solicitor', read one, 'Brian Lessiter, Chartered Accountant', the other. They did not look like the sort of men one called Trev and Brian over a couple of pints. They declined an offer of coffee with a brief shake of their heads and a glance at their watches.

'Let's get down to business, shall we? Our understanding is that on Friday last your office was effectively left unattended when all partners and qualified professional staff went to the races on what I believe is called a hospitality day for your clients...'

Blackstock's tone was clipped and official-sounding like a court clerk reading a charge sheet. He was not an old man, perhaps in his early-forties, but all the life and colour seemed to have drained from his thin face. A slight shaving nick on his neck was still covered by a dab of toilet tissue and Stephen felt himself transfixed by that particular blemish. He wondered if he should tell the man, then decided he would not be thanked for it and tried to concentrate on Blackstock's summary of events...

'Whilst the office was unattended, you gave certain delegated authorities to your accounts manager, without it appears advising the bank of the reason for this, nor indeed putting into place any back-up security systems so far as the bank was concerned.'

'The man had been with us for seven years. He'd had our total trust for at least the last five...'

Blackstock looked up in surprise as if he'd forgotten there was anybody else in the room.

'I'm not here to make judgements, Mr Kennard, merely to compile a dossier of facts. If there is a need for you to defend yourself then there will be a time and place for it. That is not now. Please allow me to continue?'

'I'm terribly sorry,' Stephen said, finding it hard to control a smile despite the seriousness of the situation. There was something about pomposity that always made him want not only to laugh but to knock it down, to do something so outrageous as to cut through the stifling propriety that faced him. He had to control himself with these men, though; innocuous as they seemed, they could destroy him with their report, and he had to appear more sinned against than sinning.

'I understand how distraught you must be by this affair, Mr Kennard, but you in turn must understand that we have a job to do. If we are allowed to approach it without interference then we can complete it all the quicker without inconveniencing your practice.'

Stephen nodded in acquiescence, surprised that Blackstock had felt the need to offer any explanation or show any sign of humanity. It was encouraging. He was not dealing with robots, however computerised they may appear.

'Arthur Kemp was not merely your accounts manager but was also your principal computer expert. I understand that he fed new code words into your system which delayed you from obtaining a printout, and even now you are not entirely certain how much is missing or indeed from which accounts. Consequently Mr Lessiter here has been appointed by us to carry out an audit of your client

176

account which will have to be reconstructed manually and then be the subject of a bank reconciliation. I am afraid that within the Law Society rules that audit may well be at your expense. Obviously, Mr Lessiter and his associates will require your full co-operation, and indeed the co-operation of your own auditors.'

Lessiter spoke for the first time. He had the face of an ex-boxer, nose flattened, lips full, his eyes narrow and hard.

'I assume they'll have working papers which will help us in the reconstruction. There are times when I despair of the loss of the quill pen—machines are so much more fragile than humans, don't you think?' The cultured tones and the slightly quavering voice simply did not go with the man's appearance, and there was almost an apologetic tone in his speech.

'I promise you, you'll have every assistance we can give,' Jeffrey said positively. 'Believe me, we're as anxious to sort this out as you are—more so if anything. We'd all like to get that bastard Arthur back here for just ten minutes before we turn him over to the police. It's like having a burglar in your home during the night—nothing can be the same again.'

Blackstock interrupted him, but not unkindly.

'Quite. As I said to your partner, this

is never easy for us, but we do have to protect the public. A client is entitled to rely upon his solicitor not only for advice but also when it comes to his money. We should be the Bank of England and the High Courts of Justice rolled into one.'

Stephen looked the other solicitor straight in the eye.

'You're absolutely right. Don't forget it was us who called the Law Society in as soon as we found out, don't forget it's us who are on the line for a hundred thousand pounds excess on our policy, so make no mistake, we want to help you. Now, when is it Mr Lessiter here intends to start his investigation?'

'Tomorrow, I'm afraid. There will be some inevitable disruption. Can you please be sure to have the relevant partner from your auditors here first thing in the morning?'

The timing did not leave any room for Paul Levy, their accountant, to claim he had a prior appointment.

'I'll call him straight away,' Stephen said.

'Good, but just before you do, we want no papers removed from the office, not even files you're working on. If you've anything at home, please be sure to bring it in tomorrow.'

Stephen's face showed his concern over

the confidential D'Arblay papers that were in his office at his house. Blackstock read the situation. He'd been there before.

'If those papers are of a confidential nature, there's no need to be concerned. I am a solicitor, and Mr Lessiter here is only interested in balances, not client information. I trust I make myself clear.'

'You do.' Stephen nodded. The threat was no longer implied: the practice was on trial.

Blackstock and Lessiter exchanged glances. Then, each satisfied that the other had nothing more to say, rose with their impeccable timing.

'Well, gentlemen, I think there's little more that we can do tonight. Shall we say nine in the morning then?' There was nothing to do but agree. They closed the door quietly behind them, like visitors leaving a terminally ill patient.

'Still feel like going to football, Jeffrey?' Stephen asked.

He shrugged.

'It'll take my mind off things. I'll see you in the morning.'

It was almost with a sense of relief that Stephen heard the front door of their offices close behind Jeffrey. He was totally alone for what seemed to be the first time in ages. He walked around the office, touching familiar items, straightening a

179

picture, tossing away an old newspaper, enjoying the feeling of what he'd achieved. He wasn't about to lose it all, just because of one man. They may have been foolish in trusting Arthur but they'd not been criminal, the Law Society must realise that. Nothing that had happened made them any less proficient at what they did. Trusting one man didn't mean you couldn't draft an agreement, buy a house, deal with a divorce. It would be all right.

Ever since he'd been a child he'd had a blind optimistic streak in him. No work for an exam? Well, the probability was they'd only ask him what he knew—it would be all right. A serious illness in the family, the doctors looking grey? What did they know? It would be all right. No money to go out on the weekend, a firm date with a girl? Well, somehow he'd win on the premium bonds—it would be all right. He repeated it to himself like a blind litany, talking aloud to give himself the reassurance he so desperately needed. The first signs of madness, but he would not give way. He'd had crises before and he had little doubt he'd have crises again. Everything passed in time.

The ringing of the telephone brought him back to reality. The telephonist had long ago departed and normally the last person out switched on the answerphone.

He hesitated over replying, reluctant to deal with a client, wary as to who else it might be. Maybe the police had come up with their results a little earlier and were seeking to interview him. It was that thought that made him realise he was bordering on the paranoid and persuaded him to answer the phone.

'Hello, Kennard & Wightman.'

'Can I speak to Stephen Kennard, please?' The voice was female, familiar and all at once his fears evaporated.

'Speaking.'

'Stephen, it's Trisha. Trisha Martin. I said I'd call. I hope I'm not disturbing anything? I thought you were the sort of person who'd be working late.'

'No, you're not disturbing anything. I am the sort of person who works late.' He felt a little helpless, not knowing quite where to take the conversation.

'I'm sorry if I interrupted your weekend. I just felt I had to tell you the result of the case.'

'No, that was good. I wanted to know.'

'You sound strange. Are you sure this is a good time to call? It was just to set up the lunch I promised. I can always ring you back later.'

'No. It's all right. It's just that I've had a hell of a day. In fact, since Friday I've had a hell of a life.'

181

'Is it anything a drink might make better?'

He hesitated. He'd promised his wife he'd try to be home early, and if he wasn't going home he ought to attack some of the mountain of work that had built up over the past few days. They were easy excuses to make and Trisha would have accepted them; easy to make but hard to say.

'A drink might just help.'

'Good, say half an hour. Any particular watering hole?'

'Groucho's.'

'Sounds fine to me. I'll see you there. I'll be the one with the red rose and even redder hair.'

He glanced at his watch. Six-thirty. Just one drink and he could still be home by eight. That was just within the boundaries of acceptability. Just one drink. But even as the thought passed through his mind he couldn't help but feel more excitement than just one drink could ever merit.

He went to the men's room, washed, carefully combed his hair, cleaned his teeth and changed into the spare shirt he always kept at the office. This was madness. With all his problems he didn't need any more complications in his life. Yet there need be no complications, there was nothing wrong with meeting a colleague with whom he'd worked so closely on a

182

case, even if she was a journalist rather than a lawyer. There was nothing wrong with just one drink. It would be all right.

Chapter Seventeen

He'd picked Groucho's because he felt safe there. He knew too many people for any meeting to be clandestine. Groucho's is an odd club in the heart of Soho which draws its name from those afficionados of Groucho Marx who stoically refuse to belong to any club that might have them as a member. For the most part members are writers, media people, but the odd lawyer slips through, and Stephen had happily applied for membership, encouraged by friends he'd met on the racecourse.

Trisha was already waiting by the time he got there, her hair a warm scarlet in the subdued lighting. She rose to meet him and he automatically kissed her on the cheek. He smelled an unfamiliar perfume and felt a sense of guilt at his own friendly greeting.

'They don't let you in here easily, do they?' she said. 'Normally I just flash my press pass and I'm in. They all seemed scared that I'd write something terrible about them.'

'They're not likely to be impressed by press passes here—too many journalists are members already. Come on, I'll sign you in.'

They moved through to the bar and she had a gin and tonic while he drank a Perrier.

'You don't look the type to be into water.'

'I'm not usually, but these aren't usual times.' He looked her straight in the eyes and posed a silent question.

'If you're asking, the question is, yes, you can trust me. I may be a journalist, but unlike some of my colleagues it's not all the time.'

'Good,' he said with relief, 'I need someone to talk to...' And then he began his story. It took three gin and tonics for her and a whole bottle of Perrier for him. He took his time over it, painting background pictures of Jeffrey, of Arthur, of Greystone's, and as he spoke he realised he was painting a picture of himself as well. Throughout the time he'd worked on the Robson case they'd never really talked about themselves, never really been alone to have the excuse to do so, but now it all poured out so that Trisha seemed to know his partners, his employees, his brother and his mother although she had never met them; but about Sarah he said little, and perhaps from the little he did say she was able to guess the reason.

'Your mother sounds a very unhappy woman.'

'She makes everybody around her unhappy, that's how she gets her kicks.'

'I don't think you mean to make her sound that awful.'

'She's not awful, that's the whole point. It's just that I can barely see the good in her any more, and that's my fault as much as it's hers.' He happened to glance down at his watch. It was eight-thirty.

'My God is that the time?'

Trisha smiled.

'Will your dinner be burned? I'm sorry, it's my fault—I didn't mean to keep you. Tell your wife you were giving an interview to the media.'

He shook his head.

'You don't know my wife. Look, I've really got to go.'

'If you have to. I was feeling a bit peckish. Do you think you could order me a sandwich before you disappear? I don't think this is the sort of place that will take an order from a non-member.'

'You're right.' He looked at his watch again as if further study might miraculously turn back the hands of time.

'Quite frankly, another half an hour won't matter. I'll join you if I may. I think my wife will have eaten by now anyway.'

He knew that if he went home his food would be in the microwave. Cathy would have taken her meal with the kids and he'd sit in the kitchen on his own, banished by his slack time keeping. Probably a phone call would help at this time. It was, on balance, worth the risk.

'Can I call home first?'

'Of course. I wouldn't like to be the cause of any problem.'

Although he smirked, he sensed for the first time in their conversation a hint of bitterness, of regret at something past, something missed, something lost.

'You always seem to be apologising to me—if it's not for interrupting me, then it's for breaking up my marriage. It's me who should be apologising to you. For what you did to help the Robsons the least I can do is buy you something to eat rather than let you foot the bill—and I think I can do better than a sandwich at a club. Have you got time for a meal?'

'I've no one to rush home to, if that's what you're asking. Are you sure you won't get into trouble at home?'

'Not if I ring. Will you excuse me?' As he made his way to the phone he saw the looks that Trisha attracted from the other members. There was something about her, beyond the hair, that he could see would attract men like flies. So why was there nobody to go home to, and why should he find that piece of information so welcome?

The line was engaged when he first rang home and he found that irritating. He'd threatened both daughter and son with financial penalties if the account for their home number rose to the same astronomic heights as last quarter's, but the effect had not been to cut down on their air time, merely rather to have the children of less Scrooge-like parents (as his daughter put it) telephone them. Quite what they found to talk about he did not know—for the most part they'd seen each other at school just a few hours before and the conversation certainly never had anything to do with homework. Yet talk they did, and for hours as well, when even the simplest arrangement to meet took up to half a dozen calls to establish who was going, then who was going with whom, what was to be worn, what time they were to meet, where they were to meet, how much they might spend and on whom, where they'd eat, whether in fact they'd eat or not—and sometimes even after all these calls one or other

of the children was still at home in the
evening, rebutting questions as to why
the arrangements had been cancelled with
abrasive monosyllables.

He tried again. Still engaged. If he was
to eat he had to leave now. He'd just
have to hope Cathy decided to have an
early night. By the time he got back
to Trisha she was deep in conversation
with a scriptwriter whom he recognised
by reputation.

'Oh, Stephen. Do you know David? I
interviewed him a year ago after his Best
Screenplay award.'

'No, we've never been formally introduced, although I've seen you around.'

The two men shook hands, although
David's eyes did not leave Trisha and
his left hand seemed to wander over her
arm. Stephen felt an unaccustomed hint
of jealousy, brushing aside any implied
suggestion that David should be invited
to join them for dinner.

'Trisha, if we're to eat, we'd better go.'

She shot him an odd look but got up
obediently.

'So I'll call you then?' the man called
David said, ignoring Stephen.

'Yes, please do. Next week some time.'

David nodded amiably enough at Stephen,
his point made, and ambled off to the
bar.

They made their way outside and he hailed a taxi.

'Is fish OK for you?'

'Yes.' She sounded less than enthusiastic.

'What's wrong?'

'Nothing.'

'Come on. I'm not stupid.'

'Very well, if you must know, you're wrong. That conversation with David Lindsay was about to lead to an exclusive interview that could have earned me five hundred maybe even a thousand pounds. You reacted to him like I was your newly wed wife and you'd found us in bed together on the honeymoon.'

He was completely taken aback by the onslaught, and for a second was inclined to call a halt to the evening and go home and face an angry but still consolable Cathy; but the thought was only fleeting and the attack made him more determined than ever to get to know her.

'I'm sorry, I didn't know.'

She calmed down a little, then put her hand on his.

'Don't worry about it. Red hair, red-hot temper, that's what my mother always used to say. It's just that I've got a job too, one I like to take seriously, and I like to be taken seriously myself. It's all about respect, you see? It may not be the most palatable of careers but it's what I do, it's

189

what I'm good at. You know, Stephen, I never sneer at whores. They also do what they're good at. I did an in-depth article about prostitutes once. I lived with them, walked the streets with them...they deserve respect too.'

He said nothing. The tone of her voice in talking about whores gave him a thrill, gave him an insight into why powerful men put themselves at risk by paying for sex.

'You walked the streets with them—did you do any more?'

The question was out before he had time to think whether it might cause offence, but her smile told him she'd been expecting it.

'That would be telling, wouldn't it? You might try and sell the story to the papers.'

He smiled as well, good humour restored to the evening just in time as they pulled up outside Wheeler's.

The maitre D' greeted Stephen with enough enthusiasm to tell Trisha that he was a valued customer then showed them to a table in the corner. He could see the telephone by the bar, but couldn't find the strength to go and make his call. She saw him looking.

'Go on. Use the phone. You obviously know the menu here. I need a bit of time to study it.'

He rose thankfully and made his way over to the phone. The number was still busy. This was a message for him; he sensed it but couldn't interpret it. It would have been simple to go back to the table and tell her he had to go home, but again the simple choice was not the attractive one. She sat running her hands through her hair, peering a little myopically at the menu, and as he killed off the engaged tone and made his way back to her, he knew he was lost for the evening.

Chapter Eighteen

As the Kennard family sat down to their Friday night meal the atmosphere between Stephen and Cathy was tense. Friday nights were the one occasion during the week that all four of them could be sure of eating together. Cathy still lit Sabbath candles when at home, although invariably at the wrong time, and whatever demands the children made they were not allowed out on a Friday night. Hypocritically, when they were away, as they had been the previous week for Stephen's birthday, the Sabbath was ignored. It was a matter of tradition rather than religion although the white tablecloth, the flickering candles, the bottle of Kosher wine and the *challah,* the plaited loaf of bread, would have fooled the casual observer into believing that this was a religious household.

It had all started in the early years of their marriage when Stephen's mother had been a regular guest, and then somehow they had fallen into a routine, convincing themselves when the children were born that they only did it for their sake. It was almost as if they were embarrassed still to carry on a tradition that most of their contemporaries had long ago rejected. Yet, in his own way, Stephen looked forward to this oasis of calm in his week: a night when clients rarely rang, when the children could tell him stories of the week about teachers and school friends that were no more than names or impressions to him.

Tonight even the children sensed there was something in the air and kept their bickering to a minimum. It was made all the worse by the fact that Stephen knew he was in the wrong, had known as the evening with Trisha progressed that there was still time to phone home, but had done nothing about it. It had been midnight on Wednesday by the time he had opened his front door, and Thursday evening had seen Cathy going to the ballet with a friend and ignoring him when she finally climbed into bed.

It was not as if anything had happened with Trisha. It could have, he knew that; knew by the way she'd touched his hand across the table as the meal progressed, knew by the way she'd snuggled close to him in the taxi on the journey back to her house. But nothing had happened and he'd gathered all his resolve and declined the offer of a drink at her flat before he went home.

'Another time, perhaps,' she said, and he'd known that she meant it.

Yet he could tell Cathy none of this. She'd still been awake when he'd got home, and as soon as he tried to tiptoe into the bedroom he realised it was one late night too many and whatever lie he would tell would not be good enough.

'Where the hell have you been? Do you know what time it is? Why didn't you ring?'

He made the added mistake of being flippant.

'Is that a multiple choice question?'

'Stephen, it's nearly one in the morning...'

'Then you don't have to ask me what time it is—and if you keep on shouting you'll wake the children.'

'Oh, all of a sudden the father really

cares about the children! You don't see them from one Friday to another. At least if I do wake them up they can come in and you can introduce yourself.'

'Cathy, it's late...'

'Well, at least we both agree on that. Now where have you been?'

'I had to work late...'

'I called the office. You didn't answer.'

'Let me finish. Then I had to do some work on Gerry's affairs...'

'I called him too. He didn't know where you were. At least I found out Jeffrey was at a football match.'

'He hasn't got a wife to report to,' Stephen said.

'Oh, so it's the chore of reporting is it, that makes you so unhappy? Hell, come on, Stephen, we've established where you weren't. Now where were you?'

'I had to give an interview to a journalist. I did it over dinner. It's as simple as that.' It was as near the truth as dammit and it was more than he'd thought he'd offer.

'And was this journalist young, female and pretty?'

'Female, yes, pretty no. For heaven's sake, Cathy, it was work.'

'It's always work with you Stephen. I've really had enough.' And with that she rolled away as far as she could.

Although their bodies did not touch he could feel the defence system she had put up, feel the barbed wire against his legs, the poisoned sticks against his back. Normally after arguments she'd sleep it off, but this time it had been different—a fact of which he was made only too painfully aware when a bowl of hot chicken soup was slammed down in front of him, half of its contents spilling out on to the cloth.

'Look what you made me do,' Cathy snapped. 'It's a clean cloth as well. You're as bad as the children.'

Stephen shrugged. There was no point in retaliating when she was this irrational. He had to accept that dinner with Trisha had been stupid. It would pass. He had done nothing wrong at the end of the day, and that was how he always balanced out his life. Yet just for the moment it was a heavy price to pay. He had so much on his mind that he'd actually been looking forward to the opportunity to slip out of his business suit, metaphorically as well as literally, and relax with the family, recharge his batteries and get ready once again to face what was bound to be a difficult week.

Lessiter and his merry men had started their audit bang on schedule and there seemed to be a perversity in their selection of files for random checks. It was always the biggest file in the biggest mess, or the file that he'd delegated and couldn't remember to whom, or the file that was misfiled and took an hour of his secretary's time to find—or, worst of all, the file that couldn't be found at all. Paul Levy had taken them aside at the end of Thursday, his face that of a mourner at a funeral.

'This guy really knows what he's doing, chaps. I just hope there's nothing to find.'

Stephen and Jeffrey looked at each other, then back at Paul.

'Paul, you've known us a long time. Are we likely to have done anything naughty? It was you yourself who told us fifteen years ago not to take any cash from clients. We didn't like it at the time but we took your advice, just as we always have. If they find anything we've done, rather than what Arthur may or may not have perpetrated, I'll eat my hat,' Stephen said, patting his accountant friend on the shoulder.

Paul's fears were not to be so easily placated.

'You may not be able to afford to eat anything other than your hat. These fellows must be costing you a fortune, and although I'll do what I can to keep my costs down, I've got to charge something.'

And so it had continued through Friday,

Lessiter and his assistants by now seeming part of the landscape, part of the team, extra mouths to drink tea, extra bodies to seat, but apart from that innocuous, a threat to nobody. The impending weekend always lulled Stephen into a false sense of security; nothing bad could happen then and everything would look fresh on Monday morning, and so it usually was.

His wife took her seat opposite him and stared fixedly into space.

'Come on, Cathy, how long are you going to keep this up?'

'I'm not sure.' That in itself was progress, a sign that perhaps he could jolly her out of her mood as he had done so many times in the past.

'When do you think you will be sure?'

'Don't talk to me as if I'm a child. Jonathan!' She suddenly turned her attention to her son who visibly ducked as if to get out of the firing line, 'sit up straight, stop slouching and finish your soup instead of playing with it. We're all waiting for you.'

'I've had enough,' the boy said, 'I'm not really hungry. All this arguing takes away your appetite.'

'You're not hungry because you've been stuffing yourself full of sweets since you came home from school. It's your fault.' Now she was back to Stephen. 'You've got

197

to stop buying a sweet shop every time you go to the garage.'

He was trying very hard to avoid a major slanging match. Normally he would have turned on her and told her to stop taking out her temper on the children. If anybody should be wearing the hair shirt, it was him. Consequently he said nothing, merely collected the soup plates, took them to the kitchen and for once in his life put them straight into the dishwasher. He had barely got back to the table when there was a ring at the door.

'Who the hell's that on a Friday night?' he said.

'How should I know? I'm not a bloody clairvoyant. It's probably somebody collecting for charity or selling crummy paintings that they may or may not have painted themselves.' Still muttering, she went to the door. Jonathan asked Stephen a question, and much later he could not remember whether or not he had ever answered it. He heard Cathy's voice at the door, heard the sound of two men, heard footsteps in the hall, and then all he heard before the room started to spin round was one of the men saying: 'Stephen Benjamin Kennard, I have a warrant for your arrest...'

Chapter Nineteen

It was only after they had gone through all the formalities and he was left in a room with only a bored constable for company that Stephen realised he had never before been beyond the front desk of a police station. A lost wallet, a polite inquiry for directions, that had been about it. Most solicitors he knew had spent some time during their articles learning the criminal ropes but that sort of work had never come his way.

He dug his nails into the back of his hand. It hurt him so this wasn't a nightmare. Yet it was a nightmare, it was pure Kafka. Somebody had been telling lies about Stephen K because he'd been arrested. And even now he wasn't too sure what it was about. They'd read him his rights, they'd mentioned the relevant sections under the Theft and the Company Securities/Insider Dealing Act 1985, but it might just as well have been in a foreign language.

All he could see was the look of horror on his wife's face, the look of disbelief on that of his children, as he was bundled away into a car. Arrested in his own house...another literary allusion. He sought for it: Lady Macbeth. There, he had it. Keep your mind on things that are constant. Shakespeare would do, even Kafka. In the world outside here, people were reading *The Trial,* thinking it couldn't happen here; people were watching *Macbeth,* disbelieving murder under their own roof, knowing nothing of his plight. Their lives went on, undisturbed, untroubled. Nobody had burst into their homes in the middle of a Friday night meal and arrested them.

Now that he was here he thought of all the things he should have said or should have done.

'It's my Sabbath, you can't take me away. What happened to sanctuary?' Again an echo from a film seen long ago. What was it? *Blade Runner,* perhaps, something like that. Keep going through the attic of your mind until you're sure. Think of movies, think of plays, think of books. Think of everything except the terrible reality of where you are.

'Call Jeffrey.' These had been his farewell words to Cathy, and by the expression in her eyes he knew that she would, knew that all the anger had faded away at the shock of what had just befallen their family.

But where the hell was Jeffrey? Stephen had lost all track of time and his watch had stopped as if to signify the end of one life and the beginning of another. He looked up and the constable avoided his gaze for there behind him was a clock on the wall. Plain, round, but showing just nine-thirty. So he had been there less than an hour. One hour and it seemed like eternity, so what would a year in prison seem like? Five years, ten? Or would it all seem the same? Innocent men did get sent to jail, as a lawyer he knew that better than most. Blind justice, blindfolded justice... He began to shake and the policeman spoke to him for the first time.

'You can smoke if you want to.'

'I don't. Thanks.'

'I'll send for a coffee then.'

'That would be good. How long do these things usually take?' He felt insane asking the question. Twenty odd years in the law and he had to seek information from a kid who looked young enough to be his son.

'As long as they do. D.I Young is a great one for detail.'

The mention of Detective Inspector Young served as an introduction for just then the door opened and in came a middle-aged man, his hair completely grey and close-cropped, slim, almost elegant, his suit looking more expensive than he ought to be able to afford on a Detective Inspector's salary.

'Mr Kennard?' Then, seeming satisfied that he'd got the right man, he ploughed on: 'Sorry to have kept you. Paperwork. But then of course you'd know all about that? The bane of our life, paperwork.' The voice was well modulated and soft so that Stephen found himself straining to hear every word. It's a technique, he told himself, don't be upset by it. He decided to take the initiative.

'What the hell is this all about? We're not living in a police state, you know.'

'I do, Mr Kennard, I do. I have to pay my taxes, keep within the speed limit, send my children to school, just like everybody else. Now if this was a police state I wouldn't be doing any of those things. My days would be filled with a mad merry-go-round of rape and pillage. I've not raped anybody today, although if you looked at the state of the WPCs here you'd quite understand that, and the worse piece of pillaging I've done was to take home a station biro without filling in a chitty. As to what all this is about, let's talk about D'Arblay, shall we?'

'I'm not talking about anything until my partner gets here.'

'Ah, that would be the plump gentleman who's been sitting outside making a nuisance of himself for the last thirty minutes.'

Good for you, Jeffrey, Stephen thought. Give them hell. I knew you wouldn't let me down. And all of a sudden the thought that there was life beyond this room gave him enormous encouragement. This was all a terrible mistake. Jeffrey would sort it out and in a matter of hours he'd be back at his own table, perhaps in time for Cathy's apple strudel.

'Yes, that's my partner, Jeffrey Wightman. Now, are you going to let me see him, or are we going to pass the time of day for the rest of the night?'

'Nice phrase that, Mr Kennard. Very poetic, very literate. Not many literate solicitors around, in my experience. No time. All rush, rush, rush, and just no time to smell the roses. Now my approach is different. I like to take my time, so before you and Mr Wightman have your little partners' meeting I'd like to ask a few questions.'

'I just told you, I'm saying nothing...'

'...without your solicitor. Yes, I've heard it all before. But humour me, will you, Mr Kennard? I don't want to be here any more than you do. The only difference between us is that I'm being paid a pittance to ask you questions and for once in your life you're not being able to charge anything.'

That was all Stephen needed. A copper

with a grudge against lawyers.

'Your young man there offered me a coffee just before you came in. What about it?'

'Did you indeed, young Hannon? Well, that was very generous of you. Perhaps you'd like to nip along to the canteen and fetch us both a coffee since you've clearly got ambitions in the catering line?'

The constable blushed, muttering a mixed acknowledgement and apology, and disappeared.

'Youngsters today. I don't know what they're coming to. Do you have the same problem in your trade—sorry, profession?'

'It's not easy to get the right articled clerks.' The words were out before Stephen realised that he was being trapped into pleasantries, gulled into the sort of small talk that neighbours from different walks of life might exchange over the garden fence.

'So while we're waiting for refreshments, the questions. You don't mind if I tape this, do you?' He spoke into a machine. 'Interview with Stephen Kennard, nine forty-five on the third of May, Mr Kennard's representative not yet present, interview kept to preliminary matters.' He gave Stephen a disarming smile.

'There, nothing you can find offensive in that, is there?'

'You know there bloody well is. Put the tape back on. I want Jeffrey in here now.'

'Want, is it? We all want. We all need. But we can't necessarily have. So...' He pressed the record button.

'We are making certain enquiries into the recent acquisition of shares in a publicly quoted company, D'Arblay Investment plc. We believe that you procured the acquisition of those shares while having information in breach of the Company Securities (Insider Dealing) Act 1985.

'Are you mad? I'm not even prepared to discuss the D'Arblay situation unless my client gives me clearance. Even that would be a breach of the solicitor-client confidentiality agreement.'

Young leaned back in his chair and applauded as D.C Hannon returned with the coffees.

'No nouvelle cuisine delicacies, no pâté de fois gras, not even a couple of delectable doughnuts? I believe we interrupted Mr Kennard here in the middle of his dinner. Are you hungry?'

'No. Can we get on with this, please?' Young turned to the Detective Constable. 'Where's Sergeant Davidson?'

'Not too sure, sir.'

'Can you get him along? I do like to have my sergeant here. Indispensable is our Charlie. Detective Constable, I was just applauding Mr Kennard's sense of priorities. Rare in this day and age, particularly amongst lawyers. But you want me to get on. Take note of that, young Hannon. Mr Kennard wants me to push on, so I'll push on and you push off and find my sergeant, will you?'

Stephen began to wonder if this man really was mad. There was a strange, almost messianic look in his eye, but the way he turned his tape machine on and off to capture the salient pieces of the interview left him in no doubt that the D.I knew exactly what he was doing.

'So about these D'Arblay shares?'

'I haven't bought any. I've no intention of buying any.'

'But your client's buying, isn't he? Mr Mortimer? Mr Gerald Mortimer?'

'I've already told you, I can't discuss my client's affairs.'

'Of course, I forgot. I must be getting old. But let's assume I know that your client's buying so you don't have to tell me, so you're breaching no confidences. And you decide to buy too? A quick buck. Helps the world go around. You've got expensive tastes, big house, country cottage, racehorse, children at private schools, expensive car. Been a bit of a downturn in the legal world so I hear, so those tastes take some financing. You can't be blamed for that. So just tell me that you gave into temptation and had a little dabble?'

Stephen looked aghast. This man whom he'd never met before this evening knew an awful lot about him, had probed deep into his life. He felt as if he'd woken up in the morning to find his home had been burgled, that a stranger was tiptoeing around his personal effects, rummaging through his dustbins, stealing his privacy.

'I did not, as you put it, have a little dabble. Now can we put an end to this farce and can I see my partner?'

Young shrugged.

'It's up to you. I've not stopped you, have I, Hannon?' The Detective Constable had returned without the sergeant in tow.

'No, sir. I'm afraid I can't find Sergeant Davidson.'

'There you are. No, sir. Can't say fairer than that. Well, if you're not going to make it easy for me and spew out a nice little confession, let's wheel your esteemed partner in. I suppose you'd like a little privacy so we'll withdraw for our supper.' He saw Stephen look around the room.

'It's all right, it's not bugged.'

The door closed behind them and Stephen was left alone for a brief moment. It was pure madness. Yes, the shares in

D'Arblay had been rising, but the first he'd heard about it was when Gerry's City analyst had called. He should have told Young that, should have told him to talk to Gerry, he'd confirm the surprise on Stephen's face when he'd heard the news; but then, policemen weren't interested in emotions, they were just interested in facts. Just the facts, man, just the facts—an echo from an old American TV show. An echo from his childhood.

As the door opened again he jumped out of his chair, his nerves finally beginning to crack. It was Jeffrey, wearing an old jumper and jeans that were just a little too tight, but Jeffrey for all that.

'You came,' Stephen said, 'thank God!'

'Of course I came. Don't the cavalry always arrive in time in the best movies? We'll soon have you out of here. Given who you are I don't think we'll have a lot of trouble in getting them to agree police bail.'

The words themselves had an ominous ring to them, words he'd only previously heard bandied around those legal circles where crime was the norm, where crime actually paid.

'I don't understand any of this, Jeffrey. Why I'm here, what I'm charged with?'

'Just calm down, Stephen. Everything's going to be all right. We won't let you down. Cathy's waiting for you at home, and the children. You've got partners, you've got friends, and you've got family. You can't lose.'

'You're right, Jeff. I can't lose.' And with that thought Stephen burst into tears and clung to his old friend with all the ferocity of a small child.

Chapter Twenty

It was the newspapers that were the worst. *Solicitor arrested in insider dealing scandal. Lawyer accused. Fashion trade scandal.*

By midday they took the phone off the hook and drew the curtains to protect themselves from the photographers and journalists who were camping out on their lawn. It had been two in the morning before Jeffrey had persuaded the indefatigable D.I Young to let Stephen go, and then it was probably only because Stephen had almost fallen asleep during the course of the last few questions. As the line of inquiry continued so the case against him became clearer. The police were, as Young made great play of saying, acting upon information received, in other words, a tip off. This information suggested that, using confidential information, Stephen had bought shares in D'Arblay for personal gain, not in his own name but through an offshore entity that he'd set up just for that purpose.

When they had finally got out, Jeffrey had been comforting.

'Look, they've nothing really to go on. Somebody's obviously got it in for you, though...'

Stephen felt a shiver down his spine as the mysterious somebody danced on his grave. Who could he possibly have upset enough to make them hate him this much? You couldn't go through life as a solicitor and expect to please all the people all of the time, but hatred...that was much stronger, that needed some desperate act to spark it off. He remembered a line from one of the *Godfather* movies; 'Don't hate your enemy, it clouds your judgement.' What sort of judgement was there in having him locked away in a cell for hours on end.

'They can't possibly link you to this offshore company...can they Stephen?' Jeffrey had asked.

'Come on, Jeff...'

'All right, I'm sorry. I shouldn't even have asked the question.'

'So where do we go from here?'

'Well, you're bailed until the fourteenth. That'll give them time to continue their investigations. Hopefully they'll find it's all a load of nonsense and then you can put all this behind you.'

'Oh, great. So I can rewrite all the headlines. You know what everybody will say: no smoke without fire. Well, I'm afraid this puts paid to the Greystone's deal.'

'Not at all,' Jeffrey replied. 'Philip was on the phone this morning saying that he was right behind you and if there was anything they could do to help, you only needed to ask. They have a connection with one of the big four accounting firms who have their own forensic accounting department, and if there is any number crunching to do or anything that needs to be investigated and pieced together to clear you, then he'll get them on to it.'

Stephen had felt an overwhelming sense of gratitude. He knew now what it must feel like to be terminally ill and to endure the kindness of strangers.

Cathy too was solicitous.

'Don't worry, Stephen. Everybody who knows you, knows you couldn't do anything like this.'

The children were quiet but fiercely loyal. Jonathan had suffered a terrible asthma attack after the police had taken his father away, and that in itself made Stephen feel worse than ever.

'It's irrational,' Cathy said, 'you can't blame yourself for something that's not your fault.' But there was a slight tremor in her voice that suggested to him that she had been doubly frightened, both for her husband and her son.

His mother was practically hysterical.

'How can I face my neighbours? My son arrested. It's never happened before in our family. Your father, may he rest in peace, must be turning in his grave.'

'He can't rest in peace *and* turn in his grave.' He regretted it almost as soon as it was out.

'Always the smart one, my Stephen. What sort of *brain-child* gets himself arrested?'

'Mum, it was me down at the station, not you. Believe me, whatever you're feeling I'm a hundred times worse. And one thing you've forgotten is that I've done nothing wrong.'

'Did I say you'd done anything wrong? It's not me you have to convince. I'm your mother. It's everybody else. I even had a reporter phone me up and ask for an interview. And when I said no, he offered me money, the little *schnip!* Like I'd sell my own son for money.'

She began to cry heartbrokenly down the

phone, and despite his irritation with her illogicality, her selfishness, Stephen began to cry as well. His father was all he could think of and in a way he was relieved that he was not alive at this moment.

Gerry Mortimer came round in the afternoon, running the gauntlet of flashing cameras and microphones stuck under his nose.

'I've been trying to call you since breakfast. What are you trying to do, push your BT shares now you've finished with D'Arblay?'

Stephen gave a weak smile, the first smile since that fateful ring at the doorbell.

'It's not funny, Gerry.'

'You want I should cry?' the older man replied in self-mockery.

Stephen shook his head.

'I just don't understand it. When Chris Kennedy phoned that day, whenever it was—I've lost all track of time—the shares were already on the move.'

'I've spoken to Chris. He's probing around for the identity of the buyer. He can't break through the nominees, and what's been bought is not quite enough to impose any obligation to disclose. Now believe me, if Chris can't find out who it is, the police won't be able to either. From what you tell me they pulled you in just because somebody called them and

213

told them you'd been buying shares. Now that could just be a crank. It could even be our friend Kinsey, who didn't exactly take a liking to you when you nailed him to the wall.'

Stephen whistled softly to himself.

'Now there's a thought. I've been going over and over in my mind just who might want to stir up trouble for me. Kinsey's one certain candidate.'

'I've tried to call him as well.'

'Somebody's been busy,' Stephen said, suddenly feeling much better.

'Somebody had to be. You've obviously been too busy feeling sorry for yourself. Anyway, our friend Kinsey's left town.'

'So that's the end of that.'

'Not necessarily. I've not lived all these years without having a few useful contacts. I've got people working on him right now, and if I find that it's our Mr Kinsey who's put you through all this grief, he'll wish he'd never been born.'

Stephen had seen Gerry Mortimer put on a hard front in business before, but he had never seen him like this. It made him feel a lot more reassured that he had him as a friend rather than as an enemy. His father had told him stories of Gerry as a young man, a street fighter, an erstwhile hooligan, a wild boy even by East End standards but until now, despite working

214

so closely with him, Stephen had thought those stories had been exaggerated by time. Right now, however, he was prepared to believe them all. If it had been Kinsey, and Gerry or his contacts caught up with him, then there was every chance that bones would break.

Gerry sipped at his lemon tea and then wiped some invisible drops from his moustache.

'Where does this leave us on your D'Arblay bid?'

Stephen bit his lip. 'I'm sorry, Gerry, I've been so wrapped up with my own problems I've not really applied myself to the repercussions of all this. I doubt I'll be allowed to act while all this is going on.'

'Then we have to put a stop to it as quickly as possible don't we? Let me give you some advice. I've seen trouble in my time, some of it with the police in my early days. One thing's for sure—you can't hide from it. You just brazen it out. Eventually everything finishes. Your dad used to say that: good, bad, indifferent, it all passes in exactly the same time, it just feels different. I can't tell you to enjoy it, but I can tell you to learn to live with it. If you were going out this afternoon, go. When it's time to go to work on Monday, get up, get washed, get shaved and go. It's the best V sign you can give to all those *mamzeyrim* out there. And Stephen,' he said rising from his chair, 'put the bloody phone back on the hook so an old man like me doesn't have to *shlep* out!'

As soon as he'd gone the depression began to sweep over Stephen again. He needed the company of people, needed reassurance like a child, to be told everything would be all right. For the first time in his life he was quite lost. He took Gerry's advice and put the phone back on the hook. Almost immediately it rang and he was tempted, for a moment, not to answer it, but in a way that was worse. Who was to say that the same malevolent force that had triggered off this train of events was not on the other end of the line? In fact it was Sarah phoning to sympathise, even her normally brittle voice soft with feeling. Only Anthony had not made contact. Knowing his brother it was quite possible he'd not even heard the news. His mother had once said that World War III might well pass Anthony by. He was not renowned for reading newspapers or watching the television, but surely somebody in his family must have seen something? Yet even if they had, would Anthony do the right thing, or would he even know what the right thing to do was? Brothers, family. You could choose your friends but you couldn't choose your family; all you could do was choose to ignore them.

The phone rang again and this time he let it ring. Eight, nine, ten times. Persistent. It was his daughter who finally took the call.

'It could be for me, you know. I do have friends too.' The tone of her voice left him in no doubt that the shock was wearing off and she was once again remembering that she was a teenager, a social creature whose demands transcended everything about her. He heard her answer and realised at once it was for him and not for her.

'Yes, yes this is Stephen Kennard's home. No. I'm not sure if he's here or not. Yes, I'll tell him if he's in. Hold on.'

She turned to her father, her hand expertly cupped over the receiver.

'It's for you,' she whispered as if any explanation was necessary, 'a woman. She says you know her. Trisha something or other.' He knew she knew the last name but couldn't be bothered to say it as that might indicate she actually had some interest in the identity of the caller.

'Martin.'

'Probably.'

He hesitated. Last night in the police

217

station, his mind in a turmoil, he'd wondered if this wasn't some kind of divine punishment on him for his illicit dinner with the journalist, a warning shot across the bows. If he promised to have nothing more to do with her, maybe it would all go away. This was another part of the test. He'd promised that invisible deity on Friday night that he'd never talk to Trisha again as long as he got out of there, and now he was being tested. But by whom, God or the Devil?

He hesitated. He'd done nothing wrong that night other than just being there, other than telling his wife a white lie of omission, so why should he have to make absurd vows? And weren't vows meant to be broken? But the hesitation was crucial. His daughter was almost jumping up and down with impatience.

'Come on Dad, you can't keep her hanging on forever.'

'No, you're right. Tell her I'm out.' And as he spoke he felt as if he were expiating his sins.

Chapter Twenty One

He realised something was wrong as soon as he got to the office. It was like boarding the *Marie Celeste*. Nobody was in reception, nobody was at their machines, the phones were ringing and nobody was answering them, doors swung open while others remained firmly closed. Finally one of the juniors appeared, looked at him as if he were a ghost, and vanished into the deeper recesses of the floor before he could even wish him good morning.

He'd slept late. Saturday night he'd hardly slept at all and by Sunday he was over the edge.

'Take a tablet, it'll help,' Cathy had said, and he'd listened. He'd never had a sleeping pill before and it was not an experience he intended repeating. He still felt he'd had a disturbed night even though he was unconscious, and when he woke his head felt thick and muzzy. The reporters had gone, moved on to cover a rail crash in Surrey, and it was only the cat he had to avoid as he manoeuvred the car out of the drive. The cat seemed to survive everything. It had appeared mysteriously nearly ten years ago, its age indeterminate. Nowadays it rarely moved outside the environs of the house but at various times it had been stuck up trees, locked in outhouses, cornered by alsations, or simply fallen asleep in a neighbour's garden and been too forgetful to come home until it got hungry. It was originally called Joseph, because of its multi-coloured fur, but that was soon shortened to Jo when the children realised it was a her rather than a him. If the cat can survive so can I, thought Stephen. This is only my first life of nine. One down eight to go.

As he drove to work he found that he was talking to himself; sometimes soothingly, sometimes giving vent to the mixture of panic, anger and frustration that seethed inside him. He switched from station to station, listening to each news broadcast, fearful of what he might hear yet equally scared that he might miss something. But all the news was of the crash, eighteen dead, a hundred injured, and Stephen felt instantly superior that he was alive, physically un-maimed while just a few miles away people mourned their losses. It was wrong to feel this way, he knew that, but as the sun slanted across his windscreen he gathered strength from it for his fight.

But all of that comparative euphoria had vanished. Ten o'clock and all was not well.

Behind the door of their board room he heard a buzz of conversation, and pushing it open he saw Jeffrey, Sarah and Anthony with the four junior partners. They looked up at him as he came into the room but only Jeffrey did not look away.

'Stephen. We've been waiting for you.'

'I'm sorry. If somebody had told me there was to be a partners' meeting I'd have made the effort. As it was, I took a pill last night and overslept.'

Nobody said anything, each looking to Jeffrey to take the lead.

'Stephen,' he said at last, 'I don't think there's any easy way of saying this to you. We've known each other a long time and quite frankly I understand less of this than anybody, but we've got definite proof that ten days ago you spoke to Interco in Jersey and asked them to establish a Liechtenstein trust.'

Interco was a company used by everybody in the practice when a client wanted to form an offshore company or establish an offshore trust. The policy was never to use Interco for anything other than genuine non-resident situations as they'd seen other professional firms come to grief with the Revenue for being parties to what was nothing short of a tax fraud.

Stephen felt nausea; thought indeed for the moment that he might well be sick in front of them, vomit up all the bile, all the lies, that were destroying his life.

'It's not true,' he blurted out. His voice sounded thin and weak to his own ears.

'Stephen, I've spoken to Jarvis Walters on the island. He swears he not only spoke to you but got a fax confirming it. The trust then bought a company—the company then bought the shares. What's even worse is that you used *our* money to do it.'

Stephen's mouth opened wide. Mistaking disbelief and astonishment for an impending denial, Jeffrey just carried on.

'There's no point in saying anything. We found in your drawer the codes for the computer that we spent hours looking for. We found a phone number for Arthur, although by the time we called he'd moved on—surprise, surprise. Maybe you thought nobody would be able to work backwards from the company through the Liechtenstein trust, maybe you thought nobody would even question the purchase of the shares, and with Arthur paid off all we were left with was an insurance claim. Quite frankly I don't know what you were thinking. Maybe even you didn't know.'

'If there's no point in saying anything, then I won't. I thought I knew you all, but clearly I was wrong.'

They've been through my desk, he

thought, and what other private things had they found there and handled and laughed over? Little things the kids had given him, an old valentine from Sarah that he'd never had the heart to throw away. Did Jeffrey and Anthony know about that piece of history as well, and would that make them trust him even less—if that were possible?

'We don't want to be unfair,' Jeffrey was droning on. 'Obviously we have to tell the insurers and the Law Society, but we'll leave it to you to inform the police. We won't do anything until two this afternoon so that you can get some independent advice.'

'Thanks,' said Stephen cynically, and to himself thought, Thanks for nothing. The Law Society would tell the police and the nails would be well and truly knocked into the lid of his coffin. He was dead and very nearly buried.

'We'll accept your resignation from the practice. We'll have to talk about things like your personal clients and your capital account but that's probably best dealt with by your solicitor, whoever that is to be.'

Stephen tried to catch Sarah's eye but she found something interesting on her finger nail. Anthony was sitting with his head bent, doodling, probably not listening. His own brother, his own lover. He had brought them both into the practice and this was what they did to him. The junior partners looked at him curiously, perhaps wondering which of them would get his room. He needed time to collect his thoughts, to come up with some explanation, to make them understand that he'd been framed.

It was all falling into place, a diabolical jigsaw that formed a picture of hell, and he was the one, the only one, roasting in the flames. This was a private hell, a personal chamber of horrors, created for him by some unknown maniac. The tip off to the police, the buying of Arthur, the share purchase, the establishment of the trust, and now this. He began thinking again, thinking like a lawyer, and a whole list of questions sprang to his mind.

'Who told you about the Liechtenstein trust?'

Even as he asked the question he realised that it sounded trite, like the denouement of a bad thriller where the murderer asks all the right questions so the reader can have his easy explanations.

'A little birdie,' said Jeffrey.

'The same little birdie who sang to the police?' Stephen asked.

'Look, Stephen. Forgive us if we feel we don't owe you any explanation. You've done untold damage to us, you and your high flying ideas. Racehorses, champagne...it all seemed a good life, didn't it? Well, somebody has to pay, and right now whatever you think, we're all paying.' Sarah flushed brightly as she launched into him, and this time she did look him straight in the face, her eyes cold diamonds carving into his flesh, through his bones and into his very soul.

Jeffrey pulled them back to business. 'This is all getting us nowhere. You've half an hour to clear out your personal effects. After that, if we never see you again, it'll be too soon. You've betrayed us all, and me the most.'

The years fell away as Jeffrey spoke. They were back at school, they'd had a row, they weren't talking for a day, maybe a week, but then it would be forgiven; but that was then, this was now, and as the great wall of silence and hostility rose against him Stephen knew with absolute certainty that nothing in his life would ever be the same again.

Chapter Twenty Two

He saved the picture of the children on his desk until last, letting their eyes follow him as he picked his way through the debris of his career. It all fitted into one box, everything that he really wanted to take with him.

So this is how it all ends, he thought, a broken man and his box. He might just as well be in a box for all the chance he had.

He'd phoned Gerry and told him the news, thinking it was better that he heard it from him than anybody else. There'd been a stunned silence, but then to his credit the old man had rallied.

'I don't believe it. I don't believe any of it. Not for a second.'

'Thanks, Gerry. I wasn't going to say so before but I swear on my childrens' lives that this is some kind of gigantic conspiracy.'

'You don't have to make oaths,' Gerry replied. 'I know you're a lawyer, but leave it out...'

'I don't know how much longer I'm going to be able to describe myself in that way. I feel as if I'm surrounded. I'm like the last cowboy in the wagon train and the Indians are moving in for the kill.'

'Very dramatic, very picturesque. At least you can take up writing as a profession if push comes to shove.' Gerry's voice took on a serious note.

'Listen, Stephen. I'll have to call an emergency board meeting to discuss the whole business.'

'I understand.' He understood only too well, understood the probable outcome.

'I can't resign, Gerry. It'd be an admission of some kind of guilt.'

'They may vote to remove you, or at best suspend you. I've only got so much sway at board level. I'll do my best.'

'I know you will.'

So there were still some people trying to do their best for Stephen Kennard, but would their best be good enough? And still on the subject of the best, he realised he had to have the best advice. A lawyer who tried to advise himself had a fool for a client. He opened his personal telephone book and began to thumb through the names. There were solicitors galore, but so many of them were specialists in company and commercial matters, and reluctantly he had to admit that what he needed was a criminal lawyer with commercial flair.

Suddenly it came to him. Colin Leigh. They had been together at Oxford and had formed an odd alliance, Stephen from his near ghetto background, Colin the son of an army officer whose childhood had been spent at a series of boarding schools. Colin had been the best there was in his year, and a first class honours degree had been followed by a scholarship in International Law at The Hague. Everybody thought Colin was going to be an academic as he resisted the courtship of every leading firm of London lawyers; but then he vanished for a year, only to resurface working for Amnesty International. He became a media figure, perfect interview material whenever a political prisoner needed a defence; but every stage in Colin's career was merely a staging place and eventually he'd set himself up in practice in London, specialising initially in immigration appeals, then gradually developing the firm until the Pan-Asian Bank Case brought him into the limelight. He'd defended three executives who'd been made the fall guys by a chairman and vice-chairman who'd systematically squeezed Pan-Asian dry over the years, and defended them brilliantly. The men had been taken back to the Far East to face not just imprisonment but death, and Colin had assumed responsibility for them stylishly as he wore the long black Dylanesque overcoat he invariably affected. He'd been advocate as well as solicitor at the preliminary hearings and even when leading counsel was instructed at the main trial, the QC in his summing up paid tribute to Colin's preparation of the case. All three were acquitted and the bandwagon rolled.

Stephen hadn't spoken to Colin for over a year. For a while they'd met for lunch and the odd drink, but Colin had married a Kenyan-Asian girl and gradually slipped into the culture of that community rather than his own. Cathy had always found him difficult.

'He makes me feel insignificant,' she'd complained. Colin had no time for trivia and Cathy's conversational subjects of ballet, theatre and fashion were unlikely to impress him. Cathy for her part was totally apolitical and once incensed Colin by telling him that one civil war was very much like another if your geography was as bad as hers. But right now Stephen wasn't choosing a dinner guest, he was choosing a lifeline. He was looking for the best and the best was Colin Leigh.

He was put straight through when he called.

'Stephen. How are you? Or need I ask. I'm pleased you called. I was going to contact you today to see if you needed any help. I hope you don't think that impertinent?'

Stephen smiled. Success hadn't changed Colin. He still had the same modest unassuming approach to life, the bemused tone in his voice that anybody would actually want to take his advice. Yet once into a case he was different; demonic, obsessive, heading for the jugular and not stopping even when the blood began to spout.

'Can I come to see you?'

'Of course, when?'

'Like now. I'm not too sure how long I'm going to be roaming the town.'

'Yes, Stephen, come right over. I'll cancel whatever I've got and give you the day. You know where to come?'

'Grays Inn Road.'

'Dead right. I'll see you in a few minutes then. And Stephen?'

'Yes?'

'I'm most terribly sorry.'

He put down the phone, feeling there ought to be something else to do. It shouldn't be ending like this, all the years of friendship, the effort he'd put into building up the practice. 'This is the way the world ends, not with a bang but with a whimper.' The phone rang and he momentarily felt the same mild irritation he'd always experienced when busy. He actually hated the telephone, rarely used it at home, even when his wife or children left it free.

'Hello.'

'Stephen. You *are* there?'

The voice thrilled him despite himself. If she was calling him, was that breaking the promise?

'Trisha. Good of you to call.'

'Very formal. I called you at home. Your daughter would make a wonderful receptionist at a theatrical agency. They groom them for years to be able to lie with a straight face.'

'She was only being protective.'

'I know and I understand. What made you think you need to be protected from me? I wasn't phoning as a journalist. Well, that's not quite true. I *am* a journalist. I was trying to see if I could help in softening the blow with any of the papers.'

'Yes, you could buy me one or two.'

'Papers?'

'No, publishing houses. Then I can write my own headlines. I think this week is going to be worse.'

'Why?'

'I can't explain on the phone and I have to be somewhere shortly.'

'Shall I call you back?' she asked.

'I shan't be here...for a while.'

'How long's a while?' she asked, catching the innuendo.

'A long while, Trish. I've been suspended. Hell, I've been kicked out, let's be honest about it.' He sounded desperate.

'Stephen, put your guilt aside. Take my private number with you. When you finish whatever you're doing, call me. We'll meet. No commitments, no obligation, just one friend helping another. From the sound of it, you need all the friends you can get.'

'Yes. Yes, I will.'

This time there was a finality in the way he put down the receiver. The last call he might ever receive in his office, or what had been his office.

He walked back into the main part of the building. All the partners' doors were closed, barring him from sight and from their minds. The girls were back at their machines, word processor screens flashing messages and words that no longer affected him. He was out in space, Planet Earth was blue, and he had just so much air supply.

Sandra his secretary came bustling over to him.

'Stephen, are you going to be all right? You look terrible.'

'Don't fuss over me, Sandy. Just look after yourself and my clients.'

She brushed some ash off her jumper and immediately some more dislodged itself from her shoulder and filled the void.

'I've given them a month's notice. I don't want to stay here on my own. I just can't believe what they've done to you.'

'It's not them, Sandy. But somebody's done something to me, that's for sure.'

She kissed him on the cheek, then hard on the lips, and he sensed that the kiss would have been longer if they had been on their own. Poor Sandy. Lost, alone, unattractive, another casualty in this guerrilla war. He'd always sensed she was a little bit in love with him. He'd done nothing to encourage it but there was an inevitability when a single woman getting on in years worked for a man for a long time.

He suddenly knew what the Americans felt like in Vietnam. The enemy was there, hiding in the long grass, hiding in the trees, swimming deep beneath the surface of the river. The enemy was there, a needle in the haystack of the world, and to prove his innocence all he had to do was to find him—or her—before time ran out.

Chapter Twenty Three

He was now part of a machine, a cog, turning mechanically, unable to function on his own. Colin Leigh had been incredible. He'd spent days with Stephen, taking statements, piecing together a history of his life, keeping him going whenever he despaired.

'Let me be the judge of what's important and what's not. Just tell me everything.'

He sat in his high-backed chair, a diminutive slender figure with a penchant for bright ties, his thin face and rimless spectacles still giving him the look of a displaced academic. And Stephen had told him everything, told him of Sarah, told him the history of his marriage, Jonathan's illness, even told him about Trisha—although there was nothing to tell.

'Not true,' Colin had said. 'As I understand it you and this journalist have closed this allergy clinic down. I don't see you being number one on Stefan Arndheim's Christmas card list. Now the Swiss know all about off-shore companies, don't they? As I see it, he could be a real suspect.'

As Stephen went over and over his career, names surfaced from the past that he'd long ago buried in the catacombs of his mind. Phil Taylor the property developer whom he'd kicked out when he began making false mortgage applications; Lennie Simons the drug-addicted fashion designer who'd always felt Stephen had abandoned him and whose obsessive phone calls at home had made him go ex-directory; Anna Tully whose theatrical career had gone downhill with the same speed that she downed drinks, and who'd become paranoid that Stephen and her agent were ganging up on her. It was amazing just how many lunatics had passed through his life although Colin thought it par for the course.

'I have to ask this,' he had said, 'but what about your present partners?'

'What do you mean?' It had simply never occurred to Stephen that anybody he knew well could be involved.

'Stephen, I never took you for naive. You're a shrewd businessman. Somebody's out to destroy you, and making a pretty good job of it. You can't overlook anything or anybody. Believe me, if your kids were a bit older they'd come under the microscope.'

Stephen permitted himself a rueful smile.

'I honestly think my kids are stronger candidates than any of my partners. Jeffrey's like my brother, Anthony *is* my brother, and Sarah—well, she's just not like that. As for the junior salaried partners they simply wouldn't have the brains. I would have trusted any of them with my life.'

Colin made a wry face.

'I don't think I would have taken their actions quite so calmly.'

'It's not a question of calm. I can understand. From their point of view there's no other explanation. Whoever's planned this has made sure of that. I keep asking myself—what would I have done in these circumstances?'

'And?'

'I'm not sure. Probably the same.'

Colin sniffed.

'I doubt it. You always were a soft touch when it came to friends—and women for that matter—so let me be a bit hard. You say Jeffrey wanted this merger with Greystone's, but you weren't too keen?'

'Well, yes, but he's hardly likely to put the whole practice at risk just because of that. I mean, with me about to go behind bars, Greystone's aren't going to be rushing into that particular marriage, are they?'

'You're probably right, but let's keep an open mind. Anthony? You've always tended to put him in the shade.'

'Anthony likes the shade. For heaven's sake, he's only a partner because I went out on a limb for him to please my mother.'

'Perhaps he knows that. Still waters and all that...'

Stephen shook his head in disbelief. 'You're going to make *me* paranoid in a minute.'

'Good. Then maybe you'll start helping me look for the key to this problem. You've got to work at this. There's too much at stake. And so we come to the beautiful Sarah. *Cherchez la femme,* as they say.'

'I've already said...'

Colin began to show a little impatience.

'I know what you've already said, but you've also said she was your mistress and you ditched her. "Hell hath no fury", and she's neither family nor a childhood friend.'

Stephen was feeling terrible. He had a permanent headache and could hardly keep his hands from shaking. He had to keep a grip on himself but this character assassination of people he liked was getting too much for him.

'So I can trust nobody?'

'Only me,' Colin said. 'Only me.'

They'd produced a list of possible enemies (and indeed friends who might be enemies) and Stephen had hesitantly asked what Colin intended to do about it.

'I'll instruct an inquiry agent. He'll prepare a report on them all: financial, emotional, even details of their movements over the last few months. It's a long shot, but we have to try everything. There are two other things we have to dispose of first...'

'Yes?'

Colin pursed his lips and played momentarily with a threatening-looking paper knife that in another's hands might well have been considered an offensive weapon.

'Look me straight in the face, Stephen,

and tell me you didn't do it.'

He didn't hesitate.

'I didn't do it.'

'Thank you. I'm sorry, but I had to ask.'

'And if I'd said anything different?'

'Then I'd have had to cease acting for you. Now to the even more difficult subject—money. If it was up to me I'd do all this for free, but I've partners myself and I can't have them accusing me of theft. Obviously, I'll be flexible and won't overcharge but I do need something on account, not just for this firm but also for the investigators.'

Stephen understood. It didn't make it any more palatable but he understood. His drawings from the practice had been stopped and his partners had made it quite clear to Colin that he could forget about his capital account until the monies were recovered. Litigation was sprouting at an alarming rate of knots. Nominee directors were being served with injunctions and his own personal account was frozen for the moment pending an application by Colin to release funds to live on. Yet, truth to tell, there was more overdraft there than cash and although the bank hadn't called that in yet Stephen was sure it wouldn't take long for someone either at Head Office or the branch to read the papers and realise that their money was potentially at risk.

He'd been duly suspended by Sidney and so had his salary which in any event always went into the practice. He had some shares, some insurance policies and a few thousand in building societies, but none of that was freed up either. That left the house which was in his and Cathy's joint names and heftily mortgaged, and the cottage which they'd bought in a trust set up for the children. Everything had been fine as long as a high income was coming in, and he had never envisaged a day when it would not. If he'd been ill he had adequate insurance to cover that, when he retired he had ample pensions to make life comfortable, but now his lifeline had been cut off and he was gasping for breath. There was always Cathy's money, but that was hers, her inheritance from grandparents, and he couldn't bring himself to touch it.

'I'll need a few days, maybe a week. How much do you need?'

'Say five thousand.'

It might just as well have been five million although Stephen was very much aware that had it been anybody else the figure would have been doubled. It was absurd. Not so long ago he'd been leading his horse into the winner's enclosure, and now he couldn't even write out a cheque for five thousand pounds.

He couldn't go back to Gerry. When they'd gone back to court to face extra charges there had been every possibility that he'd have found himself on remand until the case came up; months and months of languishing in jail. It was unthinkable, but Gerry had come through. First of all Colin had been sufficiently silver-tongued to persuade the magistrates that bail was the right option, and then when they fixed the sum at a quarter of a million pounds, only Gerry had been prepared to come forward.

'You do understand, Mr Mortimer, that should the defendant, Mr Kennard, fail to appear to answer these charges, your money will be forfeit?'

'I do.'

They'd taken their time in going through Gerry's assets, in satisfying themselves he was good for the money, but at the end of the day the police had dropped their opposition to the bail and he had his freedom, for what it was worth. The leash they allowed him though was not long. He had to surrender his passport and report to the local police station every other day. That too, Colin told him, was a meaningful concession; sometimes it was twice every day. He could not honestly say he felt particularly grateful for the court's magnanimity.

'Is that it for the day, Colin?'

'Do you want it to be?'

Stephen nodded. He'd not only had enough, he also had a good idea as to where he could get five thousand pounds.

Chapter Twenty Four

Toby Lipscomb sat in his favourite armchair in the Whitehall club that had been one of his first acquisitions. When he was absent the chair always remained empty. A new member had once had the effrontery to seat himself there whilst Toby was on the premises, had failed to move when he arrived, and then was given no explanation when his membership was not renewed. Small things like that were important to Toby Lipscomb, the trimmings of power and authority. The orb and sceptre were concepts he fully understood and regularly brought into play in his daily business life.

He was looking forward to this meeting. Nothing gave him so much satisfaction as scoring points over rivals, and when the rival was Gerry Mortimer of Sidney then the anticipation was all the greater. It had been a long time since the two of them had met face to face. There had inevitably been the odd occasion when they'd been invited to the same major lunch or award ceremony, but the organisers had been careful to keep them apart and they had merely viewed each other through a haze of smoke across a crowded room. Yet there had been no hint of romance in that gaze, there was too great a gulf in culture for them ever to have considered a merger. As far as each of them was concerned it was a fight to the death—which made the present embarrassment of Gerry Mortimer all the sweeter for Lipscomb.

He glanced at his watch. Four o'clock. This wasn't the sort of meeting you had over lunch even if he'd really wanted to break bread with the man, but tea was acceptable. Tea was civilised without in any way being intimate. He'd quite enjoyed the call making the invitation, had thought long and hard about the approach. Should it be Gerry, Mr Mortimer or Mortimer? He settled finally for Gerald. He doubted if anybody else called the man by his full name. It was details like that which kept him on top of his game. Names, seating positions, times of meetings, the minutiae of business life which so fascinated him.

It was really a quarter after the hour when Gerry was finally shown in. Lipscomb had expected him to be late, not because he was renowned for his unpunctuality but because he knew he would regard it as an opening move in their game. He understood these things. If he'd been summoned to meet Mortimer in the heart of the fashion trade he would have made sure he'd similarly kept him waiting.

As Gerry came into the room, Lipscomb rose languidly from the chair and offered the other man the armchair opposite. It looked identical until a close inspection revealed that the arms were wooden and unpadded and the legs were an inch or so shorter so that its occupant would always be looking upwards.

'Gerald, I was beginning to get a little worried. London's traffic is so dangerous nowadays, particularly when we're getting on in years.'

'Speak for yourself,' Gerry said gruffly, not knowing quite how to address Lipscomb. 'The day I can't get around in London is the day they put me down in the ground. I'm sorry I'm late, I just had a lot on at the office.'

'I can well imagine,' Lipscomb said smoothly, and Gerry realised that what he'd said to impress had only served to provide Toby with ammunition.

'Tea...you'll have tea, won't you? And perhaps some cakes and sandwiches.

They're really quite excellent here. Or is that a problem? Might there be anything that wouldn't suit your dietary requirements? I can quite easily get them to knock you up something special. I'm afraid that bagels and lox are a little in short supply in Whitehall.'

'Tea will be fine. Just tea.' Gerry said between clenched teeth. A man appeared from nowhere to take his coat and Lipscomb also gave him their order, adding a plate of scones to the tea.

'I really don't think you'll be able to resist them when they come.'

'Life's about resisting,' Gerry grunted. He'd not particularly wanted to come in the first place, and now that he was here everything told him that he should have followed his instincts. Whatever this man had to say to him was not going to be good news, and bad news was best dealt with at a distance.

Gerry sat down and sank back, wriggling with discomfort.

'Do they have any upright chairs here? I feel like I'm drowning.'

Lipscomb's eyes showed a hint of displeasure that one of his stage directions was being disobeyed but no crack appeared in the smooth external veneer. He rang the small silver bell by his side.

'Let's see what we can do to find

you a lifebelt. I don't believe the club's reputation would stand for a death at sea.'

A hardbacked chair was duly brought and this time it was Gerry Mortimer who looked down at Toby Lipscomb. The tea appeared and Lipscomb offered Gerry a scone which he declined. Lipscomb carefully buttered one for himself, spread some strawberry jam evenly and then took a bite.

'Ah, nectar. You really don't know what you're missing.'

Gerry just sipped his tea and waited impatiently for Lipscomb to get down to business.

'Well, Gerald, it's nice to talk to you again after all these years. You're carrying your age well, particularly with all the problems you've got at the moment.'

'I've had problems before, I'll have them again. It's all part of life. You can't run a business without problems, it gets boring.'

Lipscomb finished one scone and took another.

'I really do wish you'd try one of these, even if only to stop me scoffing the lot. I have enough problems with my weight as it is.'

Gerry looked at him dubiously. The trim figure relaxing in the armchair did not appear to have an ounce of spare flesh on it. He looked like a man who doubted the ability of others to care for him and therefore took the utmost care of himself. The hours spent in his garden had tanned his skin to a colour which might well have been nurtured on the Costa del Sol rather than in the Wiltshire countryside.

Lipscomb picked at a few crumbs on the plate with his finger then suddenly switched into the main thrust of the meeting.

'It's all gone terribly wrong for you, Gerald, hasn't it? If we're perfectly honest about it.'

'Why should I be dishonest? What's gone wrong can go right.'

'An optimist. You know, following the fortunes of your company over the years, I've always seen that you were an optimist. You've taken chances that pessimists wouldn't even contemplate.'

'And they've come off.'

'But sometimes failure has to make an optimist into a realist. You've tried to take over my company and you've failed.'

'Not yet.'

'Now, Gerald, that's the ultimate in optimism and you know it. All you have is what you see—a minority shareholding in a strong Public company. You did well to get Kinsey's shares, I'll give you that, but you didn't take greed and human failing into account. Your lawyer got greedy on you. Thought he'd make himself a little fortune.

246

Buy shares, push up the price, then sell and leave you holding a brain damaged baby. But it's all gone wrong. And so we're here today to talk, man to man, about realism.'

'So talk. I've finished my cup of tea.'

'Fine. I hope it was to your liking. I hope what I'm going to say is to your liking as well. Back off from D'Arblay. I'll take your shares off your hands at what you paid Kinsey plus five percent for your trouble. We'll have a mutual understanding. I leave you alone, you leave me alone.'

'What do you mean?'

'You're wounded, Gerald. You won't admit it, but you are. This Kennard problem is a minefield for you. Solicitor, director, now quasi-shareholder. You've been tiptoeing around my back door and all you've got for your troubles is a bad smell up your nose.'

'I've got a profit on the shares.'

'Try selling them. See how many you sell at a profit—that is, if you *can* sell before both our shares get suspended.'

'What did you mean when you said if I left you alone, you'll leave me alone?'

Lipscomb leaned back in his chair and wiped an invisible crumb off his fingers with a clean white napkin.

'It surely must be obvious. You and I, we're the same although you may not care to admit it. We're looking at the same face from different sides of the mirror, we play the same game. You tried to take me over and failed. If I try to take you over, I promise you, I'll succeed.'

It suddenly felt terribly hot in the room. Gerry knew if he stayed there much longer he'd faint and he wasn't prepared to give Lipscomb the satisfaction. He rose unsteadily to his feet.

'I'll find my own way out. Thanks for the tea.'

'Is that a yes or a maybe?' Lipscomb said, smiling with his mouth but not with his eyes.

'It's thanks for the tea. Perhaps next time I'll have the scones.' And Gerry Mortimer could feel the unsmiling eyes following him all the way as he made his way to the door, stumbled through the hall, then stood on the steps, sucking the fume-filled London air into his lungs as if it was fresh from the mountains of Switzerland.

Chapter Twenty Five

They'd left Stephen his car which was gracious, although he was careful to park it in a different street every night, just in case they changed their minds. That had been his own idea and it worried him that he was beginning to think like a common debtor. He called Cathy and told her he'd be late, then drove out through the heavy traffic on to the M4 motorway that led towards Lambourne in Berkshire.

Even the motorway was congested and dusk soon turned to night. Headlights glared towards him and not for the first time since his arrest he thought of suicide. It would be so easy to go out of control, to hit the central reservation at speed, or better still to find a spot to go off the road where there was a sheer drop. Nobody would be able to prove he hadn't simply fallen asleep at the wheel or been blinded by another car. Cathy would get the insurance money, the children would be well provided for, and the whole nightmare would be over. Nightmare...the word made Hamlet's warning ring in his ears. 'To sleep, perchance to dream'. What if the dream of death was just another nightmare? What if there was a special place for suicides in hell where they faced eternity, denied the final salvation? Something dimly reminded him that suicides weren't even permitted to be buried alongside everybody else in Jewish cemeteries, that he and Cathy would not be laid to rest side by side. And what if he took somebody else with him, another driver, and so not just a suicide but a murderer as well? It wasn't going to be that easy, nothing ever was.

Finally, and with some relief, he duly turned off on the road to the village of Lambourne. As soon as he entered its winding main street he was reminded of Lilliput. Everything looked small: the pub, peopled by squat, bow-legged men, their faces tanned by sun and wind alike; the houses low set as a concession to the inhabitants. Almost everybody who lived there was in some way connected with racing—trainers, jockeys, stable lads and lasses, vets, farriers, saddlers—even the ordinary shops like the newsagents and the grocers were often owned or run by men and women who'd spent much of their lives with horses.

Rory O'Donnell's stables were just outside the main village. The approach to the house was lined with trees, their heavy foliage green and healthy, delicately illuminated by hidden lighting. A fairytale dwelling in a fairytale place, and here the pauper prince came for the answer to his prayers. Rory opened the door himself and took Stephen into a much lived in study.

'The lady's out this evening so I've all the time in the world for you.'

Out or been sent out, Stephen thought, but whichever it was, he appreciated it.

'Drink?' the trainer asked. Stephen

250

hesitated, but Rory poured anyway.

'One won't harm you, and you look as if you could do with a drop of lifeblood in you.' He handed Stephen the glass and pointed to a comfortable armchair. A cat obediently moved away, leaving a generous sample of its hairs on the cushion. Stephen didn't even bother to brush them away but just collapsed, clutching his glass tightly.

'Thanks for seeing me, Rory.'

'My pleasure. At the moment you're a paying customer. Finish the drink and we'll take a walk around the yard. I like to check up on them all myself last thing at night. It reassures me that none of my owners have taken the horses away.'

'I'm the one who needs reassurance, and as to whether or not I'm still an owner—who knows? They've buttoned up all the rest of my assets. I'm surprised they've not been down here with writs and padlocks.'

Rory smiled.

'Sure, they'd not be getting past the guard dogs on the gate.'

'I didn't see them.'

'But then I knew you were coming—and the lady even baked a cake, as the old song says. Would you like some? You don't look to me as if you're eating too well either.'

Stephen nodded his assent and Rory made to cut a piece, then changed his

251

mind and moved the knife along to increase its size.

'There you are. Dublin's finest. She's never even told me the recipe.'

Rory's lady had always been a mystery to Stephen. She never accompanied the trainer to the races, and although he'd seen a shadowy figure on a couple of visits to the stables there had not been a formal introduction nor had there ever been any explanation offered as to whether she was his wife, mistress, partner, or even mother. Stephen didn't know her name, and he'd never seen her long enough to decide her age. Perhaps if Rory ever became really famous he'd read about her in the newspapers, but until then his curiosity would remain unsatisfied.

Stephen drank and ate automatically as Rory gossiped about other trainers and horses. He realised he'd never heard the Irishman talk of anything else—politics, religion or even sex. The man was obsessional to a point of boredom, but right now Stephen was gratified for the obsession. If he wanted to tell his story he could and the man would listen, but he was happy just to hear of people whom he barely knew, hear of the minor traumas in their lives, ripples on their ponds compared to the tidal wave on his sea.

'I'd have never paid 100,000 guineas for

the colt myself, in fact I told a couple of my owners not to bid, and there you are. Frank's saying he's a Cheltenham type while quite frankly he'd be lucky to get placed in a seller at Ludlow. Still, there's one born every minute and anybody who'd pay £15,000 for that particular donkey is the one. It's a fool's game, Stephen. You can't play it for the money. Just for the crack, eh?'

'Sure, Rory.' He let it wash over him. So a man he didn't know had lost eighty-five thousand pounds on a piece of horseflesh. So what? He'd probably made the same on other investments over the years. Swings and roundabouts. What he was on was a roller coaster, and he was hitting the down beat without any guarantee of ever rising again. Where was his fairground? He'd welcome a swing or a roundabout, a childish game, a game to be played with children where nobody got hurt, where there was no madman to throw a switch and leave him stranded on a ride of terror.

'Shall we have a stroll about, then? You can listen to the nags if you don't feel like listening to me.'

'I'm sorry, Rory.'

'No need to apologise, no need to explain. I understand. I've been there, Stephen, I know. I went bankrupt once.'

253

'Did you?' Stephen sounded surprised. Nowadays to get a trainer's licence you had to have led an impeccable life.

'I did indeed, though I don't publicise the fact. The Jockey Club know nothing about it. It was all a long time ago. I'd married young, was crazy about horses even then, but I had a wife who was even crazier about money. And I, poor fool, gave her everything she wanted, even when I didn't have it to give any more. I know what it's like to stare at figures that don't make sense until the last candle in the house burns itself out—and then to realise you've not even enough left to buy a new pack. She left, of course, when the lemon was squeezed dry, but that's no excuse to offer to the bailiff's man when he's knocking at your door.'

'And what happened?'

'I came out of it. The slate was wiped clean. I paid everybody back where I felt I'd hurt them, even though I was told I had no legal obligation. I wanted to look people in the eye, not to have to leave a pub when a man I'd knocked came in. I learned a lot about people in those dark times—a lot about people and a lot about myself. Now I don't pretend to understand the trouble you're in. All I know is that you're a good man, Stephen. You've always been straight with me, and as I said I've learned a fair bit about people. I've learned to tell the wrong 'uns, and there's a fair number of those and all in the sport of kings—but you're not one of them. I'd stake money on it, and I'm not a man known for betting on anything other than certainties.'

They stopped by Montpelier King's box and the chestnut head peered out as if recognising his owner. Stephen stroked him gently and not for the first time in his life thought how preferable horses were to human beings.

'Can you make the King a certainty?' Stephen asked, his voice calm.

'I beg your pardon?'

'You heard me, Rory. Can you? I need it. I need it very badly.'

'Are you talking about a mathematical certainty or a racing certainty?'

'Philosophy I don't need, particularly the Irish homespun type. If we enter the King for a race, can we be sure he'll win?'

'Not when I enter him, no, but...'

'But?'

'When I see the field of acceptors, when I talk to other trainers, gamblers, observers of the game, yes, I can tell you if your horse should win.'

'Should!'

'Should, Stephen, that's the best I can do. Despite everything we might want or think, they can't talk. He can't tell me if he's woken up with a headache or a gut ache. I can see a sore shin, I can read a temperature, but mood, appetite...well, that's in the lap of the gods. And then there's Lady Luck... Does a gap open in time, did the jockey do right holding him back, was he crossed, was he squeezed for room? And the jockey himself, is he in the best of form? Did he have a late night in bed with a lady or an even later night with a gin bottle? It's all of that which turns should into will. Depends how hard you pray, Stephen.'

He carried on stroking the horse, hoping that a genie might appear and tell him all would be well on a certain day.

'What entries has he got?'

'Well, there's Windsor on Monday. Before that there's Warwick on Thursday and the earliest is Bath on Wednesday.'

'What do you think?'

'Warwick's the easiest, but he'll be no price there, and if, as I apprehend, you're looking for a gambling win, forget it. Windsor's an odd meeting. Not my lucky track. I always find one in the pack to come and beat me. Too many casual punters there to guarantee an honest race, the bookies find one to come to their rescue just too often. Bath...Bath's the best. Decent class field, a couple of top trainers with entries but not their best stuff.

However, good jockeys up so they'll attract a bit of money. Parkinson's got one which seems a likely lad but he's already told me he's looking to keep his weight down for the big handicap at Chepstow, so I think you'll get your price there.'

'And will I get my win?'

'I can only do my best.'

Stephen was hardly listening now. It was the horse he was talking to, staring straight into its large intelligent eyes.

'You have to win. You just have to win. Everything depends on it.' And the horse pulled back its head and nodded as if it understood.

Chapter Twenty Six

It was the third time he'd had lunch with Trisha. Therapy was how he justified it to himself, but still he said nothing to Cathy. Although she was a journalist, a woman who collected and disseminated facts for a living, he still felt he could trust Trisha. He told her things he could hardly believe, not just about himself but about his partners too. He talked of Jeffrey's wives and why his marriages had failed; he talked of Anthony and his strangeness as a child; and now he talked of Sarah, and how once he'd thought he loved her.

Trisha listened, then when she felt he had spoken enough she talked back to him but told him nothing of herself, gave nothing of herself.

'You know, Stephen, I've been thinking. That day at the races, when you told me you were stopped by the police and breathalysed...'

'Yes?'

'You said you felt they were waiting for you. Well, maybe they were. Maybe that was the start of all this. Somebody sees how many drinks you had, maybe they even make sure you've had a few, enough to give off a whiff of alcohol. Then they phone the local station, tell them the number of your car, and Bob's your uncle.'

Stephen shook his head in disbelief.

'Now who's getting paranoid?'

'You don't *want* to believe it. Even after all this is happening to you, you still hate to think it could be anybody you know. But they were all there that day: your partners, your co-directors, your trainer, your clients—all your suspects.'

'Trisha, this is not an Agatha Christie thriller. You don't just assemble all your characters in one place and leave it to the clever reader. I've already told you, my money's on Kinsey, and he certainly wasn't at the races unless he was disguised as a jockey.'

Trisha lit up a cigarette and not for the first time Stephen wondered how a habit he so abhorred could be made to look so elegant by this woman.

'How's your little detective getting on? You know, the inquiry agent chap.'

'I think his name is Jones.'

'As in *Along Came...* I suppose it's suitably anonymous.'

'Anyway,' Stephen continued, smiling despite his situation. 'Mr Jones does not seem to be making enormous progress. Spying on the people I knew and liked holds very little reward. They all seem to be leading blameless lives.'

She blew out smoke and he watched it rise towards the ceiling. It was three in the afternoon and he was beginning to feel guilty that he was not back at the office, but then there was no office to go back to, no clients baying for his attention, no more rushed sandwiches between endless calls. He had all the time in the world, a whole day to fill, and he dreaded the moment when she would say that she had to go to finish some article. Then the rest of the day would stretch out before him. Each task he assigned himself spun out to fill a few more moments between waking and sleep. He felt he was holidaying in some dreadful bed and breakfast establishment, where despite the weather he was locked out all day, forced to frequent the public library or a telephone kiosk. One day he'd even taken himself down to the Old Bailey and queued with all the rest of the morbidly curious. It had not been a particularly interesting case, just an armed robbery, the evidence so conclusive he could hardly believe the defendant had the nerve to plead not guilty. The jury retired for just ten minutes and then returned to call him a liar. The judge similarly agreed when he sentenced him to ten years and harshly criticised him for wasting the time of the court. Surely his own trial would not be like that? Surely it would not come to that?

He took his time going home. Cathy was more than likely to be out, she seemed to hate being in the house in the day time, and the children would still be at school. He'd gone to meet them once or twice but they had cringed with embarrassment when they saw him waiting and smiling. Jonathan had almost swept past him with the group of hooligans who passed for his friends, and Stephen had suffered the indignity of chasing after him and hearing his offer of a lift declined. He hated the empty house, the hollowness of his footsteps as he prowled, like a burglar, from room to room, the sadness of the thought that if things did not improve, it would have to be sold.

They'd bought some ten years ago, before the market really started to move upwards in the mid-eighties. Even then they'd pushed out the boat as far as they were concerned, taking on the burden of what seemed at the time a mind blowing mortgage. They'd borrowed even more on it since then: an extension, a loft conversion, the purchase of the country cottage, a new kitchen. Solicitors didn't deal in cash, they dealt in credit. Only now he wasn't a solicitor any more, he was in limbo, and the credit had run out. He had some goodwill with the building society, he'd never missed a payment to date, and he knew from experience that it would take three months of arrears before they'd action anything; but after that he'd become another statistic unless he could persuade Cathy to divorce him and then sit tight on the matrimonial home, protecting the children with all the aggression of a mother bird.

How many times had he used that ploy for clients, watching their faces as he explained to them what they needed to do and then going into meetings, funereal-faced, to tell the mortgagee how the financial pressures had broken up yet another marriage? He couldn't do it for himself, it wasn't honest, and dishonesty for himself was different from the kind of dishonesty that was acceptable for a client.

'Lawyers and liars. There's no difference,' an elderly aunt had once complained, and she was not far wrong. They took the truth, wrung it out, then when it was neatly pegged out on the line, threw buckets of water to give it yet another different shape.

At this very moment the lawyers who had previously been his partners were gathered around the board room table. Jeffrey had taken the chair, Anthony doodled and Sarah tapped her fingers on the table to indicate she had other things to do.

'This is not easy,' Jeffrey said, 'we all miss Stephen, but what else could we have done?'

'Jeffrey, we all feel bad about it. Talking doesn't make it any better. We're under enough pressure as it is with the extra work loads. Can we just get on and decide whatever it is we're going to decide?'

Jeffrey reddened a little. He appeared naked without Stephen by his side, personality coming through in mono, being heard through just one speaker.

'Well, what we need to discuss hopefully will sort out the work problem. Our friends at Greystone's have been incredibly supportive and today Philip Greystone phoned me to say that they'd decided they'd still like to proceed with the merger.'

'Takeover, you mean,' said Sarah.

'You sound like Stephen,' Jeffrey said impatiently, 'what do you think Anthony?'

He blinked owlishly and thought for a moment as if the whole question of the merger had just been put to him for the first time.

'They do have a very good tax and trust department. I've seen some of their documentation and I was impressed. I think on the whole that I'm in favour of it.'

Jeffrey looked at Sarah.

'That's two votes...'

'There's not a lot of point in my objecting then, is there?'

'You don't sound keen, Sarah.'

'I'm not, if truth be told. I don't feel very keen on anything at the moment, and please don't make any inane jokes. I've had enough of men, and the thought of being one woman amongst—what would it be thirty, forty—doesn't exactly appeal to me. If you go ahead, as obviously you will, I'm not sure what I'll do. This whole business with Stephen has shattered me.'

'Sarah, it's shattered us all,' Jeffrey said calmly, trying to placate her. The one thing that the survivors didn't need was to start arguing amongst themselves.

'Don't make any rash decisions. What I suggest is that I go back to Greystone's and tell them we want to go ahead and then ask for some draft documentation. You know what lawyers are like. It'll take time. Give it a week or so and you'll feel differently about things. Right now we need to disassociate our name and image from Stephen if we are to keep our practice together. The deal with Greystone's will do just that. I really believe that if we go in with them we've got a chance of keeping at least ninety percent of our clients.'

Sarah gave him no encouragement to believe he might be right. She shrugged.

'Do what you like, Jeffrey. Now if you'll excuse me, I've got work to do.'

She went back to her own office and shuffled files across her desk. She missed Stephen. There had been a time when it had been painful to work with him, painful every time his wife came into the office or telephoned while she was in the room, but that time had passed. She poured herself a coffee from the percolator in the corner and lit a cigarette. Before Stephen's departure she'd managed to give up for over a year, and the fact that she'd got through half a packet today irritated her. The words on the papers in the files danced before her eyes. It was impossible to concentrate, impossible to put together the pieces of the practice, the pieces of her life.

'Damn you, Stephen. Damn you!' She said aloud, hitting the desk with her fist, harder than she'd intended and drawing blood from her knuckles. 'No, fuck you,' she whispered through clenched teeth, 'it's all fucked up.' She slammed all the files shut, pulled her jacket from the hook and hurried out into the busy street.

Chapter Twenty Seven

Stephen tried the key in the lock for the second time and still nothing happened. It was the right Yale key and the right door—or was this also part of the same nightmare? Perhaps the latch had dropped. That had happened once before when the children were young. He rang the doorbell and thought he saw a movement at one of the windows. He looked around and felt for a moment as if he were burgling his own home. Or perhaps the person inside was a burglar. They jammed doors as they worked and he had disturbed them. He put his shoulder to the door, foolhardy if they were violent, yet he felt incensed at one more intrusion into his life. Then he saw the envelope. How he'd missed it in the first place was hard to understand. It had his name on it and was taped to the post at the side of the door. Shaking his head in mild irritation, he opened it.

The message was brief and to the point. 'Stephen, I've changed the locks. I'm sure you know why but in case you've forgotten here's a photocopy of a receipt for easy reference. If you want your stuff make an appointment. I'll leave a note of my solicitors with your mother. I'm sure she'll be pleased to have you back. Cathy.'

He looked at the enclosure. A photocopy of a hotel receipt. A hotel in France. A receipt for a double room in the name of Mr & Mrs Kennard, a receipt for a room that he'd occupied on his own. What was all this? Was somebody rewriting his life for him? And attached, just in case there should be any mistake, a registration form. He remembered filling in the registration form at the hotel. It was normal in France, where every foreign visitor still technically has to be registered with the police. So much for the EEC, one nation without boundaries. The writing looked like his, but this was not the form he'd completed. There in the space he'd left blank for accompanying person was a name—Nicole La Roche—and then in brackets 'Kennard', as if to say: We're French, we're used to such matters. If you want to call this lady your wife that's up to you but we'll take her real name from her passport. And all done with a nod and a wink and 'Mes félicitations, monsieur, vous avez choisi bien.'

Nicole La Roche. He remembered the name, and if he tried very hard he could remember the face. Tall, slim, elegant in a Parisian way, carefully applied makeup that said she was not much younger than him but looking distinctly better for her years. She'd been in television and she'd been the driving force behind the French group supporting the charity. Yes, he'd stayed at the hotel, all the European delegates to the conference had, but if he'd spoken to her half a dozen times in the whole weekend that had been it. Yes, they'd sat down to dinner together at the same table, but she'd been placed at the opposite end and it had been difficult to hold a conversation across a dozen other people; but what he'd not done was sleep with her. He couldn't even remember fancying her, so why this woman's name was on his form he couldn't begin to understand.

He rang the bell loudly, his finger hard on the buzzer, the sound reverberating through the house. Nothing happened. He began to hammer at the door, his temper rising, the frustration that he'd hardly shown since his arrest surfacing finally in pure aggression.

'Cathy, I know you're in there. Open the door. Jonny, Dani, hear my side of things. Let me explain.'

He saw a next-door neighbour peering across curiously. They'd always got on reasonably well. The man had worked for British Telecom for twenty years before taking early retirement and now centred all his efforts in the garden. Stephen had admired his flowers, enquired after his family, politely sent a Christmas card without any real effort at intimacy. If truth be told Stephen was rarely there in the evenings to give rise to the opportunity of inviting him in for a drink, Stephen was rarely anywhere in an evening except at work or a meeting. The neighbour said nothing but something in his look of disapproval made Stephen crack.

'And what do you think you're staring at? This is between me and my wife. Just fuck off! Fuck off out of it!'

He couldn't believe what he was saying; he was talking like one of his clients, accused of causing an affray. Control, that's what he'd always practised, control, and now he was running wild, a car with no brakes careering down the hill with just one poor old man in the way.

The neighbour's wife, a small lady with grey hair and large spectacles, joined the battle.

'Don't you swear at my husband. He's got a heart condition. We've read all about you in the newspapers. We didn't believe it at the time. I actually said to Ken, my husband, I don't believe that of Mr Kennard, but it's obviously true. And I don't blame your wife for locking you out! You're an animal, not a lawyer. Solicitors don't use that sort of language.'

Stephen took deep breaths. He felt as if he'd been running for miles uphill. Sweat was pouring from him and he felt like a tramp.

'I'm sorry,' he muttered, knowing that he had lost this couple's respect and that mattered to him. He needed to know that nobody believed what was being written about him; he could only believe in his own innocence if everybody else believed in it too.

'I'm really sorry.' He turned his back on the couple and craned his neck upwards. The curtain twitched again and he heard Cathy's voice, cold and emotionless.

'Stephen, go away. You're causing a scene. Jonny's getting upset. If you don't go I'll call the police.'

The mention of the word sent shivers down his spine. It had not been so long ago that he too would have turned to the police for protection, but now they were the enemy. He was on the side of the underworld, he was a part of the underside of life, running in the sewers like all the other rats.

'Don't you want to listen to me? It's all wrong. I did nothing.'

'Stephen, you're pathetic! You've lost touch with reality. I don't know whether you believe your own lies. I don't know any more if anything you've ever told me is the truth. Leave us alone. Go and sort yourself out. Look in the mirror and start by telling the face you see what's really happened. If you're honest with yourself, then perhaps there's still a chance for you.'

'Cathy, you can't just throw away all our years. I deserve a few minutes.' He was pleading now, almost ready to fall on his knees on the front lawn. Even the neighbours turned away in embarrassment finding the tawdry spectacle of this grown man pleading too much to watch.

'You deserve nothing. I've eyes and I can read. I don't know who Nicole La

270

Roche was, but I hope she was worth it. Was she good in bed, Stephen? Was she better than me? Did she go down on you? Did she let you fuck her from behind? Tell me the truth.'

Her voice was rising to a scream, not hysterical, more like a stage declamation of guilt. There was no point in arguing. She was judge, she was jury, she was executioner, and his children were the witnesses. Signed, sealed and delivered, signed, sealed and destroyed, a legal deed rolled up in pink tape, notarised, everything that had to be done to make it effecting and binding had been done.

He turned his back on what had been his home. The blind windows bored into his back. The trees lining the street were the guards who escorted him away, his colours stripped from him, his sword broken in half. Until today at least he had been left with his family. Whatever else had been taken from him, freedom, profession, security, he still had the warmth of his wife in bed, the beauty of his daughter, the cheeky grin of his son. Right now he would have welcomed their arguments, smiled at their fighting, as the noise and fury filled the vacuum that was all that remained for him.

Where to go? Cathy had obviously thought he'd head for his mother's but she was wrong. He couldn't take the accusations, the nagging, the guilt she would impose on an innocent man. There was always a hotel but they cost money, and now more than ever he had to look after every penny. He'd thought that whatever was shared with Cathy was beyond the reach of these relentless hands which grasped after everything he possessed. Yet now Cathy's hands were added to those pulling at him, another set of nails tearing at his flesh, gouging at his eyes. It was tempting to let them have him, to lie there undefended, uncomplaining, while they destroyed him utterly. Yet deep inside him a still small voice told him to fight, not to give in. If he gave in they'd won, whoever they were, and he would be the victim of yet another unsolved crime. He would not allow himself to become a statistic.

He stopped by the telephone box on the corner and dialled a number.

'Please be there. Be there for me.' One ring, two, three. Any minute the answer phone would cut in. Four, five, six. It could not be switched on. Seven, eight. A phone ringing in an unknown hall, or was it the lounge, or the bedroom, nine, ten.

'Hello.' He heard the voice and could hardly speak. A tightness gripped his chest. Was he too suffering from asthma, or was this the heart attack that would end it all?

'Hello?' The voice again, threatening to replace the receiver on a nuisance call. Just in time he summoned up his voice—a strained, strange voice, not quite belonging to him, the voice of the new man who'd inherited the old body.

'Trisha? Trisha, it's Stephen. I need to see you. Can I come over?' And then when she said yes, he began to cry, wondering when the tears would stop. Wondering if he could ever find his way.

Chapter Twenty Eight

The first bottle of wine was empty and he was feeling better. The further he distanced himself from what was happening, the less the pain. He had no idea of the time but it was dark outside, the curtains were drawn and the room had induced a womb-like feeling of comfort.

Trisha lived in a first-floor converted flat in what would have been called Canonbury if she'd wanted to impress but was probably Highbury if match day parking was any accurate guideline. They were seated in a large lounge, the furniture comfortable and well worn, giving the impression of having been in place for a long time although she'd told Stephen she'd only been living there for just over a year.

'I don't like to buy new when I move. I've had some of this furniture since I first left home. It gives me a feeling of stability in a changing world.'

The music in the rack was pure sixties although she must have been too young to have been there at the time: Dylan, Pink Floyd, Joan Baez, Leonard Cohen.

'I always play Leonard Cohen when I'm depressed. He sounds so much worse off that it makes me feel better.'

He hadn't smiled. He didn't believe he would ever smile again.

'She wouldn't open the door. She wouldn't listen to me, let alone talk to me. And the children... They weren't allowed to say anything either. What kind of bastard pours poison into the mind of your wife and children?'

Trisha had allowed Stephen to outpace her with the wine, but now she poured herself another glass. The man slumped in her armchair was a far cry from the confident high flier she'd once begged to help her. Unshaven, hair uncombed, clothes crumpled, he had the air of a derelict, of a man about to go to sleep on the Embankment in a cardboard box, not really caring if he awoke to another day. She had to bring him back. He had trusted her, had called her, and it did not seem as if he had anyone else to whom to turn. Yet before she could bring him back she was shrewd enough to realise she had to let him all the way down. He had to see the bottom of the well, and if that involved drinking a couple of bottles of wine to get the perspective right, then she had all night.

'I can't blame her, Trisha. It was there, proof. And after everything else she'd gone through it must have been one blow too many.' He emptied the glass and automatically refilled it.

'I don't drink, you know...not really. Yet since this affair started I seem to have a glass in my hand all the time. Sometimes I think it's me. That I really did say what they say I've done, that I've just blotted it out of my mind—or else that I've some kind of split personality, Jekyll and Hyde. It's happened, I've read about it...' His voice trailed off forlornly.

'It's all right, Stephen, I don't think you're going mad, but you do need to relax. The wine will help. You didn't do any of those things, and you're not on your way to a drying out clinic anyway—and if you were maybe your luck would turn and you'd meet a rich movie star there. I think

275

you need some sleep. Come to bed.'

He looked up blearily.

'Come on,' she repeated, 'I've only got one bedroom but you can have it. I'll curl up on the couch. I often fall asleep watching TV anyway.'

'Oh,' was all he said, feeling stupid. 'Come to bed' she'd said, and like any man he'd interpreted it in just one way. He had to get a grip on himself. How could he believe that anybody wanted him in his present state? He wiped away a tear, the drink and exhaustion making him maudlin.

'Any minute now I sense you're going to break into a Country and Western ballad, and if you do, Stephen, I'm not sure I can keep down my supper. As my mum always says, sleep and it'll all look better in the morning.'

He didn't argue, and didn't resist when she led him into the bedroom by the hand, undressed him like a child and put his feet up on the bed. She covered him with a blanket and by the time she kissed him softly on the forehead he was too deeply asleep even to know what she had done.

Trisha was right in as much as things did look different in the morning. He awoke with the same feeling that he'd experienced in a hundred hotel bedrooms: that something wasn't quite right, that nothing about him was familiar. He fumbled for his watch but his bedside table wasn't there, his light switch wasn't there, Cathy wasn't there either. The sun filtered in through the curtains, making patterns on the dust that settled on the furniture and the floor. Cathy wouldn't have lived with that dust, the cleaning woman's head would have rolled, but Trisha was a working woman. She clearly did her own cleaning when the mood or necessity took her, and it hadn't taken her for a few weeks. His head felt bad, and as he went to move his legs off the bed the dull ache down there told him the pain was not localised.

'Hi, welcome back to the land of the living.' She stood framed in the doorway, a halo of sunshine around her head.

'Don't tell me, I'm dead and you're an angel.'

' 'Fraid not, but that's close to a joke and that's a good sign you're alive. I've let you sleep a bit. Unless I've something special on, I tend to lie in.'

'What's the time?' he asked.

'Nearly eleven. Got somewhere special to go?'

He bit his lip, feeling his stomach sink as reality was recalled. No job, no home, no family. No, nowhere to go.

'Look, Steve, have a shower. Have a

277

shave, there's a razor in the bathroom with whatever else you need. I've been out to our wonderful local shopping arcade and bought you a few bits and pieces of clothes and underwear. I hope you like my taste. When you've done all that and you're a nice clean boy, come on through and I'll make you some brunch. I must warn you, my food tends to come with a government health warning.'

Stephen didn't like what he saw in the bathroom mirror. His face was haggard and lined, the stubble slipping into the hollows of his cheeks. He needed a hair cut and hadn't felt it right to spend twenty-five pounds at his normal West End salon, and also hadn't felt he could listen to either the sympathy or trivia of Brian who usually cut his hair. Now for sure it was down to a five pound short back and sides and that was something that was high on his agenda for the morning.

The bathroom was small and soon the steam from the hot water gave his reflection a hazy distorted look. Everything he needed was there: razor, cream, aftershave, and he wondered how he could tactfully ask for which man they'd been provided. Perhaps it was better if he didn't know, and a warning voice in his ear told him there was no good reason why he should even want to. He was a married man. He just needed to prove his fidelity to his wife and he could be back in the bosom of his family. It was that simple.

Yet how? He was a lawyer, he needed to apply a logical legal mind to the problem. Find the lady. And once the lady had been found, then what? Maybe she had nothing to lose by saying she had shared a room with him. Her name would hardly have been used if she wasn't part of everything, a woman paid to support a lie. So if her story stood up, how to knock it down? Conflicting evidence, perhaps. There'd been a hundred people at that conference. He couldn't say he'd really been close to any of them, that wasn't his style, but he'd eaten with the same people on a couple of nights and he'd not said more than half a dozen words to this famous Nicole La Roche then. Affidavit evidence. Get them to swear to the fact that he'd not been with her, think like a lawyer. Yet the legal brain posed more questions than answers. All right, so they'd not had dinner together, but that didn't mean they hadn't slept together. Some of the group knew he was married, he was a respectable lawyer, he was hardly likely to parade a French mistress about the place.

So why had he checked in with her. Carelessness? The conviction it didn't matter, that nobody would know so long as they kept apart during the day. Clever up to a point, but like most deceptions, careless. He remembered, for no good reason, the old wartime slogan he'd seen painted on his father's lunch box: 'Careless talk costs lives'. So where was his life now, was it capable of rescue?

He cut his neck and swore. The razor was lighter than his own, the shaving foam a different brand, the aftershave something he'd never used. A new life, that's what he had to build, a life without carelessness.

He held up the T-shirt that Trisha had bought with its Greenpeace slogans and brightly coloured animals. More something Jonathan would have worn than him, but the crisp cleanness of the new cotton felt good as he pulled it over his freshly showered frame. The underwear wasn't his usual Marks and Spencer's either, but that also felt good next to his skin. The beige linen trousers had a crumpled look about them, even before he tried them on, but that was the style, and the total effect was not unpleasant. He looked much younger, more streetwise, what his daughter would have called more hip. Street-cred, that was what it took, that was what Trisha had tried to give him, and he appreciated it.

'Hey, not bad, kiddo. Wanna dance?' She twirled herself about, her mass of hair flying around her like an enveloping shawl.

She too wore just a T-shirt with a tight pair of jeans that showed every contour of the lower part of her body and clearly revealed that underwear was not part of her daily uniform.

'I'll leave the dancing 'til later, but believe me, Trish, when this is all over, I'll take you dancing wherever you want.'

'Moonlight cruises, first class, all expenses paid?'

'No problem.'

'You're looking better, sounding better. I like the "when this is all over". That's positive. Coming for the coffee? Watery scrambled eggs OK? I think I've managed to avoid burning the toast.'

They weren't as watery as he'd anticipated and she was right about the toast. The hot coffee scalded his throat, hit his stomach and burned straight back up to his brain. He ate quickly, like a man who'd been starved, and Trisha carelessly tossed the empty plates into a half-full dishwasher.

'It's the mean streak in me. I've worked out that by the time the dishwasher's full I've enough crockery left for one more meal, so I tend not to put it on until it is full. That can take a week or so, depending on how often I'm home, and by then it's not a pretty sight.'

She smiled as if testing him, as if saying,

This is me, warts and all. Forget romance, this is kitchen sink drama. But he didn't react. He just swept the last few crumbs off the table himself, and as they fell to the floor to join the rest of the debris said: 'Right, the decks are cleared. I need a pen and some paper.'

'Going to write your memoirs already?'

He shook his head, ignoring the joke.

'No, Trisha, I'm in a war. I'm going to map out my battle plan. They've spilled blood, my family's blood. Up 'til now I've taken what they've thrown at me. I've been arrested, practically debarred, stripped naked, and I've played it all according to the rules. But they've driven me into the wilderness, and there are no rules there, no rules at all.'

Chapter Twenty Nine

The battle plan took money and that was a problem. Cathy had moved fast. When he rang his mother she told him there was a hand delivered letter waiting for him. It meant a visit, but it had to be done. He just hoped that for once in her life his mother would listen and not accuse or question.

She waited silently whilst he tore open the envelope. It was from a firm of solicitors where one of the partners had been a not infrequent guest at their dinner table. It was good to know who your friends were. He could have recited the contents of the letter without even reading it. He'd seen hundreds of them when he'd open the post in his office, when he'd been allowed to open the post in his office.

Dear Sir

We have been instructed by Mrs C Kennard in relation to the unhappy matrimonial differences that have arisen between you. We are instructed to petition for a divorce on her behalf on the basis of the irretrievable breakdown of your marriage arising from your adultery with a Ms Nicole La Roche in particular on the...day of...and on the...day of...

We shall be issuing the petition within the next few days but meanwhile should be grateful...

The letter went on to talk of non-disposal of assets, of undertakings, of his present position, but it didn't mention the children. What did she think he was going to do, never see them again? Even if he'd actually slept with this woman, that didn't make him a leper. He felt an enormous surge

283

of outrage, and then remembered Sarah, remembered he was not without guilt and felt with fear that somebody was watching him, somebody who'd let him get away with the affair knowing that this was still to come. Never before in his life had he experienced, really experienced, the presence of God, but now God scared him and he needed God. God had proved that he could bring down retribution. Now he needed God to prove that he could also be merciful.

His mother saw the expression on his face and reached out to touch his hand.

'More *tsores?*' Yiddish again, she must be really worried.

'Yes, Mum, more trouble.'

'If you need money, Stephen, I've got a bit put away.'

'For your old age, eh?'

'Look, Stephen, I'm an old woman already. What do I need with money? To pickle it? Take it.'

He shook his head.

'I can't. It's what Dad worked for. And quite frankly, unless you've won the pools and haven't told me, I doubt if it'd be enough. I'll manage, don't worry. I don't think my credit's completely exhausted.' But even as he spoke, as he adopted a brave face, he knew at that moment he was probably the least creditworthy person in

London. Instead of money he'd accepted a smoked salmon bagel and a cup of tea, feeling curiously contented just to be with his mother. He felt closer to her than he had been in years. Closer to his mother, closer to his God. Perhaps there was after all some great pattern in the confusion.

He drove back to Trisha's flat, watching the petrol needle hover towards empty, knowing he did not have enough money on him to fill the tank. Jeffrey had also written him a personal letter asking for the return of the car, but he'd not replied. If they wanted it back let them come and take it, he wasn't going to make it easy for them.

This time he left the car near Green Lanes and Clissold Park and walked about half a mile, past the big old Victorian houses that had once been built for one family but now were converted into a multiplicity of flats. It was warm and he took off the tracksuit top that he'd had in the car and tossed it over his arm. He liked the feeling of the sun on his bare forearms, liked the way his trainers bounced over the ground, and despite everything he felt free. He was no longer restricted by timetables and deadlines, by clients ringing at all hours to press their claim for progressing their matters, by having to wear a suit, a collar, a tie. There was nowhere he had to be at any given time—except the police station.

The thought brought him back to earth. He had to report in on a regular basis, tell them where he was living, notifying any change of address. Highbury Police station was now his local and he'd already made them aware of his presence. Not that they'd been unpleasant, but when his experience of police stations had been limited to handing in lost property and asking the way it was not easy to tell them why he was there, particularly if there was anyone else around.

As he entered Trisha's flat the phone was ringing. He heard the answerphone cut in and a man's voice, a voice he felt he'd heard before, a voice he just couldn't quite place, saying:

'Trisha. I've been calling for over a week. I can explain. Please ring me.' A pause, the man's mind working overtime. 'I've something on your story that'll interest you.' Another pause. 'Trisha, I do love you.'

Stephen felt like a voyeur. There was no difference between naked limbs and naked emotions. He understood now the razor in the bathroom. Had he lived here, this man, or had he been just an overnight guest? It was none of his damn'

286

business yet something drew him to the closed drawers of Trisha's filing cabinet. If people believed him to be a thief, then why not act like one? Her filing system was in total contrast to the rest of the flat. Everything was in order, everything had a file and a cross-reference. It didn't take him too long to realise that she'd kept not only every story she'd ever filed but also every story she'd ever investigated. There was an enormously wide spread of subjects: abortion, prostitution, police corruption, gay clubs, the style varying according to the publication which had commissioned it.

Something made him pull out the drawer which contained the letter 'K', and there was a file neatly marked 'Kennard, Stephen'. He heard the door open and startled, pushed the cabinet closed without reading beyond the cover. He turned guiltily and made his way back into the living room just as Trisha staggered in laden with bags of shopping.

'Food,' she said as if any explanation was necessary. 'Can't think without food. How was your day?' She pecked him on the cheek domestically and went into the kitchen to unpack without waiting for an answer.

'There were a couple of calls for you, before I went out.'

287

'I didn't give anybody the number,' Stephen said.

'They said they got it from your mother.'

'You're right. I gave my mother the number. I'm sorry. I just thought she might need me in case of emergency.'

'It's all right,' Trisha said, without conviction. 'Anyway, Rory O'Donnell asked if you could call him as soon as possible.'

'And the other message?'

'I'm not a service, you know.'

He didn't know her yet. Here he was living with a young, attractive woman, and he didn't know her. It was absurd, but then there was little about his life that wasn't absurd.

'Your other call was Gerry Mortimer. He said he'd been told it wouldn't be appropriate to speak to you, but he wanted to help.'

'Great. Not appropriate. That's not Gerry talking, that's a lawyer. Gerry would never know what's appropriate, he couldn't even spell it. What did you say?'

'I said you needed money.'

'You said what?'

'I told the truth, Stephen. I said you needed money. And you do. You need money if we're going to sort out this problem, you need money to live, and if Rory O'Donnell's right you need money to put on your horse when it runs on Wednesday. That's why he wants you to call.'

He didn't know whether to be angry or grateful. He couldn't have taken money from Gerry. He didn't want anything from anybody who had been part of his past. When he faced them again it would be on his own terms. Yet in a perverse way it excited him. When he'd last backed his horse it had been a game, a peccadillo; now it was a matter of life and death. It was Russian roulette with an equine revolver.

'So what did the magnanimous Gerry Mortimer say to this request for a donation to the Stephen Kennard Charitable Fund?'

'He said he couldn't give you anything that might be traceable but he asked me to go down to his office.'

'And when are you going?'

'I've been,' she said, pulling a thick envelope out of her voluminous battered bag. 'Et voilà.'

'How much?' he asked, despite himself.

'He said it was ten grand. I didn't think it was appropriate to count it out in front of him.'

'The old bugger! And he told me he wasn't running a cash business any more because he'd koshered himself up for the City and never wanted to embarrass me.'

'He lied,' Trisha said starkly, 'fortunately for you.'

Stephen gave her a sidelong look. 'You're getting one hell of a story here.'

'Do you think I'll use it?'

'You're a journalist.'

A hard look came over her face and Stephen realised once more that he'd misjudged her mercurial temper.

'If that's what you think then I've no doubt a journalist *will* use it.'

'I'm sorry, Trisha.'

'Stephen, if you think I'm doing this to get a world exclusive, then fine...'

'Trisha.'

'I take in every homeless waif, every stray that can give me a few fucking lines of newsprint, you're just another in a long line. OK?'

There were tears welling up in her eyes and he saw a different person, another shift of the light to reveal another aspect.

He moved towards her and held her tight. Her head sank to his shoulder and he stroked her hair, feeling her body move against his own.

They stood like that for a long time until he sensed she was almost asleep. He kissed the top of her head, liking the smell of her hair, excited despite himself by the difference from Cathy's well-groomed coiffure.

'I'm sorry,' he said gently.

Her head came up. It was an inch away from his face, so near he could feel her breath on his skin.

'It's all right.' Neither was prepared to make the first move, and then in a voice that was so practical it hurt, Trisha said: 'Come on. Now we've got the finances it's time for us generals to make our battle plan.' And gently pushing him away, she sat down at the kitchen table.

Chapter Thirty

Arthur Kemp was a happy man. It was curious that he had never before contemplated an act of dishonesty for he was not someone who had ever set himself any great moral standards. Yet, on the other hand, he was not a man with any burning ambitions. His parents and teachers had all but despaired of him as a child.

'You've got ability, Arthur, but you don't use it.'

When he was faced with figures, however, it was a different story. It needed no effort for somebody so supremely numerate to read and understand a balance sheet, yet accountancy itself had never really attracted him. There were all those exams to take, and exams meant study, even though the arithmetical part would have been simplicity itself. And so he settled for the job of an accounts clerk, always earning a comfortable living, returning every night to his sister's house in Putney where he'd gone to live after the death of his parents.

His sister, Ethel, was glad of his company. She was, at sixty, ten years his senior, widowed, children grown up and married, and found his presence comforting.

Apart from anything else Arthur was good with his hands, mending everything that broke, and was particularly talented when it came to 'electricals', as Ethel put it. Visitors to the house were proudly shown Arthur's latest technological improvements which he'd carefully worked out and designed, or his state of the art computer.

Arthur's school days had been just after the war when the word 'computer' was barely in the Oxford Dictionary. There was no doubt in his mind that he would have used his ability to a greater degree if he'd only been given the opportunity; but the age of computers had now dawned and the dawn had given birth to a new, revitalised Arthur Kemp.

By the time he came to work for Kennard & Wightman, computer technology for him was like a third hand, a part of him. He brought to the practice a degree of order and efficiency that had been sadly lacking as they rapidly increased their turnover and client base. Yet even then something stopped him pushing to the very top. He read the appointments column in the newspapers casually, occasionally thought of applying for more senior, highly paid posts, but never did.

There were other passions in his life apart from computers: Fulham Football Club and pornographic magazines. Fulham had been for a long time the butt of popular humour when it came to their success—or lack of it—on the field. For years they'd also had the misfortune to have a comedian, Tommy Trinder, as a director, which got them off on the wrong foot when it came to being taken seriously. Then somehow or other they managed to attract oddities both on and off the pitch. Jimmy Hill with his strange-shaped chin, concealed by the beard that earned him the nickname of 'The Rabbi'; Tosh Chamberlain, a winger so bow-legged that when he sat around the house it was rumoured he really did sit around the house;

Johnny Haynes, the first player ever to earn a hundred pounds a week and endorse a commercial product. A signed photograph of Johnny, advertising Brylcreem, was one of Arthur's most valued possessions.

Although he could afford to buy a seat at matches, Arthur always chose to stand on the terraces alongside a group of die hard faithful eccentrics who had followed Fulham all their lives. They knew each other by a mixture of first names and nicknames, never even knowing what the others did for a living, just meeting every Saturday at Craven Cottage, united in their eternal optimism that one fine day Fulham would actually win something.

Whatever their secrets none would have guessed that the insignificant little man who stood alongside them, his pinched cheeks red with cold, his greying hair blowing in the wind, could have spent so much money on books that would have made his sister faint had she ever discovered the cache he kept in his bedroom. The Italian hardcore with their obsession with anal sex were his favourites, and although he didn't speak a word of the language the pictures spoke volumes. He'd say goodnight, leave Ethel watching the ten o'clock news and then close the door of his room behind him, masturbating two or three times a night as he flicked over the pages. In real life he'd never had a proper relationship with a girl.

At only five foot there weren't that many girls smaller than him, and even then somehow he could never find anything to say. All he could bring to mind in the presence of a member of the opposite sex were his computers and his beloved Fulham, and somehow he'd never had the chance to meet a committed Cottager, under five foot tall, with a penchant for database systems.

That was all over now. The days of longing, the days of imagination, were past. Nobody seemed to notice his yellowing buck teeth, nobody cared that his ears seemed to need chewing gum to pin them back, nobody was bothered that without his horn rimmed sixties glasses he was blind as a bat. Money—that was why nobody cared. He was as rich as he'd ever hoped to be and he could spend it any way he chose.

The proposal when it had come had been easy to accept. The man had slipped into step alongside him after Fulham had played Orient in some meaningless cup competition that involved only teams from the lower divisions of the football league. It was only later that it occurred to him that the somebody knew rather a lot about his habits—where he'd be, where he'd stand, his route back to the station—but that in itself was flattering, the fact that somebody was taking note of him.

'Hello, Arthur.'

He looked up without surprise. Perhaps one of his mates from the terraces had come his way and wanted to discuss their team's latest defeat. The speaker, however, was too well dressed to have been one of them. He wore a smart cashmere overcoat, and from the trousers that appeared between the bottom of the coat and his highly polished shoes, Arthur guessed he was also wearing an expensive suit.

'Good game?' the man asked.

'Not bad.' Arthur knew when somebody was interested in football and this man wasn't, and if he wasn't interested in football and he was talking to Arthur then he had to have some good reason for that.

'Got a minute for a drink?'

Arthur shrugged. It was only five-fifteen. Soho didn't get interesting until later and one of his favourite book shops had told him they might have a special delivery on Saturday night.

'Why not?'

It took the man two brandies to get

around to his point.

'I gather you're quite a ladies' man, Arthur?'

'What do you mean?'

'Come on, Arthur, we're both men of the world.' He liked that, liked the sound of being a man of the world, although he suspected it was very far from the truth.

'Well, some friends of mine have a proposition for you. Can you be trusted, Arthur?'

'Yes.' He nodded swiftly. The brandies had gone straight to his head and although he didn't even know this man's name he had the feeling he was on the brink of something momentous in his life.

'Well, this is it. If the answer's no, just say so. It'll be as if this conversation never took place. I'll walk away and you can get back to standing at your football and tossing yourself off in front of your girlie mags.'

Arthur blushed. Nobody could know for certain what he did in the privacy of his own room, but the mere fact that the man was able to guess so accurately made Arthur feel that he was under his control already.

'We need to make some money vanish from the client account of your firm—or at least the firm you work for. Now you have my word it won't vanish for ever, it'll be used for something and the something will be worth enough to put the money back. Nobody loses. You do it on a particular day, and then you're out of there.'

Arthur smiled and the stranger thought how ugly he was.

'I think that there might be a few people following me, like the police, the Law Society, the partners.'

The man nodded as if this was earth shattering insight and only Arthur's superior intellect had managed to home in on the point.

'Absolutely right, Arthur. So here's what we do. We give you one hundred thousand pounds in cash. Now that, I suggest, might give you a slight head start on anybody following you.'

'I'd have to leave the country.'

'Perhaps, perhaps not. It might be enough just to lie low for a while. And we'd be able to help you there as well...'

That conversation had finally brought Arthur to where he was today, cash stored away, the deed done, living the life of Riley and knowing that just by lifting the telephone he could bring into the room the sort of woman he'd previously only seen in the magazines. He'd been here a while now, and he'd told his contact, the stranger he'd originally met, that he felt it was time to move on, time for him really to take that holiday on which he'd told his sister he was going.

So this might well be his last night here. Perhaps he ought to make the most of it. He spoke into the phone.

'I'd like the blonde who came on Tuesday, and the redhead. Yes, the small one with the big tits.' He lay back and waited, eyes half closed, dreaming. Somewhere hot, a beach... Maybe the blonde would come with him? He felt that perhaps she really liked him. Suddenly he was fully awake or was he still dreaming? The room was full of people, of lights. He tried to rise but couldn't move, he realised he was chained to the bed. The well-dressed stranger was there, giving orders, and as the two girls, completely naked, came towards him with knives in their hands he felt an enormous wave of regret sweep over him that somehow over the years he'd sold himself short, that he'd never got to spend all that money, that Ethel would find his magazines, and that the impossible dream of Fulham winning the League would not be fulfilled in his lifetime.

Chapter Thirty One

Less than a month since he'd last been at the races but the world had changed. The colours did not look so bright although today at Bath the sun shone with a dry heat that foretold a long hot summer. Stephen kept looking around him, paranoid that he might be followed, that at any moment one of the shirtsleeved policemen would leap upon him, clasping cold metal handcuffs about his wrists.

Trisha, on the other hand, seemed to be enjoying herself thoroughly.

'I know you're not going to believe this, Stephen, but I've never been to the races before.'

'Pleased I've been able to broaden your horizons. Don't get any ideas about getting hooked on it. This is strictly business.'

A few days earlier in Trisha's kitchen the plan had been mapped out with military precision. Reluctantly Stephen was persuaded to keep Gerry's cash.

'Blood money,' he'd said bitterly.

'Come on, Stephen. You can't blame Gerry for this. I'm sure when it's all over he'll reinstate you.'

'If the City lets him. No smoke without fire and all that. If it's ever all over, that is.'

It was simple; they'd place the money on Montpelier King on Wednesday, and with the ensuing bank roll they'd launch their own investigation into the conspiracy against Stephen. Trisha was incredibly enthusiastic.

'We'll go to France, to the hotel you stayed at. Then we'll find M La Roche. We'll go to Jersey. Everywhere there's a lead we'll go. I've not been a journalist all these years without developing some good contacts. Newshounds are better than coppers when it comes to getting hard facts together.'

Stephen smiled—all these years. A hardened veteran in her mid-twenties. She sounded like a world weary hack.

'It's a shame that once they've got the hard facts together they don't actually print them,' he said, but then didn't push the point. Trisha was one journalist he couldn't afford to upset.

'There's one thing you've forgotten. I don't have a passport and I think the police might get a teensy weensy upset if I phone them from France and say I'll be a bit late reporting in.'

She touched the side of her face, a nervous habit.

'Leave it to me. There are ways, Stephen, mysterious ways. We'll work it out, trust me.'

'I used to say "Trust me, I'm a lawyer". I even had a T-shirt to prove the point.'

'And look where it got you.'

'Here with you,' he'd said, putting his hand over hers. She'd not pulled away but just left it there, placidly, until it was time to make coffee. He wasn't sure if that was progress or not, or even if he wanted progress. He didn't need any more confusion in his life.

There was only one little flaw in the plan. Montpelier King had to win. Rory O'Donnell was very confident, but then his life wasn't on the line.

'Ah, sure,' he said, 'would I be telling you he'd win if I didn't believe it? I've been through the form in this field with a fine tooth comb. There's some good horses, but the King's better. And if there wasn't good horses you wouldn't be getting any sort of price. And as I understand the situation, you need the price.'

If Rory had any nerves he certainly wasn't showing them, and Stephen felt deep down there that the Irishman was too good a friend not to care what happened. There was every chance his creditors would get the horse anyway, and if they didn't then Cathy, for once, might find a use for his equine love. Of everything that had happened he still couldn't accept that he was not allowed to see his wife and children whenever he wanted. When he caught up with the bastards who'd fixed this he just wanted five minutes alone with them.

The King did look good, there was no doubt of that. Stephen just hoped that nobody else, and the bookmakers in particular, looked at him with rose-coloured glasses. There was no point in his taking the ten thousand and putting it on in one bet. The rare bookmakers who took that sort of money might give him the best price for half of it, but after that they'd trim the odds. It wasn't easy explaining to Trisha how to place a bet when she was still staring at the tick tack man with the wide-eyed fascination of a child. Rory had a friend who'd take a bit of the money, but the three of them had to put on the bulk of it almost simultaneously to stop the market shortening.

'Shall we synchronise watches?' Trisha said, treating the exercise as one huge joke.

'Trisha, we need all the money we can get. If you only get 9-2 instead of 5-1 that means five thousand pounds less.' She sobered up then.

'I'm sorry. Rely on me.'

Neither of them voiced the thought that they were really relying on the horse.

For once Stephen didn't go into the parade ring with the horse. He didn't need to remind anybody today that he was the owner. Today it was a burden, not an honour.

From the bookmakers boards it looked like a three horse race. Senator Brady was clear favourite at 5-2, then came Catharsis at 7-2 with the King at 4-1. After then it was 7-1 bar the three. He'd hoped for a bit better than fours. Senator Brady had good form in Ireland, was extremely well bred, and his trainer, Dermot Kane, didn't send his horses over for the grass; but Rory knew one of Dermot's stable lads, and he didn't think the horse would take to the travel. It wasn't much to go on, but fortunes turn on such information. Catharsis was running over the distance for the first time, having won over a furlong less just a week ago.

'Too soon' Rory had opined. 'Look at him, he's not had the chance to put back his weight. Also I've looked at the video of his last win. I think it'll be just a bit too far for him today, particularly if the King sets the sort of pace I've planned for him.'

Stephen looked up—one of the bookmakers was adjusting his price. Len Todd, established forty years, looked as if he'd not moved from the spot for the whole of the period. Brown as a berry, wrinkled, his battered trilby and worsted jacket gave no concession to the seventy-five degree temperature. Everybody around him looked hot and sweaty, but Len calmly listened to his assistant interpreting the tick tack. Senator Brady was brought in to 2-1, Catharsis stayed firm, but he pushed the King out to 9-2. Stephen hesitated. He could wait to see if he drifted out of the market or else he might kick himself if the other punters took the 9-2 and pushed the price back.

A small posse besieged Len, people pushing money at him. Maybe the hesitation had been fatal, but no, it was the 2-1 they were taking on the favourite as all the other bookies wiped 5-2 off their board and cut him back to 7-4. Todd rubbed off his 2-1 as well to indicate he'd taken his fill, then in time honoured tradition obliterated every other fancied horse as well. The chalk squeaked on the black background 7-4, Senator Brady, 4-1 Catharsis, 5-1 Montpelier King. This was it. He nodded to Trish who moved into the neighbouring bookmaker at the right, Rory's lad moved from the left, and the three of them plunged Gerry Mortimer's £10,000 on the thoroughbred that Stephen had named Montpelier King.

As soon as the bet was received 5-1

305

disappeared and for a minute or two, the horse was out of the market. On a Wednesday afternoon at Bath, £10,000 on a horse, even spread over three bookmakers, was not a small bet. The bookmakers had laid off much of the bet which meant they'd passed on the risk to one of the big firms. That in itself was enough to trigger off fresh interest in a horse. It took a few minutes for the word to get around.

Somebody knew something about Montpelier King. Len Todd put it back at 4-1. There was a rush of takers. 7-2. Things calmed down a little. Senator Brady weakened a little back to 2-1. Catharsis drifted out to 5-1. The horses were at the start. Another little piece of racing arithmetic had taken place. The smaller lemmings had followed their larger compatriots to the edge of the cliff. Whether they survived the fall was now out of their hands.

'They're going behind.' The racecourse commentator's voice came across loud and clear. It was a small field, only eight runners, all of them with racecourse experience and therefore unlikely to cause difficulties over going into the stalls.

'Come on, let's go watch,' Stephen said, sounding a lot calmer than he felt. He took Trisha's hand naturally and led her through the crowd into the grandstand level with the finishing line.

'Just one to go on now, that's the outsider Sup With the Devil. He's in, they're under orders, they're off!'

Stephen felt Trisha grip his hand, felt her nails digging into his palms, the pain oddly therapeutic.

'Come on the King,' he said in a voice that wasn't his. 'Do it for me. Please God, let him do it for me.' And then he lifted his glasses to his eyes to watch the race.

Chapter Thirty Two

'Where is he?'

'At the racecourse?'

'Desperate measures.'

'Desperate man.'

'He got some money.'

'I know.'

'Doubtless he'll put it on that horse of his. Not that it'll do him any good. He needs more than money.'

'So there's no change in the plans?'

'No change.'

'Fine. Don't forget to check the racing results.'

They laughed and replaced their receivers.

'Two furlongs from home, it's Sup With the Devil by a length from Montpelier King, Catharsis is in third, moving up smoothly on the outside is Senator Brady...'

'What do you think?' Trisha asked anxiously.

Stephen did not take his eyes from the race.

'He's supposed to have tried to make it all. That way if he set a fast pace he'd be testing everyone else's stamina. What's happened is that this outsider's gone like a bat out of hell, but assuming he blows up, the King has to step up a gear and try and burn them off over a shorter distance.'

Trisha pursed her lips. It was hard to believe that a sport that simply involved horses trying to race faster than other horses could be so unbelievably complicated. Even giving away your money had been made difficult.

'Into the last furlong. Catharsis is weakening. Senator Brady seems to be making no impression on the first two. Sup With the Devil hanging on gamely, Montpelier King coming alongside, Sup With the Devil tiring a little, Montpelier King getting up...they've gone past together. It's a photo. Photo between number 3 Montpelier King, Number 7, Sup With the Devil.'

Stephen raced down the steps towards the unsaddling enclosure. He couldn't understand where all the people were coming from. Half an hour after the racecourse had seemed empty; now wherever he turned, people became solid obstacles.

'Stephen, calm down. You'll have a heart attack.'

He realised he was sweating, could feel the colour rising in his cheeks, his clothes sticking to his body, his feet swelling within his shoes. His heart beat was so loud that surely Trisha must hear it, surely the whole racecourse must hear it? The blood rushed to his head, to every part of his body. It was taking so long. The photo result would be given before he got to Adrian Reardon who'd ridden the horse this time around. Then the path ahead was clear, the Red Sea rose on either side, and he was standing on the little patch of sward, shielding his face from the snapping cameras. He was famous now, he was yesterday's news and tomorrow's headlines: *Bailed Lawyer's Horse in Photo Finish*. He could do the job for them, write the junk without too much trouble.

'What happened, Adrian?' He cut right across Rory who was in the middle of his own cross-examination. In turn, his own question was silenced by the tannoy.

'Result of the photo. First number 7, Sup With the Devil, second number 3, Montpelier King, third number 1, Senator Brady.'

Stephen turned on Rory with fury.

'I thought you said it was a sure thing?'

'Stephen, I'm sorry. I really believed it. This other nag had done nothing, nothing. It had no right to be in the same race, let alone the winner's enclosure.'

'He took my ground!' The jockey was off the horse now, looking preposterously small without the animal beneath him. The two men broke off their argument and focused on the diminutive Irishman with a concentration that suggested he had discovered the meaning of life.

'He what?' Rory shouted.

'He came into me as he tired. It's worth an objection. I thought the stewards might have enquired anyway...'

The voice over the tannoy echoed the sentiment.

'Stewards' enquiry. Please retain all betting slips. Stewards enquiry into the third race.'

'We'll object anyway,' Rory added. 'Come on, Ade, go and weigh in and I'll see you outside the stewards' room.'

Stephen made to go with them.

'Sorry, Stephen, trainers and jockeys only in front of the stewards.'

'I'm sorry, Rory. I didn't mean to shout. I know you did your best. What's the chances?'

'Fifty-fifty. I thought he leaned across as he got tired, but Adrian's a level-headed lad. He was on the horse and if he didn't think the result was affected I don't think he'd have said anything. He doesn't know how much all this means to you. The other jockey, Sam Duncan, he's had problems before this season. He's a kid, a bit excitable, not really strong enough to be riding at the top level. And the trainer's got no great love for authority—Barney Gilzean. He's had accusations made against him before when he's tried to pull off a long odds coup.'

'What's that got to do with the race?' Trisha asked with journalistic curiosity.

'It's got everything to do with the race, my dear. Stewards are only human as well. If it's a borderline decision they'll come down on the side of the nice guys. In this instance we're the nice guys. See you later. Go and prop him up in a bar somewhere, he looks as if he could do with a drink.'

Stephen needed three drinks, large Scotches, knocked back in record time. The first hit his empty stomach and told him he was alive, the second splashed around a bit, the third lingered in the mouth and buzzed about his brain.

'I hate waiting,' Trisha said, 'I remember once...'

'Yes?'

She hesitated. In all the time he'd known her she'd said so little about herself.

'Nothing.'

'Come on. Memories aren't nothing.'

'No, you're right. Memories are pain.' She ordered herself another vodka.

'Who's driving?' Stephen asked, remembering his last visit to the racecourse.

'Let's worry about it when it's time to go home.' Her eyes took on a dreamy look and she was staring past Stephen, past the door, to a world beyond.

'I waited once for a result. Pregnant or not. They do the tests and you wait. I was. And then I wasn't. The clinic was better than the one you sued. Did the job efficiently. No crankiness, no kindness. In, out, like the baby. He would have been three by now—he or she.'

He didn't ask about the father. He'd learned enough about her to know that if she wanted to tell him something then she would. It always had to be her decision.

'How long has it been?'

'Twenty minutes,' he said.

'Is that normal?'

'I honestly don't know. They'll look at the film, head on as well as sideways, talk to the jockeys, ask them to retire and make their decision. Crazy really. I'm a lawyer, I'm the owner, and I can't even argue my own case.'

'Here is the result of the Stewards' enquiry.' A hush fell over the bar. 'The places are reversed. First number 3...'

Stephen let out a whoop of delight and threw his arms around Trisha. She pressed her body against his, and oblivious to everybody else around them their lips met in a kiss. Neither drew away. Her hands went to the back of his head and pulled him closer. Her mouth opened and allowed his tongue to enter. He reached down to her thighs, feeling the flesh beneath her short skirt, his fingers moving back and down to just an inch away from the back of her crotch.

'Hey, come on. There are children present!' It was Rory, standing there laughing as they fell apart, dishevelled and flushed. 'Forget the sex, let's get on to the booze. A bottle of your best bubbly, my dear. Make it quick and make it cold.'

The barmaid obliged and willingly accepted a glass Rory put into her hands together with the £10 tip.

'A pushover in there. Adrian looking like an angel, the other boy with a six o'clock shadow in the afternoon and all the grace of a young Al Capone.'

He affected the plummy voice of the senior steward: '"And tell us, pray, Gilzean"—none of your Misters mind, still in the dark ages, these boyos—"can you explain the remarkable change of form in your animal that allowed it to win at twenty to one?" And me knowing it had opened at thirty-three, so not without stable support at the death, you understand. I think they gave us the race as much for the shenanigans they suspected from the trainer as the rough riding of the lad.'

'I'll be back, Rory,' Stephen said. 'I just need a bit of fresh air—and and to collect my winnings.'

'I'll come and help you count it out—you'll need a bodyguard,' Trisha added.

Rory raised his eyebrows.

'A bodyguard, is it? Well, you've a fine body and no mistake.'

'Keep them coming, Rory, we'll be back in a minute.'

They walked close together down to the bookmakers.

Len Todd didn't seem too upset. Presumably he'd cleared his books, and in any event the favourite hadn't won. Stephen stuffed the money into various pockets.

'I feel like a bank robber.'

'I still feel thirsty. I must get back to

314

Rory, I don't trust that drunken paddy on his own.'

'I've just seen on Teletext that the horse won.'
'What price?'
'7-2. If he was there he probably did better than that. It took a stewards' enquiry and an objection.'
'The boy might think his luck's turning.'
'Perhaps. A temporary diversion.'
'Can't have him getting his pecker up.'
'Very close to her today. Pecker obviously up.' There was a moment's pause in the conversation. The line seethed with venom.
'We'll just have to chop his pecker off then, won't we? See to it.'
The phone went dead, but anybody listening to the conversation would have been left under no misapprehension as to the speaker's intention. Whatever needed to be done, would be done.

Chapter Thirty Three

At first Stephen thought Trisha had read too many novels.
'It won't work. I'll end up back in jail.'

315

'It'll be fine. You go to the police station early. I'll wait outside as long as nobody reposseses my car. A mad dash to the airport. No passport needed for Jersey. We'll be in and out in a day.'

'And what happens if Jarvis Walters, over there, phones the police when we arrive? I'm not only out of the country, I'm interfering with prosecution witnesses. What happens if we have problems with the plane? If we get fogged in? It's not unknown in Jersey.'

Trisha tutted as if dealing with an irrational child.

'I'll go in first. I'll do the talking. If I think it's not going to work, he's not even going to know you've been there. You'll have had a nice day out, pick up your duty frees, and then back to the drawing board. I've personally checked the plane myself, and as for the fog, this is August, not February.'

Now as the plane circled the airport at Jersey, Stephen felt a sudden rush of exhilaration. He was doing something, it might not work, but at least it was better than just lying down and taking it all. The Jews in the Warsaw Ghetto uprising must have felt this way, badly armed, half starved, watching their houses burned—but still taking Germans with them, fighting back. And he would survive just as some of them had survived, as a glorious memory if nothing else.

It was a nerve-racking walk from the plane to the taxi. There were too many policemen there, eyes seemingly seeking out the guilty. The ones in uniform were bad, but what about the plain clothes men, the *bureau d'étrangers* as they were called in *Bergerac?* Surely one of them would smell him out, would take one look and know this was a man who was breaking bail? Trisha put her arm through Stephen's.

'Come on, darling, at least look as if you're enjoying yourself. Beautiful day, beautiful woman, beautiful island. What more could anybody want?'

It was indeed a beautiful day. The sun hit the water, the light bouncing off the freshly painted boats that smelt of money, decorated with half-naked women and well-tanned men. The taxi got stuck in a traffic jam along the sea front.

'It's never like this on the telly,' Trisha said.

'That's because they always film *Bergerac* at some unearthly hour. You'd think he'd got the only car on the island, wouldn't you? In real life it's getting like Piccadilly along here at the height of the season.' The driver glanced into his mirror to sum up his passengers.

'Here on holiday are you, then?'

317

'No, business,' Stephen replied grimly. He realised just how far he'd come from the legal stereotype. He wore a T-shirt and jeans with a light bomber jacket and trainers. The local hairdresser had chopped his hair almost to a crew-cut and he'd shaved last night rather than this morning partly to save time and partly because he rather liked the designer stubble. Trisha, as ever, looked great. Wherever she went she had a chameleon's ability to fit into the scene.

Today she was wearing tight white jeans with a blue matelot top, a bag casually tossed over one shoulder, sunglasses pushed up on her hair. Dressed to kill. He was just grateful he wasn't the intended victim.

Jarvis Walters' office was typical of Jersey. A brightly lit entrance hall of a modern purpose-built low-slung office block, the walls neatly filled with aluminium name plates, with such esoteric names as Dunkirk International Trust, Anglo-Liechtenstein Corporation, and there tucked amongst them Ashbow Investments, the company he was supposed to have formed.

'I feel stupid,' Stephen complained, 'it's like one of those really bad girl-guy TV series.'

'This is the real thing, baby,' Trisha said, out of the corner of her mouth in a mock-American accent. 'You stay out here for the moment. Let me go in alone. I don't think he'll be packing a gun.'

She gave him a hug, a kiss on the cheek, and she was gone, leaving him pacing the landing. The last time he had felt like this was in the hospital when Cathy had been expecting Danni. Now, as then, he had too much time to think. It had been folly to follow her here. What was she but a cub reporter on the trail of a career-making story? If it all went wrong she had nothing to lose, it was his life with which she was gambling, his future that she was putting down on the table.

There was the sound of raised voices, one Trisha's, the other also female—a broad Midlands accent badly disguised.

'If you've no appointment, you can't see Mr Walters.'

'I've no appointment and I can!'

'Look, if you don't get out of here, I'm going to call the police.'

'That's fine too, because if I don't see Mr Walters I'm also going to pay a visit to the police.'

It was as if the word 'police' had broken a secret code, because Stephen heard another door open and recognised Jarvis Walters' voice.

It had been ten years ago they'd first met. Stephen was flying to New York on business and Jarvis had been seated next to him. Stephen's basic tactic for long-distance flights was to take a good book, some headphones and a mass of papers. If you looked busy there was a good chance whoever sat next to you wouldn't try to strike up a conversation. There was nothing worse than sitting next to a total stranger who took the opportunity to tell you his life story and use you as a psychoanalyst's couch for six hours. Jarvis had just nodded a greeting, got on with his own work for a while and then fallen asleep. He must have been about forty, trim dark hair, a neat moustache, everything about him tidy and tanned, down to the jacket and crisp white shirt and dark tie. Everybody Stephen knew tried to make themselves as comfortable as possible during a long plane journey but Jarvis actually looked as if he'd dressed up for the occasion.

It was only in the last hour they'd got to talking. Jarvis Walters was a chartered accountant who'd tired of practice and London life and gone to Jersey to work for a company who specialised in the establishment of off shore trusts and corporations. He'd been there a year when the senior partner had decided to retire and had laid the mantle to succession upon Jarvis' shoulders. Since then Jarvis had set about the sort of expansion that his elderly predecessor had simply not been hungry enough to aim for. He'd taken on more staff, to give him time to travel the world, targetting lawyers and accountants who had clients who needed his sort of services. His quiet appearance was misleading. Deep inside him was a salesman, a salesman who could never be satisfied until he'd closed a contract. Within the hour Stephen had been persuaded that what Jarvis Walters had to offer was better than anything else he'd ever utilised, and over the years Stephen's firm had become one of Jarvis' biggest clients. Stephen also travelled extensively picking up clients and professional contracts all over the globe who had need of off shore services, and as Stephen's foreign practice expanded so Jarvis Walters also prospered. A year or so ago he'd sold a large slice of the action to a merchant bank called Rothenberg St Aubin and with that sale came even more prestige.

What Jarvis sold was discretion and trust, and the bank brought with it a reputation that stretched back to the French Revolution. A St Aubin had bought his way out of the bed of Madame La Guillotine and had lived to father a dynasty of bankers who'd joined forces with the more Germanic

321

Jewish Rothenberg while Napoleon was battling away at Waterloo. And now Jarvis was able to offer a complete service, companies, nominees, trusts, investments and banking. Outwardly, nothing about him changed. He still wore the same kind of clothes, still remained married to the quiet pretty little woman to whom he'd once introduced Stephen on his first visit to Jersey; but Jarvis was also the most ambitious person Stephen had ever met. His calm exterior hid a burning impatience to be moving onwards and upwards. There appeared to be nothing in his sights but success for the sake of success yet, but in the case of Jarvis Walters appearances could be deceptive and despite their regular contact Stephen still felt he had never come near to knowing the man.

'It's all right, Maggie, let her in. She doesn't look the homicidal type.'

Jarvis led Trisha into his office, the door closed, and all Stephen could do was read and re-read the names of the corporations registered at the office as displayed on the board outside. Anonymous names, black on aluminium, each concealing a complex web of deceit.

Chapter Thirty Four

Trisha looked round the office. She had never seen a room that told her so little about its occupant. The only pictures on the walls were dull unoriginal prints of foreign capitals where Rothenberg St Aubin had offices. The floor was uncarpeted and her heels clicked noisily on the highly polished wooden boards before she sat on an uncomfortable, but doubtless expensive, high backed chair. The desk was totally clear of files and papers save for a large blotting pad, a notebook and a gold pen. The screen at Jarvis Walters' side was filled with figures, and as if she could make anything of them, he wiped it clear with a press of a button. There was nothing personal surrounding him, no photographs of his family, no executive games, not even a desk tidy with the sort of litter that any normal businessman might collect.

'Would you like some coffee, young lady?' The tone was condescending, mildly amused, like an uncle visited unexpectedly at the office by his favourite niece.

'No, I don't think so.'

'Very well then. Perhaps you'd like to

get on with your business?' He made a praying gesture with his hands and leaned forward on the desk. She caught a hint of his aftershave, a hint of mint toothpaste. There was something terribly clinical about the man, as if he shaved twice a day, bathed three times, and cleaned his teeth every time he ate a meal. The eyes, dark and sombre, stared straight at her, giving her no insight at all into what he was thinking. All of her plans went straight out of the window. This was not a man likely to surrender easily. It was going to have to be a question of bluff rather than fact.

She introduced herself and saw a glimmer of distaste when she mentioned she was a journalist.

'I'm looking into a story about Stephen Kennard and some share dealings in D'Arblay Leisure.'

'Are you indeed? You look too young and innocent to be involved in investigative journalism. And isn't poor Stephen's case sub judice? I don't think you'll be able to write anything that might prejudice him.'

He was nobody's fool, but Trisha also had a quick mind.

'It may be sub judice now, but sooner or later he'll come to trial and at that point we want to have our story all ready. It's got the makings of a nice scandal—wealthy establishment lawyer, public company, clients' funds. That sort of thing's quite sexy nowadays. Stephen's even got a female partner who should make for a few good pictures.'

Was that something else that had hit home or was she grasping at straws? Whatever it was, she was slipping into the role of the archetypal tabloid reporter who had already made up her mind about the angle of her article and really wanted to hear anything that supported it.

'We understand,' she liked the royal we, it gave the impression that there was somebody bigger and tougher behind her, 'that you were involved in setting up the mechanics that enabled Mr Kennard to slip the money out of his clients' account?'

Walters sighed, a bored sound that said he'd heard it all before.

'I really don't think I want to discuss this.'

'We have it on very good authority that that is indeed the case.'

'I've already spoken to the police. I know the Press are supposed to be the Third Estate but I wasn't aware I had any obligation to provide them with exclusive information.'

Trisha shrugged.

'That's fine, Mr Walters, you don't have to talk to me. I'll just write it the way I see it. This is going to be a dirty

325

business. Mud sticks. You may know you're innocent, but as I understand it you've a reputation to preserve. So has the bank that employs you. I don't think they'll like the sort of story that I have in mind. There are a lot of people out there who trust you and rely on you. If they think there's any possibility of that trust being broken, you won't see their coat tails for dust. On the other hand, if you can help me put the record straight...'

'Are you threatening me?' The tone was harder now. Playtime was over. Now he perceived her as more than a passing nuisance who would be fobbed off with charm, excuses and a cup of coffee.

'Me, a little girl? How could I threaten a powerful man like you? All I'm saying is that I think there are two stories here. One's the Kennard-D'Arblay tale, and as you say that can't be written yet. So be it. The other's a major exposé of so-called reputable companies who specialise in koshering up not so reputable off shore activities. Now if I were writing that story I might well start with a list of your companies outside and see just how many of these were really just cover ups for UK residents laundering money that hadn't quite come to the attention of the tax man.'

'There are laws against libel, you know.

You start down that route and I'll have you injuncted so fast that your ink will freeze between pen and paper.'

'Oh, scary.' She'd learned a bit about injunctions in her days on the *Sun* and felt confident enough not to surrender the point. 'You'll find it hard to get an injunction when you don't know exactly what we're going to say. If a court thinks that you'll have a reasonable remedy in damages, they'll let us print and leave you to sue us afterwards. Now let's stop playing around, Mr Walters, I know all about you.'

She'd given Stephen a hard time before the meeting, examining and cross examining him about everything he'd ever learned about the man.

'What is this, a debriefing?' he'd asked, tired after two hours of it.

'Something like that,' she'd replied, and continued with the endless questions and the mass of hieroglyphics that passed for notes. She produced these now, assuming the role of a policeman interrogator.

'You like power, don't you, Mr Walters? It's all been a bit of a success story for you, although nobody quite knows how you managed to get a resident's permit so quickly. And then there's your wife—long suffering lady, doesn't ask too many questions—which is probably convenient

327

when you indulge in the sort of tastes that take your fancy abroad.' She was shooting with a scatter gun, shooting from instinct and she was hitting him.

'And then there's Rothenberg St Aubin. Were you totally honest with them when you sold out? And even if you were—which I doubt—they won't like the sort of scandal that my paper's quite capable of creating around you. Now you know what papers are like. One of them runs a story, and suddenly they're all interested. Who are you nominees for, have you been completely open with the Jersey authorities about the true identity of beneficial owners? Who knows? Maybe even the US papers will pick up on it, maybe even a TV documentary if I use my contacts properly. The IRS don't like their nationals having off shore interests they don't disclose on their tax returns. They don't like it, and the people you've given your assurances to won't like it either when we spill the beans on them. Some of them could turn rather nasty, I'll be bound.'

'You're bluffing,' he said, but he didn't sound convincing. There was sweat on his brow and his collar suddenly appeared to be a little too tight for him.

'Fine, if that's what you think, I'll bluff. We have deadlines, you know.' She rose to leave and as she did so his mask dropped. First anger, then fear flashed in those midnight eyes.

'No, I think we can, perhaps, work out a deal. What is it you want to know?'

'I want to know everything about the Kennard arrangements with D'Arblay. And I mean everything. Conceal anything and I run my story. Come clean and I'm out of here and you don't even get a mention in the small print.'

'How do I know you can be relied upon?' he asked. She smiled, she had him in the net.

'Trust me, I'm a journalist.'

Chapter Thirty Five

There had only been one moment of worry at the airport when a delay of an hour had been announced, but eventually the plane had taken off, Stephen had duly checked in to the police station, and now they sat at Trisha's big kitchen table, its surface stained and scarred by years of meals, papers spread out in front of them. They were halfway through a bottle of Chardonnay, following hard on the heels of the two Scotches Stephen had knocked back almost as soon as he'd come through the door.

'I just wish I'd been a fly on the wall,' he said.

'You can be, I recorded it all.' Trisha produced a little tape recorder from her bag.

'You never cease to amaze me.'

'I try. I find when I cease to amaze people they get bored with me.'

He covered her hand with his and she let it lie there for a moment before extricating herself with the excuse of putting the papers in order.

'It starts here. There's a fax from you authorising the establishment of a Liechtenstein trust.'

Stephen picked it up. It was on his firm's notepaper, it did look as if it was his signature.

'I didn't sign this.'

'Is it your signature?'

'I think so. If not it's a bloody good copy. But I didn't sign it. Where's the hard copy?'

'Walters swore blind he'd never received it.'

'That's odd in itself. In the past he's made a big song and dance about faxed copies. Once he even refused to release some copy documents until he'd received a duplicate hard copy from a client because the original had been lost in the post.'

'Stephen, I know you think I'm young

330

and naive in the ways of the big wide world but you learn fast in the newspaper game. To achieve this sort of effect all you need is to photocopy a blank sheet of notepaper over a sheet of paper with your signature. Obviously you can't get away with it if you see the real thing, but on a fax copy...well, you just can't tell the difference.'

'I always knew nothing good would come from technology,' Stephen said with a wry smile. 'I remember groaning when the first fax arrived on my desk. Instant pressure. No more white lies to the clients that I'd answer their letters as soon as I got them, when they were lying forlornly in my tray.'

'And I thought I was trying to clear an innocent man.'

A cloud passed across Stephen's face. 'There's no such thing as an innocent man, Trisha. That went out of date with Adam.'

'Well, your friend Jarvis Walters isn't an innocent man, and that's for sure. If he's not guilty on this little escapade I'm absolutely certain he's done some other naughties that could put him behind bars for a while. You should have seen his face when I mentioned money laundering.' She fast forwarded the tape and Stephen listened in astonishment.

'You missed your vocation. You should

have been either a professional blackmailer or a bent copper. Either way you'd have made a fortune.' He poured another glass and sat back, feeling more relaxed than he had for a week, while Walters' voice, now sounding shaky and nervous, filled the room.

'We wouldn't normally accept a faxed copy, but I did so much business with Anthony that I didn't think his brother's signature could be anything but genuine.'

'Why Anthony, Stephen?' Trisha asked, her voice deadly serious.

'No.' Stephen shook his head. 'This has nothing to do with Anthony, believe me. We're not the closest of brothers, but even he would realise what this would do to our mother.'

Trisha, though, was persistent.

'I hear what you say, but Walters only talks about Anthony. Not Jeffrey, not Sarah, not even you. Doesn't that tell you something?'

Stephen took a deep breath.

'Yes, it tells me Anthony did more business in our practice with Jarvis Walters than anybody else, but then I knew that already, so in fact it tells me nothing.'

'Very well, have it your way. Somebody other than your brother Cain—whoops! Sorry, Anthony—forged your signature and got a Liechtenstein trust fund. They chose

Leichtenstein as I understand it because you don't have to disclose the beneficial owners there. Innocent or guilty, Jarvis Walters took instructions and didn't ask too many questions because he got the authority from your office. Now to my way of thinking that means whoever set you up knew a bit about the law and more than a bit about your practice.' She leaned back triumphantly in her seat, her fingers entwined around the stem of the wine glass. Stephen couldn't take his eyes away from those fingers, long, elegant, her caressing of the stem erotic in their innocence.

'Hello, Stephen, are you there? Stephen Kennard, this is your life, this is your life we're saving.'

'I'm sorry. It's all very plausible but anybody who works for me could have got access to our notepaper. Anybody who comes into the office for that matter. We know Arthur's gone missing, perhaps he sent the faxes as well.'

'That's still progress. Partners, staff or client. We've shortened the list down from the known human universe.'

There was a ring at the doorbell and Stephen jumped. He felt like a guilty man, thought that at any moment men in blue uniform or else in grey menacing suits would take him away to some dark underground cell where in desperation he'd confess to anything.

Yes, I did kill Christ.

Yes, I did start the Second World War.

Yes, I shot Kennedy, and John Lennon, and I fired the shots that began the last World War as well. Hiroshima, that was me too, pressing buttons, killing millions. I did it all. Where do I sign? Just leave me alone. Oh, you want to close Jack the Ripper's files as well. No problem. I'll even tell you how I did it. I'm guilty, damn it, guilty as hell.

Trisha answered the door, while Stephen poured himself another drink, hands unsteady.

'Is this what it's come to,' he said to himself, 'living on drink to get through the day? That and talking to yourself.'

He heard the voices before they came into the room, and wanted somewhere to hide. Not now, not with him looking and feeling like this, not his children. They looked older, even though it was only a few weeks since he'd seen them. He was missing them growing up, and felt an awful wave of sadness sweep over him. All this time he'd been feeling sorry for himself without giving a thought to anybody else affected by the situation.

His wife thought he'd destroyed their marriage, his mother thought he'd ruined his life and consequently her own. His children thought their father was a thief, his partners must feel he'd set out to destroy their practice, and his clients doubtless thought he'd betrayed them. Yet amongst them all, if Trisha was right, there was one person who knew the truth. One person...a needle in a haystack. What chance did he and Trisha have when even the police, with all their resources, were not looking beyond him?

'Hi, Dad.' Jonathan sounded very grown up, and for once he and Danielle seemed to be united in common cause: no bickering, no tension, just brother and sister visiting the stranger who was their father.

Danni was more effusive. She threw her arms around him and buried her head in his shoulder. Not to be outdone, Jonny moved in close and wrapped both arms around his waist. Trisha looked mildly embarrassed at the family tableau.

'Can I get you two anything to drink?'

'Please,' Danni said. 'Water for me, Coke for Jonny.'

'How do you know I wanted Coke?' the boy asked.

'Jonny, you always drink Coke.'

' 'Spose so.'

Stephen smiled and kissed them both again.

'I thought that was heading for a

335

fight. I'm disappointed. I've missed all the arguments.'

'We don't fight so much now,' Jonny said. 'Mum's got a very low temper threshold. Somehow it just doesn't seem worth the effort when you weigh it against the explosion.'

'Does your mother know you're here?'

The children exchanged glances and suddenly they were once more toddlers, caught in some naughty act, looking to each other for guidance as to whether or not to confess.

'We didn't see the point in telling her.'

'So where does she think you are?'

'Out. She's not at home an awful lot herself. Grandma told us where to find you.'

'I see.' Somehow he'd distanced himself from the idea that while he lived in exile his family were existing on a parallel planet.

They stayed for about an hour. They talked of school, of their friends, films they'd seen, sport they'd played. He'd never felt closer to them, and when they were gone he'd wished they'd never come.

'We never spoke like that when I was at home. Somehow or other I was always too busy—too busy to listen, too busy to watch Jonathan play football. I was always the empty seat at Danni's school plays.' He bit his lip. There had been enough tears shed already in the saga.

'Hey, come on. Don't feel sorry for yourself. It took a lot of guts for them to come here. Dad shacked up with a strange woman.'

'You know, they didn't even ask about that. It was as if they took you for granted.'

'They took me as part of the furniture, you mean. By the way, while they were here, I was doing some thinking.'

'And?'

'You and me, we need a holiday.'

'I thought Jersey was it.'

'No, Jersey was just a trial run. We have to push it further. If we don't no one else will. Now pack your bag. The day after tomorrow we're off on another day trip.'

Stephen groaned.

'Go on, tell me. I know I'm not going to like it, but tell me. What have you got in store, New York by Concorde?'

'Nothing too esoteric. We're going to France.'

'You seem to have forgotten, I don't have a passport.'

'I know. It's no problem.'

'Whatever you've got in mind is illegal.'

'That's rich coming from somebody who's supposed to have swiped a few million of his clients' money.'

There was nothing else to say. He saw the light in her eyes, saw the youth shining in her face, and for that moment believed that she trusted in him. The day after tomorrow he would be going to France.

Chapter Thirty Six

He found it difficult to get to sleep. There was too much going on in his mind, too many questions to which there was no guarantee he was ever going to get an answer. He needed a drink, not an alcoholic one, just something long and thirst quenching. He opened the fridge carefully, so as not to disturb the woman sleeping behind the door. He still felt like a stranger, a passing guest put up for the night, his hosts eagerly awaiting his departure the following day so sheets could be whipped off the bed, the window opened, the room aired, his passing making not so much as an indentation on the mattress.

He found a bottle of orange juice and hesitated before pouring himself a glass, scared in case there should not be enough for Trisha in the morning. He'd never regarded himself as a mean man yet he'd always hated it when his children's friends had raided the food cupboard, racing through delicacies he'd bought for himself with all the voracity of locusts in ancient Egypt. He thought of his children now, asleep in their own beds, perhaps dreaming of a father they must now believe had betrayed them. It seemed like only yesterday that he'd tiptoed in every night just to assure himself they were still breathing, that no evil spirit had broken into their rooms and captured their innocent souls. Only yesterday...but yesterday was gone and they were there and he was here, the distance between them as vast as a universe.

He wandered over to the window, feeling the need for fresh air. Gently he levered up the sash until he could peer out and look up into the night sky. There was a full moon and he felt like baying towards the heavens, understanding the mind of a werewolf. They were no longer a threat, no longer the dark creatures from the graveyard mind of Edgar Allan Poe. They were creatures to be pitied, crying out for mercy like him, for an unseeing God in the heavens to release them from their torment. He gulped in the air, drinking it as thirstily as he had just drunk the orange juice. Then he saw the man.

He stood on the pavement opposite,

making no effort to hide, looking up at the window from which Stephen was leaning. He lit a cigarette, looking for all the world like a character from a Chandler novel, tossing the match into the gutter. A big man, young, fair hair close-cropped, shoulders that testified to a career in rugby, a round face, the features difficult to distinguish at a distance but with something familiar about him. He made no attempt to conceal himself although he must have realised Stephen had seen him, and that worried Stephen.

The man stamped his feet, a gesture of impatience or an attempt to shake off the chill of a damp English Summer evening, Stephen couldn't tell. He walked a few yards down the road, towards a parked car, and unlocked the door, Stephen felt sick and scared. He'd not noticed the car before because it was parked in the shadows, but now he saw it all too clearly and also saw the unilluminated sign on its roof that said 'Police'. They knew, that was all he could think. Somehow they knew that he was about to breach his bail conditions. They had the flat bugged, they could read his mind. Was it Trisha leading him into a trap or had she told anybody of the intended trip?

He tried to calm himself down, to treat himself as a client. How many times in the past had somebody sat across the room from him, their problems seemingly insoluble, until he'd probed and worked at the situation and finally found the cure?

'There is no problem that doesn't have a solution.' He'd said that almost every time as his opening gambit, never once adding that the ultimate solution was death.

'You can't hang a man who's already committed suicide,' he'd once said to Jeffrey.

He had grinned, 'You can, it's just that he doesn't feel anything. But it's still a grim warning to the others.'

He decided not to wake Trisha. If in fact his wild suspicions were correct, then she knew about this man and his safe house was no longer safe, his sanctuary violated. Stephen got dressed as quietly as he could, picking his darkest clothes, then tiptoed out of the flat. If the man's intention was to flush him out then he'd succeeded, but if he also thought to catch him he was in for a disappointment.

The main door of the house opened out on to the street, and then to the immediate left was a steep flight of stairs leading down to the basement flat. Stephen edged open the front door, waited until the man bent to light another cigarette, then ducked down the stairs. Looking around the small area in which he found himself, the options were limited. The stairs simply took him back to the street and it was hardly likely that the basement occupant would welcome him in at one in the morning. He just wasn't cut out for this sort of thing. He'd walk up slowly, ask to be arrested, plead guilty to something he hadn't done and at least then it would be all over. He'd go to jail, come out bankrupt, but there'd no longer be anybody following him, the persecution would be finished and he could start to rebuild his life somewhere abroad where nobody knew him. It was all very tempting and then he saw the empty milk bottles and realised there was another way out. Diversion. That was how it always worked in fiction, so why shouldn't it work for him now? As he faced the road, the car and the man were on the left. He lobbed the bottle as hard as he could to the right, waited until he heard heavy footsteps run by, then raced up the stairs and turned left.

It would all have worked perfectly if it hadn't been for the cat. It chose that moment to streak across the road, right into his path, and he fell with all the grace of a horse brought down at Beecher's Brook. The policeman spun round, saw at once he'd been distracted, and was after him like a shot. Stephen got up, logical enough to realise that running was a sign of guilt, yet still driven on by the primitive urge for survival.

It was no competition. He got to the corner, still within sight of Trisha's flat, when the man caught up with him. Stephen was panting and out of condition; the other man, some ten years his junior, clearly highly fit and trained, dived for him and brought him down with a crashing, perfectly timed rugby tackle.

Stephen struck out, oblivious to the thought that he was adding assaulting a police officer and resisting arrest to his long list of crimes. It was all hopeless, though, as the man's bulk nearly suffocated him. His face was pushed against the cold pavement, his arm painfully twisted behind his back. The man's voice came out in breathless gasps.

'You my friend, are nicked. One more try and I call up a few of my mates and you'll be nursing more than the bruises I've given you while you spend the night in the cells.' The policeman felt the aggression slip out of Stephen.

'Now, come on, just give me your name and we can get the formalities over.'

'Give you my name?' Stephen shook his head in disbelief. Could it be he'd made yet another terrible mistake, that the man really didn't know him, or was this a piece of Kafkaesque whimsy on the part of the police officer?

Just then he heard a flurry of footsteps, lighter this time, feminine, then a woman's voice, a familiar voice.

'Charlie, just what the hell do you think you're doing? Get off him before you do something fatal!' And there was Trisha, and the policeman was obeying while Stephen just lay between them like the baby in the Punch and Judy show.

They sat in Trisha's flat while she made coffee and suddenly it all made sense: the extra toothbrush, the shaving things, the voice on the answerphone. Charlie's voice. Trisha had reluctantly introduced them, an oasis of civility in a desert of violence.

'Charlie Davison, Stephen Kennard. I'm sorry about Charlie, Stephen, he used to live here.'

Stephen had met him before. He'd been the missing sergeant who'd belatedly joined the interview, he'd sat face to face with the man whilst he'd been interrogated by the Chief Inspector. Detective Sergeant Charlie Davison was actually on his case.

'Look, Trisha, can't we talk alone?' The voice was rough and cockney, the note of desperation impossible to conceal yet unlikely coming from such a tough body.

'I've nothing to say to you that can't be said in front of Stephen.'

'Oh, so he's the reason I'm out, is he?' She practically sneered.

'No, the reason you're out, Charlie, is you. The reason you're out is that you're the sort of person who'd spy on me. Why not use your credit card, sneak up the stairs and spy through the keyhole? Maybe you'd find me getting undressed, or if you got really lucky perhaps we'd be screwing on the floor. If you poked your nose in then you might get a sniff of pot and then you could get a drugs bust to your credit.'

She banged the coffee cup down at his side so viciously that half the contents spilled into the saucer.

'I'm sorry. I just wanted to talk to you. I came off duty at twelve, and I thought you might be up. I've left enough messages on your answerphone.'

'And I've left you enough messages by not answering. Now drink up and then go home, Charlie. I'm tired and I want to go to bed.' She saw him look at the crumpled sofa bed, then into her bedroom, and continued. 'Yes, to bed, alone. Stephen's just staying here for a while until he can get you and your cronies off his back.'

Charlie looked at Stephen as if for the first time, and the expression in his eyes made Stephen grateful that he had no access to his secret thoughts.

'I know you, don't I?' he said, searching to place him.

'I thought the police were supposed never to forget a face.'

Charlie sipped his coffee, and swore as the liquid dripped off the bottom of his cup on to his trousers.

'You've been having a bit of trouble with us lately. I thought I remembered the name, but now the face fits too. I actually sat in the room with you for half an hour, didn't I, when we first brought you in? Well, Trisha, that's from one extreme to another, copper to crooked lawyer.'

She got up, her face white with a mixture of anger and exhaustion.

'That's it! Get out, Charlie. Get out of here, and get out of my life.' She pulled the unfinished coffee from his hand and despite the difference in their size propelled him through the door.

She watched from the window until he got into his car and drove away.

'I'm sorry about that, Stephen.'

'It's all right. I don't blame him.'

'For calling you crooked?'

'That—and for not giving up on you. How long were you and he involved?'

'Three years. I met him just after I'd had the abortion. And before you say anything, he's not usually that bad. He's a big baby really, a bit of a softie for a copper. You never know, we might need a friend on that side of the fence.'

Stephen twisted his mouth into a cynical grimace. 'I think he'd rather bury me than help me.'

'He'll get over it. Now, shall we get back to sleep, unless you're planning any more midnight excursions.'

'All I wanted was a drink,' Stephen said, but she was already on her way back to her room and it was neither the time nor the moment to tell her he was sorry for his suspicions.

Chapter Thirty Seven

Gerry Mortimer fiddled with the paper knife on his desk. He did not seem to be enjoying his business life. His secretary, Mavis, had been with him for twenty-five years and she knew all the signs. She put his third cup of coffee of the day before him, even though it was only ten o'clock.

'You're missing Stephen, aren't you, Mr Mortimer?' Despite her length of service she'd never dreamed of calling him by his first name. She showed the world a stern, unyielding appearance, hair drawn back into a tight old fashioned school-ma'am bun, glasses that give no concession to fashion, minimum makeup, lips permanently pursed in an expression of disapproval of everything that went on around her. She had been in love with her employer since the first moment she met him, a fact of which he was entirely oblivious and which she only acknowledged as she lay alone in bed in her small West London flat. But today there was a softness in her tone that even Gerry Mortimer could not fail to notice.

'Of course I am. You miss him too. He made things happen. Not many people do that nowadays. I'm too old for change. It gives me indigestion.'

'I'm afraid the rest of the Board are waiting for you. Will you finish your coffee first?'

'No, it's all right. I'll take it through. There's no point in delaying things.'

Carrying the cup of coffee in one hand, he opened the intercommunicating door and went through to the board room. The rest of the directors of Sidney Developments looked up at him as if somebody had jerked their strings. That was what they were as far as Gerry was concerned, puppets, but they hadn't acted like puppets when it came to removing Stephen from the board. Suddenly they'd sprung to life with acrimony and recriminations. Yet in the past it had been Gerry and Stephen who came up with the ideas, made the decisions and then carried them through. All this lot had been good for was opening the champagne to toast another successful takeover or another record year.

'Good morning, Gentlemen.' They responded dully. They were not an imposing group. Peter Douglas, Gerry's Vice-chairman, had been with the company for years and his promotion to the board had been due more to his staying power than his ability. He was honest and industrious and could carry through a plan provided it was clearly mapped out for him. Keith Coleman had been Chairman of a textile company that they'd bought and his seat on the main board had been part of the price they'd had to pay. He travelled down from Oldham for these meetings, a thin-faced, sharp-nosed man in his mid-forties who'd screwed the last penny out of his own deal yet still continued to tell Gerry that Sidney had got a bargain. Alan Dawson was the Company Secretary. An erstwhile chartered accountant, he'd come to do an audit about ten years previously and had stayed. Stephen had once said unkindly he'd been left behind by the tide and that wasn't too far from the truth.

The fourth man in the room was David

Levine. His father, Maurice, had started the company with Gerry and had lost the toss as to choice of names. David had lived for too long in his father's shadow and now seemed scared to tiptoe out into the daylight. Maurice had done his best to groom him for stardom. David had done a business law degree, and then had lived in both the USA and the Far East, learning everything there was to know about textiles. Yet his father had taken a long time to die and it was only in the last six months that David had taken a seat on the board. He'd never hit it off with Stephen. He'd regarded him as Gerry's heir apparent, while he was at least connected to his father by blood. It had been he who'd led the pack of hounds against Stephen, and it was he again who today opened the proceedings after Alan Dawson had read the minutes of the last meeting.

'I think we've wasted enough time since the Kennard fiasco. If we're going to proceed with D'Arblay, then we should make it public. Let's get ourselves some sharp lawyers and use the shares we've bought.'

'What's wrong with our old lawyers.'

Levine laughed unpleasantly.

'You must be joking, Gerry! You're talking about the firm who let their client account be used to buy shares in a company we were taking over and made the deal twice as expensive. Sure, let's use them. Why not have the office boy there prepare all the documentation? I'm sure he's as honest as the day is long.'

Coleman lit up a cigar and puffed out smoke without any great sense of direction.

'I tend to agree with David. Things have quietened down a bit with D'Arblay, the price has fallen off again, we've got our stakes. If it was a good deal when Kennard was on the board, why is it a bad deal now? I suggest we use my old company's solicitors. They didn't do a bad deal for me when I sold out—I suppose we could have done a bit better on the price, but I mustn't be greedy. We all know Gerry here likes to get a bargain.'

'Keith, it was five years ago we bought you out. You've not done badly since then, and that was due in no small way to the same Stephen Kennard you've been slagging off. *Mamzeyrim!*' Gerry muttered the Yiddish word for 'bastards' to himself. He felt isolated among these men, none of whom were friends. They were just a random gathering of individuals with mutual business interests.

'I still think Stephen Kennard is inno-cent. There's no better way to show that

351

than to continue to instruct his firm.'

'It's not on, Gerry, we've all discussed this before you decided to join us. We've let you do things your way for a long time. You and Stephen used to play your cards very close to your chest. Now we think it's time we got a turn to deal. Do we have to put it to the vote?'

Peter Douglas had said nothing. Gerry turned towards him.

'Et tu, Peter?' he said with a surprising knowledge of Shakespeare.

The man nodded sadly, a dew drop forming at the end of his nose.

'I'm sorry Gerry, we have to move on.'

Mortimer thought for a moment, then rose to his feet.

'I'm not going to give you the satisfaction of resigning. I've still enough shares to cause a lot of *tsores* at an AGM. But if you think we should carry on and buy D'Arblay, fine. If you think we should sack Kennard & Wightman, fine. *Geh gesinterheyt.*'

He didn't know if they understood, he didn't care. He'd had enough for the morning and needed some fresh air.

He walked past Mavis who was busy typing.

'Finished already, Mr Mortimer?'

'I have, Mavis. I'll be back after lunch.'

'Will the rest of them be wanting lunch?'

'They can whistle. When they've finished, open a window in there. It stinks of cigar smoke; cigar smoke and betrayal.'

He walked out into the street. The heart of the rag trade was not what it had once been. Too many showrooms were now offices and too many of those offices had 'To Let' signs on them—'With Immediate Occupation'. It was hard for everybody. With Sidney he'd bucked the market for a long time. Competitors, friends, enemies, they'd fallen by the wayside, but Gerry Mortimer had prospered and flourished. Buy cheap, sell dear. Dear but fair. It had not gone badly adopting that motto. Now even the traffic wardens looked depressed. In the old days this had been their prize patch. Lamborghinis, Porsches, BMWs, left by owners more interested in displaying their wealth than avoiding parking fines. It had all been a game. Park it, move it, but never hide it. If you hid it from the wardens you also hid it from your competitors and they would never be able to tell how well you were doing.

Now the streets looked empty. The odd van unloading, vacant meters, the fun taken out of the contest. Proprietors looked sadly out of windows that said they sold directly to the public. No longer were there minimum orders, no longer were backs turned on foreign shop owners buying in half dozens rather than grosses. Business had to be taken where it was found. The world had turned, the world had changed, and as Gerry Mortimer hailed an eager cab for his destination he knew that for himself the world had little more to offer.

Chapter Thirty Eight

Fay Kennard was not used to visitors at lunchtime. Since her husband had died she hardly ever bothered to eat during the day. A slice of toast, a bit of smoked salmon, at most a bowl of soup when the weather was really cold. She took no pleasure in eating but it helped to fill in the time, and it was time that hung so heavily on her hands. She was not a foolish lady, she knew when she had upset one of her sons, she knew when she had upset one of her daughters-in-law—but in their case she always meant to. There was no point in getting close to them for after all they'd committed the greatest crime of all: they'd stolen her sons.

When the doorbell first rang she ignored it. It was going to be somebody selling something. The boys always telephoned first and she had a security code with her neighbours of one short ring, followed by long ones; but the caller was persistent and eventually she opened the door on the chain, preparing to see off the unwelcome caller with an onslaught from her under extended tongue.

'Fay? Were you asleep? I was just about to give up.'

'Who is it?' she asked querulously, having forgotten to put on her glasses.

'Fay, it's me, Gerry. Gerry Mortimer.'

She opened the door, still a little cautiously, then looked him up and down as if inspecting a cut of meat at the Kosher butcher's that she mistrusted on principle. In fact, she couldn't afford to fall out with her present butcher as she'd had an argument with every other one in the vicinity and she was reliant upon him to deliver.

'What's the matter, Gerry, you've not got enough business to keep you going during the day? Come on in. I'll put the kettle on.'

He grinned.

'Like old times, eh, Fay? A cup of tea in the afternoon when Leonard's out.'

She smacked him playfully, girlishly, and let him through to the lounge.

'I wish you'd told me you were coming. I don't do much with myself nowadays. Look at me, I'm an old woman.'

355

'You're as old as you feel, Fay.'

'Well, I feel old. The other day somebody offered to help me across the road. And believe me, he didn't look much younger than me. At first I thought he was trying to pick me up. But you look good for your age, Gerry. Still chasing the young girls around the desk?'

'Chasing yes, catching no. Sometimes I'm so slow they lap me.'

'You should be so lucky as to get one of them on your lap.' She was enjoying the banter, remembering better days.

He sank into an armchair feeling very tired. He remembered the chair, it had been there when Fay and Leonard had lived in their house. He had always chosen it when he visited for dinner and he had chosen it now. Seeing Fay had given him a shock. Did he look that old? She looked almost translucent, as if a strong breeze would knock her over, and he felt her touch of vanity pathetic. He was a million miles away from the brash men who probably still occupied his board room, and he wondered why he did not spend more time outside the office. Who knew if he knocked on the same door next year whether or not Fay would still be here?

She returned carrying a tray that appeared to weigh more than she did herself. She unloaded it carefully on a series of coffee tables: a tea pot, two cups, a cake, a plate of biscuits, some crackers, chopped herring, a selection of jams and honey, and a few slices of bread.

'If I'd known you were coming I'd have bought something in,' she said without a trace of irony.

'It doesn't look too frugal to me,' he replied.

'I like to keep something handy in case the boys drop by.' She didn't add that she kept the larder regularly stocked, and just as regularly threw food away when they did not come, or when they just passed by without stopping.

She poured him a cup of tea and he spread some chopped herring on a cracker.

'Good,' he said.

'Not bad. I used to make better myself when I had the strength. Now it takes me all my *koyekh* to get to the shops.'

'*Koyekh*, strength. I like to hear Yiddish. It's people like us who keep it alive. We owe the language that. It kept our people alive for years. You used to be embarrassed to use it when you were a girl.'

He finished his tea and poured himself another cup. Fay watched him with some satisfaction.

'I like to see a man with an appetite.

Leonard, *oleva sholem,* he never left a crumb.'

'He was probably too scared.'

'Nah, my Len, was scared of nothing. I miss him, you know, Gerry. I miss him more now than when he died. And with all this *tsuras* with Stephen... I can't cope with it on my own. I feel when I go out everybody's looking at me. Fay Kennard, the *gunaf's* mother. I've been so proud of the boys, and now for this to happen.' She began to cry and as the sobbing racked her body, Gerry leaned forward and covered her hands with his own. He took out a crisp white handkerchief and dabbed her eyes.

'Come on, Fay, your makeup will run. I see you once in a blue moon and your eyes become all puffy.'

'I'm sorry, it's just that there's not that many people I can talk to or cry with. My Anthony sits there but I'm never sure he's listening; the grandchildren telephone but sometimes I think that's just to make sure I don't forget their birthday presents. Stephen...now Stephen used to listen. I think he was laughing at me some of the time, but that was never a bad thing. Len always used to say I took myself too seriously. There was no chance of that happening when Stephen was around. I realise now that when he came up to see me all I'd do was moan and groan, and he never took it seriously, he always joked me out of it. I miss him as well.'

'He's not dead,' Gerry said.

'No, but they're trying to kill him, and it's killing me as well.'

Gerry's face became serious.

'That's what I came to see you about. I've never believed for a moment Stephen was guilty of anything. I've been told by all the young *pishers* that advise me that I mustn't contact him. Easy for them with their law books and their pin striped shirts with red braces. Why is it they all wear red braces nowadays? In our youth only band leaders wore red braces. He's still in touch with you, isn't he?' Gerry didn't wait for an answer.

'Tell him I'm doing what I can. It's not easy and it's not much, but it's all I can do. Tell him if it's more money he needs, I'll find it somehow. Maybe until today I didn't do enough. They're hanging him out in the sun to dry, and it's not fair.'

'Life's not fair, Gerry. We found that out years ago.'

He lifted her hand to his lips and kissed it, an odd old fashioned gesture. The hand felt like a twig in his own, dry, withered; if he held it too tightly it would snap.

He closed his eyes and leaned back in the chair. The old material moulded itself to his shape, snuggled around him, taking him slowly, slowly back to the womb until, totally relaxed, he nodded off to sleep.

Fay Kennard removed her hand and quietly cleared away the tea things. There was something more, something he was not telling her. She'd known Gerry Mortimer since they were teenagers together. She, Len, Gerry, they'd been inseparable, an eternal triangle without complications, without jealousy. Her friends had never known which of them she'd marry, and there had been times when she'd not really known herself; but although she'd felt a passion for Gerry, she'd been astute enough to realise that he would have made a terrible husband. His would not so much have been infidelity as nature taking its course. There was no way he could survive with only one woman in his life, and indeed there had been a whole succession of women, none of them quite attractive or intelligent enough to lure him away from Myrna for themselves on a permanent basis. Leonard had been dependable, Leonard had been faithful, Leonard had always been there when she needed him...so where was he now?

It was a crash of crockery that awoke Gerry. He sat up with a start, unsure of the time, unsure of his whereabouts. It was still light outside but the room seemed dark and gloomy.

'Fay, *Feygele,* where are you?'

There was no answer. He stumbled into the kitchen. She lay on the floor amidst the debris of her best china. Her colour was that of the shards of white plates that surrounded her. Her mouth opened and closed, but only bubbles of saliva formed on her lips. Her hand scrabbled on the floor as if trying to write him a message.

He sought wildly for the phone, finally locating it on the old fashioned sideboard, a piece of furniture too big for the flat but one she had refused to part with. The telephone itself was maddeningly out of date, each number having to be dialled on its black face, the wheel having to return to its last position before another number could be obtained. Nine, nine, and then finally the last nine.

'Ambulance! The address...' He sought for it and it eluded him even though he'd arrived only a few hours before. He took the piece of paper from his pocket and read it slowly and hesitantly, an old man trying to save an old woman.

He returned to the kitchen and put a pillow under her head. He had no idea whether or not it would do any good, but at least it would make her more comfortable.

'It's all right, Fay, it's going to be all

right. The ambulance will be here soon.'

It was only when they had taken her away, a stroke having been diagnosed, oxygen mask on her face, that he remembered why he had come. He had come to ask the question which she, of all people would not have been able to answer but at least with her he would not have been talking to himself. Now, as the sound of the ambulance faded into the distance, there was nobody left to ask but himself—was the plot against Stephen aimed just at him, or was he, Gerry Mortimer, a victim too?

Chapter Thirty Nine

The two brothers stood by their mother's bedside, and not for the first time recently Stephen wondered how the two of them could possibly share the same parentage. He didn't quite know how Gerry had found him but he'd moved so quickly that by the time Stephen had reached the hospital they had barely completed her admission. It had taken another two hours for Anthony to arrive.

'What kept you?' Stephen had asked impatiently. 'Were you out of the office?'

362

The inscrutable expression behind the thick lenses didn't change.

'No, I was in the middle of a meeting. I couldn't just pick myself up and leave. Unlike you, I've a job to keep down.'

'Hello, Stephen. How are you Stephen? How are you coping Stephen? Thank's for asking! And if you're at all interested, they say Mum's condition is stable.'

Anthony showed no sign of embarrassment.

'There was nothing I could have done.'

'And if she'd been dying? What about saying goodbye?'

'Well, she's not dying.'

Fay's eyes flickered open as if to object to her children's bickering.

'Mum, it's Stephen. Anthony's here as well. The doctors say you're going to be all right.'

She raised her eyebrows in a gesture that spoke louder than words.

'Doctors, what do they know?' it said.

A nurse, all starched activity, bustled into the room. She puffed up a pillow, checked the convolution of tubes that came out of Fay and spoke in impersonal tones that medical staff save for those who cannot answer back.

'There you are, Mrs Kennard, that's much better, isn't it? And I'll just show these two big boys of yours outside. Doctor will be here soon just to check up on you and we can't have you getting tired out, can we?'

As an after thought she turned to Stephen and Anthony.

'I'm afraid I'll have to ask you to leave your mother now. She's had a close call.'

Anthony made to leave the room, but Stephen leaned forward and kissed his mother on the forehead.

'Don't worry, Mum, we won't be far away.'

Outside in the corridor he checked his watch. It was only five o'clock yet it seemed as if he had been in the hospital for days. Since he'd arrived he'd managed not to think of his own problems once and selfishly gave silent thanks for the diversion, then immediately felt guilty.

Anthony sat down on one of the hard seats. Gerry Mortimer joined them, the cigar he'd gone outside to smoke extinguished in its prime.

'How is she?'

'Resting. Thanks, Gerry.'

'It was lucky I was there.'

'Why were you there?' Stephen asked. Everything had been such a blur that he had not thought to ask before.

'There's something wrong about having tea with an old friend?'

'Gerry, Gerry, you're a lousy liar.'

Mortimer shot a sidelong look at Anthony and clammed up.

'I can't talk now. Look, boys, I got her here, I'm off. I'll keep in touch.'

Anthony took his cue.

'I must get back to work as well. There's not a lot I can do here. If anything changes, I assume you'll let me know? As you can imagine, we're all having to work that bit harder in the practice.'

'How's the merger coming along?' Stephen asked, ignoring the jibe.

'Fine. Not that it concerns you. Jeffrey's handling it really well.'

'And Sarah?'

There was the slightest hesitation.

'No problem. She's looking forward to it just as much as everyone else. We're really lucky it's still in place given the problems you've caused us. I don't know how you could have done it, Stephen. I'm flesh and blood, and you've known Jeffrey so long he's virtually family.'

It was the first time for many years Stephen had seen his brother so animated; indeed it was one of the longest speeches he'd ever heard him make. Once Anthony had gone running to their father and denounced Stephen after his brother had deliberately sabotaged an unfinished chess game. Leonard had tried to calm him down but without success.

'Dad, I can't reconstruct the problem.' Even then the language was oddly formal. 'He only did it because he knows he can't beat me at chess.'

No, Stephen had never been able to beat him at chess, but he'd beaten him at everything else—until now. Now Anthony was in the driving seat and was clearly relishing the chance of refusing Stephen a lift.

'Anthony, you've never even given me a chance to explain. Not you, not Jeffrey, not even Sarah. None of you. Surely you owe me that?'

'Stephen, I know you don't like me. I know there's not between us what, for lack of a better word, I'd describe as brotherly love—but what explanation can there possibly be? Money goes missing, it turns up in an account opened for you, it's used to buy shares in a company that's about to be taken over by our best client. You're on the board of that client company. The only excuse you could offer is insanity, and that's one failing you haven't got. I've got to go. Doubtless I'll see you at the hospital over the next few days. If I do I'll be grateful if you would avoid talking about your current problems—I find it an embarrassment, and the advice given to us has been to have no contact with you at all.'

Later, back at Trisha's flat, that was what troubled Stephen the most, that was what kept reverberating around the hollow that was his mind. '"Advised to have no contact with you." Trisha, he's my brother! For Chrissakes, our mother's on death's doorstep, she's had a massive stroke. God only knows if she'll ever be able to talk again, let alone look after herself, and he's worried in case he upsets whoever it is that's giving him advice! That boy's got ice in his veins, not blood. Certainly not the same blood as mine.'

He paced the small room restlessly, making it seem even smaller as he railed against the actions of his brother.

'We can't go to France now. It was crazy thinking we could. This is some kind of sign, Trisha. I'm not religious but somebody up there is giving me a warning.'

'Calm down, Stephen. We'll give it a couple of days. If this stroke is as bad as you think, your mother will be in hospital for weeks if not months. I saw the same thing with my grandmother. There'll be ages when there'll be no change in her condition at all. Let her stabilise, talk to the doctors, and then we'll be off. We have to go, Stephen.'

'Go without me, Trisha, if you think the

367

answer to my problem is in Dijon. I don't know how you thought we'd got in and out in a day anyway. I can't leave her. If anything happened while I was away, I'd never forgive myself.'

Trisha thought for a moment.

'I'm sorry about your mother, Stephen, but you've got to think about yourself. She's had the best of her life. Yours is still to come. You saw when your kids came how much they're missing you. What we need is time. Get your solicitor to contact the police, or whoever it is he had to contact. Tell them about your mother. Say you have to be at the hospital all the time and therefore you can't report to the police every day—you'll phone in or something. It means if we're not back in a day, we're not back in a day.'

'You make it sound so easy...it's not like that.'

'Oh, I don't know why I bother.' She rose to her feet, her face flushed. 'I'm not your wife, your daughter, or your mother. Do what you like. Leave me out of it. And I'd be grateful if you could find a new hotel. I've taken another booking for next week.'

'Trisha, I'm sorry...'

'That's right, apologise, it's easy. You always feel sorry for yourself. Stephen Kennard, high flyer, big shot lawyer,

368

racehorse owner, dossing down on a settee in Islington. How the mighty have fallen. Well, Mr Kennard, next week it could be a cardboard box on the Embankment!'

She stormed out of the room and slammed the door of her bedroom. He heard her opening and closing drawers, then the sound of Springsteen filled the flat, the volume calculated to send the neighbours racing to their phones to complain.

He sat with his head in his hands. He had thought it was getting better. The visit to Jersey had given him hope: hope that there was something to discover, that he hadn't done what everybody believed during some deep, dark, walking nightmare.

It had begun to rain outside, a day more suited to February than August. Trisha had actually put on the heating in the flat and his warm spring birthday was a lifetime away. He clenched his hand into a fist and hit the table so hard that the pain shot right through him. Then, jolted into action, he strode into Trisha's bedroom without the normal polite knock on the door.

She was lying on the bed, surrounded by a wall of noise. Her jeans were tossed on the floor and the whiteness of her legs made a sharp contrast to the briefest of black panties that was all she wore. He had never seen her breasts before but she made no effort to cover herself. For a moment he thought of throwing himself upon her. He had felt no desire since the day of his arrest, and there had been times when he was convinced he would never be able to make love again. Her red hair was spread carelessly on the pillow, her eyes open and taunting, challenging him to discover the redness of her secret hair. Somehow he controlled himself, although he sensed she wanted it to be otherwise. She had hurt him and now he wanted to hurt her.

'All right, Trisha. Two days' time, if my mother's holding her own we'll go. I'll get Colin on to the police situation.'

She nodded, a small smile about her face, a victory won. Idly, she rubbed her left breast, an absentminded gesture, his presence now irrelevant, then sang along with the music, her voice low and melodious: 'Fools like us, baby, we were born to run...'

Chapter Forty

The gold in Dijon is on the roofs rather than the pavements. Long dead architects had created a city capped with shimmering ore, fool's gold in a city of rich men. The church in Dijon was rich, the merchants too, as the city buzzed with life and industry. Dijon and Beaune, the heart of Burgundy; wine and mustard; clerics and nobles. Here the grape is God, worshipped by bishops and beggars alike. The grape paid for the gold in the treasure chests and on the roofs, the grape paid for the Hôtel Dieu, the thrones of Burgundy, the wars, the women. Only the grape is constant. Dukes crumble into dust, their duchesses and courtesans age and wither, but the wine is forever; sometimes great, sometimes good, sometimes ruined by the weather, but always there, a continual birth. Planted, tended, picked, trampled, pressed, bottled, drunk—the seasons of Bacchus, as eternal as spring, summer, autumn and winter.

And now, as Trisha and Stephen emptied the last drops of the blood red wine, they too felt the surge of life, the magic elixir fulfilling everything promised by its label, a grand cru of Burgundy, *'mis en bouteille au châuteau'*, blessed by the vintner, holy communion without the water.

It had taken a week rather than a couple of days to make the trip and still Stephen could not believe he was really here. It was like being on holiday, but where was his wife, where were his children, who was this strange woman who sat opposite him at the dinner table? His mother had experienced some bad moments before he felt able to leave.

'We have to be careful of a secondary stroke in a woman of her age, but if she gets past the first three days you can probably breathe a little easier.'

There had been no second stroke but Fay had begun to run a high temperature and pneumonia had been the fear. Antibiotics and stubbornness beat off the threat, eventually the tubes were removed and she was propped up on a pillow and fed. She struggled with speech and found some words.

'Like a baby.' Tears filled her eyes at her helplessness. Stephen had combed her hair tenderly, even applied the slightest touch of makeup to her cheeks and lips. She looked terribly old and frail but he knew she hated to show a face to the world that was anything but her best.

Colin Leigh had, with the agreement of the prosecution, made an application to the court to vary the bail conditions and Stephen no longer had to report to the police station every day, merely to telephone them. He actually missed the visits, which had become part of his routine, wishing his mother better, seemingly pleased with her progress as each day passed. That was part of the problem, the days were passing all too quickly. His next hearing, which Colin had explained to him would be the committal proceedings, was due to take place in the first week of September.

'If you're going to plead guilty, that's the time to do it. At least we can make a merit of your having saved everybody a lot of time and trouble.'

'Colin, I'm not guilty and I'm not pleading guilty. By the time September comes I will have got enough evidence together to make sure you get these charges dismissed.' He sounded more positive than he felt. Colin lifted an eyebrow.

'Stephen, I hope you can, but I must tell you that from what I've seen so far of the police case, we do have—how shall I put it gently—some difficulties.'

'Forget putting it gently. I'm a big boy now, Colin. I've had to grow up a lot these last few weeks. I know you can only fight if I give you ammunition, and believe me, I'll get that ammunition together. I'll get so much together that you'll be able to make the IRA look like boy scouts.'

It had all sounded fine in the lawyer's office, but here in Dijon, in the same hotel he'd stayed the year before, he wasn't so sure. The only certainty in his life was the fact that he was there illegally. Trisha had assured him it would be simple, and indeed it was. They arrived at the airport a couple of hours before their flight. Trisha did all the talking at the Post Office at Heathrow.

'Look, my partner here has managed to forget his passport. Typical bloody man! We've not got time to get back to his house, and his wife's taking the kids to school so he can't even get her to deliver it. It's only France we're going to and it's just overnight...'

The man behind the counter was incredibly helpful, particularly when Trisha made it clear she was merely a business associate, that she was free and single, and it appeared her life's ambition was to elope with a young man with a bad case of acne who worked behind the counter at the Post Office.

All that was needed was a quick dash to the photo booth, a driving licence and the fee, and there Stephen was with a brand new travel document.

'There you go, easy peasy.'

Stephen shook his head.

'It's incredible. Don't they have a little black book or something, like Immigration in the States?'

'Maybe they do. Maybe he just couldn't be bothered to look in it, maybe he trusted me. Anyway it's worked. Are you complaining?'

'No, I just feel...'

'Well?'

'Like a criminal. It actually felt illegal.'

Trisha tapped her foot impatiently, a gesture he'd come to recognise as a danger sign.

'Oh dear. We've broken the law, have we? Why don't we run back to the nice-looking policeman with a machine gun and a guard dog and confess? Naughty, naughty me. Perhaps a kindly judge will give you a sentence to run concurrently with whatever they give you for emptying your client account, illegal share dealing, grand larceny, and the rape of your granny that they'll probably throw in for good measure!'

He didn't pursue the argument and since their arrival he'd felt more relaxed. He'd called the police station hoping the lines between Dijon and London were crystal clear, but even then he'd elaborated and said he'd been on a mobile at the hospital. Lying was becoming a way of life. It was getting back to the truth that was likely to produce a problem.

'More wine?' he asked. Trisha flicked her nail against the empty glass and he poured.

'It's good,' she said.

'If it's not going to be good here it's not going to be good anywhere.' He signalled to the waiter for another bottle.

'No expense spared, eh, Stephen? Easy to spend when you haven't got it.' The words were a little slurred and although he felt light headed himself he suspected she was actually quite drunk. *In vina veritas.* Perhaps he was about to discover the real Trisha.

'Trisha, you're in charge of this investigation. Where do we go from here?'

'I've already made some inquiries about your friend Nicole La Roche.'

'And?'

'I didn't want to tell you before we got here. She's dead. Cancer, it appears. Maybe that was why they chose her.'

She sipped her wine, and with her finger dabbed the last vestiges of the crêpes Suzette that had been her dessert.

'Sorry, I just love crêpes. Do you think it would be piggy to ask for another?' Having passed on the bad news, she was trying to change the subject.

'Where do you put it all, Trisha? There's not an ounce of fat on you.' Stephen could not believe how easily he could be led away from his mounting troubles.

'How do you know? I just do a good concealment job.' She looked at him sideways, sizing him up, flirting but half serious. 'Maybe I'll let you see...one day.' Then, as if remembering something tucked away in the recesses of her mind, 'oh, of course, you've seen it already. Well, nearly all of it. As I said, I do a great job of concealment.' She clicked her fingers and ordered another dessert in flawless French.

'You've got a great accent.'

'I know. I had a French boyfriend. No, not a boyfriend, a lover. A real lover. Aren't all the French lovers? Do you know all my best relationships have been with foreigners. English men, basically, suck. Well, they don't actually, they don't even like to be sucked, and even if they do you always get the feeling they're a bit embarrassed. Yes, a bit embarrassed and a bit dirty. I think it's something about their mothers forgetting to tell them to wash their naughty bits. Behind the ears, yes, but between the legs, no.'

Her dessert came and she wolfed it down with all the appetite of someone who'd not eaten in days, rather than a woman who'd just consumed a huge three-course meal.

'Am I embarrassing you?' She didn't wait for a reply. 'You know I think I am, but you're not really English. You're Jewish, and I suppose that makes you a bit foreign. I've never had an affair with a Jewish boy. All that circumcision. It might be interesting...'

'Trisha, we came here to work, remember? This is my life on the line. I'll ask you again. Where do we go from here?' Even before he asked the question, he knew the answer, and when she said 'Bed' and led him unsteadily by the hand towards the lift, he felt that she might have planned it that way all along.

Chapter Forty One

The man stood looking over midnight London. From the penthouse room he could see St Paul's and the river, lights reflected, late night industry and cleaners merging their cultures. He liked this time of the night, liked the power of being awake in a sleeping city. He needed help to get him through the nights nowadays, needed the buzz the white powder gave him, but there was no time for sleep, too many opportunities to be lost. While London slumbered, New York woke, Wall Street tickertaped fortunes, and it was no longer enough to rely upon the stock market here. He looked out beyond the river, the coke giving him a clarity of vision that enabled him to see far beyond the city, across the oceans, until he could smell the smoke from the bonfire of the vanities. The phone rang.

'Yes?' Non-committal, say nothing until you recognise the voice.

'He's in France. In Dijon.'

'Is he indeed? Braver than we thought.'

'Perhaps. He might just be running away from the sick mother.'

'Is he on his own?'

'No. The journalist is with him.'

'She's becoming a little problem.'

'We have it under control. There's nothing there for them.'

'Don't you think the police might be interested in a bail jumper?'

'They might, but it would take the fun out of the situation. Let him have a little holiday. And if there's a bit of adultery thrown in, well, so much the better. It's only Nero fiddling while Rome burns.'

Adultery. It was the word that kept flashing through Stephen's mind. After Sarah he'd promised it wouldn't happen again. There had been too much guilt, too much pain in facing his children, too many lies to his wife. But now his wife thought him guilty anyway, his children were across the Channel and his soul was damned if he did, and damned if he didn't.

He lay in the bed in the darkened room and waited for Trisha to finish in the bathroom. He'd heard her urinate, the long splash of water against the side of the bowl, the wine finally finding its way through the system. It was another step towards intimacy, listening to a woman on the toilet, the intimacy that developed into letting her see you naked while she slowly undressed. Even after all their years of marriage he rarely saw Cathy in the raw, sometimes a glimpse as she prepared for bed, but she always kept the bathroom door locked and would have thought he'd taken leave of his senses if he'd suggested a shared shower or bath. She was a woman who demanded privacy in every sense of the word.

Trisha came in beside him wordlessly. Her arm went around his neck and he could smell the toothpaste on her breath. Her lips found his and her tongue probed first, raking his teeth, her hands behind his neck forcing them together in an energy, a need, that said she had been too long without sex. His own hands slid down her back, feeling the crevice between her buttocks, pulling her towards him. She was a different shape to Cathy, younger, firmer, a figure not pulled apart by the birth of children, his children. He tried not to think of his children, but the image persisted: young, carefree, bouncing on their bed at some unearthly hour on a Saturday morning, interrupting any hope of making love, demanding breakfast, demanding to be read to, demanding their favourite video, their favourite game with their beloved dad who for once in a while was actually home and available.

'When you're here they don't want me,' Cathy had said at first with a smile on her face then with regret, and finally, as time went by, with a trace of bitterness. Well, now he wasn't there and he wanted them so much it hurt; he was in bed with a woman, a girl, young enough virtually to be his daughter.

Her hands went down between his legs, but even as she touched him he felt himself go limp. She stroked him for a while, her nails coursing along the sensitive skin, but still he felt no arousal, merely a sensation of tumbling over and over into a deep black hole. Her tongue was out of his mouth and into his ear, murmuring gentle encouragement.

'It's all right. I don't mind. Just relax. I'm with you.' Her mouth and tongue moved down his body, licking a silver trail until she took him gently between her teeth, willing him back to life. He threw himself backwards, legs wide open, staking himself out on an invisible cross. Even this was not possible. He had lost desire, lost the ability to love, lost his manhood. One more thing they had stolen from him.

He heard her lapping at him like the sound of the tide, but still nothing happened. He felt the tears come to his eyes and she, intent on her task, still was able to sense his distress. She moved back upon him and covered his face with small, damp kisses.

'Stephen, since I've known you, all you do is cry. I'm beginning to think it's me.'

'I'm...'

'Sorry? Forbidden word, remember. It happens. Not usually with me, admittedly, but it happens. You're under stress. That's a common problem.'

'It's not that. It's just...'

'Yes?'

He turned his head from side to side in a vain attempt to rid himself of the idea, but it would not go away.

'I'm married, Trisha. I'm bloody married! When the truth comes out and I prove myself innocent, I'll still be married. I can't blame Cathy for doing what she's done. She thinks I'm a thief, she thinks I'm a liar, an adulterer. Why give them the satisfaction of making it true?'

'Stephen, you have a remarkable talent for sobering up a girl. You've already told me about your fall from grace with Sarah.'

He said nothing but just held her, helplessly.

'Come on, Stephen. You've just avoided fucking me out of honesty, why stop now?'

'You're right. Yes, I've been unfaithful. Once.'

'Just once?'

'Well, with just one person, but no, not just once, lots of times. I thought I might leave, but I didn't.'

'The children?'

'The children. Clichéd, isn't it, staying together for the sake of the children?'

'Did she know?'

'I don't think so, but then they say women always know, so perhaps she did. Anyway, she never let on.'

There was a silence, then finally she turned away from him and it was her turn to cry.

'I didn't realise you felt that way. I shouldn't have led you on. I really wanted to help, Stephen. The physical thing came later. You were so bloody helpless, so alone. I couldn't just leave you. And then when you moved in, you made me so mad, but it was all an adventure. I've been a journalist for years but I've always destroyed, never created. And I thought I could save you and create something. Obviously I was wrong.'

383

She was finding it difficult to get the words out, her body heaving, and he put his arms around her, touching her breasts, but to soothe not to arouse. He kissed the back of her neck, trying to put the strength back in her, the strength that alone could lead him through, not just this night but all the nights that lay ahead before the sun finally rose. He felt the tension go from her, felt her relax against him, and then to his confusion found himself aroused, coming to life between her buttocks. Her breathing deepened and as soon as he was sure she was asleep, he moved his body an inch or two away, his arms still cradling her protectively. It took him a long time to fall asleep himself, but when he did it was deep, and for the first time since his arrest it was also dreamless.

Chapter Forty Two

He awoke to the sound of French being spoken. Trisha, wrapped in a soft towelling dressing gown, was thanking a waiter who managed to combine his delivery of breakfast trolley with a knowing glance at Stephen, which seemed to say: 'Congratulations. I wouldn't have minded myself.'

I didn't, Stephen answered back in thought. I didn't, and in a way I'm sorry. A couple of points for his sainthood if not for his self-esteem.

The waiter couldn't resist one last look at Trisha and a raising of the eyebrows before the door closed behind him.

'I think you've got a fan,' Stephen said.

'I think it's because I forgot to do up my dressing gown when I first opened the door. It's nice to know I can still excite somebody.' There was no malice in the comment and the smile she gave to Stephen showed there was no grudge.

'I'll do better next time. If there ever is a next time. I'm just so confused at the moment. I feel like Baldrick to your Black Adder. My kids recited Black Adder backwards. If they'd known their school work as well as they knew their scripts they'd have been out of university by now with first class honours. What time is it?'

'Just gone seven. I want to get down and talk to the night staff as well as the day people. You never know, we may get different answers. I didn't mean to wake you but I was famished. All that exercise makes a girl hungry.'

She poured herself a thimbleful of thick black coffee and tossed it back.

'My God, that's strong. I understand

385

why they give you such little cups. Do you want some?'

'Juice would be good. And a croissant.'

There was something decadent about the way she tore his croissant to pieces for him, buttering each morsel, then sat on the bed and fed him. She put her hand on his.

'Stephen, I admire you for last night. A lesser man would have taken what was on offer. I'd just had a bit too much to drink. There's one thing, though—if I had any doubts about your innocence, they're gone now. A man who won't steal a girl's jewels couldn't possibly steal his client's money.'

He ate the croissant carefully, not smacking his lips as he might have done at home, dabbing at his mouth delicately with a napkin. He still felt on his best behaviour, not knowing this woman, not knowing what might please or upset her. It was almost like being a teenager, the first couple of dates, the time and trouble in shaving, the use of deodorants—and then the gradual decline into familiarity and finally comfort.

Trisha pushed her plate away and moved over to her case. She fished out some clothes, underwear, jeans, shirt, jumper, looked at him for a moment, then shrugged and began to dress. He didn't know whether or not to look away, but as she talked to him while she pulled on her clothes he could scarcely ignore her. She squirmed into the panties, then tossed aside the dressing gown and stretched lazily, her breasts high and firm. She seemed to hesitate deliberately before putting on the shirt as if to say: 'There you are, they could have been yours. Maybe they will be again, maybe not.' Was he being moral or foolish? He didn't know. He just wanted all of this to be over, one way or another. If he was going to have to go to prison, then quite frankly the sooner they sent him away the sooner he'd be out.

She vanished into the bathroom and came out five minutes later, make-up applied and looking ready for the kill. He whistled and she made a face, pushed out her rear and blew him a kiss.

'If it's a man on the desk, you can't fail,' he said.

'And if it's a woman?' she asked.

'Invite her up to your room and hope she's gay. Do you want me to come with you?'

'I don't think so. You've got that defeated, hang dog look on your face this morning. I want somebody who would sell ice to the Eskimos.'

She closed the door behind her feeling considerably less confident than she had appeared to Stephen. A foreign country,

387

a foreign language, a wing and a prayer. She took the lift, enjoying the wait, feeling pleased at each halt on each floor, the condemned woman taking faltering steps towards the gallows.

The door opened and, taking a deep breath, she walked towards the reception desk. A woman. And then in the background she saw a man. A couple came to check in and the woman was occupied. It was now or never and Trisha moved with all the sexual power she had into the man's line of vision. 'Please, please, let him be a healthy heterosexual!'

'Vous parlez Anglais?' Why extend her efforts if she didn't have to?

'Oui, mademoiselle, très bien. Can I help you?'

She spoke slowly and deliberately, a fragile woman for once in her life, looking for a firm male shoulder to lean upon.

'I'm terribly sorry to trouble you. It's just that I'm here with my business partner. Now he stayed here some months ago, and we've got a little bit of a problem with the Revenue. You know what the tax man is like...'

'Of course.'

She had him, she knew that. In that 'of course' was every Frenchman's sympathy with everybody who had a problem with the tax man. And if that somebody was a pretty girl with red hair who fluttered her eyelashes at him then he would walk barefoot across broken glass to help her.

'Well...' She took a deep breath, blinked a few tears into her eyes and saw him lean forward, smelt the slight mixture of garlic and tobacco smoke that clung to so many Frenchman—and felt his hand touch hers.

'...you see we've claimed tax relief on a trip my partner took, and the tax man says it was pleasure, and we've lost the hotel receipt and he says that if we do not produce evidence he'll turn over our whole history, he'll bankrupt us, maybe even put us in jail!'

She didn't know quite how much he understood of what she was saying, but he clearly got the message from the words 'bankrupt' and 'jail'.

'So what is it you need, mademoiselle?'

'I need a duplicate of the receipt. Do you keep them that far back?' She gave him the exact date.

'Why, yes, I think so. Our own evil tax men demand we keep things. Just wait here and I will print it out for you. And perhaps you may allow me to buy you a drink this evening which, as it happens, I have free?'

She gave him a smile that could have meant anything from 'Why bother with a drink when we can go straight to bed?' to 'Thanks for the offer but I'd rather watch *Neighbours.*'

He disappeared into a room at the back and she idly read the framed certificates behind the desk. Touring club awards for the past five years, entries in good food guides she'd never heard of, and then a fire certificate. Well, that was good, at least they'd heard of the things here. The name on the certificate caught her eye. Not the name of the hotel, but the name of a company. Obviously that was the way things happened here. She supposed it was for the insurance.

Dunkelheit S.A. It was oddly familiar. Not because it was a hotel chain that was known to her, but because she had seen the name before, out of context. She scribbled it down again on a piece of paper, and folded it neatly into her bag.

The receptionist, whose badge said his name was Michel, returned looking puzzled and forlorn.

'Mademoiselle, we have a problem. I am desolate. Our computer, it prints out the day before your partner's stay, it prints the day after, but the day itself is, how do you say, eliminated?'

'Wiped.'

'Ah yes, wiped clean from our records. It is impossible but it has happened. I have spoken however with our accounts manager. He is always willing to help in circumstances like this. If you tell us details of the stay he will manually prepare another invoice. That will help, yes?' He smiled happily, a puppy returning a bone and waiting for a pat.

'Oh, yes, it'll help me,' she said unenthusiastically. Michel looked perplexed.

'It is not enough. If there is anything else...'

'No, no, it's fine. You've been very kind.'

'It is my pleasure. I will see you later.'

'Yes, later,' she said abstractedly. Later, they would leave; later, there was nothing to keep them here. She felt stupid. A wild goose chase down yet another blind alley. What had she expected to find? A neat little envelope which read: 'Who dunnit? Look inside.' And then there had been last night. She wasn't given to throwing herself at men, rather repulsing their advances; and when she threw herself she didn't expect to be thrown back. Married men—they were the worst, the liars and the purists, as bad as each other. She just hoped she hadn't fouled up another relationship. There were too many failures in her life for her to cope with one more.

As she rode the lift back up she thought of Stephen as he had been when she'd first seen him in professional action. Casually, but immaculately dressed in a smart Italian suit and floral silk tie, monogrammed shirt, shoes highly polished, brightly coloured socks adding a touch of eccentricity. He'd looked as if he could conquer the world, and now, if she was honest with herself, she'd wanted him to conquer her as well. To play Hannibal, to lift her up high on the back of an elephant and rampage across the Alps doing with her whatever he wanted. Every aspect of women's lib was abandoned as the juices ran between her legs and she hated herself, worse still despised herself for it. Love and hate, the twin faces of Janus' mask, and she finding it more and more difficult to tell which face was turned towards her at any given time.

The Stephen who opened the door did not look as if he would conquer any worlds, nor indeed even live in one for very much longer. The stubble on his face didn't help, but that itself could not hide the yellowish colour of his skin, the dark half moons beneath his eyes, the shaking hands with which he held a glass of whisky.

'Well, what did you get?'

She tried to make the best of it.

'Quite a lot insofar as I got nothing; but that in itself is something. Only one day's printout from the computer in the last decade seems to be missing—and that was the night you spent here. Why should that be, Stephen? And more than that, how did it come to happen? Computers don't wipe themselves, they're not toilet trained as far as I'm aware...'

He was not impressed.

'Nice try, Trisha, but I've delivered enough bad news in my time to know when I'm being told of a disaster.'

She paused, remembering the piece of paper in her bag.

'There is one other thing. The company that owns this hotel. Here, I've written it down.'

She showed Stephen the name and his lawyer's brain clicked into action.

'I've seen that name before.'

'That's what I thought.'

He closed his eyes, using all the memory tricks he'd perfected in his years of practice. He couldn't explain them to anybody but they worked. Case names, statute sections, specific clauses...they could all be conjured up by images. He never forgot names, but then he was convinced nobody forgot anything; it was all there in the recesses of your mind. The mind itself was a computer, but one that could not be wiped. All that was needed was a code word. It was not long ago. He was on his own. He was standing in a half-lit hallway. Trisha was there, but not there. She was inside a room. And then he had it! He knew where he had seen the name before. It had struck a chord then, and it struck a chord now. An odd name for a company—Dunkelheit—darkness. It was one of the companies shown on the plaque as being managed from the office of Jarvis Walters. Perhaps it had not been a wasted trip after all.

Chapter Forty Three

The journey home seemed slow. Stephen had shaved and spruced himself up, all the while thinking as he stared at his face in the mirror: Why Jarvis Walters? He'd done nothing to harm the man, nor had Jarvis ever seemed to be short of money; but then Stephen was not really interested in motives, only guilt. He just wanted to lift the guilt from his own shoulders and place the burden firmly on somebody else. He wanted to change his name from Atlas by deed poll.

As the plane landed he felt a sudden onslaught of nerves, the morning-of-examination feeling when you know you have not done enough revision; but the immigration officer just gave them both a bored look and nodded them through, whilst Customs seemed far more interested in a giant young Rastafarian whose huge carpet bag had been emptied and was now having its contents dissected.

'I'd like to go to the hospital first, if that's all right with you?'

'Of course. I'll go straight home if you don't mind. I've actually got a living of sorts to earn and if I don't knock out a couple of articles tonight then that's next month's mortgage down the tubes.'

She dropped him off in Hampstead and he walked slowly towards the huge block of buildings that was the Royal Free. They'd kissed goodbye so perfunctorily that the casual observer would have taken them for an old married couple, and indeed, without her, Stephen felt strangely alone. He'd become very dependent upon her over the past few weeks, more dependent than he could ever have believed possible.

In the office he'd relied on his secretary to fend off phone calls, to organise his diary, to make the coffee, but all the decisions had been his. Throughout the practice the decisions had been his. If he wanted something to go through at a partners' meeting then, while he would seemingly listen politely to what everybody else had to say, at the end of the day matters seldom went to a vote.

It had been the same at home. If Cathy wanted to do something that didn't interest him he would make life so difficult that any temptation she might have to repeat the experiment would soon be eliminated. He must have been unpleasant to live with at times. If this nightmare ever ended he vowed to himself it would all be different. If she wanted to go to art galleries or concerts he'd be there by her side, fully dressed in fascinated smiles. He'd give such a good impression of enjoying himself he'd qualify for an academy award; her pleasure would be his pleasure. He was tired, he just wanted to go home.

He hoped his mother would be alone but she wasn't. His brother and sister-in-law were fussing about her, the girl combing the old woman's hair with no visible sign of pleasure, his brother reading the consultant's notes pinned to the end of the bed. Anthony looked up, his expression Buddha-like behind the glasses.

'Oh, I thought you'd forgotten that you had a mother,' he said. His wife gave her mother-in-law's hair a final, testy brush, oblivious to any pain that might have been caused as the teeth caught in the thinning curls.

'You've never had any sense of responsibility, Stephen. If it's nothing to do with your horse or your business, you're not interested.'

He felt too tired to argue. She'd never been his favourite person and she had hardly moved up his hit parade this evening.

'Who can be as devoted as you?'

'We've not seen Cathy here either, have we?' she replied, rising to the challenge. 'Maybe she doesn't want to take the risk of running into you either. I gather everybody watches their purses when you're about.'

He ignored her and leaned over to kiss his mother. She looked surprisingly peaceful lying there, her hair neatly washed and combed, her skin freshly powdered.

'I like the make-up Mum.'

'The nurses,' she said, her hands making a feeble sweeping gesture, 'they like to make me look pretty. They say if I look better, I'll feel better.'

Her voice was stronger than when he'd last seen her and he felt an enormous surge of relief. If anything had happened to her whilst he'd been out of the country, he didn't feel he could have lived with himself.

There were moments when he didn't feel he could live anyway, but having imposed the shame of his arrest on his mother he didn't think he could also burden her with his suicide. At the end of the day it took no courage to end it all; the courage lay in the fight.

Anthony shifted uneasily from foot to foot, anxious to be gone now that there was any chance of conflict, but Stephen no longer had anything to lose. He was hitting out in a darkened room with one arm tied behind his back. If a blow struck a target, then so be it.

'Anthony, have you spoken to Jarvis Walters lately?'

He positively squirmed, his eyebrows twitching so badly they virtually met in the middle.

'Stephen, you never did have any taste, did you? Mum's lying here and you're talking about Jarvis.'

'I didn't know he and my mum were friends.'

Anthony virtually pulled his wife towards the door.

'That's enough. I don't have to stay to listen to this.'

Stephen put his hand firmly on his brother's shoulder. 'What is it with you? All I did was ask a simple question.'

Anthony shrugged his hand away.

'You really don't know?'

'Know what?'

'That Jarvis Walters committed suicide two days ago.'

Chapter Forty Four

He couldn't remember travelling back to Trisha's flat. He had stumbled like a drunk from the hospital, drunk not on alcohol but fear. Death was a new player in the game, and with its entry the game itself was over. Yet none of the participants could leave the table. Their pockets were emptied, arms chained to their chairs, the stakes raised without a by your leave. Nicole La Roche had died, but that was natural. There was nothing natural about suicide. He realised that now more than ever.

'You look like you need a drink. Is it your mother?' Trisha greeted him with a kiss on the cheek that had all the familiarity of long-term domesticity.

'No, it's not my mother, and yes, I do need a drink.' She poured him a generous Jack Daniels and he drank it quickly, welcoming the burning liquid into his stomach.

'Another?'

He nodded.

'What is it?' she asked as she poured.

'Walters. He's dead. I saw Anthony at the hospital. He said it was suicide.'

'But?'

'But nothing. Why should a successful man like Walters kill himself? And if he didn't, then I'm even more scared. Up to now it's just been about money and my liberty. Now, all of a sudden, it's much more than that.'

'I think maybe I'll join you in that drink.' She sat down beside him and took his hand.

'You're cold.'

'I'm frozen. It's as if summer never came.'

'Look, let me call one of my tame papers. When did this happen? They'll check on the news desk and can fax me through anything that's appeared.'

'Anthony said it was a couple of days ago.'

She made her calls and they waited in a silence broken only by the refilling of glasses. Finally the fax machine beeped into action and Trisha moved across to pull the sheets from the machine as they came through.

She stood reading them and Stephen couldn't contain his impatience.

'What is it, Trish?'

'I don't know, Stephen. It doesn't sound right. Listen: "Jersey financial adviser and accountant Jarvis Walters was yesterday found hanged in his office in St Helier.

Walters, aged forty-six, was a well-known figure on the island. Police said he appeared to have been drinking heavily and they are not seeking to interview anybody else in connection with the incident. Walters leaves a wife and two teenage children,"'

'What's not right?'

'Well, you remember when I went to see him?'

'How can I forget?'

'After I'd laid into him he actually became more hospitable. And then he apologised.'

'For what?'

'For not being able to offer me a drink. He said he'd given it up ten years ago and not touched a drop since.'

'I think you're fantasising, Trisha. If he drank ten years ago maybe something happened that made him slip off the wagon. He got to drinking, saw no way out, and called it a day. Whichever way you look at it, suicide or murder, it doesn't make my day. If he did kill himself something must have happened to make him desperate. If he didn't then it must have been desperate people who took him out.'

She took another drink.

'It's good this stuff, isn't it? I've usually only kept it for visitors. I think maybe I'll

401

put in a regular order, it does wonders for clearing the brain.

'What if Jarvis knew we were at the hotel? What if we were closer to something than we realised? He panics. Whoever it is he runs to goes to meet him. They have a drink. Jarvis drinks some more. There's nothing as dangerous as a reformed alcoholic. His drinking companion maybe didn't even plan to kill him but it's a decision taken on the spur of the moment. He stages the suicide with a man who's half drunk, and another loophole's closed.'

'You missed your vocation, Trish. You should have been a detective.'

'All good journalists have a detective streak in them. And anyway, when I was a little girl I wanted to join the police force. I think it was all that reading of *Wonder Woman* comics. I figured it was the best way of righting wrongs while wearing a sexy uniform. Look, Stephen, I know we've just got back but something tells me we ought to travel again.'

She saw the look of horror on his face.

'Don't worry, day trip only. No passports. The sea air did you so much good that it's back to Jersey. I think perhaps we should pay our respects to a grieving widow.'

'When?'

'Tomorrow's as good a day as any. At

the moment you're out of checking into the police station.'

'Why not?' He felt her close to him, felt the warmth of her thigh against his and knew at that precise moment that he was close to throwing all of his good intentions aside and leaping upon her. Then, as if she could read his mind, she moved away abruptly, kissed him gently on the forehead and was off towards her bedroom.

'Early start tomorrow. Early night to-night. I don't think we'll have a problem with the flight tickets but we'll have to get to the airport a bit before.'

The door closed behind her. The intimacy of the hotel was clearly not to be repeated and a part of him was grateful, a part filled with regret. He went to the bathroom and undressed, imagining Trisha taking off her clothes, conjuring up her body as it had been revealed to him. He lay for a long while seeking sleep, but every sound made him jump and the sofa bed seemed hard after the comfort of the French hotel. Time was meaningless. How long since they'd visited Jersey? How long since he'd last slept with his wife? Since he'd not had a care in the world...when his biggest problem had been which restaurant to choose to visit...? He drifted in and out of sleep with strange female visitors by his side. His wife's face superimposed on Trisha's body, his wife's voice saying no, as a naked Trisha sat, like a siren on the rocks, beckoning him forward... Ordinary household noises sounded odd and amplified, creaking floorboards, a tap dripping, the sound of a footstep.

There was something wrong about the footstep. He needed to sleep, needed to claw his way back to that sweet void that would refresh him, but his mind still picked out what was wrong. The footstep was inside the room. He forced open his eyes and knew at once that the man bent over Trisha's papers wasn't part of his dream, the man was solid flesh.

Even in the dark he could see that the figure was dressed completely in black, the face hooded, the hands black-gloved. An absurd thought crossed Stephen's mind. Maybe he'd just come to deliver a box of Cadbury's Milk Tray. But it was not a joke he was about to share. He didn't wait to call out, that would bring Trisha running into danger. For all he knew the intruder could be armed. Jarvis Walters had met his maker dangling at the end of a rope.

Without thinking Stephen launched himself at the figure, and in what was probably the first rugby tackle of his life brought him crashing to the ground. The man was bigger than he'd expected, and although Stephen had had surprise on his side he realised immediately he'd not done enough damage. The man lashed out at him and he took an elbow on the side of his face. He'd not experienced pain since he'd been at school, and as Cathy had often teased him, his threshold was such that he needed an injection before he had an injection. Yet the pain made him mad and recklessly he crashed his forehead into the man's face. He heard the splintering of bone and felt a cascade of blood, unaware whether it was from his own skull or the intruder's nose. The man let out a scream of pain and the noise brought Trisha stumbling from her room, holding a table lamp with deadly intent.

The man, holding his nose with one hand, saw her coming, pushed Stephen away with his other arm and made for the door. Trisha began to follow after him but Stephen held her back.

'Let him go. We don't want you up on a manslaughter charge.'

She switched on the light.

'Trust you to play the lawyer at the wrong bloody time! Look at the mess the bastard's made of my carpet. And look at what the pair of you have done to my room. Next time I'm choosing a tidier lodger.'

She saw him holding his cheek and gently removed his hand.

'Impressive. It's come up nicely already. It should look quite tasty by tomorrow. It'll scare the hell out of Mrs Walters.'

She took some ice from the fridge and made a pack to hold against the swelling. Somewhere in the distance he heard a train. A solitary car slid by in the street below, someone returning home from a club, a late shift, perhaps a robbery. The sounds of the night formed their own picture. It was three a.m.

Stephen began to laugh to himself quietly but without hysteria.

'What is it, Stephen, what's so funny?'

His laughter grew, like that of a man watching an escalating farce.

'Stephen, pull yourself together!'

'It's all right, Trisha. It's just the lengths they're prepared to go to. First me, then Walters. A robbery, assault. You know, I think we've really got them worried.'

And then she too began to laugh, her head shaking from side to side, until finally she burrowed down beside him and, holding each other tight, they fell asleep until it was time to leave for the airport.

Chapter Forty Five

Marion Walters must have been very pretty once, but now as she opened the door to them, eyes red from weeping, without make up, wearing a simple black sweater and skirt, she looked what she was: a woman in mourning. A girl of about ten clung to her arm, her face pinched and pale, a wordless picture from a Dickensian novel.

'Look, I don't know who you are, but I've nothing more to say. I've told the police everything.'

It wasn't the moment for Trisha to tell her she was a journalist but Stephen had to admit that she carried the introduction off magnificently.

'We're not here to ask questions, Mrs Walters. We're here to try and find you some answers. Stephen here knew your husband.'

'I met you once as well, when I first visited the island. Don't you remember?' he interjected. Marion Walters clearly did not remember and Trisha took up the conversation again.

'I met your husband just a couple of

weeks ago. We don't think his death was as simple as the police would have us believe. Now, can we come in? We've come all the way from London just to see you.'

Trisha looked her straight in the face, woman to woman, both of them born to suffer, her expression said, and as the message got home, Marion Walters stood aside and ushered them in. The small girl still held tightly to her mother as if to say she had only lost her father because she let him out of her sight.

An older boy was slumped in an armchair, the TV on but his eyes looking beyond the programme into a world where he still had both parents.

Mrs Walters flung out her arm.

'Excuse the mess. Since Jarvis—died—' she had obvious difficulty with the word, '...since then we've found it difficult to get ourselves organised. I don't know what we're going to do. The insurers say they won't pay if Jarvis...if he did what they say he did.' Her voice dropped to a whisper in a vain attempt to conceal the ghastly words from her children.

'Maybe I can help. I'm a solicitor, after all.'

She looked at him, not unkindly.

'Yes, I know who you are now. The police asked lots of questions about you as well. I probably shouldn't even be talking to you, but quite frankly I don't care any more. I'd talk to the devil himself if I thought it would bring my husband back, or even just clear his name.' She started to cry, then remembering the child at her side, noticeably got a grip on herself.

'Carrie,' she said, addressing the girl, 'do you want to make yourself really useful?' She took the girl's silence for acquiescence. 'Just go into the kitchen, put the kettle on and get some cups out for coffee. And pour yourself a Coke and one for Ian as well.'

The girl reluctantly disengaged herself from her mother and slowly moved towards the kitchen, with several backward glances to satisfy herself this was not a ruse to enable her mother to make a bolt for the door.

Marion sighed.

'I'm so sorry, Miss...'

'Call me Trisha.'

The woman gratefully homed in on the familiarity, hugging the newfound friendship to her.

'Trisha. Yes. It's been just awful. Nobody seems to want to know us. It's as if we've been stricken with the plague. There's been one death already, and they're just waiting for the rest of us. Then maybe they'll all come to the funeral. People we've known for years. Yes, they phoned once, but after that it's been a wall of silence. It's the silence that's the worst, not having anybody to talk to. I can't say too much to the children. You can see what the little one's like, and Ian has hardly been out of the house since this happened. He just sits like a zombie in front of the television, I don't think he even knows what he's watching. It's as if the noise is just there as background to his trance.'

'I've got a son like that as well,' Stephen said, and for the first time since their arrival Marion smiled.

'If I wanted to be unkind to Ian I'd say he was like that when his father was here, but he wasn't. He was always up to something, tennis, cricket, football. Not one for schoolwork is Ian but show him anything with a ball and he's happy as a sandboy. Happy.' She tested the word with the curiosity of a wine expert sampling a fresh bouquet.

'I don't think we'll ever be happy again.'

'What are you going to do?' Trisha asked.

'I'm not sure. I need to get off this wretched island. There's nowhere to hide here, and we just need to be somewhere where nobody knows us. Where nobody knew Jarvis. Somewhere where there are no questions to be asked. But until I can get some money together...I don't even know if I can sell this house, or how much Jarvis owed on it, or even what other money he had. Before we got married I taught dance. I knew that if I had more than eight people in my class then the hall was paid for, and with another six I'd covered the pianist's fee. After that it was all profit. That was the extent of my business knowledge. Jarvis dealt with everything: the post, the cheques, the banks. He had it all on his wretched computers. I'm not even sure how to turn them on.'

Trisha and Stephen exchanged glances.

'Where are the computers?'

'At his office, but he also kept duplicates here. He said something about never relying on back-ups. He was a very careful man. He'd learned lessons the hard way. About ten years ago he was drinking heavily. He said he had pressures that I wouldn't understand. Then he had the courage to go to Alcoholics Anonymous. For a man like him it was the ultimate embarrassment, but although he never told me names there were quite a few other people on this island, people more famous and far richer than Jarvis who had the same problem. He kept at it, and gradually he became the man I'd married until...'

'Until?' Trisha could not stop being the journalist. She had a willing subject, and she knew it. All she needed was to probe at it.

'About a couple of months ago, he changed. He wasn't drinking, I'm sure of that. That's why I can't believe the story about his death...but he was different. He started staying away nights, visiting the mainland more often. When he was home he'd have no time for the children, pick faults with them. He'd never shout at the kids. He spoiled them terribly, particularly Carrie, but they couldn't do right by him. If they said black he'd say white. If they wanted to watch something on TV he'd turn over—and he wasn't a TV person. We'd talk in the evenings or he'd play on his bloody computers, but television was a waste of time to him. Now we won't have any more time. There was so much to say, things left unsaid. I can't believe he'd have left the kids like that, knowing they'd remember him for the arguments and not for the love.'

Stephen covered her hand with his own. 'Marion, let me be honest with you. I think you've had enough mystery and lies in your life. I really *do* want to help you and if I can get you out of this mess, believe me I will. But I also need to help myself. I don't know why your husband died any more than you do, but I'm sure it had something to do with me. I'm sorry if

412

that hurts, but knowing me at the moment seems to be a dangerous occupation.'

'You don't look a dangerous man,' she said, smiling wistfully, a smile that took years off her age and gave him a glimpse of the young dancer who'd stepped out so optimistically with Jarvis Walters not so many years ago.

'What do you want me to do?' Marion asked. 'If I can help you and you can help me, that strikes me as a bargain.'

'Just give us the run of your husband's records. Neither of us are computer experts, but Trisha here knows her way around word processors and there must be some books around that tell us which button to press and in which order.'

Marion Walters didn't hesitate.

'It's all in the cellar. It's quiet and cool down there. Take as long as you like. I'll bring you some lunch down.'

'Please don't bother,' Trisha said kindly, her hand on the other woman's arm, bonding with her.

'It's no bother. I'm glad of something to do, glad of the company. I understand how people who live on islands go rock crazy.'

She led them down the stairs into a large square room and as she flicked on the light it looked for a moment as if they were in the command centre of a

413

spaceship. Everywhere there seemed to be electronic equipment, screens, printers, racks of computer hardware, a lifetime of memory.

Stephen let out a whistle of amazement. 'Where do we start?'

Marion nodded in the direction of a large screen.

'That was where he always seemed to be working. Over there on the left is the filing system. I think it's coded so you'll have a hard time finding anything.'

'Did the police come down here?'

Marion shook her head.

'I didn't tell them about it. They spent hours at his office. I just couldn't face the thought of them trampling about here. Nobody was suggesting that Jarvis had done anything criminal so they seemed quite happy to leave me alone and just close the file on another suicide. I'll leave you to it. Good luck.'

She left the room, a sad figure, dignified in her mourning.

Stephen looked at his watch.

'It's nearly noon. We need to be away by four to get the plane.'

'Let's start then,' Trisha said. 'Needles and haystacks have always been such fun.'

They fed disc after disc into the main computer, at first methodically then at random. Information sped through the

414

machine, unknown companies, unknown faces behind them.

'We've probably got enough here to blackmail half of the United Kingdom if we only understood the code words,' Trisha commented.

At two o'clock, Marion brought them some food, smoked salmon, rolls, a salad, but as the clock ticked inexorably on, by three it was still untouched. Stephen loosened his collar, feeling claustrophobic in the windowless room, the air conditioning keeping it cool but airless.

'I feel like a cross between a bomb disposal officer and Gary Cooper in *High Noon*. There's something here, I know it, but where?'

Trisha pulled out drawer after drawer of the filing cabinet. Tucked at the back of the first drawer, lying flat under a whole series of files, was an envelope. It was addressed to Jarvis Walters, and as she flipped through the glossy photographs it contained it occurred to her that perhaps this was what had pushed him over the edge. The Jarvis Walters in the photographs was a far cry from the efficient businessman she'd seen on her last visit to the island. Naked, he seemed much younger, more vulnerable, curiously more innocent despite what was being done to him by a woman and what he was doing to another. He could not have been aware of the photographer so intent was he on his task.

'The game widens. Death *and* blackmail,' Trisha commented.

'Or was it blackmail and death?' Stephen murmured.

Trisha continued her search then paused. 'Stephen, come here. Come here quickly!'

He tore himself away from the corporation on the screen that began in Jersey and ended in Liechtenstein, trading its way through Ireland and Gibraltar on its journey. Jarvis Walters had the sort of mind that must have made it difficult for him to go into the kitchen without passing through the bedroom.

He peered into the drawer and there under 'R' saw a file that made him go cold, too cold even to feel the man walking across his grave. The file had just one word on it, 'Rabbi', the same code word Arthur had used to block off the practice computer. Trisha flipped the file open. It was empty save for one piece of paper with a reference number: CP 3742/001.

'Great, that makes perfect sense,' Stephen said in despair. 'All we have to do is to find a disc with that number—always provided he doesn't have some reverse code from file to disc.'

He moved back to the screen, and

made to clear it when he saw the number—100/2473PC. He shook his head in disbelief. After all the bad luck he'd suffered these past few weeks he needed a break but he hadn't truly believed he'd ever get it.

He moved the computer past the on-screen information but all that came on screen was 'Enter password'. He typed in 'Rabbi', held his breath, and then the information began to flow through. Trisha and Stephen watched mesmerised and after two minutes began to realise the enormity of the web that was being spun around him.

'Let me call Charlie,' Trisha pleaded, 'he'll know what to do.'

'Yes, he'll probably dump all this information in the sea just to make sure I'm banged away and he can move back in with you!'

'He's not like that.'

'They're all like that, Trisha. All coppers are bent. You learn that when you spend any length of time around them. We're going to do this my way. I've let other people direct my life for too long. Now come on, let's get that plane. I've things to do and people to see back in London.'

'What about the photographs?'

Stephen paused, thought of Marion Walters, thought of her children.

'Some mysteries are best left unsolved. We take them with us.'

Marion saw them to the door.

'Did you find anything?'

'I think so. I think at the end of the day it's going to help us all.' And as she kissed him gratefully on the cheek Stephen knew that his decision regarding the photographs was absolutely right.

Chapter Forty Six

Stephen should have felt tired when he got back to the flat but he was travelling on automatic. There was too much to be done to sleep. He was on his own personal high, no amphetamines, no cocaine, just the gradual discovery of the truth.

Trisha put on the kettle and played back the answerphone.

'Trisha, it's Charlie. I'm sorry. Please give me a ring. I've something to tell you that may help your friend.'

'There, you see, I said he wasn't all bad.'

Stephen was not impressed.

'What's he going to tell you? To tell me to plead guilty and reduce my sentence? I told you, they're all liars. Bigger liars even than lawyers.'

Dead on cue, another voice came on to the tape.

'Stephen, it's Jeffrey. Give me a ring. Not at the office. Call me on my mobile between seven and eight. We've got to talk.'

Stephen looked at his watch. It was a quarter to eight. He flipped through his book to find Jeffrey's number then dialled it through as Trisha stood by anxiously.

'I still think you should let me ring Charlie before you call Jeffrey. I know which one I'd rather have on my side.'

Stephen felt a painful dart of jealousy whenever she mentioned the policeman's name.

'The Vodaphone subscriber does not answer. Please try again later.'

He hated that message, had hated it when he'd been at work in his prime. It meant that somebody wasn't where they'd promised to be, it meant that they were there but they weren't receiving, it meant they'd switched off their mobile because they didn't want to receive calls. That bland message in cold impersonal tones meant so many things.

He looked at Trisha, saw the expression on her face and knew what she was about to say.

'All right, try Charlie.'

She did, but he was off duty. She rang

419

his home and again it annoyed Stephen that he felt any emotion at the fact she knew the number off by heart. There was no reply there either.

'Too mean to install an answerphone, is he?'

Trisha blushed. Charlie had always said that if people left you messages you had to call them back and pay for the call. She'd never been too sure whether or not he was joking.

Stephen almost grabbed the phone from her hand and tried Jeffrey's mobile again. This time it rang out and Stephen imagined him in his car, travelling home after a day at the office, a day spent with familiar staff, familiar clients, familiar problems. He felt an enormous wave of nostalgia sweep over him, a man watching a Movietone News of his youth. He wanted to be back there, back even further than that, to the days of their schoolboy innocence. Stephen, Jeffrey, Cathy, joined by unknown girls on Jeffrey's arm who drifted in and out of fours. All of them forgettable, even the wives, chosen for one purpose only: the ease with which he could get them into bed. Yet, for the most part, they knew that before they got involved with Jeffrey, for his reputation preceded him, a choirboy with a machine gun, an angel with a pitchfork in place of a harp.

It was odd how he'd pushed Jeffrey and the practice to the back of his mind. Their behaviour had been logical, it was he who'd committed all the crimes, but now regret set in as he knew that whatever else might happen in his life, the clock could never be turned back.

'Hello.'

It had been so long since he'd heard Jeffrey's voice, that last brutal day in the office when he'd gone to collect his belongings, that it sounded like a stranger's. But then it was different: no longer friendly and confident, but scared, querulous, unsure whether or not to assume a false identity.

'Jeffrey, it's me, Stephen.'

'How are you?'

'I've been better.'

'We need to talk.' The tone of Jeffrey's voice said it all.

'When?'

'Tomorrow morning. Before work. I'll meet you in the car park. Not our usual floor. On the roof deck. Say eight o'clock.'

'Very MI5 all this Jeffrey.'

'Don't joke, Stephen. It's not a joking matter. There's no laughs in this any more for any of us.'

'Was there ever?' Stephen asked, but Jeffrey had already gone.

'Well?' Trisha asked.

421

'I'm seeing him in the morning. He sounds scared.'

'Are you?'

He hesitated.

'I'm not sure. I ought to be, but I don't think I am. When all this first happened, when I was arrested, I thought I couldn't live with it. I couldn't sleep, and the more tired I got the more impossible it became to cope. Then one night I slept through. Everything suddenly became part of my normal life. I guess if you're put in chains for twenty years, the last nineteen don't count. It's the twenty-first, when they free you, that's the problem.'

He stretched out on the couch, his legs aching. He must have dozed because the ring at the doorbell brought him back to the world with a start.

'I'll go,' he said, rising so quickly that his head swam, he nearly fell down the stairs and opened the door without using the intercom. The two men standing there were large—so large that they might have had difficulty getting through the door together, and certainly one of them could not have got in without bending his head. The larger one, broken nosed, patchy eyebrows, scarred cheek, could have been none other than an ex-boxer, although by the look of him his licence should have been withdrawn a long time ago.

'Stephen Kennard?' he asked.

'Who's asking?'

'I am, and I reckon you're him. We're here to recover a car. No payments on the lease, so no little automobile for naughty boys.'

Stephen swore softly. The car had been the only thing he'd kept from the practice and despite all the recent requests to return it, he'd refused to give it up. He'd banked on his ex-partners not being mean enough to take any action on recovery and he'd been right—until now. It had actually been his idea to put all their cars on lease. It helped the cash flow and it still meant they could indirectly buy them back from the leasing company at a reduced price when the time was right. What had obviously happened was the practice had just stopped paying the lease instalments on his, ignored the letters, and now these two thugs were being sent to collect. Yes, the partners had a clean conscience.

'Look, this is all a mistake. How much is owed?'

'You know as well as we do. You've had all the letters.'

'I've had nothing.'

'That's what they all say.'

'Just tell me what the arrears are and I'll pay.' He still had the money from his winnings in cash.

The smaller of the two smiled, revealing teeth that had obviously had only passing acquaintance with a dentist.

'They all say that as well,' he added. 'If you think you're hard done by, contact the company, and then if you pay up like a good boy they'll let you have your toy back to play with. Now Billy here, he gets a bit impatient when he's kept waiting, and when he's impatient he shows it a bit. Show him, Billy.'

Billy clenched his fist into a massive ham and smashed it straight through the glass at the side of the front door. It all happened so quickly, so professionally, that he was able to withdraw his hand neatly without even a scratch.

'He's always sorry afterwards, our Billy, really regretful, but when you can't help yourself it's often too late.'

Stephen decided not to argue. It was probably not a sensible thing to offer these two heavies cash, and he'd contact the company himself in the morning. It would all be a minor inconvenience. He couldn't even report the broken window to the police when he shouldn't have had the car in the first place. He felt in his pocket for the keys.

'Just let me get a box from upstairs so I can empty my personal stuff out of the car.'

'Sure,' grunted the man called Billy. 'Why not? We're not thieves.'

Trisha was at the door when he got back.

'I was just coming down. What on earth was that about?'

'Better you don't know. I'll explain later. For the moment I just need a box.'

'To fill or bury yourself in?'

'Just a box, Trisha, not the jokes.'

'In the kitchen, under the sink. Stephen, just tell me what's happening?'

'When I get back.'

He took the stairs two at a time and reached the street just in time to see his car screech into a left turn at the T-junction and vanish from sight.

'Not thieves, eh?'

Trisha was behind him now, looking at the debris of broken glass. He told her what had happened.

'Stephen, you've got to tell Charlie. It's obviously a matter for the police. It's one thing repossessing a car, it's another threatening you, breaking personal property, stealing your belongings.'

'It doesn't matter. I didn't have a lot in there. A few maps, some tapes, an old pair of shoes, an umbrella. It's my own fault. I should have taken the car back. I'll sort it out tomorrow. Let's get to sleep. I've got to get up early for work.'

It was only later, lying in bed, brain working overtime with sleep refusing to come, that he realised that he'd neither asked for, nor been offered, any form of identification by the two men.

Chapter Forty Seven

It was odd getting up to go to work again. He showered carefully and even put on a suit and tie, taking ages to select the right combination.

'Are you sure you're meeting Jeffrey and not some floozy?' Trisha asked. He smiled nervously. 'Where's my packed lunch?'

'I didn't...'

It was her turn to smile, but then it faded quickly as she imagined a thousand lunches Cathy must have made for her husband, a thousand breakfasts together, a thousand goodbye kisses. They had nothing like that, the two of them; all that held them together was a mutual sense of danger, and when the fear was removed what would be left?

Stephen was tempted to take the tube but in the old days he'd never been able to face travelling in the rush hour on packed trains and he didn't feel able to start now.

He hailed a cab and, giving his destination, sank back on the seat.

'Nice day, Guv,' the driver said, pushing aside the glass partition that separated him from his passenger.

Stephen groaned. It was a nice day. Summer had come very late but it had come with a vengeance and now people walked about in short sleeves even at that time of the morning. Plain girls looked pretty in their flimsy dresses, making male heads turn that in winter would stoically have ignored them. But he didn't need a talkative taxi driver this morning. He just wanted to be left alone to his thoughts.

'No car this morning?' the driver asked chattily.

'No. Not this morning.'

'Wife took it, did she?'

'No. It just got taken.'

'What line of business you in, then?'

'I used to be a solicitor.'

'Retired, are you?'

'Sort of—but about to make a come-back.'

'I wouldn't mind retiring myself. I've been doing this job for forty years. Plays havoc with your piles. Not like it was when I first started. Used to be a bit of courtesy on the roads then. People let buses pull out, gave signals, nobody in too much of a hurry.'

Stephen was about to point out that he couldn't recall any taxi driver he'd known ever giving a signal or letting a car out unless the only alternative was a major collision, but that would only have encouraged the man to continue with his conversation.

'Yeah, it's speed what kills. What sort of lawyer were you? Had a judge in my cab the other day. Told him I thought they ought to bring back hanging. He didn't object. What sort of lawyer did you say you were?'

'I didn't.'

A good one, a competent one, an honest one—at least, as honest as the breed went. He didn't always tell the truth, but he didn't lie either. Silence was as much a weapon as speech. You took your clients to the brink but when they jumped you stayed at the edge of the chasm, looking down, throwing them a line, and all the time charging for the privilege. Days rushing by as the hour glass turned first this way, then that, watching the sand pile up, watching the money grow. Although a part of him longed to get back, another part of him believed he could never do the job properly again. He could see through walls, see through people and all he saw was dirt and decay. He wanted to take the time to smell the roses, to watch the girls in their pretty summer dresses.

'I used a solicitor for my divorce. Knew how to charge he did, but he didn't do a bad job. The old woman left me after thirty years, can you believe it? Took herself a toy boy. The solicitor got more out of it than she did, but I didn't begrudge him. He earned it, making her life a misery. The other fellow's moved on. Down the pub the other night she comes up to me, asks if I want to try again. "Try again?" I says. "We tried everything last time, and unless you've learned some new tricks you've got nothing to offer."' He laughed wheezily at his joke, and as if to help the wheeze lit a cigarette.

'Do you smoke?'

'No.'

'Very wise. Killing me this is, but I can't stop. Too much aggravation in the world. Yer, too much speed.'

And then, as if satisfied that the conversation had come full circle, he lapsed into a meditative silence punctuated only by coughs and critical tuts at other drivers.

He dropped Stephen off at the entry to the NCP, and feeling slightly guilty Stephen overtipped him.

'Thanks, Guv. Do you want a receipt?'

Stephen was about to say no, then changed his mind. If he had any thoughts of going back into practice then he had to start behaving like a businessman.

The car park was still virtually deserted at that time of the morning. Most of the commuters were still struggling through suburban traffic and as he climbed past the first floor where the practice had half a dozen spaces he noticed only Jeffrey's car there. By custom the first space had always belonged to Stephen, it was slightly bigger than the others and easier to get into, but this morning Jeffrey had parked there. Clearly he was stepping into more than Stephen's shoes. It all had to change, it all would change.

By the time he reached the roof Stephen was out of breath. That was something else that must receive his attention. He missed his squash and tennis, disliked the slight paunch he'd developed, knew that he was half a stone overweight. He'd had too much time to eat, and eating itself had become a nervous habit. Instead of burning up his nervous energy, he was constantly fuelling it with a steady stream of chocolates, nuts, biscuits, crisps, any junk food that came to hand and required neither plate nor cutlery. Trisha had tried hiding it, stopped buying it all together, but the little corner shop was too near, too convenient in staying open all hours, and the short walk down there was both a diversion and as much exercise as he ever took.

He paused on the roof, gulping in the fresh air, enjoying the panoramic view. The Post Office Tower looked so near that he could reach out and touch it; to his left was the green expanse that was Regents Park; and away in the distance, eastward he could even pick out the roof of St Paul's, a slight heat haze shrouding its dome like a halo.

This was his city and just for a moment he felt like a king, lord of all he surveyed. Whatever else they'd taken from him, they'd not taken away this view. What the unseen teachers had taught him was that it was all transitory, this sense of power. God gave and God took away. The rich either got poorer or they died. Everything was finite, everything transient. He and Cathy had once visited Egypt on holiday and had seen the ruins of a lost civilisation crumbling into the desert. They too had thought in their time they were indestructible, they too had finally met their maker, doubtless crawling on hands and knees, faces buried into the dirt.

'Jeffrey,' he called. He had to be here unless he'd parked his car and gone to get a paper or some of the cigars he smoked endlessly. There were only a couple of cars scattered around the large expanse of the roof. Parked out of the way by regular customers on holiday, left after a dinner where the owner had had just that bit too much to drink. But one car had not been left for any such reason. Stephen recognised it yet did not, because he didn't want to recognise it, even though he'd only seen it the night before. It was his BMW, parked tight up in a corner.

He walked towards it, looking nervously over his shoulder. Perhaps Trisha had been right. Maybe he should have left it all to the police rather than walking into what might be another trap. He was becoming paranoid, envisaging a mass of people all over London, sitting around hatching plots just to catch him. Kennard catching, a new national sport. Join in, join the fun, it's fresh, it's novel, you can't lose. Everyone a winner. Except Stephen Kennard.

By the wall there was a cigar, half-smoked, a Villager—just as he had seen Jeffrey smoke so many times since they were young. Only he never half-smoked them. Jeffrey puffed away until his fingers almost burned on the stubs. At first it had been because he was smoking something he could not afford and didn't want to waste, but then it became an affectation, explained away by him as being because he really enjoyed them. No, never half-smoked.

Stephen tried the door of his car. It was open, the keys in it. Nothing had been taken, the tapes were there, his driving shoes. All that had happened was the car had moved from Trisha's flat in North London to this West End car park. He found the key and started the engine, without thinking pushing the gear into reverse. The car moved a few inches, then stuck. He hit the accelerator and this time there was a terrific crunching noise as it bumped its way backwards. He immediately got out of the vehicle to see what was wrong and vomited as he realised that what he'd just driven over had been the body of his sometime school friend, sometime partner, Jeffrey Wightman.

Chapter Forty Eight

Gerry Mortimer sat with his new advisers looking like an old, old man. He was not enjoying life at the moment. When Stephen had been around there had been a sense of adventure, a feeling that there were still mountains to climb; but Stephen was not around and he no longer had a taste for mountaineering.

It had been a week before Len Kennard

died that he'd phoned Gerry and asked him to visit. Fay was making a shopping trip to town and Len knew the two of them would be alone.

'Gerry, why don't you give Stephen any work?'

There was nothing like coming straight to the point. Len Kennard and Gerry Mortimer went back a long way. They'd been born in the same hospital, Stepney Jewish in London's East End, and then had been brought up in the same road. Jubilee Street in the 1920s had been a seething hive of Jewish life where doors were always open, housewives bustling in and out of each other's homes with steaming bowls of food, new recipes, gossip, and comfort when times were bad. The boys had gone to the same Hebrew classes, played truant at the same time, and struggled reluctantly towards their barmitzvahs in the same Synagogue. It had been at the Synagogue Youth Club they'd met their respective wives and the four of them had been inseparable since, even when the Kennard family moved upwards to Stamford Hill and the Mortimers eastward to West Ham. They'd not been Kennard and Mortimer in those days, it had been Kesselman and Moskovich, but new environments brought new names, and gradually they grew into their new identities.

434

All of that was now in the past, but to the old, the past is more important than the present and the future is just a game of Russian Roulette.

'I've never liked to mix business with friendship. If anything went wrong it could affect our friendship.'

A spasm of pain passed across Len's face.

'Look, Gerry, I've not said anything to Fay but I've been getting some terrible chest pain.'

'Have you been to the doctor?'

'Doctors, what do they know? They'd have me in bed before I could say anything, and once you're in bed then you're a sick person.'

'You're a stubborn man, Len. After that angina attack last year you were told to be careful. You've slowed down as much as a taxi driver at an amber light.'

'If your number's up, then your number's up,' Len said philosophically, 'but I just want you to promise me something. If anything happens to me, look after Stephen.'

'Does Stephen need looking after? I thought he had everything? A nice wife, lovely kids, a good practice.'

'Call it a father's instinct. Just make me the promise.'

Gerry had promised and in a week

Len was dead. Gerry had never regretted the promise, and instead of his being an honorary nephew Stephen had rapidly become a surrogate son to a man who had never had children himself.

He felt, in a way, that he was breaking his promise to Len by cutting Stephen off now, but what could he do? His whole battery of advisers had told him to distance himself if his company was not to be dragged into the scandal. He'd offered money and the boy had refused it. Stubborn like his father. And so he'd persuaded the girl to take it.

Now, sitting with his financial adviser, Chris Kennedy, and the company's new solicitor, Arnold Petrie, Gerry longed for it to be all over. Everything, the takeover, the business, life. He had no stomach for it any more. Kennedy had done his best, but then he always would. He didn't forget how Gerry had rescued him, but he had his limitations. He reacted rather than planned and what Gerry needed right now were ideas. The sort of ideas Stephen would have brought to the table, ideas that stimulated, progressive thoughts that took him along a primrose path, shedding years along the way.

Arnold Petrie had been recommended by the company's brokers. He was a humourless man in his early-fifties and one of the senior company partners in the City firm of Jennings, Fraser & Douglas. His practice represented many Public Companies, had been established for over two hundred years, and now listed some two hundred partners at offices that straddled New York, Paris, Hong Kong, and even Moscow and Tokyo. To have found somebody as far removed from Stephen as Petrie had been a real challenge but there was no doubt that the brokers had succeeded.

'If you're to retain any sort of credibility in the City you need to show the market that you're taking a serious and responsible approach. Jennings is the firm, Petrie's your man.' Robert Allen, a partner in his brokers, had said, and weakly, almost listlessly, Gerry had floated with the tide.

'I simply don't understand how you've got yourself into this position, Mr Mortimer.' Petrie had been asked to call him Gerry, had duly noted the invitation, but regularly declined to take advantage of it.

'You had to be there at the time,' Gerry grunted.

'Doubtless. I think I'm rather relieved I was not.' He spoke in a clipped tone that just failed to hide his Scottish antecedents. His grey hair was neatly cut, meticulously parted on the left, and had his face been a little fuller, the small moustache would have cast him as Adolf Hitler in any movie. Yet there was no kind of fanaticism in the steady grey eyes. They were calm and unemotional, critical but without any concern.

'Let us look carefully at what we have here. You hold a substantial stake in D'Arblay investments which you acquired by certain means that are not within my terms of reference, but which you have assured me, and I accept, were quite legal if a little amoral. These were acquired at a price of £2.65. You were anticipating making a bid for the whole company, hopefully at a price of some £3.20, but you had budgeted for a maximum price of £3.50. There appears to have been substantial support for the shares, initially using money that was, how shall I put it, "borrowed" from your own solicitors, but luckily from different unknown sources. Consequently the share price is now £3.75 and you are advised that on the current profits and net asset situation of the company, no bid is economically feasible.

'I am sure that with all the whispers and rumours surrounding this company, the present activity and the dubious sources of money used to acquire shares, the Stock Exchange must have given some thought to suspending them. That would, of course, mean you could neither buy, nor, of course, of more importance in your case, sell. Obviously as the company is a competitor of yours you would like to know who is buying as if you are not to acquire the company you may well be faced with a more aggressive opponent in the market place, and indeed one with considerably more money to play with than has heretofore been the case. Consequently your own company's ability to expand may well be indirectly hampered, a fact of which the market already seems to have taken some cognisance. Hence a down turn in your own shares of some ten percent.

'It therefore follows that the market is not confident of your ability to acquire this company at a reasonable price, and where the market itself lacks confidence, investors may well find themselves similarly inhibited. So it would appear you have three alternatives. You make an offer for the company at a price it is hardly worth, you retain your stake for another day and merely make yourself a nuisance as a minority shareholder, or you simply sell your shares, take a profit, pay your capital gains and live to fight another day. If you do take the latter course, although you would seem to be making some money, it may well be perceived as a defeat and while you are licking your wounds the predators that abound in the City may sniff blood themselves...'

'You mean?' Gerry asked, despite himself fascinated by the lawyer's expert analysis.

'I mean you may become victim to a takeover bid yourself, perhaps even from D'Arblay. We are dealing with serious players here, players with large stakes on the table.'

'So what do you suggest?' Gerry asked.

'Ah well, there you have me. I am merely a lawyer. I can only point out the alternatives, and the potential effect of selecting any one of them. The commercial choice, I fear, is yours.'

'But Stephen always...'

'Indeed, Mr Kennard did. Hence the plight in which he now finds himself. I, fortunately, am not Mr Kennard.'

'No indeed you're not,' Gerry said in humourless mimicry. Whatever the decision he made he knew it would be his own, for despite his having the best advisers money could buy, he felt for the first time since the death of his wife, truly alone.

Chapter Forty Nine

'Charlie, he didn't do it, believe me.' Trisha sat in the wine bar with Charlie Davison, trying desperately to get her ex-boyfriend over to Stephen's side.

'Trisha, maybe he did, maybe he didn't; but innocent men don't run. Innocent men can explain away allegations of guilt. This guy seems to have some power over you that's made you toss reason to the winds. Whilst we were together you were all logic when it came to a story. I'll never forget how you pieced together the investigation of that phoney clinic, how you felt the medical director was too good to be true. That was your instinct working full strength.'

'You made fun of my woman's instinct.'

'I made fun of lots of things with you, Trish. It didn't mean I didn't care.'

She touched his face affectionately.

'Poor dear Charlie. I never doubted for a minute that you cared. But you cared about lots of other things too. You cared about the force, your snouts, the victims. You even cared about the villains sometimes—cared too much in your desire to put them behind bars. I couldn't compete with all that caring, and you couldn't live with my ambitions either. I wasn't cut out to be a copper's wife and you weren't meant to be a journalist's husband.'

'But you reckon you could live with being a lawyer's wife?'

She bit her lip.

'He's got one of those already, and kids, and a Jewish mother. I don't fit into the frame, Charlie. He's just a friend. A decent bloke who's got his back to the wall. Somebody hates him, somebody's doing their best to destroy him, and you've got to help.'

He hesitated.

'He still ought to give himself up. He doesn't know what it's like to be on the run. He's white collar, Trisha, he can't live rough. If he tries to bed down in a cardboard box it'll kill him—if his sleeping companions don't. This is a small country, we're a big force, and believe me if you're wanted on suspicion of murder there's nowhere to hide.'

'I've told you, two men came to take his car away the night before. They threatened him.'

'You've only his word for that. He tells you they smashed the glass but you didn't see it. He tells you he gave them the keys to his car because he was frightened but you didn't see them. He tells you he didn't even see Wightman's body before he ran over it, but we don't know if he was dead or alive before he got flattened.

'Let me paint you another scenario. You and Kennard go to Jersey. Whatever he saw on that screen told him a story but he didn't let you into the secret. Let's say he saw something that put him in the dock for everything: theft, blackmail, you name it. Jeffrey asks to meet him. He realises Wightman knows a fair bit too, so he sets up this elaborate charade with the car, goes along there, they argue, Kennard runs him over. He knows you'll believe him, knows you'll come to me to help clear his name, and he thinks you'll convince me.'

She shook her head vehemently, dismissing the suspicion that Charlie was trying to put into her mind. She'd seen the look on Stephen's face when he'd come back from the car park: the stunned horror, the somnambulistic quality to his walk.

'Trisha, Jeffrey's dead. They've killed him. Killed him with my car—or maybe *I* killed him with my car. I don't know. I can't let you be involved in this any more. It's too dangerous. I'm getting out of here. I'll stay in touch by phone. If you think there's a tap on the phone, just ask about my mother when I call.'

'Stephen, calm down. If you vanish they'll think you've definitely done it.'

'You call your friend Charlie. Tell him where the body is before anybody else finds it. They've made it easy for him—it's even on his patch.'

'Where will you go?'

'I'm not sure. And even when I decide, it's better that you don't know. Don't worry about me. I've got the money. I'll survive.' He'd kissed her, hard on the lips, then left.

He was a survivor, far more resilient than Charlie Davison would ever have imagined. He'd seen violence and he'd seen death all at close hand and they didn't frighten him any more. He was angry. A line from a movie came to him: 'Don't get mad, get even.' Despite everything he conjured up a smile as he saw himself dressed in Rambo-style costume, bandanna around his head, rifle across his chest. If he had a gun he wouldn't even know how to use it. No, the only ammunition he had was his wits. He'd just have to rely upon them. He needed transport and without credit cards car hire would be difficult. He got on a bus at random, not really caring where it took him, waited until he'd put a fair distance between himself and Trisha's flat, then alighted as soon as he saw a secondhand car showroom.

The proprietor might have been a prototype for Arthur Daly, pork pie hat firmly fixed on his head, showbiz-length cigar unlit in his mouth, probably lasting from week to week. Every car was: 'A little cracker. A gem.' Every price: 'An absolute giveaway, just to get a little bit of cash flow, you understand. If you come back next week, you won't find the same price.'

Stephen had no intention of coming back the next week. He wanted something anonymous and reliable, and whereas he quickly formed the opinion that reliability here was likely to be comparative he finally settled on a three-year-old Ford Escort. He asked for and got a ten percent discount for cash and then felt mildly annoyed with himself that he'd not asked for more.

He needed some time to think, to work it through. He believed he knew now what there was at the eye of the storm, he just needed to get there in one piece. He found a public phone box and called home, praying that Cathy wouldn't answer the phone. It rang and rang and he was just about to replace the receiver when his son finally answered.

'Jonny, it's Dad.'

'Hi, Dad, how are you?'

'Could be better. Look, you're likely to read things about me in the paper for the

445

next few days. I've never lied to you, have I?'

'No.'

'Well, I'm not lying now. There's no truth in anything they say, and what they say will be much worse than last time. Just trust me. I'm working at it. If you get the chance, try and explain it to your mother and sister as well.'

'Dad, when are you coming home?'

'Soon, Jonny, very soon. And Jonny...'

'Yes, Dad?'

'I love you.'

He blew a kiss down the phone just as he had done when the children were small. He could not tell whether or not it was his imagination but he thought he heard his son kiss the receiver at his end.

He counted his change, knowing he still had another call to make, then dialled Gerry Mortimer's direct line. The voice that answered sounded tired and depressed.

'Gerry, it's me, Stephen.'

'Stephen, am I pleased to hear from you! I miss you.'

'I'm glad. You'll get me back soon enough. Listen Gerry, I've not much time. Jeffrey's dead.'

'What?'

'Dead, killed. It's all getting out of hand. They're trying to lay the blame on me.'

'That's *meshige!* Anybody who knows

446

you would realise that.'

'It was just as crazy to suggest I'd steal all that money or cheat on my wife.'

Even as he spoke the final few words he felt again the guilt he'd experienced when in bed with Sarah, but now was not the moment to worry about a touch of hypocrisy.

'Gerry, it's going to be all over the papers tomorrow. Make sure Mum's kept away from them. Have a word with the hospital. The shock of this could kill her.'

'Leave it to me. Where are you going to be if I need to contact you?'

Stephen hesitated. He'd already decided to make for the anonymous bed and breakfast land of Muswell Hill in North London. He'd toyed with the idea of Paddington or even Brixton, but he felt lost in the west and south of the city and Muswell Hill was familiar enough territory for him to feel at home. Somehow he knew that if he felt comfortable he wouldn't stand out in the crowd, and he needed to pull anonymity around him like a cloak.

'I don't know yet,' he lied. It was crazy that he trusted Gerry to protect his mother but didn't feel he could trust him all the way. He couldn't trust anybody any more. Only himself. Himself and Trisha. He trusted her, and feared for her if he trusted her too far. That was why he'd pushed her back towards Charlie. Whatever else, he never doubted for a moment that Charlie would protect her.

Charlie was doing his best to do just that.

'Forget him, Trisha. He's trouble. If he's innocent he'll be cleared. If he's guilty he'll take you down with him.'

'Justice isn't like that, Charlie. You and I know there are a lot of innocent men behind bars. Now I'm a big girl. I can look after myself. I'll ask you one more time, will you help me?'

Charlie sighed.

'I can't put my job on the line.'

'Nobody's asking you to do that. You know you can get me information without doing that.'

She looked him in the eyes, the look that had said a hundred times in their relationship that if he'd just do her one little favour she was his forever. He chewed his lower lip, and as soon as she saw the habit she knew she'd won.

'All right, Trisha, you always get your way. What do you want?'

'Simple.' She reached into her bag and pulled out one of the photographs they'd removed from Jarvis Walters' study.

'Pretty girls, lucky man.'

'Not so lucky. He's dead. That's Jarvis Walters.'

She quickly filled him in on Walters and he made a few notes.

'What am I supposed to do with this?'

'Try Vice. See if they know the girls. Blow up the picture. See where it was taken. If you have anything on Stephen's case, anything about anybody connected with it, just let me know.'

'You're not asking a lot, are you?'

'I never did.'

'I love you,' he said, reaching out to her.

'I know. I'm sorry.'

'Yeah, well, I'll get on with it then. Tell him if he calls, to give himself up.'

'I suppose you have to say that?'

'What, that he should give himself up?'

'No. That you love me.'

She flashed him a mischievous smile, insisted on paying the bill, and then went back to the flat to wait for the phone to ring.

Chapter Fifty

Philip Greystone and Toby Lipscomb sat in the same room overlooking the City and the river that had housed the meetings between Stephen and Jeffrey and the Greystone's

449

partners. The long table, the pads and pencils set up in readiness for a dozen people, seemed testimony to the ghosts of the plans that had been discussed that spring evening.

'Tea?' Greystone asked.

'I'd rather have something stronger,' Lipscomb replied.

Philip went over to the cocktail cabinet, pressed the security code that prevented the cleaners or junior staff raiding it for a drink, and poured Lipscomb a large Scotch.

'Water? Soda?'

'No, why spoil it? I think everything's better if it's simple. Food, drink, business, sex. I don't like complications, Philip.'

'My dear Toby, I've acted for you long enough to realise that.'

'Kinsey selling his shares was a complication. You shouldn't have permitted that.'

Greystone adjusted the cuff of his sparkling white shirt and brushed an invisible speck of dust from his lapel.

'You sometimes have an exaggerated view of my capabilities, Toby. How should I have prevented a sale that I wasn't even aware was happening?'

'You get paid to know what's happening. The girl should have known.'

'She says she didn't.'

Lipscomb seemed to lose interest in the conversation momentarily.

'I assume that after the misfortunes of poor Mr Wightman, you will no longer be taking his firm under your wing.'

Greystone rose and walked to the window as if the answer to the question lay in the skyline.

'I'm really not sure. I've already spoken to young Anthony and offered my con- dolences to him and the beautiful Sarah. We have a meeting arranged for the day after tomorrow. I think they may well be desperate enough to do any sort of deal I suggest.'

'And what will you suggest?'

'I'm not sure. I'm not sure that with Kennard out of the picture and Wightman out of the world they really have too much to offer.'

Lipscomb nodded. He was not a polite man and considered he'd paid enough lip service to what he considered polite trivia.

'You're quite sure that we've seen off Sidney and that ridiculous Mortimer fellow?'

'Oh, yes, we've got the share price up to a level that would make it suicide to launch a bid. Once we know what he's going to do with Kinsey's shares, we can gradually unload and take a profit ourselves.'

451

'Mortimer won't have done too badly out of it if he sells now,' Lipscomb grumbled.

'Rather him than Kinsey. Where's your old friend now?'

'Monte Carlo, we hear. Enjoying himself.' There was a pause, and if a pause could be described as unpleasant this one was. 'Yes, enjoying himself. For the moment.'

'You sound as if it's to be a temporary state of affairs?'

'We live in hope, Philip, we live in hope.'

'Lipscomb picked up a paper.

Lawyer sought in murder inquiry was *The Times* headline. He flipped through, seeking something more sensational, and found it in the *Sun*.

Car Park Killer Manhunt.

'Not quite up to the usual standards,' he commented, 'but the photograph is not unflattering.'

Across the City Sarah was also looking at Stephen's photograph, and remembering other times. She had never regarded herself as sentimental but she could not help but recall his body beside her in bed, the warmth of his arms around her, his tongue in her ear while his hands caressed her body. And now it had come to this. Anthony came into the room and

452

immediately she pulled herself back into control, became once more the ambitious businesswoman who was clawing her way to the top of her profession.

'It's lucky you don't look like your brother, otherwise you might have found yourself hauled off the street.'

Anthony just blinked, speed read the paper then tossed it aside.

'You don't care, do you, Anthony? He's your brother and it still doesn't make any difference to you. Jeffrey's dead, Stephen's on the run for murder, and I still don't know what's going on in that head of yours.'

'No,' he replied, 'you don't. Greystone rang me. I've arranged to see him the day after tomorrow.'

'You're not serious, are you? What have we got to offer them now?'

'I'm not sure, I'm thinking about it.' His voice had taken on a robot-like quality.

'Anthony, are you all right?'

He shook his head and sat down at a desk.

'When Stephen was here, I could just get on with things, my things. Even Jeffrey let me do that. But now...' He gestured around him, looking for guidance. He seemed terribly vulnerable and for the first time since she'd known him Sarah saw the link between him and Stephen.

He put his head in his hands, the picture of utter despair, and began to rock backwards and forwards, making small moaning noises.

'Anthony, pull yourself together. If you let go now what happens to us? Stephen's coming back. We've got to hold it in one piece until he gets here.'

He raised his head a little, his eyes looking up at her. With his glasses removed there was a glossy, distant look to his pupils, a struggle to focus on a world that now seemed permanently blurred.

'Do you really think he's coming back?'

She nodded. Now was not the time to tell him that she'd decided to leave. She couldn't take any more of the family drama. She also had a life to lead and she had no intention of being sucked into the anonymity of the Greystone machine that called itself a law firm. She'd been thinking about it for some time now. Nobody thought she'd had anything to do with taking the money, nobody would suggest she'd killed Jeffrey. She could leave and approach other firms with a degree of sympathy. She had her own niche market in the matrimonial field, there'd always be clients for her, always be divorces. Everybody got divorced. Except Stephen. She had to get involved with the one moral man in England—although

454

not so moral that he'd not tumbled into bed with her when the opportunity arose. But then, not many men would have said no to her in those days. She watched as Anthony gradually calmed himself, and idly wondered if he would say no, wondered what he would be like in bed. Would his mind still be on tax schemes or whatever it was that went on behind the smoke screen that passed for an expression on his face?

Perhaps that might even bring Stephen back to her, seducing his brother, making him realise what he was missing? It might do them both some good, jolting the one back to the real world, the other to her side.

It was all fantasy. Everything that was going on around her was fantasy. She patted Anthony on the shoulder, made to say something then held back. She had said too much in the past and now was the time for silence.

Chapter Fifty One

Charlie Davison kicked the coffee machine brutally. Detective Constable Terry Moore, waiting his turn, looked on with some amusement.

'Hold on, Sergeant. It's not some likely lad we've pulled in for questioning, you know.'

Charlie turned on him, and Moore realised immediately he'd made a mistake. As far as Charlie was concerned the machine was Stephen Kennard and the young constable's comment had struck too close to home.

'You think you're so clever, you make the fucking machine work! And when you do, mine's black without. I'll be at my desk.'

There had been a time when he'd thought he was over Trisha. He knew he'd been lucky to get her in the first place. Bright young journalist, university graduate, intellectual, she'd read books, seen plays that they'd never even heard of in New Cross where he'd been brought up. But Charlie knew people. That had always been his greatest asset. People related to Charlie Davison. His teachers at school had related to him, realising that he had a sharp brain even if he didn't speak too clearly, even if he didn't sound his 'aitches, even if he'd sometimes wear the same shirt for a whole week.

Nowadays, as if to compensate, he'd sometimes change twice a day, always had a whole fresh set of clothing hanging up, just in case he got too hot or too dirty.

It hadn't been anybody's fault really when he'd been younger. His mum had died when he was seven and his dad had done his best. It wasn't easy for him, working down at the docks and bringing up four children, and for the most part he'd let them fend for themselves. It hadn't really done them too much harm, although it had been hard at the time. Charlie's eldest brother had joined the navy and was now a first lieutenant; not bad for somebody who'd left school at fifteen and worked as a deckhand. One of his sisters was a staff nurse at a large teaching hospital in Yorkshire, married to a vet, while his pretty baby sister was making a good living modelling. Charlie hadn't done too badly for himself either, a Detective Sergeant, bordering on promotion to Inspector, needing just that final career push to see him really take off.

Yet he hadn't been able to cope with a career and Trisha. There was a selfish streak in her that made it impossible for her to see that he couldn't always be around when she wanted. She also went off on stories, stayed away, travelled abroad, but that was her job. When she'd cooked a meal or bought theatre tickets and he didn't turn up until late, then it was him and his 'bloody villains'. If she got a call at three in the morning it was because the news was hot and she was grateful. If one of his snouts called after ten it was 'some unearthly hour'.

Although the relationship had been ended before Stephen moved in, although Trisha denied there was anything in it, he still blamed Stephen. He'd never really spoken to him socially yet he still hated him. Hated him for his opportunities, for his education, for taking his place. And Trisha expected him to help her clear his name! That was Trisha all over, and he smiled inwardly, knowing that despite everything she still had a hold over him. 'You lucky bastard, Kennard,' he said quietly to himself. 'You don't know just who it is you've got in your corner.'

The pile of papers on his desk seemed to grow bigger every time he went out for a drink. He was sure there was some little demon watching until he got up to leave the room, then leaping across with more unsolved puzzles, dumping them on Charlie, then vanishing to get a good view of the joke.

He sifted through them miserably, hoping that a change in order might give him some inspiration. He understood what it must be like to be a writer with a block. That was exactly how he felt today. Too much to do; so much that whatever he did would make no impression, and therefore the temptation was to do nothing but stare at it. But staring at piles of paper wouldn't get him promotion and that single thought kick started him into action.

He pulled open an envelope that had landed on his desk whilst he'd been at the coffee machine. At least it had the merit of being fresh. It was a note and a photo from Ray Wexell in Vice. Ray was a good mate, and he and his wife had often formed foursomes with him and Trisha in the old days. Trisha had loved his stories and when they got home after an evening with Ray her lovemaking had always been that bit more passionate, a bit more inventive. He'd had a drink with Ray only last night and told him all about his problem, all about Trisha and Stephen. He'd left him the photograph of Walters and the girls, knowing he had more chance of coming up with something than ordinary CID. One part of him hoped he'd draw a blank, that was the part that wanted Stephen out of the way; but the other part, the copper in him, hated any unsolved mystery. He hoped it would be solved by laying the guilt on Stephen, but he had to get an answer.

Ray had returned the photo with a simple note: 'Got it in one. Call me.'

The pile of current papers seemed to

459

have grown just that little bit higher while he'd opened the envelope. There was no real point in starting anything. He dialled Ray's number. There seemed to be a party going on at the other end of the line as Ray answered the phone, laughing.

'Ray, it's Charlie.'

'Hello, Charlie. Sorry about the noise. The boys just raided a lock-up in Brixton and they're trying on some of the more unusual items they've brought back. I've seen most things in my time but some of this stuff beats it all. I don't honestly know how the punters who use this gear can get it up for laughing.'

'Sounds like fun.'

'Come and join us. It's a man's life in Soho.'

'I got your note.'

'Yeah, interesting little photo that one too. We had it blown up here. It's amazing what those blow ups show. The action there isn't in a room.'

'No?'

'No. It's in a lift. Obviously that's what excited your Mr Average here. The old *Fatal Attraction* scenario. Do it between the second and third floor. I reckon the camera was in the ceiling and that's how it got taken. Nice job. Lovely detail. Anyway, you know how all of those lifts have to be checked out every so often? Well, we even

460

managed to read the safety certificate, date of last check, right down to the signature of the examiner. Just called them up, got the date, got the man. Got your place.'

'Where is it?'

'Ah, well, that's where it gets less helpful. It was the Sapsford Clinic, some kind of allergy place. Looks like a strange way to treat an allergy to me. Place got closed down a while ago.'

'I know,' Charlie said.

'What do you mean, you know? You been going there for hay fever or fear of lifts?'

'I just know. Thanks, Ray, thanks for your help.'

'No problem. See you around soon. I'd love to see Trisha again as well sometimes. Lisa sends her love.'

Charlie looked down at the picture in front of him, looked at the name he'd scribbled down on his pad. The Sapsford Clinic. He knew it all too well. It was over that bloody clinic that Trisha had met Stephen. It was closed because her article had closed it down. He picked up the phone and dialled Trisha. He'd promised to let her know if he found anything, and wherever the trail was leading, he was a man of his word.

461

Chapter Fifty Two

Stephen laid all of his papers out neatly on the chest of drawers. He'd bought himself a fresh writing pad, a new pen and a set of coloured pencils at W.H Smith in the main shopping centre, treated himself to a smoked salmon sandwich, and now felt ready for work.

He'd been like this when he was studying and it was the same in the office. The preparation for a major job was in itself a ritual, the dressing of the High Priest before he entered the Holy of Holies, any error dooming the project to failure.

On one sheet of paper he wrote neatly the names of all the people that had in any way been involved in his life since the money had disappeared.

Jeffrey, Anthony, Sarah, they wrote themselves, then he added Arthur, and Eddie his assistant. That dealt with the office. Gerry, Chris Kennedy, Kinsey, Lipscomb. They summed up D'Arblay and Sidney. Jarvis Walters, in splendid isolation now and for always. He thought, then added the names of Philip Greystone and those of the Greystone's partners he

462

could remember, he tapped the pad, hoping to draw further names from his pen, but succeeded only in producing a series of random dots. Rory O'Donnell, Trisha... Why not add the names of friends? But who was the real enemy?

One of his children had bought a tape that taught the concept of mind mapping a subject and on a different sheet of paper he drew his own mind map now. In the centre of a big circle with a man inside, the trapped man, the prisoner. 'I am not a number.' Drawing had never been his strong point but he knew that the man was himself and this map was for his eyes only.

He drew a line out of the centre in blue. He'd always found blue comforting and drew a picture of two adult stick people holding hands with two stick children, then wrote the word 'Family' and their names. Leading out of that he drew a red line and wrote down the name of the woman he was supposed to have slept with in France—red, a danger to his family, then ringed it in black for death.

In purple he drew a law book, then wrote Jeffrey's name in black while sticking to purple for everybody else. Again he branched out from that line and still in black wrote Jarvis Walters' name. He used green for Trisha, a fresh colour, reminding him of fields and trees and the countryside. When all this was over he'd take her for a ride in the country, down to the Cotswolds. An innocent ride. They'd walk down to the stream that ran at the bottom of the field near his home, look up at the clear sky and laugh about all they had shared. And all this would be over.

The picture came together and he tried to work out the connections. Every map had a connection. Sea or land, it all led somewhere and this one had to be no different.

Finally he set out the information he'd pulled off Jarvis Walters' computer. Dead men did tell tales. Dead men who liked secrets, dead men who couldn't resist storing information, they could talk from the grave. As a child he'd been fascinated by old movies where the long dead star was there, up on the screen, his face, his voice, his body, preserved by celluloid as surely as the ancient Egyptians had preserved their Pharaohs.

'Speak to me,' he said to the printouts. 'Come on Jarvis. Explain it all to me.'

The money had gone out of his client account straight into Jarvis' account, no effort to conceal it. Money had gone that route before for clients so he supposed there was no reason for that to cause any raised eyebrows either. Just another transaction for another client wanting to pay as little tax as possible. The money went out to brokers to buy shares in D'Arblay in the name of the company he was supposed to have formed; but then on the same disc there was more, as if Walters had been stockpiling information for himself for a rainy day. Only the rainy day had not come before the storm that had washed him away.

The Jersey company had been incorporated as being owned jointly by two companies, one in Ireland, one in Gibraltar. Those companies themselves were owned by a Liechtenstein trust. There had been nothing in the letter to tell Walters to set it up this way, so this was something he'd obviously done before. And if he'd done it before had he done it for the same person?

Stephen tried to put himself into Walters' mind. When had the blackmail started? What if he'd been deliberately covering his back by setting up the companies as he had? If he was being blackmailed then he was about to hit back. Perhaps he'd tried to hit back at that meeting, shown what he'd done on his screens at the office. Somebody killed him, made it look like suicide, then wiped the tape. Only they didn't know there was a duplicate at his home, didn't know what a very careful man he was.

He moved on down the printed sheets. Other names, other companies, dozens of them, but one stood out amongst the others: Dunkelheit SA, the company that had owned the hotel in France. Reams and reams of paper. It was inconceivable that such small machines could hold a wealth of information. Computers never ceased to amaze him. Jeffrey had never wanted to computerise the office. Jeffrey never had the patience.

'I've used pen and paper for years. I don't see why I should change now.'

But they had changed, and although Jeffrey was the last to fall into line, eventually even he could see the sense and advantage in time costing.

Stephen moved to the final sheet of the printout—an analysis of English properties owned ultimately by the Liechtenstein trust, some of them vaguely familiar, some totally unknown, but one in particular a name engraved on his heart—the Sapsford Clinic. There were several clinics, hospitals, casinos, clubs, not just in England but across the whole of Europe, a whole network of properties. Then, at the very end, as if Walters had himself been working out a puzzle, was one name, printed in block capitals and followed by an exclamation mark.

He paced the room, the television droning in the background. He couldn't understand how the kids managed to sit through a diet of *Neighbours, Home and Away* and *Eastenders* while they were doing their homework, but then he'd always watched *Emergency Ward 10* when he was a kid and that had probably been just as bad. He needed to talk to someone and there was nobody to talk to except Trisha. Cathy would have to wait for another day, although if he was right in what he thought was happening, that day wouldn't be too far away.

The answerphone message began to play and he groaned. He needed the real Trisha not some recorded message. It was as though she read his mind because as he spoke, she cut in.

'Stephen, I've been waiting for you to call. Where are you?'

'On my own.'

'You have to call Charlie. I've got his private number.'

'Why, so he can make a personal arrest? Sorry, but I'm still sorting this out on my own.'

'Don't be so bloody stubborn and listen to me! This isn't a competition between you and Charlie. People are dying here. I don't want you to be the next—nor me for

467

that matter. We've made some dangerous enemies.'

'We?' he said. Somehow it had never occurred to him that she was in any way a target. His own problems had made him selfish.

'Yes, we.' And then she told him what Charlie had told her.

'It all makes sense,' Stephen said.

'I'm pleased it makes sense to you. Stephen, if you can see it, so will the police. I'll meet up with you and go with you to the station if it helps. Let's leave it to them.'

He hesitated, it was so tempting, but there were some debts he wanted to collect personally. She sensed his hesitation.

'Just tell me where you are. I won't tell anybody, I promise. I'll come on down there on my own and we'll talk it through.'

'All right. I'm at the Caernarvon Hotel in Muswell Hill. Room thirty-four. I'll be waiting for you. Come on straight up.'

He felt an enormous sense of relief in telling somebody where he was. The isolation had got to him, the thought that if he died there in the night nobody would know who he really was, the ultimate dread of being buried in a plain pine box in a pauper's grave.

He walked over to the window that

468

overlooked the street waiting for her already although he knew it would be at least half an hour before she arrived. The two policemen he saw seemed to show a sense of purpose in walking towards the hotel and his stomach sank. He couldn't let it end like this. Perhaps they'd go past but they didn't, they simply waited outside, looking up, looking towards him as if to say: We know you're there, we're waiting for you, either you come down or we come up.

He wasn't going to wait. Like any good fugitive he'd checked the hotel out thoroughly. The main entrance at the front led from a flight of stairs straight down to the street, but at the back was a small car park from where the porters brought through the heavy luggage. It could be reached without going through the main lobby along a short corridor that connected the kitchen and the dining room. He didn't know how much time he had but he couldn't afford to wait for Trisha. He pulled on his jacket and ran, taking the stairs two at a time, hurrying past an astonished porter, running too fast and too far to hear the policemen ask the receptionist if she knew to whom the van illegally parked on the double yellow lines belonged.

Chapter Fifty Three

Trisha reset the answerphone. She'd been tempted to call Charlie and get him to go with her to Stephen, but she knew that he would regard that as a betrayal. She felt confident that once she met up with him she'd be able to persuade him. The doorbell rang and, swearing softly to herself, she flipped on the intercom.

'Trisha, it's me, Charlie. I've got to talk to you.'

'Charlie, I was just going out.'

'It's urgent. Really urgent. Can I come up?'

She pressed the door release and heard his heavy policeman's footsteps on the stairs, just as she'd heard them so often before in the past.

He seemed too big for the flat as he filled the doorway and just for a moment she wanted to throw herself at him, to feel him enfold her in a gigantic bear hug. She knew, however, he'd misinterpret it, would think the next stop was the bedroom. All she could say was: 'Do you want a coffee?'

'I'm not sure we've got time. Look,

Trisha, no games. Do you know where Kennard is?'

She shook her head.

'Trisha, just tell me the truth. I'm on the up, honest. You asked me to help you. I told you about Walters and the photo—he's dead. Now, you remember Arthur Kemp?'

She searched for a moment, the name coming to her out of context.

'Arthur, your Stephen's accounts manager. Well, they've found his body too. In a lake out near Hoddesdon. He'd been dead some time.'

'I don't understand.'

'No, you don't. I'm not sure Kennard does either. Or maybe he understands too much. We know how Arthur died. I've *seen* him die.'

She slumped into a chair.

'What do you mean, you've "seen" him die?'

'I saw it on film. They filmed it, Trisha, a snuff movie. They filmed and sold it. We circulated Arthur's details when the body was found and, bingo, Ray comes up trumps again. His crew had just seized a stack of blue movies in a raid: kids, animals, the lot. Real heart-warming material. but amongst it there's this little vignette of poor old Arthur. Ray realises it's a genuine death, he's seen enough of them, compares the photos and it's our man.'

'How did they do it?'

'Do you really want to know?'

She nodded, and he gave a half smile.

'Still the old Trisha, eh? Into vicarious thrills. Well, believe me, this was a little thriller. They carved him up.'

'I'm sorry?'

'I think you heard me, Trisha. Two girls, naked, with knives. All the time they had him tied up, it was all very slow, very artistic.'

'What about the girls?'

'Oh, it's all very cleverly filmed. Oscar award stuff. Backs to the camera, nice shadows, even background music, would you believe? So now we've got three people dead, Wightman, Walters and Arthur. Can you spot the link? Yes, you've got it, they all knew Stephen Kennard, all played a part in his life. Now do you want to tell me where he is?'

She remembered her promise then looked at Charlie. Had she ever loved this man? She'd slept with him often enough and at the time she'd convinced herself she loved him but now he just appeared to her to be what he was, a big, burly, ungainly policeman, a man whose job was to arrest Stephen Kennard. She shook her head at first, not to give Charlie a denial but to clear her mind of the thought that she cared more for Stephen than for Charlie. He was a married man. He loved his wife. He'd told her so, if not in word then at least in deed, and when this was all over he was going back to her. He'd go back to his life and she'd return to hers. And whatever happened Charlie played no part in that any more. She'd get rid of that razor in the bathroom, the few other bits and pieces he'd left around the flat, she'd purge herself of him for good.

'No, Charlie,' she said, 'I can't tell you where he is because I don't know.'

'You're lying to me, Trisha. I've always known when you were lying, even in bed. I'm still not sure exactly what Mr Kennard's got himself into or how far he's involved himself, but obviously you want him in one piece.'

'Yes. Yes, I do.' She paused. 'But I still can't tell you where he is.' Now her tone was confident and she stared him straight in the face, 'Thanks for your help, Charlie. If I find him and we need you then I'll tell you.'

'For crying out loud, Trisha, this isn't a game! You came to me, remember? When you wanted a favour you didn't hesitate to ask. You're not some cub reporter. I don't care what you think about me but I know what I still feel about you.'

'Yes?'

A little smile played around her mouth as her mind went back to their first meeting. It had been at court one day when she was covering a rape trial. She had fancied him as soon as he entered the witness box to give evidence. Tall, well built, his hair persistently falling forward over his brow despite his constant efforts to push it back. He had been calm then in giving his evidence, professional despite the horror of the case. It had all been part of a series of articles she was writing about rape victims and interviewing the policeman who had been first on the scene was, she convinced herself, a necessity.

He had not been keen, and although she'd thought he was just playing hard to get, later, when they were lovers, he told her he had just not been interested.

'I don't like red hair,' he'd said, but by then it was not her hair that fascinated him the most. She quickly discovered that he'd never met a woman like her. Charlie was used to meeting his women in pubs, getting them drunk on the cheapest concoctions available, taking them to bed and then hoping they wouldn't remember enough to want to see him again. He'd then talk about it to his mates, point out his victims as they came into the pub, raising dirty laughs with crude jokes.

Trisha had taught him how to appreciate a woman's body; she'd lectured him that there was no difference between him and the men he put behind bars for rape.

'You get them drunk so they don't know what they're doing because you're sure you wouldn't score with them if they were sober. That's rape, Charlie, like it or not.' But she'd taught him far too well. Whatever time of night or morning he came home she wanted him, and he wanted her, and when he didn't come home the wanting got too bad. She couldn't take the pain, and knowing that the job would always be the most important for him she told him it had to end, that she couldn't share him. He hadn't believed it then, and he didn't believe it now, she could tell, could sense him watching her, his mind mainly on Stephen, but also still thinking of her.

'I've a good mind to arrest you as an accessory after the fact. If I bang you away for a few days, at least you'll be safe.'

'Ooh, safe—with all those big meaty jailers? I don't think so, Charlie. You do your job, I'll do mine.'

His face was growing red with frustration. He'd always lost a battle of words with her. He turned to leave.

'All right, Trisha. Be clever. Have it your

way.' Then as he made to close the door behind him, he said more gently, 'But take care, you hear me? Just take good care of yourself.'

Chapter Fifty Four

Trisha arrived at the hotel in thirty minutes. Highbury to Muswell Hill was close, but all the lights had been against her. It took her nearly another quarter of an hour to park her car but eventually when no space appeared she just dumped it on a double yellow line outside the hotel and hoped for the best. As soon as she got to the hotel entrance she realised she had a problem. Stephen had not told her in what name he'd booked his room and he was hardly likely to have used his own. She'd just have to wing it. She dashed through the lobby, trying to look dishevelled and confused.

'Good morning, Madam. Can I help you?' The girl was in her late-teens, a determined effort at sophistication failing to hide either her youth, her acne, or her cockney accent.

'Look, my husband checked in this morning. He's a writer, likes to be on his own from time to time. It's just that

476

he's, he's...' She searched, then it came to her. 'He's asthmatic. He forgot his inhaler and his drugs. I wonder if I could take them up?'

'Of course. What did you say his name was?'

'His name?' She pretended to be coy. 'I can't tell you. You know what writers are like. If I told you who he really was it'd slip out, he'd be besieged, and he'd kill me. I tell you what I'll do...' she checked the girl's name tag '...Tracy'—it would be Tracy—'I'll make sure you get a signed copy of the new book just as soon as it's finished.'

The girl looked impressed.

'Wow, a famous writer here.' She looked down the register. 'We've not had that many people check in today. Stephen Cole, Room 6?'

'Yes, that'll be him. Stephen's his first name. I'll just go up. I don't want him to have time to get mad with me.'

She took the stairs thinking, Thanks a lot, Stephen, for putting me through that. If we're going to play spies then at least we should be getting the passwords right. She knocked on the door, at the same time trying the handle. It was unlocked and for the first time she regretted that she was alone and did not have the bulk of Charlie standing in the corridor behind her.

477

The room looked barely lived in. A bottle of water taken from the fridge, a half eaten packet of nuts, the abandoned sandwich wrapper in the waste paper basket, an empty Marks and Spencer bag that had contained the few clothes he'd bought. The window looking onto the street was half open and along the ledge were scattered papers and notes, the final sentence unfinished.

'What scared you off, Stephen?' she said to herself, looking out of the window, trying to put herself in his place.

She went down to Tracy who by now appeared to regard her as her closest friend.

'My husband's not in.'

'Oh, I didn't see him go out. I'm sorry. Would you like a cup of tea while you're waiting?'

'I don't think I'll hang around. I've all sorts of things to do today, you know what it's like.'

The girl nodded sympathetically although by the precise colouring of her long nails and the slightly unnatural sun tan, her basic outside exercise would appear to have been taken in a beauty parlour.

'I wonder if he had any other visitors today? Sometimes he likes to get together with somebody from his publishers or his agents.'

'No, nobody like that. It's been really quiet today since your husband checked in. The only human beings I've seen were the two policemen who came in.'

'What did they want?' Trisha asked, trying hard to conceal the trembling in her voice.

'Oh, nothing much. Never there when you want them, are they? There was a real set to outside the night club I go to in Enfield last Friday. My boyfriend gets in the way of a flying bottle. Where were the police then? By the time they got there there's just me and Kevin left and he's still on the ground. Kept us for hours at the station when they should have been out looking for the real hooligans...'

'So what did these two want today?'

'Just asking about an illegally parked van outside, just where you've left your car it was. I told them it was nothing to do with us, they gave it a ticket and off they went.'

So that was it, Trisha thought. Stephen saw them from the window, saw them come in and panicked. She just hoped he didn't think she'd put them on to him. If he was running and felt he was entirely on his own then there was no telling what he might do.

'I'll just pop up and leave his things in his room, then I'll be on my way. Thanks for all your help.'

She left the girl filing her nails with great concentration and returned to Stephen's hideaway. She looked carefully at the papers on the ledge and spread them out on the dressing table. There was no doubt that if Stephen were looking to learn a living as an artist he should not be giving up his day job. There was a mass of colours, lines, doodles, tiny pictures of people, houses and other items that were less easily identifiable. She bit her nails as she tried to translate Stephen's sketches into something recognisable. Tracy would have torn her own heart out rather than deal in such self-mutilation, but it helped Trisha to concentrate. There were the names Charlie had thrown at her, Nicole La Roche, Jeffrey and Jarvis Walters in black coffin-shaped boxes connected by different lines. Arthur was there too but obviously Stephen did not know that he was dead. All victims. Charlie dealt in victims. Should she talk to him now, tell him what she'd found? But he wasn't committed to Stephen's cause. He'd be calm, detached, just another job. And to him the job had always been everything.

She lifted the phone to dial his number, still holding the computer printout in her hand. The words and the names jumped off the page towards her. She could see exactly what Stephen had seen;

exactly how his mind had been working. Desperately she scoured the room for the floppy disc but Stephen must have taken it with him, his insurance policy. She swept up all the rest of the papers and shoved them into her bag. As she made her way out of the hotel the girl was still attending to her nails whilst making a call to book a session on a sun bed.

'Bye, Tracy, thanks for everything,' she said, just hoping Stephen had paid in advance for the room. As she came out a traffic warden was pasting a ticket on the car behind her. She smiled sweetly and pulled away with a careless wave, feeling that perhaps the tide was turning, but praying it turned quickly enough before Stephen drowned.

Chapter Fifty Five

Stephen was running, running harder and faster than he'd ever done on any tennis court in his life. He might be sitting in his car, his right foot might be pushing an accelerator rather than pounding a track, but he was running for all that. He'd taken the disc and his wallet but very little else as he'd fled that hotel. He couldn't phone Trisha again. Maybe she had kept her word and not told Charlie, or maybe her phone was tapped. In his confused thinking the possibility that the police might have arrived by coincidence or not even have been looking for him did not even cross his mind.

Where to go? What to do? He was on his own now, truly on his own. He realised that until now he'd not been alone during this whole nightmare. At first he'd had his partners and his wife, then only his wife, and finally Trisha. It didn't pay to rely on others. Neither family nor friends. There was nobody he could trust. Only he, Stephen Kennard, could get himself out of this mess, but like the leader of a defeated army he needed time to regroup, to think, time to put together his resources and plot a new campaign.

He had to steer clear of familiar places, yet at the same time he longed for friendly territory. Play them at their own game. Do the unexpected, live on your wits. That's what he'd done for years as a lawyer, as a tennis player, that's what he'd done for Gerry. His mother had taught him that if nothing else. The thought of his mother threw him into guilty confusion. He should talk to her, see her, reassure her, but if he tried to get near the hospital they'd be waiting for him. It would be the same if he approached his wife and kids. They must by now be watching all his escape routes. Did they know about his place in the Cotswolds? He had to assume they did, although the thought of sleeping in his own bed in his own cottage was very tempting. Yet he knew the Cotswolds well, he'd driven around and around the area for years, walked across the Cotswold Way for miles, forgetting about cars and clients, forgetting about the twentieth century.

Almost automatically he headed out towards the M40 going west, driving carefully within the speed limit, like a drunk who knows in a blurred instinctive way he must draw no attention to himself. He avoided Oxford and the city streets. Too many police, too many squad cars with nothing to do but look for him. He prayed for a crime wave to take the pressure off him. Come on, rape, pillage, burn. Do what you have to do, but buy me some time. He had to be selfish, to be single-minded to survive. The police were not the real enemy, they were just another obstacle that had been put in his path, and he was determined to get round them just as he'd got round everything else. Jeffrey hadn't been able to avoid the enemy, but why had they killed him? What could Jeffrey have done or said to line him up with Jarvis Walters? Stephen felt no sorrow any more for the casualties of war. He felt anger, struggled with it, he had to think like a lawyer and act like The Terminator.

He stopped at Chipping Norton and bought himself some supplies at random, a tin opener, some cans of food, drink, a portable radio, a sleeping bag, a torch. Changes of clothing. He frantically searched his mind for memories of his days in the cubs. He'd never been too attracted to the idea of living rough, never graduated to the boy scouts, but he'd attended camp a few times. Apart from the smell of burning sausages, uncomfortable toilets and silly songs he could remember little. Once he took cover he didn't particularly want to surface every minute to go on a shopping spree. He suddenly realised that he'd accepted he was going under cover, that he was a fugitive. Somehow it was important that the enemy should not know of this, should get no satisfaction from the total destruction of his life, his ultimate degradation.

He loaded up the boot of the car, looking around him cautiously, trying to wipe the memory of his face from the minds of casual shoppers. He drove on, taking a right turn towards Moreton-in-Marsh, determined not to go all the way through Broadway in case he saw somebody he knew—no, that was the wrong way round, in case somebody he knew saw him. He toyed with the idea of an anonymous bed and breakfast place, but they had landladies who watched TV, who bought papers, and who was to say when his picture might appear? It had to be rough. There was enough woodland around to hide Robin Hood and his outlaw band let alone one frightened lawyer. Then he saw the sign and realised he could do better than that.

'Barn conversions for sale'. The sign had been there for years. Nobody was rushing to buy barns to convert nowadays, the whole concept was a throwback to the eighties, to the days when Mrs Thatcher had ruled the world, when yuppies gobbled up these country properties with the same appetite they gobbled up each other. Then greed was good, and now greed was bad. Times changed, but the barns were still there. He turned off the road and saw no sign of recent habitation, nor even of any recent visits. There were no locks on the doors, but there were roofs and even some old straw littering the floor. If the properties had been in London they would have been occupied by squatters but not here in the country. It was considered bad manners to live somewhere without the owner's permission.

'Consider me ill-mannered,' he muttered to himself, parking his car out of sight behind one of the barns. He threw his possessions to the back of the building that seemed the least dilapidated then walked to the end of the drive to see if anything was visible. Not a thing in sight, nor indeed was there anybody around to see anything. The site lay between two villages, just outside Bourton-on-the-Hill which wasn't the busiest of places at the best of times. Cars passed through at speed but few stopped and he just had to bank on nobody suddenly deciding to view the 'desirable site', as the estate agent's board described it.

He went back to the barn, pulled out his sleeping bag, took a swig from a can of mineral water and lay down to sleep. For the moment he was safe. For the moment.

Chapter Fifty Six

On the Tuesday Trisha had visited the hotel she returned to her flat hoping Stephen would call. She tried to keep the line clear, cutting short potential commissioning editors with a speed that left them not only breathless, but convinced that she must be in demand. Work didn't bother her. She was becoming obsessed with one story and one story only, and that one she could never write.

But Stephen didn't ring. She had to do something. She called his cottage number but the phone just rang and rang and eventually she realised he'd have had more sense than to go there. She rang Gerry Mortimer who sounded depressed.

'No, he's not called me. I wish he would. Stephen's not a killer. He'd go for the jugular in business, but in real life, never. If there's anything I can do...'

The offer, well meant but meaningless, hung in the air. She hesitated then rang Stephen's home. It was a long shot but she had to try. A young voice answered the phone, his son she guessed.

'Is your dad there?'

'Are you the Press?'

'Sort of. But a friend. We met at my flat, remember?'

'Mum says you can't trust any journalist.'

Trisha smiled to herself.

'She's probably right. Is your mother home?'

'No.'

'Look, don't tell her I called, but if your dad gets in touch, tell him to call Trisha.'

'Trisha,' the boy repeated. 'Dad's in big trouble, you know, Mum says so.'

'If your mother says so it must be right, but I'm trying to help him out of that trouble.'

'That's good.'

'So you'll tell him.'

'Sure. 'Bye, Trisha.'

' 'Bye, Jonny,' she said, remembering his name.

She was crying by the time she put the receiver down. No wonder Stephen was always crying, always saying sorry. He had had a family and he'd lost them. The kid sounded nice. Maybe she could get to know him properly some day. A big maybe. They belonged to another world, another life, a life she had to save in the knowledge it would almost certainly destroy her own world. 'Heroic stuff, Trisha,' she muttered to herself. She needed a drink. She always wrote best with a few drinks in her, thought more clearly. She went to the fridge and took out a bottle of wine. Normally she wouldn't waste a whole bottle on herself, but what the hell? If she had to get to the bottom of the bottle to get to the truth, then that was where she would go.

She poured the first glass and spread out all that she had taken from Stephen's room on her kitchen table. She had the papers, he had the disc. She had to use them. By the time she'd got to the fourth glass she had worked out the idea, but it needed the sixth glass to give her the confidence to make the calls.

She'd known Simon Burton a long time. They'd started together on the same provincial rag, had served time on the same tabloid, had even contributed to the same Sundays, but Simon had moved onwards and upwards using his economics and politics degree to good advantage. He was now the guru of the City pages. Where Simon led others followed. Inevitably they'd had their fling when they were both younger, but when it had ended, after a disastrous weekend in Venice when the constant rain through a leaking roof had threatened to turn their hotel room into another canal, they had eventually become even firmer friends. Any financial stories Trisha immediately passed on to him and he reciprocated by treating her to regular expensive meals at restaurants she selected. He'd married and divorced twice, but had never tried to rekindle the flame with her. She enjoyed his company, enjoyed the lack of pressure. It was a question now of how far she could make him trust her.

'Simon, it's Trisha.'

'Good to hear from you,' he said in muffled tones.

'Are you eating, Simon?'

'Always eating. Helps to keep the old adrenaline pumping. Eat today, diet tomorrow.'

'But tomorrow never comes, eh?' she added, laughing, thinking of the slim, good-looking boy she'd first known who'd now turned into a plump balding journalist who could resist neither wine nor desserts. Even when they went to the movies together he couldn't sit through the film without a bag of popcorn, a large Coke, and a seemingly inexhaustible supply of chocolate. She'd long ago given up accepting his invitations to the theatre where the audience were more discerning and tended to become somewhat aggressive over the constant rustling.

'Listen, Simon, this conversation's not about food.'

Suddenly he became businesslike. 'What have you got, Trisha? It's a bit quiet on the old market place today. Is it something good?'

'Real good, but dangerous. Your editor's going to hate it, your lawyers are going to freak out, but trust me. It'll be the biggest story of your career.'

'And you're giving it away?'

'I'm too close to it, Simon, and anyway, it's more your line than mine.'

'Anything to back it up? The lawyers are sure to ask.'

She hesitated for a second then grasped the nettle.

'Don't worry. I've got enough. There's no way you'll be sued.'

'Will I be able to see what you've got?'

Another moment's pause.

'Simon, just for once, don't push me. Tell your editor you've seen it. Believe me, it's better that way.'

'Trish, no can do, not even for you.'

She bit her lip anxiously, chewed on it. Another life in danger. Could she do it to a friend?

'OK. Meet me at the usual wine bar in Convent Garden. When does your rag go to bed?'

'I'll see you there at five. If it's good I'll knock the story out and it'll be in tomorrow.'

'Fine. This isn't one story, Simon, it's a whole series. I'll see you later.'

She looked at her watch. Just after three. She had a few minutes to get ready, a few minutes to decide just how much she told Simon, how much she really knew. She shoved the papers back in her bag. She knew enough. One more call to make, then a shower, then a cab.

She dialled the number and to her relief heard Gerry's voice.

'What, you again? You fancy me or something? No, I've not heard from him, but then you only called me an hour ago.'

'Gerry, do you trust Stephen?'

'What you want me to say is I trust him with my life. Believe me, I've got things that are more valuable than my life. That there's not much left of. If I have to be serious, then the answer is, I'd trust Stephen with anything.'

'Good. And do you trust me?'

'Stephen does. That's good enough for me.'

'It shouldn't be. He trusted his partners as well.'

'The fact you'd say that makes me trust you more. And one of his partners is dead. It's all a waste young lady, a *schmutzige* waste.'

'I speak German, not Yiddish. But I understand. Now just listen to me. Over the next few days there may be some movement on your D'Arblay shares. Don't panic, don't sell. Buy. But don't buy too many that the price gets pushed up.'

'This is complicated stuff. Are you sure you know what you're doing?'

She took a deep breath.

'Gerry, I *have* to know what I'm doing. Will you do it?'

'Agh, what's money? Sure I'll do it. I'll have to talk to somebody to make sure I don't get so many shares I have to make a bid for the whole company. Life's complicated when it comes to Public Companies.'

She thought again of Stephen's notes, of the papers in her bag, of the coffin-shaped boxes, of dead men and women she had never known.

'Yes, Gerry, when it comes to Public Companies, life and death are very complicated.'

Chapter Fifty Seven

It had all seemed a good idea at the time. A schoolboy adventure. But the early September nights were cold, the sleeping bag on the ground hard, a far cry even from the lumps and bumps of Trisha's settee. He missed the luxury of a shower, a proper toilet, a table upon which to eat his breakfast. Small things, things which he had always taken for granted. Like his family. He missed them too, and Trisha...did he miss her most of all? He still could not understand why she had betrayed him. There had to be a reason for the police turning up at the hotel, there was no way they could have arrived by chance. He had no links with the area, had never stayed there before. They had come because they'd been sent, Stephen was convinced of it.

He washed as best he could in drinking water that he'd bought in large quantities, changed into the clothes he'd bought at his pit stop in Moreton-in-Marsh and shaved with a cheap safety razor that had been another of his acquisitions. He still had some cash on him but he had to be careful with it. He knew that to use a credit card was dangerous, even assuming they hadn't all been stopped. Thank goodness for Gerry and the horse. Since the day Montpelier King had won he'd kept a fair amount of money on him, somehow anticipating the position in which he now found himself. Always anticipate the worst, run it through your mind, play your doomsday scenario to an audience of one, and somehow it won't seem so bad when it actually happens.

He listened to the news on the radio. He was no longer an item. That was good. Clearly he couldn't compete with allegations of corruption against a Government Minister, another Royal divorce and transfer rumours of Gazza's return to English football. Automatically he tidied the barn, storing his few belongings neatly in a corner. Then he realised he had nothing to do. The day stretched in front of him endlessly, a day without clients, without phones, a day curiously without pressure considering his position.

The sun appeared from behind a cloud and he stood at the door of the barn taking in deep breaths. There was that odd autumnal smell in the air, a hint of burning fields when the summer is not quite forgotten but winter is pushing to get in. He'd hated that smell when he was young. It meant that the summer holidays were coming to an end. It was a scent associated with shopping for winter clothes, for a new school blazer, a scent of days when everything that had been put off for weeks had to be crammed into a few hours.

He couldn't just stay here listening to the radio. He knew it was safest, but then was there any real risk in his walking the countryside? He really wanted a newspaper, a book to read, some little luxuries that might improve the quality of his life. He remembered when he and Cathy had gone to see Robert Redford in *Jeremiah Johnson*—the story of a man who'd turned his back on civilisation.

'I could be a mountain man,' he'd said as they'd left the cinema, and her eyes had not dried from tears of laughter by the time they'd got back to the car. Well, he was a mountain man now, although the rolling hills of the Cotswolds were a million miles from the snow-covered peaks of the American mid-west.

Well, everybody had to start somewhere. He was talking to himself, laughing at his own jokes. The first signs of madness. Perhaps he was mad, perhaps he'd committed all the crimes of which he was accused, that the men who'd taken his car were figments of his imagination. No, the men were real, the damage to Trisha's flat was real, Jeffrey's death was real. He would have remembered if he'd run him over with his car, but did Dr Jekyll remember Mr Hyde?'

Shivering, he found despite himself he'd walked to the end of the drive. No cars, no people. If he was going to come into the open this was the moment.

He turned left towards the village. There had to be a shop there. He could go there once, maybe twice. After that people would ask questions, perhaps even recognise him. Village people were notoriously curious and a persistent stranger would be a talking point. He walked for a few moments, enjoying the feeling of total freedom, the lack of responsibility. Whatever was happening was happening without him, was out of his control. Let the gods decide. Whatever the oracle contained, it contained, and that was it. The oracle or the Bible. The night before, in the barn, he'd woken just after midnight and lain there unable to get back to sleep. As a child he'd never been able to get to sleep until he'd said his prayers—not the formal Hebrew prayers he'd learned in classes but his own version, pleas for his parents, pleas to pass exams, to make a particular girl like him, selfish, selfish prayers. Last night, to send himself to sleep, he'd run through the Ten Commandments, trying to remember them like long forgotten litany.

'I am the Lord your God. You shall have no other God before me.' They were two, but only one was really a commandment, the first was a statement. Had he had other Gods? Was mammon a God? If so, then he was guilty.

'Don't take the Lord's name in vain.' He'd done that too, time after time, used it in jokes, used it to swear. He was guilty.

'Remember Sabbath'—the fourth. He'd remembered it only to forget it. He and Jeff, teasing the orthodox kids at school, laughing at them as they left school early on winter Friday afternoons, taunting them for missing football matches, Saturday just another day of work. He was guilty.

'Honour your father and mother.' He'd loved them when he was a kid, but honour, obey? No, not for a long time. And now his mother, his unhonoured mother, was mourning for him. He was guilty.

The sixth. He had sought for the sixth but couldn't remember. Seven was adultery. He had tried to block the memory of Sarah from his mind but again he was guilty. He'd tried to focus on eight calling back long forgotten days at Hebrew classes, but then you never forget anything. It's always there, tucked into the mind.

Nine: 'Don't lie.' He'd lied to Cathy, lied to clients, lied to himself. Guilty.

Ten: 'Don't be jealous.' Yes, that too. He'd wanted what his neighbours had, and more. Enough had never been enough. That left six and eight. He had finally got them. 'Don't kill, don't steal.' The two he'd never broken, the two for which he'd been condemned by the world. It wasn't fair, and he had fallen back to sleep protesting his own innocence.

As he ran over them again in his mind he found he'd walked the distance to the village shop, which turned out to be a general store and sub post office. An old lady looked up as the door rang on his entry.

'Morning sir, nice day.'

'Very.' Keep it minimal.

'Can I help you?'

'I just need a few things.'

'You take your time, sir, no hurry. Never any sense in hurrying in life. You hurry,

498

you scare the sparrows away.'

Just what I need, he thought, a country philosopher. He picked up a couple of papers at random, a quality and a tabloid, bought some chocolate, paper cups and some serviettes.

'Picnic, is it, sir? Good day for it. When the clouds scurry then you must hurry, that's what my nan used to say. No wind today so I reckon you'll be all right.'

He smiled politely. Would she be able to describe him? He imagined the conversation with the local bobby.

'Oh, yes, he was here, right here in my shop. I thought it was odd a man like him buying cups and things. He looked sinister, he looked desperate. Can you imagine...' and then perhaps some more wise words from her grandmother.

'Anything else, sir? We've some nice pork sausages in that fridge over there. Fresh from my brother's farm. Talked to the pig on Sunday and I'm eating him today.'

'No, that's fine.'

He walked out quickly, controlling himself from breaking into a run. Pork sausages! It would have to be pork sausages. He arrived back at the barn breathless, relieved to see nothing had been touched. He poured himself a drink, emptying a can of Coke into the cup. It just seemed more civilised that way. He took a deep breath. He was getting away with it. Getting away with what? He hadn't done anything. So, he was just getting away, like the old phrase in another life on the lips of another man.

'I'm just getting away for a few days.'

He turned unhurriedly to the papers. It was a long time since he'd read a newspaper from cover to cover. He was going to enjoy it.

Chapter Fifty Eight

By Friday morning Toby Lipscomb was not enjoying the newspapers. He was not a happy man and when he was unhappy those around him were similarly so. He'd virtually thrown his cup of coffee at his secretary telling her she needed to be in earlier to percolate it, and if she gave him instant coffee one more time she wouldn't have a job for which to be early.

Now it was the turn of Philip Greystone. It took a lot to ruffle Greystone's feathers but today they were not merely ruffled but threatening to leave him fully plucked.

'Look at it, just look at it! Who the hell is Simon Burton?' screamed Lipscomb.

'He's a very well-respected City writer.

He carried a lot of weight in the market.'

'I know he carries weight in the market. I just have to look at our shares to know that. Today's Friday. This is the third day running he's had a tilt at us, the third day! Wednesday morning he says that there's likely to be a mass walk out of our exhibitors in England because our fees haven't come to terms with the recession. OK, I take that as whistling in the dark. Maybe he knows something we don't know. The shares fall 10p. It's acceptable. It happens, vagaries of the market. They fall, they rise. Then Thursday, according to Mr Burton, we're under pressure with our gaming licences. We're delaying our half-yearly results while we negotiate. That was 30p's worth. I ask you to write a letter before action, to threaten an injunction.'

'I did it. I faxed it across.'

'So what happened?'

'Odd response. Normally they'd say they're looking into it, making a full investigation and then they'll get back to us. This time, like a shot, fax comes back and says they stick by their story, they've got more to come, and in due course they'd be interested in our comments.'

'So what does that tell you?'

'It suggests they're either confused or bluffing.'

'And what do you think, in your

considered legal opinion?'

'I think they've been fed these stories. I think they're bluffing because they've gone so far down the line they can't turn back. So at the end of the day we'll sue them. You just have to be patient, Toby.'

'Patient, patient? I'll give you fucking patient! Have you read today's little effort?'

Greystone had never seen his client in this mood before. He'd seen him angry, but it was always controlled, always a loss of temper almost contrived for effect. This was a crazy sort of rage, a rage that stripped off his veneer, stripped away his flesh, stripped the man down to his bones and beyond.

'Yes, I've read it.'

'Oh, he's read it! The great lawyer has read it. Maybe I should get myself a real lawyer like Stephen Kennard? At least I'd be sure of some bloody action. Today the whole business world is told that our exhibition halls are about to create a sealed tender for bids and that we're likely to lose them. I've had the brokers on the phone saying we need to put out a statement and put it out quick. They've only been trading an hour and we're down another 28p.'

'All right, we'll work on a statement.'

'Well, that's good. That'll make it better. And what are you going to do about the banks? I've had all three on the phone today saying they'd like to see me. They didn't even mention lunch so I don't think they have anything social in mind.'

'We'll deal with the banks. I've been dealing with banks since I was an articled clerk. They're like babies, they just need reassurance.'

'Well, you go and change their nappies for them,' Lipscomb said, his voice still high, bordering on the hysterical. 'You reassure them with your assets, they've got all mine!'

'Just calm down, Toby. We'll deal with it all in the proper manner.'

'No, Philip, we'll deal with it all now! You get this Burton on the phone. I want him stopped before it gets out of control. It's not just the shares, and the banks—I've even had bloody trade creditors phoning me, money up front, deposits, bonds, before they'll give us space. I've never had this sort of thing in my life.'

'It's just panic. It'll wear off. The shares will stabilise. By next week Burton and his paper will just be yesterday's fish and chips.'

'Philip, you're not listening to me. I sometimes think you forget who pays you. I'm your biggest client. You may be in the City but you're not some mega firm with a hundred partners. I move and I leave a big hole for you to fill. Have you done any shovelling lately?' He didn't wait for a reply, he was not in a mood to listen to replies or reason. 'No, I don't think so. Now lift that fucking receiver and phone Burton! Don't say you're with me. I'll listen on the loudspeaker.'

'Toby, for the last time, this is not a good idea.'

Suddenly Lipscomb's voice was quiet and cool, the words turning to icicles as they left his mouth, sharp icicles with points and edges that could pierce a man's flesh.

'But it's *my* idea, Philip, so do it. Now. There's a good boy.'

The lawyer lifted the phone and asked the receptionist to get the number.

'Don't bother, Philip. I took the trouble to get his direct line before you came. Just dial.'

He dialled.

Chapter Fifty Nine

Trisha was disappointed. The plan had worked up to a point, but she'd clearly not thought it through all the way. She knew bits and pieces but not enough it seemed. She was on a treasure hunt, but she'd not been given all the clues, or maybe she had all the clues and didn't know it. Either way it had failed. She knew that somehow D'Arblay was the key to it all, and so she'd targeted the company in the best way she could. It had all seemed so simple: hit D'Arblay in its corporate solar plexus and see who reeled with the punch. Somebody would come out in the open and somehow she'd hear of it. And that was where it had floundered.

Simon had met her, looked at her material and been satisfied. He'd done everything she could have wanted and more. The shares had fallen and she knew from a call to Gerry that he'd bought.

'I must be *meshige*. I'm buying shares in a company where I've already got shares. The company's in *dreh*, in dead *stooch*, and like a *shmock* I'm getting in deeper and deeper just because a pretty redhead tells me to do it. I want to talk to my lawyer, but no, he's wanted for fraud, theft, embezzlement, murder. You name it, he's wanted for it. Oy, am I getting old?'

'Ride it, Gerry, just ride this roller coaster and I promise you you'll get off it feeling good.'

'Good is nice, rich is nicer.'

'Yeah, that too. I'll keep in touch.'

And still Stephen didn't phone. He could be dead for all she knew, lying in a ditch somewhere, or a wood, the kind of corpse the police find twenty years on and need dental records to identify. She didn't even know who his dentist was. There was so much about him she didn't know, and yet she was putting everything on the line for him. That itself was frightening.

Charlie had called.

'It's official, Trisha. Have you heard from him?'

'No.'

'OK. I believe you. If you do, just tell him to get in touch.'

'What, so you can arrest him?'

'No, so I can help him.'

'Sure, Charlie. A pig's just flown by my window.'

'Book a ticket on its next flight. I'll call you in a couple of days. Don't forget what I told you.'

She'd not forgotten. Call, Stephen, call! She tried to focus her mind on him, trying to connect across however many miles there were. It was just possible he'd left the country. He had the documents to get to the Continent. There'd be watches on ports and planes but that wasn't to say he wouldn't get through. She poured herself a drink. She'd done a lot of that. On a Friday evening she wouldn't normally be on her own at home. She'd have gone to a wine bar, a journalists' drinking hole, swopped stories, listened out for leads. She was features more than news and so she wasn't seen as a rival by the journalists who worked on the dailies. Their stories were quick, under-researched, a wham, bam, thankyou mam approach reflected in lurid headlines. She was patient, she got beneath the surface, never hurried, never rushed a story. It had to be conceived and born and the birth could be painful, sometimes dangerous, but never as dangerous as this. And it wasn't even her story any more. It was Simon Burton's. She felt suddenly guilty in case she'd put him in danger. She tried to call him but the line was busy. She tried again impatiently but almost as she picked up the phone she heard Stephen's voice on the line.

'Hey, it didn't even ring,' he said, and she felt a shiver go down her whole body at the sound of his voice. Was it just relief or was it something more? She didn't think right at that moment that she really wanted to know.

'Where the hell have you been?' She couldn't keep the note of anger from her voice.

'Hell and back. Don't be mad with me, Trisha. I just had to get my head straight. Country air, doctor's advice. You don't think the phone's tapped, do you?'

507

'No. Charlie wouldn't allow that.'

'Is it in Charlie's gift?'

'I'm not sure, but no, I don't think I'm bugged. The line sounds the same as normal.'

He hesitated.

'OK. We'll just have to take a chance. These D'Arblay stories. Have you had a hand in them?'

'How did you guess?'

'Perhaps I know you better than you think.'

'How have you been?'

'I'm fine. Better than I could have expected.'

'Stephen, those stories. I need the disc. A friend has done me a favour. I showed him the papers you left at the hotel.'

'Why do you need the disc?'

'I've sort of half told him the truth. He's running these stories as flyers for the real hit. He doesn't want to put his head on the line for that one until he's seen what you've seen.'

'How did you get the fix on D'Arblay?'

'I'm not stupid. Your mind map was good. I followed it through. There's just one thing more. You left out a black box. Charlie tells me Arthur's dead.'

There was a silence.

'Look, Trisha, I don't want you staying on your own. We're both getting out of

508

our depth. We're throwing punches in the dark. Have you got a friend you can stay with?'

'Male or female?'

'Don't play games, Trisha.'

'Stephen, I want to see you. I told you, I need the disc.'

'Do you want to see me or the disc?'

'I'll tell you when I get there, only you have to tell me where there is.'

Again he hesitated. She was probably right. He was fantasising when he thought she was bugged, but he'd been careful up to now and it had paid off. If she did bring a cavalcade with her there was no way out of the barns.

'Trisha, this is what you do. Drive down to the Cotswolds. Head for Broadway. Just before you get to the village there's a left turn for Snowshill. Take it, then turn back on yourself towards Broadway. On your left-hand side you'll see the Broadway Tower. You can't miss it. It's closed at night but you can walk up a little hill from the road. Take a torch. There's barbed wire, but only a couple of strands. It's more to keep the cows in than to keep people out. Flash your torch from the road, twice if you're sure you've not been followed. I'll flash back twice, then come on up.'

'Do you need anything?'

'It's Friday night. Some chicken soup would be nice.'

'Sorry, I'm not your wife. I'll be there in a couple of hours, traffic permitting. It'll be dark by then.'

'Trisha...'

'Yes?'

'Come on your own, promise?'

'I promise.'

'Drive safely.' It wasn't what he'd meant to say, but it would have to do.

Trisha put down the phone. She was angry with herself. No, she wasn't his wife but she didn't need to tell him that. He'd made her nervous. Slowly she walked to the window and looked out. Apart from a few parked cars the street was empty. A door opened and a child appeared with a tricycle. She didn't think the police or anybody else were recruiting them that young. Slowly she drew the curtains, balancing possibilities in her mind. She'd not delivered Charlie's message, but then she'd promised Stephen she wouldn't involve him. Again she peered out through the curtains. There was nothing to be seen. Ten minutes later, dressed for a cross-country hike, she turned on the answerphone and was heading for the motorway.

It was five minutes or so after she left

that Simon Burton heard her recorded message. He swore softly to himself. Just like a woman, never there when you want them.

'Trisha, it's Simon. I think I may have made a mistake. I had D'Arblay's lawyer on the phone earlier. I've been out most of the day and perhaps I should have told you before. He got a bit heavy and I had to play a card or two. I mentioned the Sapsford Clinic and then he hung up... Just take care. Call me when you get back.'

Burton sat back feeling that he'd not done quite enough. He hadn't liked the sound of the lawyer's voice nor had he liked the whole tone of the conversation. He automatically distrusted people who spoke over loudspeakers. It was as if they needed an audience. That was it. It had felt as though Greystone was performing to an audience...

Still with the feeling that something was wrong, he sat down before his screen and began to type tomorrow's story, hoping that neither he nor Trisha would be a part of it.

Chapter Sixty

The Broadway Tower is an old man's folly. It guards nothing but is merely a testimony to man's pride and foolishness, like so many other buildings scattered around the countryside. Yet as the autumnal dusk fell and a chill wind began to blow it had a ghostliness about it that belied its age. During the daytime families picnicked, children played, visitors admired the William Morris designs. It had no age, no atmosphere. But now it was different.

Stephen remembered the stories he'd heard of nineteenth-century grave robbers crossing the Cotswold Way to the old church of St Ethelbreda, and then carrying their ghastly burdens back along these paths. Maybe that was what he felt, the souls of the disturbed? Or was it the souls of Jeffrey, of Jarvis, of Arthur? How had he died? He couldn't feel angry at the man, just an all consuming sorrow that he'd been driven to do what he did. He had no anger at those ghosts with faces; it was the faceless ones who enraged him.

He was excited at the thought of seeing Trisha again, excited not just by her but also by the surroundings in which he'd set the scene. The dark tower silhouetted against what was now a dark sky, beyond down Fish Hill the lights of the village, in the distance the church clock sounding the hour. The stillness of it all, the absolute stillness of the country at night.

He poured himself a coffee from his thermos. He'd learned a lot about survival in the last few days, had actually begun to enjoy it. When this was all over he'd take Jonny camping; when this was all over he'd do lots of things with the kids; with Cathy too, although he couldn't envisage her sleeping rough. He realised he was making plans, assuming it would all be over, and that was something new, something positive. And where did Trisha fit into all this? If he didn't see Cathy sitting around a camp fire he also couldn't envisage her inviting Trisha around for a cosy meal.

He heard a car and instinctively shrank back against the wall. It stopped. A door slammed and he thought he heard a female curse. Then a light flashing, once, twice. He flashed back, and then he heard her scrambling up the bank.

'Couldn't you have chosen somewhere quieter? I've just ruined a hundred pound pair of slacks on the barbed wire.'

'I'll buy you a new pair. Were you followed?'

'No.' There was the slightest hesitation.

'Are you sure?'

'I thought there might have been a car behind me all the way to Oxford. I saw a blue Merc in my rear mirror a few times and I was a bit surprised it didn't go past me, but after that it wasn't there.' She flashed her light up and down in a cursory inspection.

'Hey, you look good, considering. Where have you been all week?'

He told her of his flight from the hotel and she told him about Charlie, and Arthur, and Simon Burton.

'I've brought us some wine. I couldn't get the chicken soup but I stopped at a deli for salt beef sandwiches. I hope it's ethnic enough.'

'It's perfect, Trisha.'

'And you've got the disc?'

'I've got the disc.'

'Oh good, I am so pleased.' They hadn't heard the speaker approach, but now they found themselves caught like moths in a powerful cross beam of light.

'I don't think I've ever had the pleasure, my dear. Toby Lipscomb. I can't say I'm delighted to meet you, although I am quite pleased that my trusty drivers were able to follow you here. And the next question I believe you should be asking is how, and after that why? Well, we have a moment

514

or two so let's fill them, shall we?'

Trisha moved closer to Stephen and he put his arm around her protectively.

'Lipscomb, if it's me you're after, fine. Just let the girl go.'

'No, it's actually both of you, I fear. But everything in its time, I have a kind of mental agenda for this meeting. You as a lawyer—and I believe you are still one, although that would not have lasted for long even if I hadn't intervened tonight—you as a lawyer will appreciate the necessity for order in any meeting. Oh, yes. I will take questions at the end.' He smiled, his teeth shining white in the light, his face a mask of crazed enjoyment.

'So first, I'm afraid your reporter friend let you down, Ms Martin. He happened to mention he had a story about Sapsford Clinic up his sleeve. Now my able lawyer Philip Greystone—I do believe you've had the pleasure, Stephen. You don't mind if I call you Stephen, do you, although we've never ever been really introduced? I do so want this last meeting to be amicable—well, Philip picked up on that. Now it was you two who got Sapsford closed down, and as you seem to have guessed from that little disc you have there, Stephen, Sapsford was actually one of ours.'

He opened his mouth to speak but

the words would not come. When he'd been faced with imprisonment he'd have settled for bankruptcy, but these were finite problems compared to what faced him now. The game had changed and he had been too slow to recognise it. He should have realised when Jarvis and Jeffrey had been taken off the board. Trisha had known it, she had tried to warn him, but he could not bring himself to ask Charlie for help. He didn't want to be indebted to a man who'd shared her bed, who'd entered her body, who, for all her protestations, might still be in her mind.

It was absurd. He'd never spoken more than a few words to Lipscomb in the past. Their paths had rarely crossed, yet here he was at the man's mercy.

'It's such a shame your good friend Mr Mortimer can't be here to share this farewell party. Gerry and I, though, we go back a long way. Wherever I turned he'd pop up, stealing companies from under my nose, hiring my staff, taking my profits. You know, I once nearly went under because of your good friend, Gerry Mortimer. Seems a pity really that you have to suffer for his sins, the sins of the father and all that. But then he's not your father, is he? Just a substitute. He and your mother had something going years ago, I

516

understand. Maybe that's why he took you on—out of guilt.'

Stephen made a move towards him but Lipscomb held up a hand and Stephen saw two large figures looming behind him.

'No, not just out of guilt. Gerry never did anything unless there was some advantage to him. You were good. We all saw how good you were. Things were looking up for Sidney from the minute you got there. We were going to head hunt you, Stephen. Did you know that? But would you have played with us? No, I don't think so. You were always going to be the game keeper, never the poacher. Too honest to be in this dirty business, and look where it's got you.'

Stephen took a step backwards, holding Trisha even more tightly.

'So sweet. Our little lovebirds. Well, you led us to your turtle dove, Trisha. As soon as I heard mention of Sapsford I realised your sweet white hands were behind this, so I put a watch on your flat...'

'I looked out of the window.'

'Did you? Well, you could hardly have expected my lads to be carrying placards. They do their job well. They know what happens if they don't.'

'And Arthur did his job well, and Jarvis,' Stephen said.

'Arthur did it exceedingly well, but he

517

was never really a member of the club. There was always a chance Arthur would have one drink too many after one of those dreadful football matches he seemed to enjoy so much. And Jarvis was getting out of line, becoming nervous. We owned Sapsford through one of the trusts that Jarvis Walters set up and administered for us.'

'He didn't kill himself, did he?'

Lipscomb smiled, an expression without warmth or pity.

'No, Jarvis didn't kill himself. As I said, he just lost his nerve.'

'Perhaps because you were blackmailing him?'

Lipscomb raised his eyebrows.

'Well done. I didn't realise you knew that too. Yes, we were putting a little pressure on Jarvis. There's never anything wrong with insurance; but Trisha's visit did him no good at all. He didn't like the police snooping around either in respect of the money that came from your client account.'

'So why send it there?' Stephen asked, curious despite himself.

'We controlled him. It was logical. It pointed the finger firmly at you. Jarvis wasn't difficult. A few drinks down him. Once he'd slipped from the wagon we could do anything with him. Make him do anything to himself.'

'His wife won't get the insurance money if it's suicide.'

'Shame.'

Stephen tried to control the anger in him. Everything told him that the longer he kept the man talking, the more he'd learn. However remote the chance of survival he had to cling on to the hope that one day he'd be able to pass on the knowledge.

Lipscomb seemed relaxed and smiling.

'If it's any consolation, Arthur died the way he would have chosen surrounded by pretty ladies. You see, D'Arblay is two businesses—well, several really. It's what you and the shareholders see and what they don't. And what they don't see they don't share in. Yes, we have lots of interests: clinics, bordellos, movies. That's how Arthur went, starring in one of our little snuff productions. It would have been a shame to miss the opportunity of his demise. Perhaps I should have brought some cameras with me tonight, although I doubt if these lights are really up to the demands of our discerning viewers.'

'And Jeffrey, why kill Jeffrey? He was on to you, wasn't he, you and your bent lawyer. He was about to tell me.'

Lipscomb laughed, a harsh cawing sound

that sent some night birds scurrying from their branches.

'On to us? Your dear friend Jeffrey? On to us? Jeffrey was *part* of us.'

Chapter Sixty One

It was at that moment Stephen realised there was no hope. Everything he believed in suddenly slipped away into a deep dark chasm. Jeffrey, his school friend, his partner. He would have walked over broken glass for him, yet he had been betrayed by him. He felt a deep sense of depression, knowing that Lipscomb could see he'd dealt a deadly blow. He wriggled on the hook one last time.

'Simon Burton will know that we've both disappeared. He'll put two and two together.'

'The arithmetical skills of journalists are notoriously weak, I fear. And anyway, who said you're going to disappear? Nothing so melodramatic. We have a screen play for you and I'm sure you'll both play your roles to perfection. Now we don't have time for any rehearsals so this is how it goes—murderer on the run gets tracked down by journalist looking for a story. He kills her, then filled with guilt and remorse, kills himself. Nobody else involved. Neat and tidy. Mr Burton can surmise all he wants, but if he surmises too far we end up with a libel action and even more tax free money for me. You see, sometimes I will take a lawyer's advice. Greystone wanted me to leave you alone. He felt the police would take care of you in the end, but I couldn't leave it there.' His voice was rising. 'Nobody, but nobody, has got under my skin the way you two have.'

It was now or never. Stephen launched himself at Lipscomb, and taking him by surprise fell on top of him, the torch dropping from his grasp. He got hold of the man by the neck and gripped him tight, suddenly becoming a person he did not recognise, a person who could kill to save himself. The first blow from behind he hardly felt, so intent was he on destroying the evil in his hands, but the second blow to his temple sent him reeling away, one hand feebly flailing at Lipscomb's face. A boot caught him in the stomach.

'Leave him be,' Lipscomb said, 'we can't have him too badly marked if he's going to kill himself. We'll have to make it seem as if the young lady here inflicted those injuries before he overpowered her.'

Stephen looked up and saw the two men by Lipscomb's side, the same two who'd taken his car. They seemed even bigger now, mountains towering over him, Stephen Kennard, mountain man. The idea now seemed even more absurd.

'Enough,' Lipscomb said, 'I'm bored. Let's put an end to it. First of all the girl. I think perhaps you beat her to death with a piece of wood.' He looked around thoughtfully. 'Ah, there's one handy.' He nodded to the bigger of the thugs who picked up the large piece of wood with as much effort as Stephen would have extended to a matchstick. He lifted the weapon. Trisha screamed, and Stephen threw himself in front of her in a futile attempt to ward off the blows.

It was at that moment that the police siren cut through the night, headlights blazed from the road, and suddenly Charlie was there accompanied by what appeared to be most of the police force of the surrounding counties. Lipscomb put up no struggle at all, but it took eight hefty policemen to bring the two heavies under control. Dusting himself down from Stephen's attack, Lipscomb regained his cool.

'Thank goodness you've come. I dread to think what might have happened to the three of us if you hadn't arrived. These two villains brought me here against my wishes...'

The largest of the heavies threw off the policeman who was sitting on his head.

'You lying bastard, Lipscomb! This was all your idea.'

'Excuse me, did I ask you to bring me here?'

'You got your bloody mouthpiece that lawyer to do it...'

Stephen looked ruefully at Charlie, the blood still streaming down his face from the cut on his temple.

'Don't worry about Mr Lipscomb here. He's told Trisha and me enough to put him away for life. And as for these two, they were the guys who took my car. I've no doubt they killed Jeffrey too. I trust you'll be paying a visit to Philip Greystone?'

'Who's leading this investigation, Kennard, me or you? I've had a hard enough time getting the locals to allow me in on this when it's a hundred miles from my patch. And you're not out of this yet by a long shot. There's still a warrant out for your arrest, and as far as the Met are concerned you're still public enemy number one.'

'Give it a break, Charlie. Look at him. You must know now he had nothing to do with any of it,' Trisha said.

'I don't know. Tell me.'

'I acted for Gerry Mortimer and his company, Sidney. They wanted to take over D'Arblay which was run by Lipscomb. If that had gone through they'd have lost their cover for their underground operation. Trisha and I had already upset them by closing down one of their clinics which had a life all of its own.'

'Sapsford was one of theirs?' Charlie asked.

'Believe me, I didn't know that for sure until today.'

'Go on.'

'They flattered me. They thought I was crucial to the takeover. They got to my partner Jeffrey, God knows how. Got Greystone to offer to take over our firm, flattered him, bribed him, threatened him. Who knows? He can't tell us now, poor Jeffrey. They or Jeffrey paid off my accounts man, Arthur Kemp. Money goes out, they use it to buy D'Arblay's shares. I'm set up. They even go so far as to try and ruin my marriage—they pick a dead woman who can't talk back. Isolate Stephen, that's the game. Then they get hold of Jarvis Walters in Jersey, blackmail him into handling the money, he tries to put it right and they kill him—maybe even Lipscomb himself did that. He seems to enjoy that sort of thing. Even if he didn't put the rope around his neck, I think he was there. They think I'm getting close, they even break into Trisha's flat to see what we've found. Jeffrey wants to talk to me, he's scared too, maybe he's seen what's happened to Jarvis.'

'He should have seen what happened to Arthur.'

'We just heard.'

'Yes, his first and only role—his career came to a dead end.'

'I see. I rather liked Arthur.' Stephen paused, reflecting on the chats he'd had with his former employee. The coffees shared, the drinks at Christmas. The man's genuine excitement and pleasure when his team had won. He stared at Trisha, her face that of a young girl at a story teller's knee. 'Anyway, Jeffrey was about to talk to me. That was against the rules. They stole my car and killed him too. So much death...'

Charlie looked almost convinced.

'Back up here yet?' he asked one of the police.

The sound of cars down the narrow country roads answered his question, the insistent shriek of the ambulance siren following close behind.

'You look as if you could do with a ride,' Charlie said to Stephen.

'I'm fine.'

An ambulanceman appeared at his side.

'Shall I just take a look at that wound, sir?'

'I'm OK honest.'

'Come on down to the ambulance. Let's clean it up and get you down to hospital for a check up.'

'Clean it up, but no hospitals.'

Charlie sighed.

'You really are a stubborn bastard. Check him out,' he said to the ambulanceman. 'If you find he's got a pulse and a heartbeat, let him do what the hell he wants. If he's keen on killing himself, I'm all in favour of that.'

Stephen made his way unsteadily down the slope, watching without emotion as Lipscomb and his two men were pushed into the waiting police cars. Charlie put his hands on Trisha's shoulders.

'Are you all right?'

'I'm fine. They never touched me.'

'Lucky for them. I might have wanted a few minutes alone with them before they made it to the local nick if they had.'

'Thanks, Charlie. I didn't know if I was doing right calling you or not. I'd promised him I wouldn't.'

'Some promises are better broken. Fancy coming out with me tonight—or at least what's left of it?'

She shook her head sadly.

'I can't. I really can't. It wouldn't be fair on you. I'm grateful, but that's it. Gratitude, not love.'

'It'll do for the moment. I told you before, he's going back to his wife.'

'I know. I think I need to get away for a while. This hasn't exactly been a holiday for me, no fun in Dijon and Jersey.'

'Even with your friendly lawyer?'

'It's not been like that.'

'Sure.'

'Charlie, I don't have to lie to you.'

'But if you didn't it might hurt.'

She touched his cheek.

'I just want to slip away quietly. Tell Stephen I said goodbye. I don't want to hurt him or you. Ever.'

'Too late for that.' Suddenly he got a firm grip on himself.

'Are you guys finished? We've got a lot to do here.'

'Yeah, we're finished. Your friend's here as healthy as he's ever been.'

'All right, Steve.'

'I can go?' he asked.

'I shouldn't let you, but I will. I want you down at West End Central first thing

Monday morning. First thing. Always assuming that nobody tries to bump you off between now and then. Where are you going in such a hurry?'

'Back to my life,' he said. 'Where's Trisha? I wanted to thank her for everything, even breaking her word about you.'

'She nearly didn't, you know. She was on her way here and stopped at a garage to give me a ring. We broke almost every speed limit to catch up with her. Lucky the traffic was bad and it's amazing what a blue flashlight and a siren can do even in a solid jam. Everybody thinks they're after them and moves aside.'

'You didn't answer me, Charlie, where's Trisha?'

He smiled this time, a rueful grin that for the first time in their relationship said they had something in common.

'She said to say goodbye.'

'That's absurd. After what we've been through! Where's she gone?' He made to race after her, but Charlie's hand restrained him firmly.

'Leave it be, Stephen.'

'I won't. Just tell me where she's gone.'

'Back to her life,' Charlie replied, and looking down the road Stephen thought he glimpsed her red hair behind the wheel as her car turned the bend.

Chapter Sixty Two

It was nearly midnight when he got back to London. He should have gone home first, he knew, but then he'd been away for so long that another hour or two would make no difference. And so he went to the office, his office, in an attempt to reconstruct his life, to rediscover the man he had once been.

With some surprise he found his key still fitted the front door. Maybe they'd thought he'd never again try to get in, maybe they'd just forgotten to change the locks. Even the security number on the alarm pad was still the same: 941947. His birthday. Not Jeffrey's, not Anthony's—his. His firm. Perhaps that was what had been the mistake, a benevolent dictator rather than a partner. Was that how they'd seen him? He couldn't ask Jeffrey now. It was too late to ask Jeffrey anything.

The main office was as untidy as ever and absentmindedly he switched off the VDUs and the photocopier. The practice always gave the impression of a nuclear disaster when the last person left at night, a scattering of papers, files, half-typed letters, unposted stamped envelopes...yes, they were there, still using stamps. He'd had that constant battle with Jeffrey—'Let's move on to a franking machine'—Jeffrey would never agree it. Stamps were a way of him taking a little cash out of the business after they refused it from clients.

'Nobody can check how much petty cash you draw for stamps, so we take an extra £50 each and it goes into our pockets.' And Stephen had humoured him, almost thought it was amusing, Jeffrey never coming to terms with the fact that they had responsibilities, a reputation, that it was no longer possible to bend the rules. He should have seen Jeffrey's larcenous tendencies coming through in those little things but the problem was he'd always seen his friend with schoolboy-tinted glasses; but they had both grown up and only Jeffrey had noticed. It seemed to him now that Jeffrey had noticed many things, that it had been Jeffrey who had always had the eye for the main chance, not him.

He pushed open the door to Jeffrey's office, half expecting to see him sitting there, feet up on the desk, telephone in hand, writing the hieroglyphics that only he could read. The room was, of course, empty. The desk still covered by papers, some evidence that somebody—perhaps the police—had tried to bring some order to the chaos. Although there were no photographs, there was still the unmistakable print of Jeffrey's personality on the room. The sign that said: 'First we kill all the lawyers', the little clockwork man with a billboard that served as a memo pad, his desk top bowling game that could make even the most difficult client compulsive in a matter of moments. But no photographs. His ex-wives did not rate any memorabilia and there were no children. If Jeffrey had to die he should have died mourned but unforgotten by friends. Yet what friends did he really have?

Stephen seated himself in his late partner's chair, hoping to get some insight from the things he had gathered around him. He had thought himself Jeffrey's friend but when he came to list any others it was difficult. Everybody who met him claimed to like him.

'Great company, Jeffrey—good for a laugh. Nobody better to spend an evening with. But to spend a lifetime?'

Three women had tried and failed. Stephen idly wondered who'd inherit under his will. He'd not been known for his charitable tendencies, so perhaps he'd selected the wife who'd stung him for the least. It was, of course, possible that there had been another great love in his life. Even before his problems they'd shared very little social life. Whenever he'd suggesting inviting Jeffrey over to dinner Cathy had demurred, and eventually he'd given up. He'd never understood what it was that had driven a wedge between his wife and his partner. They'd grown up together, after all. It had, in its way, been like his mother, his father and Gerry, history repeating itself.

Cathy. He ought to get home, try to talk to her. How did he explain everything to her, that living with Trisha had somehow rescued his marriage. Not easy, but then nothing would ever be easy again. He shuffled papers, knowing that he was delaying the inevitable, grateful that at least at this time of night—morning—the children would be fast asleep. It was going to be difficult enough anyway without having them there as well.

'Daddy's home, kids. He didn't steal, he didn't kill, and this has all been a nasty dream.' His mind felt oddly empty and he realised that for too long it had been filled with fear. Now the fear was gone, drained away, but still there was a nagging doubt, a voice that told him he should be feeling better than he did. Relief was there, but so was sadness. Lipscomb, Greystone, he'd never really known them, just stumbled across their path, and having got in their way had to be removed. Jeffrey, though, was different. He was something else, he was family. Family might argue, family might scream and shout, sometimes even come to blows, but families didn't steal, families didn't kill. It was impossible to believe that Jeffrey had ever been a part of the killings. Cuddly, laughing Jeffrey, a man who wanted to love and be loved. There had to be a clue somewhere. Jeffrey was always a hoarder, dumping stuff at random in his desk drawers. Then he remembered. He'd always had a little hiding place for his really confidential stuff—'the dynamite' as he'd put it.

The left-hand drawer was sticking and as he pulled it the whole thing came out in his hand, spilling the contents on the floor. As if somebody was guiding him he looked into the empty space in the desk and saw an envelope tucked at the back, wedged between top and bottom drawers. It looked clean and uncreased, not in any state that could be explained away by something falling behind there and being forgotten.

He pulled it out, an envelope. An envelope with one word written on it: 'Stephen'. It was crazy, this feeling he had that Jeffrey was here, taking him step by step towards a conclusion, towards the answers to all the questions he wanted to ask. Or was it in fact just one question?

He weighed the envelope in his hand, tempted to throw it in the waste paper basket, consign it to the cleaner's mercy. Maybe it was better that he didn't know. He tossed it away and as it hit the bottom of the metal basket it made a slight clanging noise. As if the noise told him something he retrieved the envelope almost immediately. If Jeffrey had wanted to tell him something enough to die for it, if Jeffrey had been sufficiently scared to risk his life to get to see him, then Stephen owed him a duty to find out what he wanted to say.

The decision made, he ripped open the envelope. A tape, wrapped in paper. A few words only, the writing surprisingly legible for his late partner.

'Stephen, if you get to read this I suspect I'll be dead. Dead or jailed. There's too much to write, and you know I was never one for writing unless it was making team changes on a football programme. Just listen to the tape. I doubt if you'll ever understand, doubt if you'll ever believe me, but I'm sorry. I'm truly sorry.'

Stephen felt a lump come into his throat. He was about to cry again, the tears pricking against his eyelashes. He needed Trisha there to shout at him but believed that this time, hard-headed journalist though she was, she might understand.

He put the tape in the machine and there in the gloom of Jeffrey's office began to listen to his dead friend's explanation of why he had tried to destroy him.

Chapter Sixty Three

Stephen had been walking for hours in the general direction of home. Taxis slowed down then accelerated again, like kerb crawlers threatened by the police. Head down, hands in pocket, Stephen did not even see them.

Jeffrey's voice still echoed in his ears; a voice from the grave, bringing with it another small death. At first there had been no surprises. Naive he might have been, but Stephen still had his lawyer's wits and had been able to piece most of it together. Lipscomb's boasting in any event had not left a lot to the imagination. Yet somehow, as Jeffrey spoke, a condemned man with his final message, it all became more poignant, somehow more understandable. If it had been his own life at stake Stephen could almost have sympathised.

'Steve,' Jeffrey begun, 'you know, your trouble was you'd never listen to me. You'd never listen to any of us, to anybody in your life. You made up your mind, and once you'd decided then that was it. Not once did we ever shake you. Partners' meeting after partners' meeting we all sat and listened, and afterwards it was as if you'd never have let us been there unless it was to be your audience. Your ego always needed an audience, even when we were kids. It was your ball, your game. That's why you liked acting so much. You had your audience then and you never wanted to lose them.

'It came so easy for you, I worked my balls off and got Bs, you did bugger all and got straight As. Even in those days I'd have loved it if just once you'd failed something, just once you'd not got the girl you wanted to get.

'You had it easy at home as well. I used to love to come to you for tea. Loved it and hated it. Your parents were always there for you, your mum always managed to be home by the time you got back from school, tea on the table. Remember her egg and cress sandwiches? I used to look forward to them. I even liked to be there when your dad got home from work. Tired as he was, he always had time for you, time for me too. Always interested in what I was doing. I think I spoke more to your parents than I ever did to mine, not that I saw that much of my father after the divorce.

536

Like father, like son, eh, only more so. Even my wives liked you, Stephen. They all hated me by the end, but you—oh, you they spoke of kindly.

'Even the horse wasn't fair. You knew my problems and you bought me out. That was fair enough but another man might have given me something when it started to winning. You probably didn't even remember I'd ever had a share.'

Stephen had shaken his head then and spoken to the unhearing Jeffrey. Or was he hearing? Was this all a final joke bringing a smile to his face while Stephen wept unashamedly.

'Not fair, Jeff. Not fair. I overpaid you on the horse—you knew that. I didn't tell you to get into property. If I'd ever sold the horse you'd have still had your share...' But Jeffrey was continuing without a pause.

'It was me who phoned the local police that day at the races and told them to look out for your car. Childish really, but it was all a kids' game then. Oh, by the way, you'll find a letter on your desk from the police telling you they're taking it no further, so at least that didn't hurt, maybe it even prepared you a bit for what was to come.

'And then they came along with their offers, so what was I to do? It all seemed so easy. Greystone's would make me an offer I couldn't refuse. I'd become a senior partner there, and they'd take in everybody else as well.

'Before you say anything, it wasn't just the money. It was that at first they seemed really to want me, for what I was. I'd have had responsibility, power, everything you'd denied me, Steve. Maybe you thought you were doing it all for the best. Maybe you didn't think at all. That's more likely. Did you ever think of anybody but yourself, Stephen? Sorry, this was meant to be an apology, not a lecture. Perhaps you've learned from all this. Perhaps you're a better person. All credit to me, eh, Steve? Good old Jeff. Always could be relied on. You believed you were sweeping up behind me, but it was me with the brush behind you all the time. I don't think you ever realised how much I had to explain when you were dashing off for Mortimer or running to see your horse. Here, there, everywhere, but never behind a desk, never in the office when the chips were down!

'Sarah and Anthony put up with it. I knew about you and Sarah. You tried to hide it, but you weren't ever very good at hiding things. Bit of hypocrisy there, Steve, loving family man, screwing his articled clerk. Still, she was a bit tasty back them. I tried myself, you know, but she wasn't having any of it. One up to you yet again. Anthony idolised you but you never realised that either. You took his isolation for indifference, but it was you who isolated him. You cut him out of your life when he wanted to be in it, and Anthony, in his own way, never forgave you for it. You didn't understand his way any more than you really understood anything that went on around you.'

Stephen had pressed the stop button. He hadn't smoked since he'd left university, but he'd needed a cigarette then, a cigarette or a drink, probably both. He'd settled for a cigar from Jeffrey's stock and a whisky from his cabinet. The drink had gone straight to his empty stomach, the smoke choked him as he forgot to exhale, yet the combination had brought him back to life, made him aware of where he was. Had Jeffrey been telling the truth, or were these the ramblings of an embittered man? Had it all really been an apology or some kind of death bed confession that lay midway between truth and imagination.

He'd emptied his glass, refilled it, then hit the play button once again. It had to be heard through to the end, however painful it might be.

'They promised me that nothing serious would happen to you. They said they had it all worked out, how they'd blame Arthur. That the money would go back, that Arthur was being well paid for his services not to have to come back. At the end of the day you'd have had a fright, a few sleepless nights, and nobody would have been permanently hurt. I believed them, Steve, honestly I did. And then Jarvis died, and Arthur turned up dead, and I realised it was all lies. The money wasn't coming back, Arthur wasn't alive and well and living in South America, and you weren't coming back either.

'That's why I want to see you. I want to tell you all this face to face. That way I think you'll understand it better. We used to be able to talk, we used to be able to laugh. You remember in school what we did in History? Who could first cover the ceiling with chewing gum. I never forgot things like that. You did. That was the problem. I never forgot my roots. You never wanted to acknowledge yours. You didn't deserve to have happen to you what has happened, but you didn't deserve all that happiness either. If you get to listen to this then enjoy the rest of your life. Remember me, remember us as it was, not like it became. Not a lot to ask really. That's if I'm entitled to ask anything.'

There had been a pause on the tape, and for a moment Stephen thought it had ended, but the sound of breathing had continued, a sharp intake of breath, as if

Jeffrey was steeling himself to say one last thing, and then his voice, unsteady, full of emotion, telling Stephen one final dreadful truth...

Chapter Sixty Four

It was nearly two in the morning when he got to his front door. The light was still on in the main bedroom, in their bedroom. A thin drizzle had begun, cold for the summer. He felt tired, dirty, like a tramp who'd slept rough for days. A police car cruised by, seemed to hesitate, then decided it had more urgent business and moved on by. He was a fugitive once again, unable to come to terms with the fact that, subject to the formalities, he was no longer pursued. He could come and go as he wished, leave the country without subterfuge.

He stood on the pavement looking up, then picked up a handful of gravel and tossed it up to Cathy's window. He thought he saw movement at the curtain and waited. A sound of feet, reluctant, the door pulled open a fraction on the safety chain and then Cathy's voice.

'Oh, it's you.'

'I suppose so.'

They stood looking at each other like strangers, not touching, the distance between them as huge as Stephen's suffering.

'Am I interrupting something?' he asked. She shook her head, her own face pale, her eyes red. She looked older than he remembered, but then they probably both did. She showed no surprise at his arrival, and released the chain to let him in.

He needed to wash, to shower, shave, to change back into clothes that he'd not worn for months, to sleep between clean sheets in a familiar bed. He went up the stairs to the bathroom and splashed water on his face. Everything in the room was vaguely familiar, like a hotel revisited once a year for a holiday, but the face that stared back at him was strange. He'd grown used to his reflection in Trisha's bathroom, the battered mirror, the toothpaste squeezed in the middle, her lady's razor, the casualness of her sex. So different to the precise order that surrounded him now.

He went into the bedroom. There were clothes strewn everywhere, two cases on the floor, lids open, half-packed.

'Finding it difficult to decide what to take?' he asked.

'More difficult to decide where to go.'

She refused to meet his gaze. Her eyes moved everywhere but to his face. The bed, the cases, the window, the door, the escape route.

'You know, don't you?' she said finally, her voice flat, emotionless.

'Yes.'

'And?'

'Why Jeffrey? If it had to be somebody, why him?'

'He was available. I cared for him, though that came later. And now he's dead and you killed him as surely as if you'd driven the car!'

'Why anybody, Cathy? What had I done?'

Now her eyes flared and he remembered all the passion she'd brought to their bed.

'Sarah, that's what you'd done—who you'd done! She told you, you know. Never trust a woman to keep a secret from another woman. She thought she was helping. That I'd understand. That you weren't coping with the guilt. I knew there was something wrong at the time. You're not a very good actor, Stephen, you never were. Did I ever tell you that? It was because you were so awful in that play at school that I fell for you. I thought then you needed someone to look after you. I wasn't wrong.'

'But you're a good actress, Cathy. You pulled this role off beautifully. Jeffrey left me a tape. He told me everything. How he let you into the little secret of what they had in store for me, how you played along, pretended to be the loyal little wife, knowing even then you had that phoney hotel receipt. Did you have a good laugh in bed that night, the two of you? "Oh, I wonder how Stephen's getting on in cardboard city."'

Cathy sat on the ends of the bed, playing with a silk nightdress, running it through her fingers, remembering nights with her men, crying now, crying for them both, both lost to her.

'Who are you crying for, Cathy, him or you? You know, what you did to me was nothing. Maybe I asked for it after what I'd done to our marriage with Sarah. Yet what you've done to the kids is unforgivable.'

'The kids are all right. Children are resilient. They'll get over it.'

'Were you going to take them with you?' She didn't answer.

'Did they know about you and Jeffrey?' he continued to probe.

There was still some fight left in her.

'Did they know about you and Sarah?'

She looked ready to play Lady Macbeth, still beautiful, her figure a wonder for a mother of two teenage children. He understood what Shakespeare had intended when he had made Macbeth kill for her.

'There was nothing real between Sarah and me. It was an affair. Men have affairs. I felt bad about it, I ended it. I tried to push it to the back of my mind, to make up to you for what you didn't know I'd done.'

She rocked backwards and forwards, clutching her knees, and he thought she might be about to lose touch with reality, but her voice, although strained, was still controlled.

'There was something between Jeffrey and me. Whatever we did to you, he at least showed some feelings for me. He was human, Stephen, fallible and human. He made mistakes. One of them cost him his life. But when did *you* ever make a mistake? When did you ever make a decision you hadn't thought through a million times? Even in bed it was all mapped out, wasn't it? The same order of foreplay. The same positions. The same time for you to come—I could set a stopwatch and hear it ring when you spilled into me. I came to hate it. Everything about you became predictable. The late nights, the early mornings, the apologies for missing a kid's play, an open night at school. You were never here for me, Stephen, nor for them, and the worst thing is you didn't even realise it. Stephen Kennard, perfect husband, great provider, wonderful father. His wife and kids never lack for anything. Well, Steve, we lacked for one thing—you. Is it any wonder I replaced you?'

'Replacing me is one thing, destroying another.'

She shrugged, past caring, unrecognisable from the girl he'd married.

'Are you going to turn me in? Isn't that what happens to the bad girl in the movies? I'm probably an accessory to half a dozen major crimes.'

He ran his fingers through his hair. He should call Charlie, he knew, but then there'd be a trial, the kids would see their mother paraded through the courts and the papers. The tabloids would love this one, it had every ingredient: theft, sex, death. And if he did nothing, who would know? Jeffrey was dead. Lipscomb was unlikely to drag her into things. She was too far removed from the main plot.

'Being a judge isn't easy, is it Stephen?'

The tone of her voice made it easier for him. She was under control, she would survive.

'Keep packing, Cathy. I want you out of here by the morning. This is the deal. You find yourself somewhere. I don't care where, but not in London. Just let me know where you are and I'll send you an allowance—God know's you don't deserve it but it'll keep you off the streets, maybe keep you from destroying some other poor bastard. I'm taking responsibility for the kids. They'll live here with me. I'll tell them we're getting divorced, that you've decided to make a new life for yourself, that you need some time to be on your own. Maybe in a few months I'll let you see them. Maybe. This is one decision I've not thought through a million times.'

'Can't I stay here? We could piece it together for the sake of the kids.'

He didn't hesitate.

'No. As you said, I'm not that good an actor. It's not negotiable, Cathy. That's what's on offer. That or I call the police.'

She seemed to shrink within herself and it was hard to imagine that she'd plotted to destroy him. Then, gathering herself together, she began automatically to fold clothes and put them in the cases. He looked at his watch. Three a.m. It was a long night and he still had another visit to make.

'I'll be back at seven. Don't be here. I hope for your sake you find yourself—I've lost you.' Then, taking from the dressing table the key to his house, he turned his back on the debris of his marriage.

Chapter Sixty Five

He'd phoned for a cab. He not only needed to be there quickly but also to put distance between himself and Cathy. If there'd been two people he'd trusted in his life it had been his partner and his wife. He couldn't believe he'd been such a fool. The cobbler and his shoes... But then he'd been too busy with other people's problems even to realise that his own existed.

His intuition had been right, his timing impeccable. Trisha was just loading her bags into the boot of her beat up old Renault when he arrived. He saw her in slow motion as the cab pulled into her street, caught in the shadows of the street lamp. A final shove of the cases, the boot slammed shut oblivious to the neighbours at that unearthly hour of the morning, a glance up at her window to say goodbye, and then she was in the driver's seat, turning the key. He threw the money at an astonished driver, who gladly took the £50 note for a £10 fare, and saw his passenger race alongside the car pulling away from the kerb.

Stephen knocked on the window and

she began to accelerate, perhaps not even realising it was him, thinking it was just another late night drunk. Then she glanced sideways, her mouth opening a fraction, still not slowing down. He couldn't keep up the pace, it had all been too much for him, his chest felt as if it was about to explode. As her car turned the corner he sank to his knees on the wet ground, finally beaten.

She offered herself to him and he'd said, no, thinking he'd still had a marriage. It wasn't fair. He'd put an end to his relationship with Sarah because of guilt, he'd never begun with Trisha because of guilt, and now he had nothing. He eased himself onto the pavement and sat with his back against the lamppost, not even aware of the drizzle soaking into his clothes. To have battled through everything and still to have lost the one prize that had been available to win; to be left like this, just another derelict in the rain.

The drizzle turned into a downpour, the water sluicing into the gutter beside him. A light went off in the house opposite, the last light in the street, for Stephen the last light in the world. His shoes were filling with water, his clothes sodden, pounds heavier, his hair as wet as any drowning man's. He leaned back and opened his mouth to catch the water, to drink it in. Acid rain. Was this a very special form of suicide? A line from a poem half-remembered:

'And all the time I was too far out of reach
And not waving but drowning.'

A film, *Death by Drowning,* the images all merging. He felt so tired, his eyes closing, blurred by rain. He needed to sleep, to disentangle the poem from the film, extract them both from reality. That was what frightened him the most, the reality of being alone. No wife, no partner. He could have coped with it all twenty-five years ago. That was when he'd been single, unqualified, setting out lightly on the yellow brick road; but the road had led not to Oz but to this miserable wet night in London where only ghosts walked the streets.

He didn't even hear the car pull up, the door open, the footsteps. Only the voice brought him out of his delirium.

'Not enough sense to come in out of the rain, eh?'

She'd reparked her car and now stood over him, rain pouring down on the umbrella she held. He tried to get to his feet but the cold and weakness had got to him and they simply gave way under him.

He felt like a baby learning to walk. She pulled him up and touched his face with her hand.

'Wet, so wet.'

He leaned against her for support, his arms around her neck, and she staggered under his weight. Supporting him, she led him back into the flat. He stood there miserably, swaying from side to side, an ever widening puddle forming on the floor.

'Hey, let's get you undressed.' She took off his clothes gently as if he'd been scalded rather than soaked, then brought a huge bathrobe and began to rub him dry. As warmth and feeling came back into his body and his mind he told her about Cathy, forgetting she was a journalist, forgetting everything but the fact that she was a woman and he was here with her, just where he wanted to be.

She put her arms around him, and rocked him slowly backwards and forwards.

'It'll be all right,' she said, over and over again, a litany of reassurance, then took his hand and led him through to the bedroom, not stopping when the robe fell away to leave him naked.

They made love as if they had always been lovers. Her breasts seemed so familiar, small, comforting; the whiteness of her skin; the red hair standing out like a beacon between her legs. His tongue played its way over every inch of her, eating hungrily, satisfying an appetite that had seen no food for a long time. She sat astride him, head thrown back, riding him rhythmically with all the expertise of a jockey who knows the race is won.

Afterwards, despite his exhaustion, sleep would not come. He held her in his arms, her head on his shoulder, smelling her hair, the sweetness of her perfume, the tang of her sex still on his tongue.

'Where were you going?' he asked.

'Away.'

'Where?'

'Anywhere.'

'With Charlie?'

'No. Not with Charlie.' She paused. 'I was just going away from you. I couldn't stand the thought of your being with her. I'd never met her, but I hated her. I hated her since that night in Dijon when she was in bed with us. I never doubted you, and couldn't understand even then why she should have.'

'So why didn't you say something then?'

'Would you have believed me? Woman's intuition.'

'Probably not.'

He kissed her full on the lips, his hand going to her breast, teasing the nipples back to life.

'So what happens now?' he asked.

'It looks like you're already decided,' she replied, her hand moving down his body.

'We can't stay in bed for ever.'

'We could try. Who'd find us?'

'Charlie for a start. He's one hell of a copper.'

'I never thought you'd appreciate him.'

'I envy him, you know. At least he's doing something with his life. What have I ever done except make money and destroy lives around me?'

'You won the case for the Robsons, Marion Walters will get her insurance money, Gerry's company will now take over D'Arblay and their shareholders will breathe a sigh of relief. You're not the worst son in the world, and you're not the worst lover either.'

Almost absentmindedly he rolled on top of her and eased into her body again. As they moved together in perfect familiar rhythm, he made his decision.

'I'm not going back.' He felt her body arch, her muscles contract, and knew instinctively she was about to climax.

'I'll leave the practice to Anthony and Sarah. I'm not going back. I'm not going back.' He repeated the phrase with each triumphant thrust, and as he came, shouted them out in a fanfare of glory.

'I'm never going back.'

This Large Print Book for the Partially sighted, who cannot read normal print, is published under the auspices of

THE ULVERSCROFT FOUNDATION

THE ULVERSCROFT FOUNDATION

. . . we hope that you have enjoyed this Large Print Book. Please think for a moment about those people who have worse eyesight problems than you . . . and are unable to even read or enjoy Large Print, without great difficulty.

You can help them by sending a donation, large or small to:

**The Ulverscroft Foundation,
1, The Green, Bradgate Road,
Anstey, Leicestershire, LE7 7FU,
England.**
or request a copy of our brochure for more details.

The Foundation will use all your help to assist those people who are handicapped by various sight problems and need special attention.

Thank you very much for your help.